The Bookish Bandit

by

Erica Dansereau
& Britt Howard

Identifiers:
Library of Congress Control Number: 2023921484
ISBN: 979-8-9858237-7-6 (paperback)
ISBN: 979-8-9858237-8-3 (ebook)

This is a work of fiction. Any references to historical events, real people, real publications, or real places are used fictitiously. Other names, dialogue, characters, and events are products of the author's imagination. Any resemblance to actual persons, living or dead, is purely coincidental.

Cover design by Brittany Howard

"For God so loved the world, that he gave his only begotten Son, that whosoever believeth in him should not perish, but have everlasting life."
John 3:16

Authors' Note

Dear Reader,

In these pages we hope laughter finds you and brightens your day, that this love story sparks a light within your soul, and that the messages of faith leave you hoping for a greater world to come.

Love,
Britt and Erica

1

Andrew

Winter

"Andrew, this isn't a story I can publish." The novel I've been working on for months lands on the desk with a thump that reverberates throughout the spacious corner office.

"You published a story about mating snails last quarter, for crying out loud!" The door is open, and I know my raised voice just carried through the mahogany paneled walls of CityLight Press, but I don't care who hears. It's late, the wintry sunset hours long past, though New York City never goes fully dark. Most of our employees have gone home for the night. I lean forward, knuckles planted on the desk. "Why won't you give my book a shot, Dad? Your own son?"

He leans back in his chair and looks at me. My maternal grandfather, after accumulating a great deal of wealth, founded CityLight in the eighties as publishing became more and more mainstream. Through upheavals in the market and the emergence of online publishing services, he manned the helm and stayed the course, making our family business one of the largest and longest single-owned publishing houses of the century. Ten years ago, he stepped down and made my father, Gary E. Ketner, the CEO of CityLight. Grandfather passed away the following year.

Dad sits in his wingback chair before me, shaking his head and rubbing his thinning temples. His silence causes the blood to drain from my face. I drum my knuckles on his desk and glance at the wall behind him, which is decorated with various prestigious literary awards and accolades CityLight has accumulated during its duration in publishing.

"Your grandfather never handed anything out to me," Dad says as he follows my gaze to the wall. "And it made me a better man because of it. I had to start at the bottom and work my way up, even after I married your mother. I proved my worth." He sighs and leans forward. "I don't understand your obsession with becoming an author anyway, Andrew. Wouldn't you much rather be on the publishing side of things? Follow in the family's footsteps?"

I grip the edge of the desk and mull his words over in my mind. Why do I want to be a writer so badly? Is it because of Mom and the impact books had on me as a highly anxious child? Or is it because I know Dad secretly admires the crafters of the word more than he does the publishers, despite being one himself?

I look down, trying to process my whirling thoughts. Or do I want to see my words in print because writing is the one thing in life I've actually given my best to, but it still isn't good enough? At least not for Gary Ketner.

My tone reflects my frustration. "Do you want me to get a literary agent? You want me to jump through those hoops? Maybe I'll wind up at Penguin Random House. Would you like that? Would that be a good look for your son to get published by the competition?" Maybe the threat will force Dad to reconsider. I've given my all to writing this novel, and I believe in it.

A pained expression slides across his face, and he pinches the space between his eyes. "That's not . . . it."

Heat crawls up my neck. "Then what is it, Dad?"

"You're just . . . not . . . Hey, you know what?" he says, his tone suddenly shifting. "Remember Alba? Let me give her a call, and we—"

"Alba? As in Alba Esterez, the writing coach? You . . . you think I need a writing coach?" I'm floored. "What are you trying to say here?"

He licks his lips and hesitates for a moment. "You just don't understand," he finally says.

"Try me." I fold my arms across my chest.

Dad stares at his steepled fingers for a moment, avoiding my pressing gaze.

"Come on," I prod. I can feel sweat collecting at the base of my neck. "I'm a man. I can take it."

His brow furrows. "Alright, fine. You want the truth, Andrew? Your writing isn't good enough. You just . . . don't have what it takes. At least not right now. And I'm not publishing something you've decided to write on a whim simply because you're my son, and I own this company."

Whoosh.

There it is. His words knock the air from my lungs. My brain goes static, and it takes me a moment to recover.

"I'm sorry, Andrew. I really am." His tone is regretful, but it doesn't lessen the sting of his words.

"You know, Mom always told me to keep writing. She believed in me." My voice falters, and I clear my throat. "Guess she was the only one, huh?"

Dad sighs and cradles his forehead in his hand. "Andrew, I think you should focus your efforts elsewhere. You're a bright kid. But if there's any chance that I'm going to trust you to lead this company one day, like your grandfather did with me, you have a lot to prove."

"Thanks for the pep talk. I feel like I can conquer the world now." I knock my fist on the top of his desk and shake my head.

"What more do you expect?" He's frustrated with me, and it shows. "You treat your job like it's optional. You take advantage of your position as my son, coming and going as you please. Let me guess, you're still ducking out of town next week? Will you even be back in time for CityLight's spring events, or should I start finding a replacement to cover you for the ones *you've* set up?"

Heat flares again along my skin. "I'll be there, don't you worry." Sarcasm is my second language at this point. "But you know I don't like being here this time of year. I . . . I can't take it."

Dad looks me in the eye. "A real man could."

I let the door slam as I storm out of his office. The rest of the twentieth floor is dark, each executive office locked up for the night. CityLight occupies three levels of a high-rise building in downtown Manhattan. I tap the call button next to the elevator. There's a ding, but though I wait, the doors never open. Impatiently, I press the button a few more times to no avail.

I can't stand still long enough to wait for the elevator, so instead, I turn and head for the stairwell. I barrel down the stairs, my shoes clattering on the metal steps. When I reach the stairwell one flight down, I poke my head through the door on a whim and see a single office light still on. It doesn't surprise me that she's working late. I feel a twinge of guilt as I speed walk toward her office.

"Hey, Ava. Late night?" I poke my head through her open door.

Ava Fox is one of CityLight's senior acquisitions editors. We've been friends since college, and though I work in the firm's public relations and marketing department on the upper floor, I manage to find my way to her office at least once a day.

She looks up now from an envelope she's opening. "Andrew, hey." A warm smile spreads across her face. "Yeah, finally getting the chance to go through the last of my mail today, and then I'm heading out. You okay? You look all . . . hot and bothered."

I smirk and cross my arms, leaning casually against the doorframe. "You think I'm hot?"

She sets her lips into a straight line. "Thanks. Now I'm bothered."

I chuckle and grab a piece of candy from the dish on her desk. "I much preferred the M&M's, just so you know."

"Sorry to disappoint you," she says, reaching for another piece of mail. She grabs a thick manila envelope and opens it. She peers inside, then pulls out a stack of printed computer paper. I watch her roll her eyes as she reads the cover letter. "These authors really need to learn how to read a website," she grumbles, stuffing the giant stack back into the envelope.

"What's that?"

"Oh, just another unsolicited manuscript, which we don't accept. Our policies are written clearly on our website, but still, every day, some aspiring author thinks they'll take the chance and mail their full novel to us anyway." She huffs and tosses the entire package into the wastebasket. "I'll take it to the shredder on Monday morning. I'm ready to get out of here tonight."

She yawns, stands, and walks around the desk toward me. She reaches for her coat from the hook behind the door. "Are you sure you're alright?"

If anyone would understand the impact of my dad's rejection, it's Ava. Still, I can't find the gumption to tell her the full scope of my fight with my father. Not tonight.

Instead, I shake my head and try to ignore the hole forming at the base of my sternum. "Just had a, uh, little disagreement with my dad."

But Ava knows me too well. She stands in front of me, combing through her blonde hair with her fingers. "Is it about writing again?"

I pop another candy into my mouth and shrug.

"Why don't you take a stab at editing?" She peers up at me. "I think you might have a natural knack for it."

"So, you think I should give up on being an author too?" I frown and cross my arms. If even Ava doesn't believe in me . . .

She sets a gentle hand on my arm. "I never said that. Just think about it, okay?" She shrugs on her coat and zips it to the top. "Will you walk me out?"

"Of course."

We take the elevator down to the main lobby on the first floor, waving goodbye to the security guards posted at the desk. As we step through the revolving front doors, the icy winter chill hits me and rattles me to the bones. It is a bitter reminder of the night that Mom left this earth. I just want this night, this day, this season to be over already. I close my eyes against the cold, trying to push away the frosty hand that clenches my lungs. Winter in New York City has always been cold, wet, and dreary. It's doubly miserable now.

In a week's time, though, I'll be on a plane to somewhere the sun can pierce through the darkness again.

"Any fun plans tonight?" Ava asks, a puff of air appearing in front of her face. It's the start of the weekend, and the streets are crowded with New Yorkers headed out for a night of fun. "A few of us are meeting at The Rusty Elephant to humiliate ourselves with karaoke. You're welcome to join."

"Thanks, but I think it's best I just head home tonight."

"You sure? A fun night with friends could be exactly what you need."

I shake my head and note the flakes of snow that are falling from the sky. The last thing I want is to be around anyone else tonight. "Maybe next time."

The lounge isn't far away from the office. I walk with her all the way to The Rusty Elephant to ensure she gets there safely. Ava puts a hand on the door and opens it a smidge. A Garth Brooks song blasts through the crack, spilling into the night.

"You sure?" She smiles at me encouragingly.

I nod. "I'm ready to call it a night."

"Okay." She begins to push through the door but

suddenly releases the handle and throws her head back with a groan. "Shoot." She smacks her forehead with her palm. "I don't think I locked my office door."

I don't hesitate. "Don't worry about it. I'll go back and take care of it for you."

"Are you sure?" Her face is hopeful.

"Absolutely. Have fun tonight."

"You're a lifesaver. Thanks, Andrew."

With a smile, Ava ducks inside, and I walk back toward CityLight through softly falling snow. As I take the steps to the entrance, I wonder if my father is still upstairs, burying himself in his work so he doesn't have to face the pain of our reality. All the work in the world won't bring Mom back. I often wonder if he works so tirelessly to honor her memory or just to dig himself further into denial.

I greet Mattias, one of the security guards, as I reenter through the heavy front doors and head to the elevator. The doors open readily when I press the call button. When I reach Ava's office, I try the door. Sure enough, it's unlocked. The lights flicker on automatically as I take one quick glance into the room. She also forgot to power off the essential oil diffuser sitting atop her filing cabinet. It's billowing puffs of something minty into the empty office air. I stride across the room and flip the switch. As I turn to walk back through the dark, empty building, my eyes settle on the lonely manuscript discarded in the wastebasket.

What a waste. Never truly given the chance. Just like me.

The depressing thought floods my brain. Curiosity gets the best of me as I stare at the plump package, and I find myself grabbing it from the trash and sliding the stack of pages out of the envelope. A clatter from somewhere in the building distracts me. Briefly, I glance over my shoulder, but the hallway is empty and dark. Quickly, I flip past the cover letter and title page, taking note of the book's title. *Love Between the Pages* is written in bold lettering.

Not a bad title, I muse. Curiosity tugs at me again, and I flip to the first chapter, intending only to scan the first few lines of the rejected novel. Maybe seeing someone else's dream in the trash will make me feel better about the dumpster fire that is my own.

I read, and I keep reading. Within the first few lines of the book, I am completely hooked. How could anyone simply discard this? It's . . . *an undiscovered treasure.*

The sound of footsteps down the hall sends a jolt of panic through me. Without thinking, I stuff the manuscript back into the manila envelope and shove it into the messenger bag slung over my shoulder. I speed walk out of Ava's office and lock the door. As casually as possible, I walk down the hall toward the elevator just as my father rounds the corner.

"Andrew. You're still here?" He sounds relieved and claps me on the shoulder when he catches up to me. "The elevator button upstairs doesn't seem to be working. Look, son," he pauses. "I . . . I feel terrible. If you get me a story—a really good story—I'll consider giving it a shot, okay? But if CityLight is going to compete with these other houses, we've got to step up our game. We need to publish something with real grit, real heart."

"I hear you, Dad."

The manuscript hidden in my bag feels like it is burning a hole through the leather. Maybe I have what it takes to be an editor as Ava suggested. "I think I might surprise you one of these days. I might just have CityLight's next bestseller under my sleeve."

Dad chuckles. "Son, you know bestsellers aren't just written; they're made."

We part ways on the street after leaving a note for maintenance to check the elevator controls, and by the time I get back to my dark, quiet apartment, I've sweated through my undershirt despite the frigid winter temperatures of early January. But I don't have time to shower off the stress of the day right now. There are more pressing matters.

I shake the snow off my clothes and climb the dozen steps that lead up to Winters Tower, the residential building I inherited from my mom when she passed. I take the elevator, making a mental note to check in with the super about using extra salt on the steps and walkway outside during the heavy winter weather.

This building is yet another reminder of Mom. She left me so much, passing down the wealth inherited from her father in the form of pristine New York City real estate on the Upper East Side. With my inheritance and the likelihood that CityLight will one day be passed to me if my father can keep it afloat till then, I would never have to work another day in my life if I didn't want to. However, due to Dad's humble upbringing, he taught me that wealth is a valuable tool but not to be depended upon. After remodeling a few of the units for vacation rentals, I chose one to make my permanent home.

A bead of sweat rolls down my spine, but funnily enough, the interior of Winters Tower feels colder than the outside, and I know it has nothing to do with temperature. Without Mom, I've lost so much of the warmth in my life.

Her absence has shown me that more sometimes means less.

I step off the elevator and pass the doors of the other apartment units on the top floor. A few are leased to permanent renters, and a few are listed as short-term, furnished rentals and bring in a sizable monthly revenue. My door is the last, leading to my penthouse apartment situated on the corner with a sweeping view of the Upper East Side and Central Park. I punch in the code. The door shuts and self-locks behind me. The open floor plan is lit only by the soft haze of a snow-stricken sky and endless city lights that twinkle through the wall of windows on the far wall.

Life didn't discriminate when it came to my mother's heart. Even the best doctors that money could buy couldn't stave off the grim reality she faced as her condition grew weaker. And now, even the most stunning location can't mend my broken heart.

I lean against the glass and look out over the view of the city that never sleeps. Snow blankets the world beyond my window. Mom always loved this time of year. She thought it was serendipitous that the season matched her maiden name: Winters. But to me, it just represents sadness now.

Resolutely, I turn away from the windows and pull the manuscript from my bag. Hours later, I flip over the last page and lean back in my seat, inhaling as emotion stirs deep within my chest.

I wasn't wrong to rescue this manuscript from the trash. It's pure gold.

I sit at my laptop as it whirs to life. I've kept most of the lights off, so the bright backlight of the screen against my dimly lit home makes me squint. Ignoring the protest of my tired eyes, I open up a fresh document. A plan is forming in my mind. If I'm really going to edit this novel and present it to my dad, I need to have it in a computer formatting program exactly as it is before I begin. If he wants CityLight to produce bestsellers and me to take on a bigger role in the company, this is a good start.

I take a deep breath and look at the title page. My fingers dart across the keys as I type the first words.

Love Between the Pages
by
Charlie Blaire

"Okay, Charlie Blaire, whoever you are, let's show the world what we're made of."

2

Charlie

Fall. Ten months later.

"Do you want me to put Hank into his kennel for the night, Maeve?"

She looks up as I walk through the door to the wood shingled building that serves as Pleasant Hollow's veterinary service. The valley's animal shelter is built onto the back. The door swings shut behind me with a soft thud. I swipe my muddy boots on the utility rug before continuing. Heavy rain last night soaked the nearby forest trails. It will probably be the last rain of the season, as our first snowfall is predicted to arrive as early as next week.

Hank, a medium-sized border collie mix, strides calmly at my side. Gingerly, he sidesteps the colorful display of pumpkins and gourds piled atop a bale of hay in the entryway. When I pause at the high-top reception desk, the shaggy black and brown dog comes to a standstill, his fluffy tail proudly dusting the air. Glancing downward, I raise my hand, signaling for him to sit. After a moment's hesitation, he obeys my command.

"You two are done already?" The blonde, curly-haired woman who serves as both receptionist and office manager stands to peer over the counter at him.

"Our boy here was quite the angel today." I look at him affectionately. "His manners have already improved. I think he'll be ready for adoption within the next few weeks if Doc doesn't mind giving him room and board for a while longer."

"I'm sure she won't mind," Maeve assures me. "Charlie, you're an angel for using your time to train these homeless pups so they have an advantage going into their new homes."

The middle-aged woman presses her palm dramatically to her chest, and I see her take a heaving breath. We are both animal lovers through and through. It's the reason I volunteer at the shelter several hours a week to put new canine guests through my obedience training school. While it would be more profitable to spend the time working on my ever-expanding business, I get too much satisfaction from volunteering to consider stopping.

"You know it's my pleasure." I feel my cheeks warm at her praise.

Maeve gives me a grateful look. "If you don't mind taking him back to his kennel, I'll finish closing up for the night."

"I don't mind." I unlatch the half gate separating the reception area from the door leading to the kennels. "Heel," I say to Hank. He falls into a brisk stride next to me.

We are greeted by a cacophony of barking dogs as we step

into the large space. Rows of spacious kennels house dogs of every shape, size, and breed. Some of the residents simply wandered away from home and are waiting for their owners to remember to check the shelter. Others, like Hank, are permanent residents, abandoned or surrendered, waiting for their new forever homes.

I lead him back to his kennel and give him an affectionate head rub before checking that his water bowl is full. As I make my way back, I pause at a few cages to offer words of praise or head scratches to some of the other dogs, several of whom have already passed my training course with flying colors. When I reenter the office, Maeve is turning off her computer and stacking her purse and lunch bag on top of the desk.

"So, where does a pretty young lady like yourself spend her Friday nights?" She flashes me a grin and a wink. "You probably have a hot date waiting for you."

An involuntary chortle bursts out of me. "Um, no. Unless you count a date with myself, *You've Got Mail,* and a tub of pumpkin pie ice cream?" I tilt my head, the dark waves of my hair falling over my shoulder with the movement. "I guess I am planning to stop at the bookstore on the way home, though. I think I deserve a few new books for the weekend."

Maeve makes a *tsking* sound and shakes her head. "You spend too much time alone, Charlie Blaire. You should go out with your friends. Live a little."

It's my turn to shake my head. "You know I'm a hopeless homebody. I'd much rather stay home and read or write on the weekends."

I linger by the desk as Maeve gathers the last of her

things. We walk out together, and I wait as she locks the door. A sharp chill nips at my face as we turn toward the parking lot. The sun has nearly set, and the temperature is dropping rapidly. I pull my heavy flannel jacket tighter around me. As much as I love autumn in Vermont, I miss the warmer days and long evenings of the summer season. The scent of crispy fallen leaves mixing with the aroma of a wood-burning stove catches my nose as Maeve drops the keys into her purse.

"I forget that you writers are a reclusive lot," she exclaims. "Have you been writing anything new lately? Did you hear back about that one book you sent in?"

Her small sedan and my aging F-150 are the only vehicles still in the lot. At her question, my lips purse, and I shrug as I throw the dog leash and collar I'm still holding into the back of my truck.

"I'm revising a book I finished writing this summer. I didn't hear anything at all from the publishing houses I queried for the manuscript I sent in last winter, go figure." I shake my head. "I discovered after I had sent out a half dozen copies that most mainstream publishers don't take unsolicited manuscripts, so that was my mistake." I smile ruefully. "Getting a publisher to look at your book without an agent is apparently harder than getting a date in this town. I don't know. Maybe I need to give up."

"Any publisher who passes up a writer as talented as you is a darn fool. Your bestselling novel is just around the corner. I can feel it. You just have to give it to God and let Him take care of the details," Maeve declares emphatically, hugging me as we part ways.

I climb into my truck, giving the wheel a pat as the

engine roars to life. The leather seats inside the cab are scratched and faded, the passenger window doesn't roll down anymore, and the forest-green exterior paint is chipped, but I can't imagine giving it up.

Despite her aged appearance, the truck's engine purrs as we bounce over the road leading back to town. To accommodate the shelter, Doctor Meltzer built the clinic a few miles into the countryside surrounding Pleasant Hollow, the tiny but growing Vermont village I've called home since girlhood. As the miles pass and the fading sun dips lower over the mountains, I let the scenery soothe my brain, pulling me into a meditative lull as I marvel at the beauty of autumn in Vermont. The state puts on its best dress this time of year, painting the foliage of the sycamores, birch, red maples, and oak trees with brilliant sunset-colored hues. It's late in the season, with winter weather on the cusp of blanketing the whole state in crisp, white snow, so I'm soaking up the views as long as I am able to.

The idyllic scenery has certainly provided ample fodder for the settings of my own novel writing over the years. I sigh, thinking of the multiple finished manuscripts collecting dust in the drawer of my desk at home. In typical writer fashion, I have finished and unfinished writing projects, all of them waiting for the day I finally get the courage to really pursue publication. Maybe Maeve is right. Maybe God does have a big plan for my future success as an author.

But I can't help but wonder if I lived in a big city and could cross paths with some literary agent, would I finally have a chance to see my name on the cover of a novel in the bookstore? The thought of relocating my life to a noisy, smelly, congested city like New York or Chicago is about as appealing as reading *War and Peace* for a second time. I'm a country girl through and through, and I just want to snuggle into my tiny cottage and write.

The twinkling lights of Main Street welcome me in the distance. I can't imagine a more perfect town to call home than Pleasant Hollow. The seasons committee outdid themselves this year with the autumnal theme. The entrance to almost every storefront along the cobblestone street has been decked out with rustic crates, bales of hay, cornstalks, and, of course, our beloved pumpkins, each grown by one of several locally owned pumpkin farms around the valley.

But perhaps my favorite display of all looms ahead as twilight officially falls over the town, and I approach my last stop for the day. Bluebird Books sits nestled between the bakery and the coffee shop, an ideal location for a bookworm to feed her book-buying habit, in my opinion. A parking space is open in front of the shop, and I pull the truck into the stall.

I take a moment to appreciate Lora's talent. As the owner and operator of the bookstore, she asked the seasons committee to allow her to design her own autumn display. The effect is pure magic every time I see it. Soft blush and white heirloom Cinderella pumpkins pile generously on either side of the door. Nestled among them are pots of deep pink and purple chrysanthemums, which have happily burst into brilliant blooms. Pampas grass waves gracefully to each passerby as fairytale lights twinkle in welcome.

Even the bookstore's interior lights cast a warm, golden glow over the street. In a world of digital reading and many distractions, I love that our village wholeheartedly supports our local bookshop. There's nothing more welcoming than the sight of rows and rows of bookshelves, each representing new worlds and characters to explore.

As I pull open the etched glass door, the merry twinkle of a bell greets me. Warmth instantly brushes away the autumn chill. Instinctively, I inhale, searching for the intoxicating scent of paper and ink.

"Charlie, why am I not even surprised to see you here tonight?" A soft, cheerful voice calls out from behind the counter. I look over to return Lora's smile with one of my own. My friend is busy stacking the receipts she's just pulled from the register.

"You know me well," I reply. "Am I too late? I just wanted to grab a couple of new books for this weekend."

She waves her hand in my direction. A short pencil is tucked behind her ear, the soft waves of her pixie cut peeking around the edges. "Not at all. I am just getting a head start on closing up. Go ahead and browse. I'll let you know if it starts getting late."

I turn toward the rows of wooden bookshelves, scanning the signs hanging above them. Lora is very good about bringing in fresh, new titles regularly. She and I share a particular love for indie authors. Tonight, I stopped by with the intention of picking up an inspirational, coming-of-age, historical fiction novel set in a tiny gold mining town in Nevada that I keep seeing rave reviews for on social media: *Come Forth As Gold*. The title is on the to-be-read list I keep in the notes app in my phone. Bookstagram keeps me informed on all the must-read latest releases, but who knows how many other titles will tumble into my arms and come home to live on my TBR shelf tonight?

"Do you like the new release display I just refreshed this

week? Isn't it perfect for autumn?" Lora calls as I walk away. She is a true artist at creating seasonal displays that are perfectly themed and far more creative than anything I've ever seen in another bookstore. I see her wave toward the space in front of the registers, so I veer off my course. I'll take a detour past the display to admire her work before I hunt down the book I'm planning to purchase.

I see it before I reach it. A round table holds stacks of strategically displayed books, with a sign announcing "Sweater Weather Books." Lora has crafted a paper mâché autumn-to-winter-inspired tree for the center of the table. Her sculpture is complete with individually hand-cut leaves, bark that looks like it's been hewn from real wood, and a cascading blanket of faux snow on one side to represent the impending seasonal shift. The tree rises several feet above the center, catching my eye almost more than the covers of the latest novels to hit the shelves. I circle the table, admiring Lora's artistry and peeking at each new title, waiting for one to catch my eye.

"Do you like it?" she calls.

"It's incredible," I say over my shoulder. "You should be working at Strand or one of those fancy pants bookstores in the city. But don't you ever think you can move away and leave me here, though."

Her laughter carries through the shop. "What am I supposed to do when you eventually get the travel bug and move away?"

"Oh no. I'm planning to live out my days in Pleasant Hollow."

I'm still circling the display, brushing the tips of my fingers over the hardcovers. Briefly, I wonder if publishers compare notes before they release books because this season's covers look perfectly coordinated. Forest greens, deep burgundies, and vibrant golden hues adorn the book jackets. A cover that looks like a walking advertisement for autumn catches my eye. The ombre wash of sunset colors cascades down to a row of watercolor trees in the foreground. The design is minimalist without being pretentious.

I reach for the hardcover, its matte jacket scratching softly against my fingers. An endorsement across the top from a notably popular author declares the book an instant bestseller: *Watch out for A.C. Frost.*

Love Between the Pages. The sight of the pretty title makes my stomach drop immediately.

"What are the odds?" I murmur to myself. My lips twist into a grimace. The title page of a certain manuscript in a certain drawer in my desk at home reflects identical words. *Love Between the Pages* is the exact name of the manuscript I sent out last winter before I realized how difficult getting a publisher to look at a novel really could be and lost my courage for the endeavor.

The idea that someone else successfully published an identically titled novel hurts more than a little. Under my breath, I huff, "At least one of us is successful, A.C. Frost."

The back cover is lined with more raving endorsements from a few popular authors I recognize. Turning the book over in my hands, I let it fall open to the back flap first. No author photo, just a succinct, to-the-point, but vague biography. I flip toward the front flap, looking for the synopsis. I'm curious to know what critics currently consider an instantly successful book.

I'm only a few lines into the blurb when I feel my heart

catch painfully in my chest. My head gives an involuntary shake, and I go back over the lines I just read with careful attention.

Her soul was between those pages, and he wouldn't rest until he found the woman who had penned the words that brought him back to life.

"What in the world?" My eyes fly to the top of the paragraph, and I reread the words for the third time. A throbbing pulse begins to pound erratically in my neck. *Thud, thud, thud.* Each beat is a warning that something is terribly wrong.

The words are familiar. More than familiar. I can recite each one by heart. They are ingrained in every fiber of my being because . . . I wrote them.

Is it possible for two writers to identically title a novel and pen the same words?

Frantically, I flip through the book, scrambling through the pages with feverish haste. It's there. It's all there. My book. Every word that I labored over is contained within the pages of this newly published novel.

Except there are minor differences. Even I can tell this book has been professionally edited. It's smooth in places where my words were still unedited. But it's here. This is my manuscript with someone else's name splashed across the front cover. This is the book I wrote to honor the memory of my parents.

I struggle to hold back the sudden lump in my throat.

I flip to the copyright page, searching for the name and insignia of the publishing house.

CityLight Press. New York City, New York.

"Did I send them a copy?" I whisper, struggling to

remember which publishers had made my list of potentials. I'm struggling to remember anything or even think clearly at all right now. My temperature loops between feverishly hot and numbingly cold. I realize my hands are shaking.

I need to get home. I need to check my records and confirm that I sent a manuscript to CityLight.

With a shaky stride, I approach Lora. She's still sorting and counting money from one of the registers and looks up when I approach.

"You found a book," she exclaims happily. "Do you want me to ring that up for you?" Alarm spread across her expression at the sight of me. "Wait, honey. You look like you've seen a ghost. Are you feeling okay?"

Tears sting the edges of my eyes. I twist my lips, trying to get out the words that keep falling short on my tongue.

Lora's expression intensifies. "Honey, talk to me. What is it?"

I finally get my tongue to cooperate. I lift the book in my hands. My eyes are wide, my voice surprisingly hoarse. "This is my book. Someone has plagiarized my entire manuscript."

3

Andrew

The wrought iron gate screeches as I shove it open. It slams against a stone post and rattles the tune of my anger throughout the otherwise peaceful cemetery.

Autumn in New York City has always been my favorite season, but today, even the scent of chrysanthemums and the decadence of changing leaves is doing nothing to boost my mood. Today, all I see is death—the death of my future. Leaves crunching under my boots, I weave among the headstones. A bell rings in the distance, the deep, resounding chime emanating from the cathedral on the other side of the cemetery, which is near the church where my mother used to attend services. Briefly, I look in its direction and see the aged stone building rising before me. But I quickly turn my head and resume my walk, too miserable in my current state to heed its call. I haven't attended any church services since Mom passed. Add that to the tally of failures I'm racking up.

I try to focus on the disaster spinning in my mind. But it's no use. The familiar chimes count off in my head until they stop at eleven. The day isn't even half over, and already, it's ruined.

The marble monument we had engraved and installed to mark Mom's grave looms in front of me. Numerous flower arrangements decorate her headstone. She was beloved by many and clearly still is.

Today, I've arrived with no flowers in my hands. I do have a book tucked under my arm, though. Months ago, I thought it was the story that would offer me restoration or at least a way to get my life back on track. But it's proven to be nothing but a nail in the coffin of my own making.

I shove my hands into the pockets of my charcoal slacks, fighting the urge to yell and shatter the quiet composure of the cemetery. I wish I could talk to my mother. She knew how to fix things. No one could take something broken and make it right, heal a heartache, and remedy the worst mistakes like her. But could even she fix *this*?

I pull the book from under my arm and trace a finger down the spine. *Love Between the Pages.* The book I knew would make an impact on the world when I first rescued it from Ava's wastebasket and snuck a glance at its pages. But it was never supposed to end up like this.

For the next week, after rescuing the discarded manuscript, I sat at my computer, painstakingly typing every last word into a document. The novel brought me to tears at times. I tried my best to professionally edit it. Then, almost ten months ago, right before my trip to our family vacation home in Destin, I left the newly edited version on Dad's desk with a note: *Maybe this is worthy of CityLight's approval?*

I hope it's something you can finally be proud of me for.

I never heard a word. How could I ever have known that my father would take it to mean I'd written the book myself? Even I couldn't have predicted Gary Ketner pulling the mother of all Gary Ketners by going behind my back to "surprise" publish what he mistook as my own work. And now CityLight has committed the worst offense a publisher ever could: plagiarism.

"This is too far gone, Mom." My voice shakes with anger. "You know how Dad can be. He's even worse without you here to reel him in."

Love Between the Pages feels like lead in my hand, and if the words hadn't planted themselves so deeply into my heart, I would chuck it across the cemetery out of pure spite. "I don't see a way out of this one without destroying everything Dad and Grandfather built."

It isn't lost on me that I'm largely to blame. I was gone, away on another one of the trips that drove Dad crazy. When I didn't hear from him after I'd poured my best effort into preparing what I thought was a brilliant find for CityLight, I made myself as unavailable as I could. His silence proved to me that no matter what I did, he didn't plan to give me a chance. I shut Dad out completely for months.

And now, my bare-minimum approach to life and responsibility has finally caught up with me. Maybe if I had been *a real man*, as Dad had insinuated that night in his office, I would have stuck around instead of running like the coward I am to the distraction of Florida's Emerald Coast. If I had just *been* here, I could have stopped Dad from making this irreparable mistake. It was too easy for me to stop caring. I never even looked at the full list of upcoming books on CityLight's catalog.

Instead, I was blindsided this morning by the news. Taking a deep breath, I stand on a bed of drying leaves and replay the last few hours in my head.

After months in and out of the office and handling my role in the PR department remotely as much as I could, I've finally been feeling like I am regaining my footing. Lately, I've actually felt like trying again, so I showed up to the office today for the first time in weeks.

The sheer number of memos and emails I'd missed caught me off guard, so my first task of the day was to go through those. Ava bounded breathlessly into my office before I'd even made a dent, excitement splashed over her face.

"Andrew, can you believe it?"

"Yeah, I know. Pumpkin spice is back." I glanced up at her with a smirk.

She deadpanned, but her elation was back within seconds. "No. Have you seen our sales for this quarter? How many lists we've already made?"

I looked up from the Fantasy Football lineup on my phone screen and shrugged. "No. But I have a feeling you're going to tell me."

After returning from Florida, I'd fallen into a weird state of half-not-speaking, half-avoiding-every-awkward-interaction with Dad I could. I knew my production had nosedived, my drive to succeed nothing short of nonexistent. He clearly didn't believe in me, so what was the point in trying? His odd behavior over the past couple of months when we have crossed paths has further emphasized his disappointment. His quirky attempts at kindness and his uncharacteristic hands-off approach to managing me have been an obvious giveaway that he doesn't consider me or my ideas worth his time.

The patronizing has only made me block him out more and block out CityLight too. Other than the PR events I'd already coordinated, like the Pups and Paperbacks author event (where I somehow wound up adopting a mischievous golden retriever), I dipped in and out over the summer, not really paying attention to much happening at the company. This morning, I had a feeling Ava was about to get me up to speed.

"You're going to freak out." She toyed with the ends of her blonde hair and bounced from foot to foot. "For starters, do you remember how I got promoted a while back from senior acquisitions to production editor?"

"Yes. Congratulations, by the way. I don't think I ever properly congratulated you." Shame burned through me. I've neglected so much this year, friendships included. "I know it's always been your dream job." I lift my hand to give her a high five.

"Thank you."

"So, what's the big news for today? Let 'er rip."

She clapped her hands and squealed. "Okay, okay. Well, your father handed off a special book as my first project months and months ago. He didn't really explain how CityLight acquired the book, but he believed it was going to be a global smash. And Andrew . . . it is!"

"What book?"

She gave me a wry smile. "You don't pay much attention around here, do you? It's called *Love Between the Pages*."

The general office clatter outside my door went still. Was

I hearing her right? "Wait, wait. What . . . what did you say the title was?"

"*Love Between the Pages* by some unknown author. A.C. Frost? Whoever this Frost is has gone through tremendous lengths to keep themselves anonymous. Like, I'm talking legally binding contracts on our side. Even I don't know who Frost really is."

Love Between the Pages . . . The title is uncomfortably familiar, identical to the book I edited. But that was by a Charlie Blaire, not A.C. Frost. It could be a coincidence, I told myself. It wasn't *that* unique of a title. But a nagging in my gut told me that something wasn't right.

"Anyway," Ava prattled on, "it's a true shame this author doesn't want to be recognized. He or she is taking the book world by storm right now."

"What's this book about?"

"It's beautiful." She sighed wistfully. "Two missionaries, an impossible love story, the ultimate sacrifice . . . You really have to read it."

I didn't hear the rest. My ears rang with a high-pitched noise that I'm sure only I could hear. Had Dad really taken the manuscript I'd left him and passed it on to another editor? Did he give it to someone more suitable for the job? And he feels guilty for it, hence his weird behavior lately.

My heart sank as I processed the news. The fresh wave of Dad's rejection felt worse than any before. Saliva pooled in my mouth as my glands tightened, and nausea gripped my stomach. I thought I might actually lose my breakfast right in front of my long-standing friend and colleague.

"Wow, Ava, that's so awesome. I'm so happy for you and this company that I obviously care so much about," Ava said sarcastically as she snapped her fingers in front of my face.

I came out of my trance and shook my head. My stomach churned. "Sorry. I . . . uh . . . I am truly happy for you, Ava. Thanks for telling me."

"Man. Tough crowd." She set her hands on her hips and flipped her hair over her shoulder. "Maybe I'll have better luck in another department."

"Stop it. I'm thrilled for you. I think I'm just coming down with something. I don't feel well today."

"I wasn't going to mention anything, but you do kind of look like trash right now."

I smirked as she turned to leave. When Ava reached the door, she swung back toward me, snapping her fingers.

"Oh, before I go, I sent you an email this morning. Did you get it?"

I glanced down at my Fantasy Football app. "Haven't had a chance to check. Been busy."

Ava rolled her eyes. "I've been running this author's social media accounts for a couple of months, but your dad wants you to take it over. I sent you the login credentials."

"Me? Why?" A frown pulled my eyebrows together as I processed the unusual request. There were still a few old school authors CityLight worked with who didn't run their own socials, but that was unusual in this day and age. What was going on? Was this his way of sticking it to me? Was he planning to force me to run the account of a book he had excluded me from, punctuating his continued disappointment in me? My mouth went dry. How long had this project been going on? How long had my father been hiding this, not man enough to tell me himself?

I cleared my throat. "Ava, when was this book published?"

"A few weeks ago. Early October," she replied nonchalantly, drumming her nails on the doorframe. "Anyway, I've got loads of work to do, but I just wanted you to know. Also, you should connect with your dad. Stop stonewalling. You Ketner men really need better communication."

"Yeah," I grumbled, my head spinning. "Clearly."

She gave me a quizzical look then left. Once she was out of sight, I made a beeline upstairs to Dad's office. I didn't bother to check in with his secretary but barged into the room.

"*Love Between the Pages?*" I blurted out, the words a sharp accusation.

Dad was standing, obviously preparing to leave before I walked in. "My son finally speaks to me again!" Dad moved from behind his desk and wrapped me in a hug, catching me completely off guard. We haven't hugged in probably two years.

"It's been killing me to keep this surprise from you, but I knew you'd start paying attention and come around eventually!" He clapped a hand on my shoulder and beamed. "It took you long enough to come to thank me and quit blocking me out though. Andrew, I always knew you had it in you, son."

"Had . . . what in me?" My head spun. What universe was this? "Dad, what have you done?"

The smirk couldn't have been wiped from my father's face if he had tried. He moved to gather his briefcase, sliding a folder inside. "I feel so bad that I can't stay and talk. This is the worst time to catch me today. My car is waiting downstairs, and I'm already running late for my flight."

"Your flight? Where are you going?"

"Big book conference in Boston this weekend. I emailed you about it a while back, asking you to consider joining me. But that's when you weren't speaking to me." Dad winked and reached for a book on the far corner of his desk. He looked up at me, his expression suddenly back to the serious one I'm used to. "Andrew, your mother would have been so proud of you. Not as proud as I am though. Your pen name needed some work, but don't worry. I took care of that and changed it to something that honors your mom."

Dad handed the book to me. It was a hardcover copy of *Love Between the Pages*, the manuscript I'd rescued from Ava's wastebasket and edited months ago. I flipped through the pages, taking note of passages whose words I still hadn't forgotten. "Pen name?" I asked.

"Charlie Blaire made you sound too much like a woman," Dad replied, striding around the desk.

My breath froze in my lungs. "You . . . you . . ." I fought against my constricting throat. My brain could hardly keep up. "You published it? As . . . me?"

"I wanted it to be a surprise. You really proved yourself. When I found it on my desk and gave it a read through, I could hardly believe you'd written it! My own son."

"What did you do? It . . . it . . . never occurred to you to *call* me?"

"You were away in Florida. It was the anniversary . . ." Dad stopped himself and shook his head. "Trust me, son. There are things you mustn't waste time on. Decisive action is why CityLight has been such a success." He moved toward the door. "I thought you'd be happier than this. Becoming an author is what you've always wanted."

"No, Dad." My vision blackened, and he faded for a moment. The room began to spin. "You don't understand. You . . . you can't. I . . . didn't write this book!" I held it up, the pages ruffling as I shook them.

"Of course you didn't." He turned around and winked at me. "A.C. Frost did. Besides, as poor as your first choice was, I think having a pen name is smart. A nice touch. I don't want to be accused of nepotism."

I opened my mouth to speak but choked instead on my rapidly closing throat.

Dad opened the door. The ambient sounds of the offices beyond filled the room. His staccato tones sent his parting words toward me briskly. "Look, you need to take over Frost's social media account. I'm all for preserving the anonymity we've already built, and you have a marketing degree. Ava has the details. Chat with her. I think the anonymity angle is already creating buzz and working in favor of sales, but I need you to continue to build hype for the book. It's the least you can do after all I've done for you. See you Monday."

And then, in true Gary Ketner fashion, before I could get in another word, he'd walked out the door, leaving me alone in his office, shaken to my core.

The memory of this morning swirls in my mind as birds flit and chirp in the balding nearby trees. Burying my face in my palm, I berate myself for my inability to make him listen and blame Dad for not trying to hear me. And now, it's too late. Already, I can see the irreversible damage done to the company my father loves so much.

Plagiarism. The most forbidden, dreaded word in the publishing world. After Dad left, I stewed for a moment in my anger-fueled panic before racing back to my desk. I discovered that not only is *Love Between the Pages* already published and distributed, but it is also ranking higher than any book we've published in the last decade and flying off shelves. I want to dissolve into the earth, to fall into this grave we've dug for ourselves and pull it in after me. Inadvertently, we've set a train in motion, and I have no idea how to stop it.

The office walls felt like they were closing in, so I left and came to the only place I could think of to run. My only intention in presenting the manuscript I'd discovered to Dad was to prove that I could discover upcoming talent and that I have a rightful place within CityLight's walls. Charlie Blaire deserved to have the chance for publication I couldn't earn for myself.

"Mom," I plead through my fingers to the ground at my feet. I drop to my knees, and the book falls open across the crunchy leaves. The chilly breeze catches the pages and sends them turning. "What do I do?" But the ground before me is silent. Answers, I know, won't come from looking down, but in my despair, I can't quite bring myself to look up.

When I first read the rescued manuscript, it was its characters' bold exploration of the very questions that have plagued me since we lost Mom that gripped my attention and wouldn't let go. Questions about the meaning of hope, the origin of faith, and the certainty of a future beyond this life that I didn't know how to answer without her presence. I know to whom Mom would turn in this moment of turmoil, but the prayer is stiff on my unpracticed lips.

"What do I do, God? Is there any way to fix the mess I've made?"

My eyes fixed on the ground, I notice an envelope

peeking out from between the pages of the book. I lift it free. My name is scrawled across the front in my father's handwriting. I open it and read the note out loud.

"*Andrew,*

The depths of my pride cannot be found. This is an unconventional approach to repairing our relationship, but how conventional have I ever been? I know these past few years have been hard. I haven't been the father you need. Your struggle is evident. But you've taken your grief and created something beautiful. I didn't want to spoil any of that with the stress of bringing this book into the world. I wanted to surprise you by publishing your novel to show you how deeply invested I am. I appreciate your discretion with this publication process. You know how the world would respond if they thought I'd pushed it through because of our relationship as father and son.

Proud of you.

Dad"

I hold the note in the air and shake it. "Did you hear that, Mom? Dad finally believes in me, and it's not even me he believes in!" My laughter rings sarcastically through the cemetery. I pick up the book, dusting dirt from its cover. The gravity of what has happened cements itself in my core. "CityLight has plagiarized a book."

The rest of the afternoon and evening is spent at home frantically pouring over the internet. Sergio, my oversized and unruly golden retriever, brings me toy after toy to throw for him as I sit at my laptop and sweat bullets. I find next to nothing about Charlie Blaire, except for a dog training page run by someone of the same name from Vermont, but I do find plenty of reviews, viral booktoks, and the like about *Love*

Between the Pages. Apparently, it's caught the public right in the feels and is going viral. I research the implications of plagiarism and understand enough to have a very clear picture that CityLight and, by extension, my father, is in deep trouble.

But at the heart of it, I know I'm just as guilty as Dad.

I scour the internet until my eyelids droop and the early twilight has descended beyond the windows, then decide to give it a rest. I'm still angry that Dad's refusal to communicate with me has led to a disaster of this proportion. Maybe a little trouble is what he deserves after all. Maybe that's what it will take for him to finally come to his senses. I know that's not true. As frustrated as I am at my dad, I can't help but feel protective over my family's legacy.

As I lay on the sofa staring at my ceiling, I rack my brain for a solution that doesn't involve completely destroying Dad's reputation and the company he's dedicated his life to. It isn't as simple as hunting down the real Charlie Blaire and fessing up to our mistake. Once the news is public, the scandal and lawsuit could crush us. Suddenly, I remember that tomorrow is Saturday, which means my weekly basketball game with the guys. A group of guys which happens to include one of the best attorneys on CityLight's legal team, Josh Lance. Maybe he'll have some advice.

Reluctantly, I allow myself to rest, though I toss and turn most of the night. In the morning, I take Sergio for a jog before heading down to the court. It's five-on-five, and I play lousy. Blame it on stress or lack of sleep, I am an asset only to the opposing team.

At the end of the game, Josh tosses me a ball. "What is with your game today? You okay, bro?"

I dribble and make a jump shot. Airball. Josh cringes.

"I have a question," I say, not entirely sure if I should divulge the situation yet.

"Alright, shoot. Or, actually, maybe don't." Josh laughs.

"Hypothetically speaking, if an author accuses CityLight of plagiarism, what's the next step?"

Josh lands a three-pointer. He retrieves the ball, pausing in front of me with a thoughtful expression on his face. "Pending an investigation, we would determine if the claim is true or not. If we can prove it's untrue, of course the case will be dismissed, and in certain circumstances we may even have cause to pursue legal action against the accuser. There are a lot of leeches out there. You don't know the half of what I've seen throughout my career.

"But say the claim is found to be true, CityLight could be found liable for damages and would be forced to terminate all ties with and pursue legal action against any party knowingly involved—author, editor, literary agent, etcetera. The work in question would be removed from distribution, and we'd have a lot of cleaning up to do. In short, it would be a disaster. Why do you ask?"

I freeze and clear my throat. "I was just reading some articles last night. Got me thinking about worst-case scenarios."

He snorts. "Might want to stick to what you know, which clearly isn't basketball. Leave the legal stuff to me." He smacks me on the back and jogs up the court to retrieve the ball again.

I jog after him, but my shoes feel like lead. This is all going to be so much worse than any of us can imagine.

4

Charlie

The scent of freshly baked oatmeal chocolate chip cookies intensifies when I open the oven door and slide out the baking sheet pan. I'm on my fifth batch, and it isn't even noon yet. Every room in my cottage is saturated with the scent of cinnamon, vanilla, and chocolate. The kitchen countertop is strewn with dozens of cooling cookies. At about seven in the morning, I started with snickerdoodles and have now moved on to baked good varieties that include chocolate.

Because it's a drown-your-sorrows-in-chocolate kind of day.

"A plagiarism claim is a big deal, Charlie," Nate says through the speaker of my phone. I have him propped up on the wooden stand I usually use for holding open recipe books. Except today, I don't need instructions. I've stress-baked enough cookies in my lifetime to have my go-to recipes memorized.

We've been on the phone for almost an hour. After discovering the book that I spent years writing already published and hitting bestseller lists in Bluebird Books last night, I didn't know who else to call. Nate is a professional ghostwriter living on the Oregon coast, but he grew up in Pleasant Hollow. He's a lifelong friend and has at least some experience in the mysterious world of publishing, even if his name doesn't appear on the covers of the books he writes.

"Their lawyers are not going to take this lightly. Expect to have a fight on your hands and to bend over backward to prove this book is yours if you take this to them," he continues. His advice isn't making me feel any better about the situation. If anything, I feel worse than I did last night.

I turn toward the fridge to pull out more eggs and butter. Our local fire department is going to be thrilled with a fresh delivery of baked goods when I drop them off later today. At least someone will benefit from my habit of stress-baking whenever disaster hits. If our conversation keeps going in this direction, I'm going to have to take out my tension on a loaf of bread. Punching down some freshly risen dough would feel really good right about now.

"What do I do, Nate? I can't afford lawyers, but how else would I prove that the book is mine?"

"You could print your manuscript and take it to them. Show them the date you created the file."

I glance over at my friend on the screen. He's walking on the beach, holding me at face height as we talk. The sound of wind and waves crashing on the surf compete with his voice. Gray skies and deep green pines on the cliffs dot the scenery in the background. I know Nate walks when he feels stressed. It makes me feel a tiny bit better that someone else besides me cares about this catastrophe. I shake my head.

"Realistically, I don't see how even that would work. Who is to say I didn't just copy the novel, put my own tweaks into it, and then use an old document file to try to claim it's mine?"

"It would be the same thing someone did to you," Nate muses, and my heart drops for the hundredth time since last night.

I managed to drive myself home last night after stumbling up to Lora behind the counter at Bluebird Books to announce that one of her latest featured books is actually mine and has been plagiarized. How and why, I had no idea. Even with a cursory glance, I could see that my words had been professionally edited. There were tweaks here and there, but the core of the book was the same. My words. My story. There was no doubt in my mind. *Love Between the Pages* was my book. Someone stole it and published my book baby, taking all the credit for themselves. Lora must have thought I'd suddenly gone crazy to make such an outrageous claim.

I paid for the book—the cruel irony of which did not escape me—got back into my truck and left. When I arrived home, I threw myself onto the sofa without even taking off my shoes and began reading. I never even went to bed. I stayed up all night reading my book. The first time, I read through it rapidly, turning page after page as my eyes tore through the words. When I finished the last page, I took a deep breath and turned back to the beginning. During my second read through, I took my time, each word memorized and imprinted on my heart long ago.

By the time dawn broke through the forest of trees

behind my cottage, I went to the kitchen to make a cup of coffee. My nerves were still too abuzz to even consider sleep, but my body was starting to protest. I haven't pulled an all-nighter since studying for final exams in college.

As the hot, steaming elixir of life, aka coffee, dripped slowly into the carafe, I opened the back door and leaned against the frame, staring at the soft morning light filtering through the bare branches and firs beyond the deck. Trying to still the panic in my chest, I considered my options. The problem was I had no idea what options were available to me. How did anyone approach a situation like this?

After reading the book for the second time, I went into the tiny back bedroom I use as an office. Combing through my records, I found proof. Earlier this year, I sent a manuscript—a foolishly unsolicited manuscript—to CityLight Press. CityLight is well-known and prestigious. The thought that they would be part of this farce is unbelievable. Stealing an unknown author's manuscript is unheard of for a reputable and well-respected publisher, and it will ruin their credibility when the public finds out.

One thing I knew: The first person I planned to call was Nate. If anyone could figure out what to do, it would be my friend. And if he didn't know, I could trust him to have plenty of ideas. Nate relocated from Pleasant Hollow to Oregon a few years ago. Something about needing to live near the ocean, feel the salty breezes on his skin, etcetera. I love our little Vermont valley home, but I couldn't blame him for craving the sense of freedom and awe the ocean invoked.

The urge to bake hit me halfway through my second cup of coffee. It wasn't even sunrise on the West Coast, and I didn't have the heart to wake my friend before dawn. I'd stress-bake my way through a few pounds of flour and butter and sugar and then give him a call.

I was sliding my third batch of cookies into the oven when he answered on the first ring. His hair was mussed, and he rubbed sleep out of his eyes as the Facetime call connected.

"What's up, Charlie?" he said. "I didn't expect to see you ringing my phone this morning. Is everything okay at home?" Nate's mother and father still live in the valley. I try to check up on them often.

His question sparked the tears I'd held back all night. The salty liquid stung, and angrily, I dashed them away. Nothing felt right anymore, and I wasn't sure if anything would ever be right again.

"Hey, hey." Nate sat up immediately, instant alarm spreading across his face. I saw his eyes drift to the scene behind me. "Wait. Uh-oh. Your kitchen looks like it has turned into a full-on bakery. You only bake that much when something's wrong. What's happened, Charlie?"

And I'd be baking a heck of a lot more than this before I even remotely felt better.

"Do you remember that novel I told you I was writing a couple of years ago?" I began to blubber.

Nate rubbed his hand across his face. "Yeah, the one about your mom and dad?"

I nodded, the hot tears streaking down my face now. "I finished it at the beginning of the year, and I sent it to some publishing houses to see if anyone had an interest. I knew it was in a super rough state, but it was a total whim. I was completely unprepared, but I felt that if I didn't just do it, I'd find some way to talk myself out of it."

"Okay," Nate tried to hide his confusion. "Did you get a rejection letter or something? Is that why you're crying?"

"No." My sobs came harder. All night, I'd managed to hold back my tears, the shock rendering me emotionless. Stoically, I'd read through my stolen novel like a robot, absorbing the words but never letting myself connect with them. As soon as Nate's kind, sympathetic face filled my screen and he asked what was wrong, every emotion I'd held back all night bubbled instantly to the surface. The tears rolled across my chin, and I watched as they dripped into the mixing bowl of freshly creamed sugar and butter for my next batch of cookies.

"What is it, Charlie? You're really freaking me out right now. Did you get an offer letter? Are these happy tears?"

Wildly, I shook my head. "Someone stole my manuscript. I don't know who or how, but they stole it, and CityLight published it. The book just came out, and critics are calling it an instant bestseller." I didn't even bother to hide the bitterness in my tone.

Nate's end of the line fell silent for a long, breathless moment. "Tell me everything," he finally said.

"Who is this A.C. Frost," Nate says after I've poured the whole story out to him. We've progressed past the initial shock, and he is in full research mode at this point. "I'm searching on my phone, and I can't find anything substantial on this woman, or I guess it could be a man as well. Is it a pen name?"

"Maybe? Even the author site redirects me back to CityLight's main website. There just isn't much. Even her (or his) social media accounts are generic posts more for PR than anything."

"Have you tried getting in touch with CityLight?"

I nod, using a spoon to portion out a fresh batch of cookies onto a baking sheet. "Nothing but the runaround from their customer service. To talk to anyone there, you have to have an extension, and no one would give me a clear answer."

"It's all about who you know in the industry," Nate says thoughtfully. "Honestly, Charlie, I only see one choice for you. You have to get a lawyer, tell them everything, and file a lawsuit against CityLight."

I chew on my lips for a minute, processing the advice. My gaze drifts through the window over my sink toward my backyard. The branches of the red maples and oak trees that crowd among the spruce trees are nearly bare of leaves, the muted hues of the crisping leaves covering the ground like a sunset-colored carpet. I'm not sure if I'm ready to pursue a lawsuit.

For many years, Pleasant Hollow has been my safe place, my shelter to weather out the storms of life. Even though I've dreamt of seeing my name in print, pursuing fame was never part of that dream. The last thing I want is to go public with my allegations and end up a pariah in the publishing community. Pursuing the rights to my novel is risky. I could make the trip to The Big Apple and come away with nothing but rejection and a broken heart. Worse, what if accusing CityLight and A.C. Frost of plagiarizing my novel lands me in the hot seat? Could they countersue me if I can't prove that *Love Between the Pages* is mine?

A little voice in the back of my brain begs me not to go. It begs me to curl up in a little ball in my safe Vermont village and cry away my sorrow until I have the strength to get up and write again. Clearly, one of my books has already made it, even if it has been stolen right out from under me. Maybe I can write another bestseller and protect the legal rights to my work this time. I could get published for real. Is getting justice worth the potential heartache?

For the book that is my love letter to my beloved parents? Yes. Yes, it is.

Using the back of my flour-dusted hand to dash away the last of my tears, I straighten my shoulders and look toward the phone screen. Nate is watching me quietly, his brow furrowed as he waits for my reply.

"Okay." I take a deep, steadying breath. "I'm not sure what I want to do yet. But suppose I pursue a plagiarism claim. Walk me through everything I need to do to make this right."

5

Andrew

"You can't hide out forever, Andrew," Dad whispers in my ear with coffee fresh on his breath. "I mean, look at this. This is all because of you. Don't you want to revel in your success?"

I take in the main floor of the office just beyond my doorway. Banners were carefully hung over the weekend, and the desks were decorated with balloons and flowers to celebrate landing on *The New York Times* Best Sellers List. Today, smiles are plastered on the staffs' faces and for good reason. I've tried without success to tune out the bubbling conversations about the mysterious CityLight author who has beat multiple sales records and is now crowned with the ultimate prize. *Love Between the Pages* has created such a splash that there is already speculation about which prestigious literary awards it will win this year. The scene is out of a movie. It's so jovial and over the top I could puke.

How am I going to burst everyone's bubble with the news of this plagiarism?

Someone extends a tray of gourmet donuts toward me, and I wonder if the sugar will help calm my nerves. I pick a maple bar from the tray, but as I take the first bite, a fresh wave of guilt rises from a place deep inside and nearly makes me choke. Dad claps me on the back and shoves a steaming cup of coffee at me. The liquid burns on the way down, but the ball of sugar in my throat dissolves. I'm left sputtering for only a moment.

"Alright there, bud?" Dad asks.

"Crisis averted," I rasp and take a deep breath. "I'm going to look for some water and maybe get some fresh air."

He leans in closer to me, a proud grin peeking through his graying beard. "Just don't be too long. This party is for you."

I cringe and attempt to return the smile, but I know it doesn't quite meet my eyes. This office-wide celebration is the first time I've seen Dad since Friday, and I know I need to tell him the news. But the thought of coming clean with the awful truth has me choking on the words even now. Before he can press me to be proud of myself yet again, I stride out of the room, grab my coat from my office, and head downstairs, the hot cup of coffee still in my hand.

So far, Dad is the only soul who knows that *Love Between the Pages* is mine. Well, not *mine-mine*. In a million years, I never predicted the nightmare this turned out to be. When I rescued Charlie Blaire's manuscript from Ava's wastebasket, I thought it might be leverage . . . something I could do to prove myself as an asset to CityLight and make Dad take me seriously.

I took Blaire's work, which was already an excellent start, and refined it enough to show Dad that I am capable of finding good manuscripts too. I should have known he'd take it and turn it into the masterpiece that is flying off the shelves worldwide.

As I speed walk toward the elevator, the coffee sloshing around in a paper cup branded with the CityLight Press logo, I notice that every office is empty. Everyone is gathered on the main floor, talking and laughing and eating catered donuts and coffee from The Drip, the firm's go-to coffee shop down the street. I can't blame them. They are gathered in honor of an overnight success, the elusive, albeit imaginary, author A.C. Frost. Though A.C. Frost isn't entirely made up. Dad was trying to pay homage to my late mother, Alexandra Celeste Winters, and her favorite season.

I press the button for the elevator, and it opens right away. Every part of this week has been a nightmare I wish I could wake up from. I close my eyes and let the elevator carry me downward and closer to my freedom from this suffocating building.

I've no sooner stepped off the elevator when a tangle of shouting voices draws my attention toward the front desk, where Mattias is trying to prevent a small-statured woman from approaching the elevator bank. He lifts his arms to block her while Lacey, the building's main receptionist, watches in horror.

"You can't go up there, miss!" Mattias' voice pleads as she tries to dart around him. "Please stop before I call the authorities!"

"I should be the one calling the authorities!" the woman shrieks. "You don't understand what they've done!"

I approach from the side, trying to assess the situation before I intervene. As I close the gap, I see that despite her slight frame, the young woman's face is set and determined. She has locked eyes with Mattias, and if I had to bet, my money would be on her winning whatever dispute this is. I also take note that she is pretty and well put together, with long, cascading coffee-colored hair that flows over her almost-blush hued sweater. Long leather boots, jeans, and a wide-brimmed hat complete her look. She looks like an adorable L.L. Bean model. Mattias glances over and catches my eye with an exasperated frown on his face.

With caution, I approach the scene. "What is going o—"

Before I can finish my sentence, the woman swings to the side, breaking free from Mattias with a momentum that carries her smack into my chest. Caught off guard, I stumble backward and feel the hot burn of coffee saturate my crisp white shirt as the woman struggles to find her footing.

I reach out to steady her, lightly cupping her elbow. "Is this love I feel brewing between us or just my spilled coffee?"

She peels herself off me, her cheeks burning red. Strands of her long, dark hair stick to her face where it was pressed against my wet shirt. Her brown eyes widen in horror as she takes in the mess. I stare down at her in amusement, thinking that her deer-in-the-headlights look is rather cute and a welcome, though stark, contrast to the MMA fighter mode I just witnessed.

"I . . . am . . . so sorry!" She pushes the sticky pieces of hair away from her face, and her hand comes to rest in front of her mouth. "Can I . . . I am . . ." She shakes her head and mutters, "I can't believe this is happening."

Nor can I. I look down at my ruined clothes and almost

laugh at the irony. Today, of all days, I deserve no less.

"It's fine," I reply. "Turns out the coffee here wears better than it tastes."

She winces and hides her face in her hands. A beat passes before she finally brings them down, heaving a heavy sigh in the process. She looks from me to Mattias, who now stands by my side with his hands on his hips and a heavy frown across his brow.

"I am so sorry to both of you," she groans. "I, um . . . It hasn't exactly been my day. Or week, for that matter."

"How about your month? Even your year?"

My joke brings a tiny smirk to the corner of her mouth. "What? Is it a requirement to be a *Friends* fan in this city?"

Her lips are pretty, and I catch myself staring at them before I pull away my gaze and arch an eyebrow. "Okay . . . so we can establish that you're not a *Friends* fan, nor are you from the city. Are you some sort of"—I lower my voice an octave and bend toward her—"criminal?"

Her mouth drops open, and the fire returns to her eyes. "Excuse me?"

I hold up my hands in surrender. "Hey, I'm not the one dissing one of New York's most famous sitcoms, let alone attempting to break past security."

She works her jaw and smooths the front of her knit sweater with a nervous gesture. "Fair enough," she affirms. "But today's outburst is more because I'm just a simpleton from Vermont with a plagiarized manuscript."

My heart drops into my stomach. Surely, I misheard her. "I'm sorry. What did you say?"

Fire flashes in her eyes. "*Love Between the Pages.* Ever heard of it?" She is seething, and I feel the weight of her wrath settle on me. "Of course, you have." She lifts her hands with exasperation. "Everyone has! But that's my book!"

My lips part. *You are Charlie Blaire?* I nearly blurt the words aloud but catch myself just in time. This woman, with her fiery brown eyes, adorable pout, coffee-infused hair, and black jeans—is that dog hair on them?—is the writer whose dream I have accidentally destroyed? I swallow hard, my temperature rapidly jumping between hot and cold. Fresh air is needed now more than ever.

Immediately, I know I need to tread carefully. People have already thrown us a few glances in the lobby. Mattias flashes me a look that says even he knows this type of accusation would ruin the reputable CityLight name that my family has worked so hard to build. If she blurts the full truth out loud . . . *Think fast, Andrew.*

"That's quite a serious claim." I furrow my brow, racking my brain for a way out of this disaster. Whatever happens, I've done enough research into the legal ramifications of plagiarism this weekend to know that our best bet is to settle quietly. The public can never find out about this. If word gets out, our company will be forever ruined as a leading force in publishing. It would take years to regain CityLight's reputation. And my relationship with Dad, strained as it is, would be destroyed.

"It's a very serious matter," Charlie Blaire snaps.

It's time to take control of the situation. I reach into my shirt pocket and withdraw a damp, coffee-stained business card, giving it a small shake before handing it to her. "You spilled the beans on the right guy, it seems."

I have got to stop with these coffee puns.

I extend my hand to her. "Andrew Ketner, public

relations for CityLight Press." Inwardly, I wince at the sound of my last name, wondering if she'll immediately recognize the surname of CityLight's CEO.

I half expect her to step away from me in horror and shout, "He's the one! Plagiarizer! Book thief!"

To my relief, Charlie barely glances at the card. Visibly flustered, she slips her free hand into mine, giving it a shake while stuffing my soggy card down into the purse slung over her shoulder. "You work for CityLight?" she says, clearly skeptical.

"I do. Rather than continuing to cause a scene and making Mattias here call the police, would you like to sit down with me and discuss what is going on? I was just stepping out for some fresh air and . . . a new coffee, apparently. There's a coffee shop down the street. Care to join me over a cup, and we'll discuss your matter?"

Charlie lifts her chin and searches my face. I can't help noticing the striking espresso hue of her eyes as they flicker back and forth. Even infused with deep anger and resentment, they're beautiful. *She's beautiful.* And she's nothing like I expected the mysterious Charlie Blaire to be when I first read her manuscript months ago.

That seething anger is pointed at CityLight and at you, Andrew. Snap out of it, man!

Still, I can't suppress the brief flutter in my chest when she draws a deep breath and says, "Sure. Let's go."

6

Charlie

If this is how all New York City men look and behave, I may have to consider relocating. I can train dogs anywhere, can't I? Andrew holds the door open for me as we exit the building and make our way down the sidewalk. There's something familiar about him, but I don't know what it is. Surely, I would remember meeting a man like him? He is certainly memorable in the looks department: over six feet, broad-shouldered, with a combination of tan skin, milky chocolate eyes, just the right amount of stubble, and wavy golden-brown hair that looks like he just threaded his fingers through it.

I shake my head at my inner thoughts and refocus on avoiding the waves of humanity walking briskly along the city sidewalks. My experience with big cities is limited to occasional trips to Burlington, and I'm guessing the small, friendly city could almost fit into a few blocks of NYC. Once,

I visited Nashville, but even that city seems small in comparison. Andrew, however, seems unfazed by the rush of pedestrians who seem equally unconcerned about bumping into, stepping on, and otherwise pushing past everyone in their line of sight for more than five seconds.

It is a lot to take in. A woman stops short in front of me, and I nearly bowl into the back of her.

"Whoa there." Andrew's smooth, deep voice falls on my ear. I feel his hand gently cradle my elbow as he guides me around her. The warmth of his touch reaches me even through my sweater. He pulls me gently around the woman, his fingers lingering for an extra moment as we pass her. "Good thing she wasn't carrying coffee."

It takes me a second to realize he's joking. The rich scent of the coffee stain now on his once crisp white shirt lingers under my nose against the smell of car exhaust, pavement, and people. I feel a painful twinge of guilt over ruining what was clearly an expensive item of clothing by my clumsiness. Glancing from the corner of my eye, I eye his wool camel coat, checking the lapel for any signs that the coffee has ruined that as well.

To my relief, it doesn't look like I will be on the hook for a dry cleaning bill for the coat. Good. I've been in New York for all of a couple of hours, and already, I'm racking up a bill.

Andrew catches me eyeballing him and flashes me a smile. It's the kind of smile you can't help but smile back in response to. An unexpected sensation flutters in my stomach as the expression lights up his face. This handsome man looks like a walking advertisement for an autumn-themed magazine shoot. He's the picture of upscale city life in his brown slacks, once stain-free white shirt, and that elegant coat. Andrew looks like summer warmth fading into the cooling off of fall, with hayrides and caramel and bonfires just around the corner.

And his warm, friendly personality is like golden retriever energy meets GQ. My face flushes. Immediately, I drop my eyes and turn back to the sidewalk, reminding myself silently to stay focused on the task at hand. Getting distracted by this good-looking man is only going to derail what needs to be done.

"Are you walking me all the way to Central Perk?" I hear myself say in a tone a bit snarkier than I intend. Too late, it occurs to me that I just walked away with a perfect stranger into the crowded, oblivious rush of New York. He could be hustling me toward a windowless van waiting on the curb right now. Does the public relations department of a company like CityLight even handle issues like this?

Just as I begin to panic, his caramel voice reaches me. "I would," he counters before I can sprint off and run yelling, "Stranger danger" down the sidewalk. "But I think they are closed today. You'll have to settle for our local bean water instead."

He pauses in front of a modern looking storefront and grasps the door handle. I look up to see a sign reading "The Drip" hanging above the door. He pulls it open and stands to the side. His free hand makes a little motion. "After you."

I eye him again, wondering if his chivalrous, friendly personality is all an act. Aren't big city men supposed to be self-absorbed and aloof? Despite his handsome looks and expensive clothing, there's a small-town charm to Andrew's mannerisms that would probably make me googly-eyed in a hot second if I wasn't in New York for a very serious matter that I do not intend to allow myself to be distracted from.

With a nod, I step into the coffee shop. The scent of freshly ground beans, brown sugar, and baked goods hits me immediately, and my stomach growls. I haven't had much of an appetite the past few days, and the delicious scents make my mouth water.

The space is elegant and modern. A black and white marble floor leads to the counter, which is constructed of glass display cases, white marble, and wood. Even the walls are lined with white subway tiles. Gold light pendants hang from the ceiling. A multi-station machine hisses as streams of rich, dark espresso pour into tiny cups.

"Not in Kansas anymore, are we, Charlie?" I mutter under my breath as I greet the barista, a bored college-aged woman behind the counter.

"I'll take a double espresso with sugar. And . . ." I lean back to take in the baked goods and treats stacked temptingly behind the glass. "I'll take a butterscotch cookie and a pumpkin spice cookie too, please."

"That'll be twenty-twenty-four," the barista drawls.

"For two shots of espresso and two cookies? That is like one dollar's worth of ingredients." I stare at her until Andrew's voice behind me draws me back to reality.

"Please. My treat. I'll add a double espresso to the order," he says.

Swinging around, I don't even attempt to hide my frown. "I can pay for my own."

He glances down at me as he hands the barista a black card. "I invited you. My treat," he replies, his tone final.

Irritated, I shake my head. "Well, thank you."

I'm not sure if I'm more annoyed with myself for racking

up a twenty-dollar bill at this pricey coffee shop or with him for not letting me assert my independence. I turn away before I say anything else and walk over to a small iron and marble bistro table near the window. If I have to be in New York, I might as well people watch while I'm here.

Instead of joining me, Andrew waits at the counter for our order. When he walks over, he is balancing a tray on one hand with more precision than I would have given him credit for. Still resentful, I wonder if my treats are laced with gold or if these are just big city prices.

He settles on the wicker chair across from me. I take a sip of the strong, sweet espresso and eagerly reach for the golden butterscotch cookie, hoping it will satisfy my hunger until I can find a proper meal. I take a bite and grimace. I reach for the other cookie and sample a piece. It earns the same frown.

"Everything okay?" Andrew asks, his own cup and saucer balanced in his hand.

I wave my hand. "It's fine. I could just make a better butterscotch cookie at home in my pajamas on a Friday night blindfolded."

Before I can blush over the realization that I just admitted to having no social life, Andrew throws his head back and laughs. The sound is rich and throaty and clear. "Somehow, I have zero doubts of that being true, Charlie Blaire."

I think he is complimenting me, but I'm still offended. "Here." I shove the small plate with the cookies across the table toward him. "Taste it and tell me what you think."

He breaks off a small chunk of the butterscotch cookie and pops it into his mouth. "If you can bake a cookie better than that one, I'd sure like a batch of those," he says a moment later. There's amusement on his face, but his eyes are serious.

I roll my eyes. "Believe me, if I had a kitchen, I'd prove it to you."

"I have a kitchen," he says. The warmth in his face draws me in. "I'm too busy to cook most nights, so it would be like working in a brand-new space. If you stick around, maybe you should show me how to bake a butterscotch cookie that's up to your standards."

"If I stick around? As soon as I get the rights to my book back, I'm out of here."

Andrew purses his lips. "I didn't mean for that to sound . . ." He blows out a breath and rubs the back of his neck. "I'm sure you have a whole life—husband, job, and all—to get back to in . . . Where is it you're from again?"

"Vermont." My eyes briefly flicker away from his curious eyes. "And no husband or boyfriend, for that matter," I mutter as I break off another chunk of pumpkin spice cookie just to decimate it between my fingers. "Not that it's any of your business."

He clears his throat and shifts in his seat, the corners of his mouth downturned ever so slightly.

"I like to bake," I revive the subject, suddenly nervous. *I like to bake?*

"Do you work in a bakery?"

"No, I own an obedience training school for dogs, and I volunteer at the animal shelter." Even I hear how lame it sounds. *Wow, exciting life, Charlie.*

"Do you ever make homemade treats for the dogs you work with?"

I nod, unsure why I'm suddenly blushing.

Andrew leans forward, resting his elbows on the tabletop. "Spoiled dogs. I'd consider myself very lucky if you were baking treats like that for me."

As my brain imagines Andrew leaning against the counter in my tiny cottage kitchen while I bake trays and trays of the most delicious cookies ever, I force myself to stop drowning in his milk chocolate eyes and come back to reality. I frown and firmly shake my head at him. "I don't care about the cookies. My book has been plagiarized. What are you and CityLight going to do about it?"

His reaction is like a veil has been dropped over his face. He shutters his expression, pushes the espresso cup aside, and leans back in the chair to assess me. Briefly, his eyes dart to somewhere behind me. His side of the table suddenly feels distinctly cooler than it did a moment ago. "What makes you think the book in question is taken from your manuscript?"

My hands fly up in exasperation, and I try not to raise my voice. "Because it's almost word for word. Every chapter. Every scene. Almost identical. But whoever this A.C. Frost is was clever. They edited just enough: a word here, a word there. But the core of the book, the heart of the plot, it's all mine."

"CityLight isn't in the habit of publishing plagiarizers." Andrew frowns. He closes his eyes and takes a deep breath. "Do you have any actual proof of the allegations you're making?"

I lean down and rifle through the leather purse I'd set on the floor. "Believe me, I already know what a legal battle this is going to be. I don't expect this to be easy. But I have my manuscript here. I started writing this book several years ago. It's all here. You can even compare it to *Love Between the*

Pages. I have that here too."

I'm babbling, but I don't care. I hand the folder containing all three hundred and fifty-seven pages of my original manuscript to him. Andrew takes the sheath of paper and stares at the title page for a long moment, his expression somber. He turns the page, his eyes scanning the text before he turns another.

The steady hum of voices and machines and car horns on the street echo behind me, but my heart is pounding too hard in my ears for me to hear the din. I watch the man in front of me closely.

After flipping through the pages, Andrew places my manuscript on his knee. "I don't have to tell you how serious the allegations you're making are. Besides this manuscript— and I don't want to offend you, but anyone could have typed this up and slapped their name onto it—do you have any further proof that you wrote this book?"

Briefly, I close my eyes to gain control over the flood of emotions I feel building inside my chest. He's right, but I don't want to admit it out loud. Why should he believe me, a stranger, when CityLight has been publishing some of the biggest names in publishing for decades? They have a stellar reputation, and their lawyers will fight tooth and nail to protect it. A sense of dread pushes aside some of the anger I feel rising. Do I really think I can win this battle when they have endless lawyers and funds to contest my claim?

The truth is that while I make a good enough living in Pleasant Hollow, I'm just a tiny minnow in an ocean of sharks right now. A nobody thinking she's going to do battle with an army of the rich and influential. Nate is right. The only chance I have to reclaim ownership of my book is to bluff my way through this or find the right person to buddy up with who is willing to take on my cause.

My eyes fly open, and I catch Andrew watching me. He quickly shutters his expression again, and the flutter that automatically began in my stomach dies down instantly. Sternly, I remind myself that as polite as he's been, Andrew is front and center in the enemy's camp. I have no doubt that he hustled me away from CityLight's offices on purpose before I could create more of a scene.

And like a fool, I let him because he charmed me with *Friends* puns, and there was something irresistibly swoon-worthy about the way he gripped my elbow when I crashed into him and spilled coffee everywhere. He didn't even act like it bothered him.

I feel a scowl begin to work its way across my features. I sit up straighter and pull back my shoulders. Neither intimidation nor false charms are going to work on me.

"On the counsel of a trusted adviser, I don't think I'm going to say anymore." I hope my tone reflects the confidence I don't feel. "My friend Nate advised me to retain the services of a lawyer, and that's what I'm going to do. CityLight isn't going to get away with stealing the book I wrote. Be prepared to be served with papers any day." I'm slightly bluffing because I haven't found a lawyer and don't even know where to start looking. Resolutely, though, I press my lips together and stare straight into his eyes.

Andrew's face has paled noticeably. He lifts his hand and strokes his jaw, then leans forward and props both elbows on his knees. When he opens his mouth, his question catches me off guard. "Who is Nate, Ms. Blaire? Is he the one pushing you to do this?"

Instantly, I'm furious. Standing abruptly, I shove my chair away. The coffee shop swirls around me. "Why does it matter to you who Nate is? He has nothing to do with this nightmare inflicted upon me by CityLight. This is three years of my life. No, this is my family's entire history wrapped up in three hundred and fifty-seven pages, and it was taken from me. By your company."

Bending, I snatch up my purse and grab my manuscript from Andrew's fingers. I turn away and then whip back toward him. He's staring at me again with an expression I can't read. "Any decent person would want to make this right," I snap. "When someone knowingly allows injustice to continue, it says a lot of not very nice things about their character. Thanks for the coffee."

It's late morning, and the day is bright against my eyes as I burst onto the sidewalk. Someone bumps into my shoulder. Immediately, I feel the press of bodies moving me down the street. I blink back against fresh tears, trying to keep my footing as the pedestrian traffic propels me forward. Looking around, I can't spot a single friendly face in the river of people on the sidewalk. New York City is already proving to be treacherous, and if I'm not careful, I'm going to end up washed down river, beaten and bruised against the current.

A wave of claustrophobia chokes me. I get caught in a pocket of walkers, and I feel like I can't breathe. Catching sight of the other side of the street, it seems more open. I know I need more elbow room before I have a meltdown right on a New York City sidewalk.

"Excuse me," I gasp, my arms shooting out to push people aside. "Please let me through."

Ignoring the grumbles and sarcastic quips, I shove and

break a path, trying to reach the street.

There's a sudden opening. I dart toward it. One more step, and I'll reach the curb. I lunge forward and . . . feel myself lifted off my feet and yanked backward . . . just as the front fender of a yellow cab whips by and narrowly misses my legs.

"Hey, let me go!" I yell, instinctively kicking and reaching down to claw at the strong arm surrounding my waist. I can feel the plane of a broad chest pressed firmly against my back. Panic sets in, and a mist swims over my eyes. My hat shifts, nearly falling off my head in the struggle to free myself. My feet finally hit the concrete again. I try to twist to see who just rescued me from getting taken out by a cab. Either that or this person is trying to kidnap me. I don't know if I'm grateful for the rescue or upset that this person still has his arm around me.

A warm, caramel-coated voice hums low in my ear, his breath a whisper against my hair. "Whoa there. It's okay. I've got you."

Andrew releases me, and I stumble around in shock to face him. "Th . . . thanks," I stutter. "I didn't even see that cab." A few looky-loo pedestrians are lingering, staring at us as if they think drama is about to unfold. Two women have their cell phones out and pointed in our direction. I try to regain my composure so they go away. "Are you following me?" I hiss.

"Yes." Andrew nods seriously. "And it's a good thing I did. Wouldn't want a cab to take you out on your first day in the city. What kind of welcome is that?" The sun glints off an unruly curl of hair brushing his forehead.

"But why are you following me?" My teeth are clenched,

and I feel the beginnings of a migraine pounding at the back of my brain.

Andrew notices the people watching us. He steps closer to me, his frame shielding me from the view of the onlookers. I have to tilt my chin back to look up at him.

"I want to help." He shrugs. "Will you let me help you, Charlie?"

7

Andrew

Her words burn as she storms away from me. *Not very nice things about my character?*

I guess I did just throw bold face lie after bold face lie at her, but what else was I supposed to do? I tried my best to think like a lawyer, but I fear I've only made an already horrible situation even worse. A knife twists in my gut, and I want to melt to the floor. No one has trained me on how to handle a corporate-wide mistake of this degree. It's not like I could just admit the truth to her over a casual cup of coffee. Josh would have my head.

The sashay of her long, dark hair disappears into the swarm of passersby on the sidewalk outside The Drip. Yet the crowd doesn't swallow her completely. I still see the top of her wide-brimmed hat as she weaves and ducks and stumbles into bodies around her. New York City is ruthless to newcomers who don't know how to navigate as a pedestrian, and Charlie looks like a deer suddenly thrown into the middle of the city.

What is happening? In the last hour, I've gone from celebrated, unintentional, rising-star (without a clue until last week) author to coffee-stained poser by the fierce and fiery woman who deserves my every apology and is . . . currently being swallowed alive by the crowd outside.

I push away the wicker chair and jog out the door. I need to catch her to tell her I want to help—although help might be a loose word. Can I help my father not find out about my mistake, help his company not go under, help repair the damage I've done to this woman who clearly doesn't deserve it? I have to smooth this situation over the best I can. But how can I do that if I let her go?

I weave through the pedestrians, keeping my eyes trained on her small figure just ahead. How can I get lost in those espresso-colored eyes again if I let her walk away? It's crazy, but I want to dig deeper into the heart of the true author of *Love Between the Pages*. I want to know the writer who made me feel more hope than I've felt in so long . . . since Mom died.

Can I find a way to solve this dilemma if I let her . . . get hit by a cab? *Shoot!* I lunge forward, sliding my arm around Charlie's waist and yanking her backward just in the nick of time. The cab zips by with a quick, annoyed tap of its horn.

I'm not sure whose heart is beating more wildly—hers or mine. I don't release her right away, and with her back pressed against my torso, she flails like a madwoman against me. I'm tempted to say, *"Beating up the man who just saved your life says a lot of really not nice things about your character."*

But I refrain, and when she finally wriggles free to face

me, I see that not even the fright of death has buried the fury inside of her. Realizing who just saved her, she musters a timid apology and then proceeds to accuse me of following her.

I can't help but be glad that I did.

She's okay. She's safe.

Her wild eyes glance nervously around us, and I take a step toward her, wanting her focus to be fully on me. I lean over her, my voice low, "I want to help. Will you let me help you, Charlie?"

Her lips part, eyes widening in shock. Another flash of fire moves over her face as she eyes me with caution.

"That would be . . ." She draws a deep breath, still obviously shaken from her near run-in with the cab. Nodding curtly, she finally says, "Yes. Thank you."

Relief floods through me, and I resist a sudden strong temptation to hug her, because:

1.   She would probably pummel me.

2.   The nosy onlookers would get even more of a show.

3.   It's vital I get my emotions in check because I'm on the verge of blurting the full truth out to this beautiful, completely unexpected woman, and . . . doing so would be a disaster.

"Alright, then." I drop my voice an octave and lean closer to her. "Shall we take this somewhere we are not the main attraction?"

"Right," she says, smoothing the front of her oversized knit sweater. The color is caught between cream and the softest of pinks, and I'm struggling to take my eyes away from the glow it casts on her delicate face.

Gently gripping her elbow, I direct her back toward the

coffee house. First things first. I am determined to finish a whole cup of coffee today, both for the sake of buying myself time to decide what to do and for the dull ache that's forming in my skull. Come to think of it, water might serve me better, but what says this day is going poorly more than stress drinking a double espresso?

Once we've reentered the shop, Charlie sits across from me with a sheepish look on her face. I still can't believe it's *her*. *The* Charlie Blaire who months ago sunk me to my knees with the words she'd penned. She tucks her hair behind her ears and watches me drain the cooling espresso left in my cup. I know she's waiting for me to express exactly how I plan to help her, so I clear my throat.

"I understand how serious you are about pursuing action in regard to this plagiarism claim, Ms. Blaire. And if these claims you make are true, I want you to know that I am on your side and committed to making this right." I mean every single word.

She remains stoic, but the smallest flicker of hope in her eyes tells me she believes me.

I continue, guilt racking my stomach, the full truth just a few words away. But I can't spill it now. Not until Dad knows and CityLight's lawyers are involved. "My intention is to contact our lawyers and the appropriate parties immediately and launch an investigation. In the meantime, I ask for your cooperation. Can you honor the process by remaining silent on all of this until our internal investigation is complete? I will warn you that our lawyers will first draw up a nondisclosure agreement for you to review and sign before an investigation can even begin. Are you willing to cooperate with us to proceed?"

I feel as if I'm pulling random words out of a hat. Only a sliver of those espresso-colored irises shows through her thick lashes as she narrows her eyes and ruminates for a moment.

She reaches out and fiddles with the edge of the table. "I need you to understand something, Mr. . . .?"

"Please call me Andrew."

"Fine, Andrew. I need you to understand that this book—*my book*—means the world to me. It's not just some arbitrary story I cooked up in my spare time."

"Then what is it?" I steeple my fingers and lean in, truly not wanting to miss a word she says. I feel that I already know the answer. I knew it months ago when I first read through her manuscript.

Through *Love Between the Pages*, she had cracked open her soul and offered the world a look inside.

"It's . . . it's . . . my heart on the page. It's the story of the hard-fought battle my parents waged to fight for their love. It's wildly personal and intimate, and most of all, it's *mine.*"

Tearfully, she looks away through the window. Her hair falls over her shoulder and creates a wall between us. I wish I could reach out to tear that wall down. Guilt burns in my chest, and I have to close my heart to the scene.

"I've read your book," I hear my voice saying.

What am I doing? I try to regain my composure. I can't admit my guilt here and now. I have my father to protect. My family's legacy. I clear my throat and clarify, "I've read the book you claim is yours."

Charlie's head swings back to me. If looks could break a heart, she just obliterated mine. "And?" she asks.

"And I think the person who wrote it is more than just

a writer."

"What are they then?"

"A . . . literary gardener."

"A literary gardener?" Her full lips part, and she stares at me with a deadpan expression. "I think you're trying to flatter me, but that's literally the stupidest term I've ever heard."

"Just hear me out," I hear myself pleading, and I must admit that the term sounded much better in my head. "Anyone can be a writer. But not everyone can be a literary gardener, capable of cultivating a field of blooms in soil unfit to grow anything but weeds. And whoever wrote that book accomplished exactly that."

Charlie covers her mouth. Peeking out from behind her hand, I see the edges of her smile.

"What's so funny?" I ask, confused.

She shakes her head and continues to fail to suppress her smile. I feel my face flush in the way it only does when I'm embarrassed. I sit back, shaking my head and trying to look unconcerned. This only encourages her. Giggles erupt from her mouth, and her small hand is no match to keep them in.

"I'm sorry," she finally wheezes. Tears are now streaming from her eyes. "That's just literally the . . ." She holds up a finger as another round of laughter hits.

The wicker chair creaks as I lean back. My cheeks continue to burn, but I can't be completely offended. I stare at her. Charlie is positively adorable when she laughs—even if she does sound part hyena. As her laughter continues to bubble, I can't help but crack a small smile of my own. And this smile doesn't feel like I'm wrenching out my soul to conjure it up.

She finally settles and manages to say, "I think I needed that comedic relief today. Thank you." She wipes the corners of her eyes. "We can tell which one of us *isn't* the writer."

My smile drops. Charlie takes a sip of what's left of her espresso, blissfully unaware that she just twisted the knife that has been lodged in my heart for years. It's not her fault. How could she know? My pulse throbs in my ears, overpowering the voice in my head telling me to pull myself together.

I wink at her. "With all due respect, Miss Blaire, we have yet to prove you're a writer at all."

Her eyes widen like saucers, and I assume it's more in response to my tone rather than my words. I continue nonchalantly. "As we were discussing before, would you like to proceed with an investigation? I'd like to see to this matter as soon as possible."

She sets her cup down and folds her hands in her lap, all evidence of her laughing fit now gone save for the tiniest smudge of mascara beneath her left eye.

"Yes," she answers resolutely. "And I intend on staying in the city until this is dealt with."

"Is that so?" I look at her in surprise. "Do you have a friend you're staying with? Extended stays in New York City aren't cheap. I can't be sure how long an investigation like this will take."

She frowns, and a storm of what looks like panic clouds her eyes. "I'm actually staying at the Crescent Garden Motel. Which, come to think of it,"—she gasps—"where is my bag?"

"That bag?" I point to the leather purse on the floor.

"No. My duffel bag! My luggage. It's gone!"

Frantically, she stands and scans the coffee shop for any

sign of her belongings. Light from the hanging pendants illuminates the glistening tears brimming in her eyes. Suddenly, I wish she was crying from laughter again, even if it was at my expense.

"How is this happening?" she mutters. "How is this happening?"

I stand as well and reach instinctively for her arm. She doesn't flinch when I touch her. "We will find your bag, Charlie. Please sit down. Let me make a quick call."

She sits down, and I dial Mattias at the publishing house. Charlie's eyes are dark and worried as she watches me. I don't think she's relinquished all hope as she leans forward, elbows on the table, eager to find out who I'm calling and why.

When Mattias answers his cell, I say, "Hey, do you remember the woman who was trying to pay CityLight a visit this morning?"

Charlie's eyes linger heavily on me as I listen to Mattias reply with a simple, *"Yes."*

"Yeah, the screaming, unruly one. That's her," I say.

Her mouth drops open as I toss her a wink.

"No, no, Mattias, I don't think she has rabies. Actually, let me ask. One sec—" I cover the phone with my hand and whisper to Charlie, *"You're clean, right?"*

Her stare could level a man. "My criminal record won't be if you don't ask about my bag right this second," she hisses.

"Yeah, she's clean. What's that though? You're really hungry? For raw meat? Mattias! Stop howling so loud. It hurts my ears!"

Reaching over, Charlie smacks my arm. She's glaring, but I catch the hint of a smile lurking just beneath her angry surface. She's so cute that I can't help but laugh, and my chuckle makes her laugh again too.

I can practically hear Mattias rolling his eyes on the other end as I resume my call. "Okay, all jokes aside, the reason I'm calling is because I'm wondering if the lady in question left a duffel bag there by chance?" I perk up at Mattias' response, and Charlie sits up straighter. "Oh, that's great! We'll be back in a jiffy."

When I end the call, Charlie looks so relieved that, for a moment, I think she might hug me.

"Is it there?" she asks.

"It's there. Apparently, in the theatrics of it all, you forgot it. Mattias has it safely secured behind security. Why did you have your bag with you anyway? Have you not checked into your hotel?"

She shakes her head. "I literally stepped off the plane and took a cab straight to CityLight. Check in wasn't until this afternoon, so . . ."

"I see." I gesture toward the door. "Let's rescue your bag and get it dropped off where it belongs then, shall we?"

8

Charlie

I sneak a glance at Andrew as he holds the cab door open for me and retrieves my duffel bag from the trunk. When I made the reservation at the motel, I didn't realize just how far away from the city center it was. He insisted on both accompanying me and paying for the ride through the hustling, loud streets of the city.

When we had arrived back at the main floor of the highrise building CityLight shares with a number of other firms, I longed for answers. Is someone in one of those luxurious corner offices harboring a plagiarizer? Do they know they are hiding the identity of a book thief?

Mattias' eyes bored into me as we approached the security desk, probably watching me carefully in case I started foaming at the mouth again. I took the opportunity to apologize for my earlier behavior. New Yorkers may be infamous for their no-nonsense approach to manners, but as a lifelong resident of a small country town in Vermont, I don't have it in me to tolerate even my own rudeness.

It took over an hour by cab to reach the motel. At least I didn't have to navigate the city, trying to find my destination by myself, but I'm slightly carsick by the time we reach my home for the week.

Andrew leads the way into the lobby of the small motel I'd chosen. It's a little dingy and rundown, but I tell myself beggars can't be choosers. Another thing New York City is famous for: overpriced, overbooked hotel rooms. It was enough of a challenge to book a room last minute, let alone find one I could afford. The Crescent Garden Motel is nowhere near any of the centrally located places I figured I would need to get to this week, so add daily cab fares to the bill that I am not looking forward to fronting. It's either paying for cabs or hoofing it. Navigating the city on foot is not ideal, but I guess I brought my walking boots for a reason.

As Andrew approaches the reception desk to inquire about my room, a deep, cloudy sense of exhaustion washes over me. I was skeptical about his insistence on helping, but gratitude seeps over me as I watch him talking to the day manager. I feel like I'm suddenly walking through fog, and all I want to do is take off my shoes, collapse in a heap on a comfortable bed, and shut out the world until tomorrow. Apparently, traveling is exhausting for a homebody like me.

"Terribly sorry . . . reimburse . . ."

I catch the tail end of the manager's apologetic voice trained in my general direction. I pull myself back to the present and realize that Andrew is looking at me with an expression that can only be interpreted as regretful dismay on his face.

My eyes dart between the two men. "What do you mean that my room is unavailable?"

"I'm afraid that the guests above you had—ahem—shall we say a little too much fun with the bathtub last night?" the manager replies. "There has been a substantial water leak down into your room, and the structural integrity of the ceiling may have been compromised. Of course, we will issue you a full and immediate refund."

"Why can't you just give me a different room?" My voice is noticeably strained, and I can feel my exasperation growing by the second. I'm too tired and too overwhelmed to deal with this nonsense right now.

"I'm afraid that's not possible," he says after typing rapidly on the keyboard in front of him.

"And why not?" Without warning, the heel of one of my boots clicks against the ground in a firm stamp as exasperation shifts into irritation. From the corner of my eye, I catch Andrew's gaze flickering down and up again. Embarrassed that he's caught me in my immature habit, I do my best to rein myself in. I take a deep breath. "What I mean is, I'm perfectly happy switching to another room."

A fresh wave of regret flashes across the manager's face. "That's just the thing. All our rooms are booked this week. We simply don't have another room to give you."

Shock renders me speechless for a moment before I find my voice again. "Where am I supposed to sleep tonight?"

"Perhaps another hotel . . .?"

"I don't want to find another hotel. It was hard enough to book this one on short notice." Another involuntary heel stamp. My head is pounding. I realize that all I've eaten today is coffee and sugar and the little baggy of nuts they gave me on the plane. My hands rise to cover my face before I let out a scream.

I feel the sudden grip of warm, strong fingers as Andrew's hand lands on my wrists and tugs them down from my face.

"Will you excuse us for a moment?" he says to the manager, who nods in obvious relief that someone is stepping in to rescue him.

Andrew takes my hand in his and leads me toward a quiet corner, still holding my duffel bag in his free hand. When I sit on a nearby chair, he bends over me. Concerned lines etch the corners of his eyes. The man is a complete stranger, but I stare up at him anyway, finding immediate comfort in his kind eyes.

"Charlie, I'm sorry. This is terrible."

"Yeah." One side of my mouth lifts in a sarcastic smirk. "Welcome to The Big Apple, Charlie Blaire."

"Flooding your room and leaving you stranded is a terrible welcome. Can I help you book another hotel?"

I resist the urge to groan out loud. "I guess that's what I'm going to have to do. I chose this hotel specifically for the price, so hopefully, I can find something within my budget." A deep sigh escapes from my chest.

Andrew tilts his head, studying me, eyes narrowed slightly. "If I suggest something a bit unconventional that could help, are you going to be mad at me?"

A short, sharp laugh escapes me. "Despite the fact that you work for the enemy,"—his eyebrows lift as he gives me a pointed look—"you've been kinder than I ever expected anyone would be considering my reason for being here, so, um, no, I could never be mad at you for trying to help me."

"In the building I live in, I have a couple of extra apartments—"

"Of course you do."

He ignores my interruption. "I use them as short term, furnished rentals. One of them is open for a few nights this week. I was shocked no one had booked it yet, but maybe it's a happy coincidence? You're welcome to stay there if you like."

I shake my head, but my insides flip over once or twice. His offer is generous. However, sleeping in the same building as a man employed by the company I'm preparing to go up against in a legal battle is just a little too crazy, even for me. Also, just the way he bends over me with that warm expression gives me butterflies. I really don't need the distraction or the complication.

I try to keep my voice firm. "I already know I probably can't afford to pay you for the room, so I'll pass. Thanks for the offer, though."

"Who said anything about paying?" He smiles at me, and I wonder how any woman is supposed to resist that expression. "It's my city and my company that brought you here. The least I can do is to make sure you have a safe place to sleep. The best part is that I'll cook you dinner tonight while we make a plan to handle this situation. And if you want to leave in the morning, I'll help you find a new hotel."

"Are you a good cook?" I eye him skeptically.

He lifts one muscular shoulder in a casual shrug. "I get by. You'll have to tell me how my skills hold up."

"And you think the offer to cook for me is better than the endless plethora of exotic and international food options in NYC that I could simply order in?" Rather than accept his invitation, I hem and haw around in a tone I realize too late sounds decidedly flirtatious.

Keep it professional, Charlie. You're here on a mission, and Andrew is simply a nice guy doing you a favor.

Why is he so nice, though? I find myself wondering as he flashes me another boyish grin.

"How can you resist such an offer?" he says.

Because he's simply trying to do damage control for the company he works for. Despite my internal dialogue, I pretend to ponder out loud. "Hmm, well, how can I refuse an offer that even comes with room service and a private chef?"

Andrew pulls me to my feet. He tugs me toward the exit, tossing my duffel bag over his shoulder. "Let's not waste any more time then."

———

The building Andrew calls home is exactly the type of luxurious building I would expect an obviously sophisticated city-gent like himself to occupy. CityLight must be paying him a heck of a lot to PR for them because, based on the tree-lined streets and snooty, well-dressed people milling about this section of the city, an apartment here costs a pretty penny. And he said he owns more than one unit in this building.

The cabbie drops us off, and I follow Andrew up the steps to a white limestone building. On a gold plaque above the door, I catch the name "Winters Tower" as my new landlord pulls me toward the elevator in the lobby. As we wait for the gold-paneled door to open, I do some quick mental calculations.

One of my favorite useless hobbies is to sit in front of the television at night with the laugh track of one of my favorite classic shows only a murmur in the background while I scroll through the most expensive real estate listings in big cities just to get a peek at the photos and see how the other half really lives far away from my tiny village home. I don't have the travel bug like my parents, but I do love a good real estate browsing session. Based on what little I know of neighborhoods in NYC, I could probably purchase ten houses in Pleasant Hollow and still not reach the price of a swanky city apartment.

Maybe he comes from money? I muse, eyeing him discreetly as he slides a card into the elevator panel and pushes a few buttons.

The elevator doors *whoosh* open to reveal a long, carpeted hallway. It's been painted a soft gray with softer gray doors at regular intervals. Andrew leads me to a door marked 1207. He keys in a code on the lock panel. When it beeps, he pushes the door and holds it open for me, flicking a few switches just inside the entrance. A lamp flickers in the foyer, and I catch sight of a gourmet kitchen and small living room just a few steps away.

"There are clean towels and toiletries, plus water bottles and snacks in the fridge," he says, handing my duffel bag (which he insisted on carrying) over to me. "Feel free to freshen up and relax for a few hours until dinner. Unless you have something else you need to do . . .?"

After this day, the only thing I want to do is hide away in this pretty apartment and not have to face the stress of everything that is to come. I accept the handle of my duffel bag from him, trying not to notice the warmth of his fingers as they brush mine. "I think I'll stay right here for a bit.

Where will dinner be served, Chef?"

His eyes lighten in amusement. "I'm just down the hall in 1212. Just come on in. Will five o'clock be too early?"

"That's perfect. Thank you." I didn't expect to be such close neighbors for the week, and I wonder if his offer of a place to stay could somehow constitute me accepting a bribe or be a conflict of interest. Did I make the right call in coming here?

Before I can second-guess the whole arrangement, he turns away. I force myself to take a step inside the apartment. I need a place to stay for tonight, at least. I'm in no mood to wrangle a new motel tonight. I can reassess the situation in the morning.

"Oh, and one more thing . . ." Andrew's voice stops me in my tracks. I pop back half through the doorway to look at him. "I have a dog who is half-wild, half-bumbling idiot, depending on the day. We're working on his manners with company . . . and just about everyone and everything else. I can put him in his crate if you like."

A genuine smile creeps across my face for what feels like the first time today. "I love dogs. I already told you I train them for a living. As long as I don't end up on his menu for dinner, I can't wait to meet him."

He throws me a wink and a laugh, turning away with a wave over his head. "I'll let him know guests are strictly off the menu tonight."

I watch his broad, muscular frame walk down the hall toward a door at the other end. When I see him turning back to look in my direction, I quickly duck back inside the apartment and shut the door so he doesn't catch me staring after him.

9

Andrew

The marble surface of my kitchen island is cool to my forehead. In just a couple of hours, Charlie will be knocking on my door, expecting dinner and a game plan that preferably doesn't involve suing the pants off CityLight Press. I groan as Sergio whines at my feet. Peeling my face from the countertop, I reach down and scratch him between his golden ears.

"And you, mister, had better be on your best behavior." I look at him sternly, all the while knowing Sergio is the least of my problems right now. "None of that psycho behavior you pull out when guests come over. You hear me?"

Sergio stares me down, his brown puppy dog eyes gleaming with the sheen of innocence.

"Yeah, I know. Why should I expect you to have your stuff together when I clearly don't?" I say, giving him one final pat on the head. Sergio's fluffy tail pounds against the cabinets, and he whines again, but I don't have time to devote to him at the moment. "Sorry, bud. We have a guest coming over tonight, and it's imperative that we impress her. You hear that? *Imperative.*"

Shooing Sergio out of the way, I assess the food situation. As today's luck would have it, the cabinets and fridge are mostly bare, though that's nothing new. Contrary to what I led Charlie to believe, the extent of my cooking experience in this gourmet space involves warming up leftover takeout or pouring a bowl of cereal. I can cook a couple of eggs, but that's about it.

Well, this is going to be nothing short of a disaster.

Though I've become a little too comfortable with ordering takeout lately, I dial Gustinelli's like a reflex and schedule a three-course Italian meal for delivery.

When I hang up, Sergio follows me into the bedroom, and I change out of my coffee-stained shirt and into a fresh one, forgoing the desire to slip into my usual at-home attire: sweatpants and a Knicks t-shirt. If there has ever been a day in my life when it's important to dress to impress, today is the day.

"Alright." Sergio looks at me expectantly, his tongue lolling out, mouth pulled up into a smile. "Dinner: check. Outfit change: check. Now I can focus on you, big boy. Let's go for a walk."

At the magical word, my apartment marvelously transforms into a giant pinball machine, with Sergio being the actual pinball and my furniture being the bumpers, flippers, and slingshots all at once. Despite the boulder of dread currently sitting in my stomach, I can't help but smile and shake my head at the fluffy lunatic. He may be destructive and next to impossible when it comes to hosting guests, but life wouldn't be the same without him.

He shakes with excitement as I leash him up and walk him downstairs. Central Park is only a couple blocks away, and out of force of habit, we turn in its direction. Bold and brilliant, the autumn leaves greet us as we enter the park.

I purposely didn't tell Charlie that the building I call home is part of my inheritance from Mom. It is bad enough that I'm aware it's only a matter of time before she puts two and two together and realizes I'm more than just a PR manager for CityLight. When she realizes I am Gary Ketner's son, I'd rather she doesn't assume I'm also just a rich guy who is trying to buy time while he figures out how to protect his family's company.

While Sergio sniffs every surface imaginable and does his business, I dial Josh.

"Finally calling to congratulate me," he says as soon as he picks up the phone. "Nice to hear from you, Ketner."

"Congratulate you for what? Paying off the umps?" I already know Josh's characteristic song and dance phone ritual.

"That's what all losers say." He laughs in the way only a reveling sports fan can, and I bite my tongue as his jesting continues. "I mean, how bad of a childhood did you have to become a Mets fan?"

"You don't even wanna know, bro."

He snorts. "What can I do for you?"

I grimace at both the question and Sergio, who is insisting on marking yet another tree along the pathway.

"Look. We messed up. Messed up big time." I keep my voice as level as I can manage.

Josh huffs. "What'd you do this time, Ketner?"

"Remember that question I asked you on Saturday?" I clear my throat. "You know, about what would happen if an author accused CityLight of plagiarism?"

I hear papers rustling in the background. Josh is probably still at the office. "Yeah?"

"That may or may not be actually happening as of today. And by may . . . I mean, definitely is."

On the other end of the line, Josh curses. I hear him take me off speakerphone, and his voice amplifies in my ear. "Andrew, what are you talking about?"

I give him the basic gist of the situation, which only makes Josh curse again.

"I'm heading over," he says.

Sergio tugs on the leash as panic builds in my chest. This is a disaster. "No, no. You can't. She's over here. You can't show up here."

"Her? You have this alleged author *with you?*" The confusion and annoyance in his voice is more than evident.

Sergio lunges for a squirrel that has appeared from around the corner and yanks the leash from my hand. He darts toward the small animal. The squirrel scrambles up a tree and stares at my fluffy lunatic as he tries to leap up the trunk. Angry squirrel chatter hits my ears.

"Darn dog." I jog after him. "Sorry, Josh. I've gotta take care of something, but can we meet first thing tomorrow? It's extremely important."

"This had better be one of your stupid jokes. Get here before eight o'clock. I have meetings starting at nine."

"See you by eight then. Gotta go." I end the call and drop my phone into my pocket so I can save this poor squirrel from a heart attack. Retrieving Sergio from his mission is an embarrassing struggle because, quite frankly, I have no idea what I am doing with this dog. He's the first and only pet I've ever had, save for the exotic fish my parents bought me at seven, although I'm not sure those count.

By the time I drag him homeward, the afternoon sun is waning. As I ascend the white limestone steps to the door, I hear my name over my shoulder. I turn to see Bart from Gustinelli's jogging down the sidewalk toward me. His shoes kick up drying leaves scattered across the path.

"Good timing!" he says when he reaches me. "Bigger order than usual, eh?"

I take the giant paper bag stuffed with takeout containers from him. Sergio, thrilled at the prospect of pets from a new person, jumps around like a bumbling idiot. I know it's only a matter of seconds before I trip over him and scatter this food all over the sidewalk.

"Yeah, I have company tonight," I finally manage to reply.

Bart slips the receipt into the bag, thanking me for the tip I left when I paid over the phone. Awkwardly, I trek upstairs, taking special care to slip quietly and quickly past Charlie's door.

Please don't look through the peephole. Please don't look through the peephole.

Once I'm safely tucked back into my apartment, I wonder why I care so much if she knows I've ordered takeout or if she realizes that I am completely incapable of caring for a dog that's half my size. I tell myself I care because the impression I give Charlie tonight may help or hurt her future lawsuit against us. Maybe the judge will be more lenient if she likes me. And maybe I care, too, because even though I met her for the first time today, it feels like I've known her for so much longer.

When I walk in with the food, the clock says she will arrive at the door within minutes, so I get to work. I dump the salad into one of my mother's crystal serving bowls. Carefully, I dish fettuccini onto plates, throw the leftovers into a pan on the stove, and lay out the fresh bread on a cutting board. I make my own mix of oil and vinegar, then set the table as though I use it on the regular rather than what realistically happens: me eating alone in front of the TV watching sports highlights most nights.

Still wanting to keep up my cooking ruse, I toss all the evidence of Gustinelli's into a trash bag and stuff it into the butler's pantry out of sight. Just as I'm setting out a pair of wine glasses, there's a knock on the door. Right on cue, Sergio goes ballistic. His intimidating bark is a weird mix of, *"Oh, great! A friend is here!"* and *"Don't worry, Dad. I'll rip their throat open!"*

"Just a sec!" I yell over his ferocious bark. Grabbing Sergio by the collar, I drag him away from the door and out to the balcony. As I'm pushing the glass door shut, trying to block the wild dog with my knee, I yell out, "It's open. Come in!"

Charlie wastes no time. I see the waterfall of her dark hair first as she peeps her head through the doorway. The rest of her follows, and she stands nervously in my foyer wearing a simple ensemble of black leggings, an emerald sweater that drapes over her figure, and ankle boots. Her long hair is tucked away from her face with pins. It takes my brain a second to connect again, and Sergio capitalizes on my momentary inability to function. He bursts through an opening between my knee and the door and aims straight for Charlie.

It's all too fast. By the time I've opened my mouth to call him back, Sergio's already within pouncing distance. I see a second lawsuit pending with the heading, "Man who plagiarized a novel sends his dog to attack rightful author of book."

Just as it seems like Sergio is about to tackle her, Charlie raises a hand and bellows a striking command. It's powerful enough to make him halt in his tracks and lay down in submission, though his body shakes with kinetic energy held at bay.

"What are you? A dog whisperer?" I say as I bridge the gap between us.

Charlie doesn't make eye contact with me. Instead, her focus remains solely on Sergio. "Something like that," she mumbles, then crouches down to greet him.

"Horrible with coffee, great with dogs. Got it."

She lifts her head to look at me now, a playful look in her eye. "I'm great at a lot of things, Andrew. Baking . . . dog training . . . book writing . . . "

Outwardly, I laugh. Inwardly, I die a little more.

"Let me get Sergio outside for now." Pathetically, I struggle against the dog's powerful might but finally manage to securely lock him outside. He promptly lies in front of the glass door and lets his sad face rest on his front paws.

"Poor guy," Charlie looks over her shoulder at him. "Locked out on a beautiful evening, stuck with a beautiful view of the New York City skyline."

"Yeah, the mutt's got it rough." I shake my head at his

pathetic—albeit heartbreaking—plea for attention and direct Charlie to the dining table.

She walks around and eyes my handiwork. "Wow. This not only smells but also looks incredible. Did you do all this?"

"Yep." I say because, technically, it's true. I did it by pressing a few buttons on my phone. "Here, take a seat." I pull out a chair and wait for Charlie to sit, but she holds back, staring up at me with a serious look on her face.

"I just want you to know," she begins, her voice firm, "that I've let certain friends know where I'm at tonight. So if you end up murdering me, you are going to get caught."

She's so pretty and adorable as she says it that I can't help almost laughing. I smother my smirk and try to match her serious expression. "I promise that you are safe with me." Inwardly, I wince. After what my irresponsibility has inadvertently taken from her, *is* she safe with me? "Care for wine? Lemon water?"

She thinks for a moment and opts for the water. After I fill both glasses, I sit across from her. For the first time all day, I have entirely nothing to say. Thankfully, before the moment of awkward silence gets too long, Charlie speaks first.

"Can we say a blessing over the meal?"

I'm caught off guard, but I immediately nod and bow my head, though I haven't thought to pray over a meal since before Mom passed. It's easy to get immersed in Charlie's melodious voice. When she finishes with, "Please provide wisdom for both me and CityLight as we work this situation out. Please help me to trust You in all things. And thank you for sending Andrew to help me today," the words cut extra deep.

"So, what's his story?" She twirls a forkful of fettuccine.

"Whose story?"

"Your dog," she laughs. "What did you say his name is? Sergio?"

As though he can hear us talking about him, Sergio lets out a long, dramatic whine on the balcony.

I shake my head at him as I begin to explain. "Earlier this year, we put together a community event on CityLight's behalf. It was called 'Pups and Paperbacks.' We set up in Central Park and partnered with a local animal rescue who brought their hard-to-adopt dogs in hopes of finding them a forever home. A few authors agreed to speak at the event, sign books, all that fun stuff. Save for author royalties, CityLight donated all the proceeds to the rescue foundation and found twelve of their dogs a home. Including Sergio, who came home with me."

Charlie presses her hand to her chest. "Wow. That's literally the sweetest idea. Wait, did you come up with that?"

I shrug and feel my face heat. "Yeah, I mean, it's just, you know, one of those public relations things."

"You're cute when you're humble." Charlie grins. "Somehow, you just made me hate CityLight a smidge less. Though, I think that's less to do with them and more to do with you. Anyone with a heart for animals is a good person in my book."

I choke down a bite of fettuccine as her words burn in my ears.

10

Charlie

Gosh, he is a charming man. Does he have to be so handsome?

Trying not to be completely distracted by Andrew's chiseled, bearded face, the thought bounces around in my brain as I listen to him describe a wild chase Sergio took him on through Central Park the week after he adopted him. The story has me laughing and glancing toward the fluffy dog. Sergio is still posted at the patio door, his tail wagging despite his obvious disappointment at being banished from the dining room for the evening.

Despite the waves of emotion I've gone through since discovering the theft of my book and my uncertainty that this trip to the city is going to get me any answers, I can't help but feel myself pulled into the tale, which is complete with comical physical pantomimes of the race through a crowded park.

He talks with his whole body. I observe with amusement as

Andrew pushes his chair back yet again to stand and imitate the cyclist who tried to dodge the charging dog, only to end up nearly catapulting into a pond.

"Needless to say, there were a couple of unhappy police officers and more than a few passersby who thought the best place for Sergio was anywhere but posh Central Park. Total dog snobs. Good thing I can talk my way out of anything." Andrew grins as he resumes his seat across from me.

"Good to know," I reply, cocking my head and eyeing him pointedly.

His eyebrows lift. He drops his fork and raises both hands in a surrendering motion. "Hey, being diplomatic and good with words isn't a bad thing. I'm in public relations, after all."

"Never said it was a bad thing," I quip back. "But tell me, is all of this"—I motion to the table setting, which includes a crystal salad bowl and dinnerware that I would consider fancier than my fanciest Christmas china—"secretly just a ploy to butter me up so that I go easy on CityLight and this Frost-wanna-be-author?"

And if it is a strategy, I must admit it's probably working. It's hard not to be charmed by Andrew's animated and welcoming presence. I'd pictured myself going into battle when I arrived in the city, shields ready, guards up. I didn't expect to be quickly swept into a scene that is so . . . enjoyable. I never expected to be invited to dinner by an actual CityLight employee, let alone accept it. I'm having fun, and it feels . . . odd. I wouldn't trade my quiet life in Pleasant Hollow for anything, but I don't exactly have a vibrant social life. I keep silently reminding myself to stay focused on the mission that brought me here in the first place.

At my question, his eyes go wide. Andrew leans forward, stretching his hand across the table to me. His fingertips barely brush the back of my hand, and a little tremor shivers up my arm. Before I arrived, he had switched the coffee-stained shirt for a crisp, fresh one, and the luxurious material shifts across his muscular shoulders as he stretches toward me. I'm glad I opted to wear something a little dressier for dinner rather than the flannel shirt and jeans I'd be more comfortable in. It's obvious that Andrew is comfortable with wealth. He carries himself well, and even his apartment is well-designed and pleasing to the eye, though I suspect he hired an interior designer. The living space is scattered with aged leather furniture and plush rugs. Framed black and white landscapes are featured on the walls.

I'm struggling not to feel like the homely country cousin in this posh environment, and I don't want his suspiciously extroverted charm to distract me from what I'm really here to do.

Andrew is speaking now. I pull my attention back to his voice. "It's nothing like that, Charlie. Believe me, I'm taking this as seriously as you are." He sits up abruptly, breaking eye contact to reach for his water glass.

His expression is so sincere that my trademark suspicion is soothed for the moment. If I am honest, I don't envy his position or CityLight's. If it turns out that A.C. Frost deceived them as well, they are in for a rough time straightening it out. I'm going to be as polite and respectful as I can, but I'm not leaving this city until I have answers. Or until I run out of money, which is highly likely to come first. But justice is justice, and I am going to make this situation right. For the memory of my parents' legacy if no one else's.

My question has caused a cloud of discomfort to settle over the dining room. Andrew is the first to break the lingering silence.

"Can I ask you something?" he says.

I nod. "Of course."

"You seem to have a relationship with God. It's highly evident in your book. I take it you are a Christian?"

"Since I was a young girl." I set down my fork. "My parents did a lot of missionary work. I was basically raised in a church building, but I personally made the decision to give my life to the Lord when I was about seven years old."

Andrew stares across the table at me. He opens and closes his mouth a few times. I get the feeling he wants to say something, so I wait patiently.

"How can you be so sure of it all?" he finally blurts out.

I frown and shake my head. "Sure of what?"

"Jesus, life after death, a place we can't see that people who believe in God will supposedly go to when their lives end on earth? I just . . . is there any proof that Heaven is real?"

Holy Spirit, please give me wisdom right now.

I breathe the silent prayer as I try to gather my thoughts. Andrew clearly has knowledge of the Bible but seems to be struggling to connect the dots between what he can see versus his faith. I didn't expect to have the opportunity to share my faith tonight, but I try to rise to the unexpected challenge.

"There are countless witness accounts of Jesus' presence here on earth. We have access to a Book that has been preserved for centuries. In it, Jesus' words are recorded. He said, 'My Father's house has many mansions . . . I am going there to prepare a place for you.' In that same chapter, He instructed us not to let our hearts be troubled, not to be afraid." I pause, trying to sense how Andrew is receiving my words. His expression is carefully fixed and unreadable.

"It's easy to demand physical proof that Heaven exists. But what if all that is standing between us and the confident trust that it is where we will spend eternity together is the willingness to surrender our human longing for answers to God and allow Him to grow our faith in the things we cannot see? What good is faith if we don't ever have to exercise it?"

He nods, his lips pressing together. A silence falls over the table again until Andrew breaks it, saying falteringly, "Thank you. I . . . have had a lot of questions about all of this since my mom passed away."

The mention of parents brings a lump to my throat. I blink away the quick tears. "I have my own experience with that. But I can confidently say that if we have personally accepted Jesus' invitation to be reunited with the family of God after our sin separated us from that birthright, we will be reunited with both our Savior and our loved ones in Heaven for eternity. Any questions you have, please feel free to ask me." Before the emotions of the day make the tears begin to fall for real, I veer off into a less-threatening topic.

"This fettuccine is delicious. Is this your recipe?" I twirl another bite of the creamy, nutmeg-infused noodles onto my fork, wondering if I can wheedle the recipe out of him before the end of the night. The meal is delicious, and I have to admit I'm secretly impressed that he could whip it up for a stranger.

Andrew chokes on a drink of water. I watch him sputter for a moment before he can reply. "Uh, honestly, it's just a little of this and a little of that. Pinterest is everybody's best friend nowadays, you know? Who even uses family cookbooks anymore when you can try a different recipe every night?"

He trails off, and we both nod aimlessly, as if he's just made a profound and insightful statement about the state of the world's cooking heritage. Before the silence can stretch out too long, Andrew clears his throat.

"So, while dinner was cooking, I put in a call to our legal department. I have a meeting with them tomorrow, and I'll start the ball rolling then. I don't know exactly how they'll proceed with an investigation, but I'm guessing it's going to involve a lot of questions."

To buy time, I take a sip of cold lemon water before replying. The ice clinks loudly against the glass in the silence. "I'm ready for all the questions. Throw them at me. Is there anything special that you think I need to prepare for?"

He shakes his head. "Just be prepared for this to be a painful and challenging process. CityLight has never had a plagiarism claim nor any lawsuit of significance. The onus will be on you to prove you have a claim to this book. And you will be strictly forbidden to talk about it with anyone other than us."

"Thank you," I say softly. I let my eyes linger on his face, taking note of the attractive curl of dark caramel hair that keeps swooping across his forehead even though I've seen him brush it back half a dozen times. "I mean it. You've been really kind to me, Andrew. I know I probably seemed like some crazy lady when I walked into the building this afternoon. Thanks for not sending me straight to jail for disturbing the peace."

"Well . . . " he smirks. "I did have nine-one-one on speed dial just in case you got a little too rowdy and started throwing cookies."

I roll my eyes and shake my head. "Can we put aside business for a little bit? I want to hang out with Sergio on the patio and stare at the skyscrapers peeping into your windows."

"Hey," Andrew says as we push away from the table together. "If you stand on the balcony and look down yonder, you can see right over to Central Park. We're practically rural over here, Ms. Blaire."

11

Andrew

The inkling of sunrise is only beginning as I sit at my desk in the living room, pressing pen to page. As much as sleep would do me good, I can't rest. Not with this disaster hanging over my head. Through the long, empty hours of the night, overwhelming, unsettling thoughts paralyzed me in my bed. The voices in my head played a competitive game of which one can drive me insane first. In protest, I rose early. I put on a pot of coffee and am now attempting to silence the anxious voices by doing what I always do when they get a little too loud. I put them on paper and try to empty my mind of their ability to control me.

The glide of my pen is soothing in my otherwise silent apartment. I fill in another page of the leather journal before I pause and let out a breath. My journal collection is extensive. I've kept one since childhood, a technique Mom taught me to stave off the panic attacks. My completed journals are stored away in a box that hides beneath my bed. Mom always asked me to keep them, but now that she's gone, I'm not sure why I do.

I flip back toward the beginning of my current leather bound and journey into the past until I reach a page with a single quote scrawled in the middle. It's one of the many *Love Between the Pages* quotes that have made it into this journal.

"For me, the night dripped with sorrow, the bitter taste of loss a tragedy so great I could not fathom surviving it. But on the other side, for them, it was a new beginning. That sun-soaked, glorious day marking the start of forever," – Charlie Blaire.

On the following page, I'd written:

Mom told me, as she lingered in that fragile state between life and death, not to fear. She was sad, but she wasn't afraid. She had a faith that marched to the same beat it seems this Charlie Blaire marches. I long to know I'll see her again. I want to believe that this . . . this life we live isn't all there is. Mom seemed so sure of that, as does Blaire. It's a comfort to think of Mom in that glorious eternal afterlife, to know that her faith carried her through the gates of forever. Is there a place up there for me?

In the final pages of Blaire's manuscript, he or she has written an author's note rich with Scripture. I think it's the first time the holy words have ever felt real, and that is something I'm ashamed to admit. How unsure I've been about what comes after this. How much disbelief and doubt I've harbored in my heart.

The entry goes on, but I don't continue reading. Instead, I flip back to this morning's entry and finish filling in the details of the past twenty-four hours.

Of all the people to meet in this big world, of all the people to spill coffee on me . . . it had to be her. And I write that not tritely, but with awe. It had *to be her. That's the feeling I can't shake.*

That this meeting wasn't by happenstance, and yet I'm filled with an inexplicable dread. The task ahead of me today could make or break her, could make or break my father, CityLight, and myself.

But all I really want to do is tell her, "Thank you" . . . Because I have never felt closer to God than when I read her words. I'm completely stricken by her, which makes this all the more difficult. I don't see how this ends well for anybody.

I set the pen down on the desk, and it rolls as I drop my head into my hands. My chest feels tight. My breathing is shallow. Sergio scratches the floor with his twitching paws, a light whine escaping his mouth as he dreams in his bed on the other side of the living room. He's probably envisioning catching the elusive squirrel we chased in Central Park yesterday. When he wakes up, I'll take him for a run. Then, I'll head down to Josh's office and face what feels like a bleak future.

—

Josh paces his office as he listens to me detail the situation at hand. His face is grim, his lips set into a tight, straight line. And as I catalog the disastrous domino of events that have led to this moment, I feel myself slip further into despair. How many of the problems in my life have been caused by my incompetence and laziness? If only I had been a better employee, a better son . . . It's a truth that doesn't feel good to face.

Josh doesn't help the matter when he finally speaks once I finish my spiel. "This is your fault. You realize that, right?" He doesn't bother to hide the sharpness of his tone.

Spots appear in my vision. I close my eyes and take a deep breath. "Trust me, I know." The words come out as a shiver.

"I have important meetings all morning that I can't

reschedule." Josh sighs and sinks his hands into his trouser pockets. "What is she doing today?"

"I . . . have no idea."

"Well, let's hope she isn't blabbing this to the world as we speak, or everything I'm prepared to do will be futile. Can you get her in here this afternoon? I'll have her sign a nondisclosure agreement right away and make her think we're taking this seriously."

My muscles tighten. "We *are* taking this seriously, aren't we?"

Josh throws me a look of disdain. "Obviously we are, but we're going to fight tooth and nail to work this into a favorable outcome for CityLight."

"But it is CityLight's fault."

"No. It's *your* fault." He levels me with a glare that makes my blood run cold. "Will you let me do my job here, Ketner? Because ultimately, it's your future and your father's future on the line here, and that spills over to every single employee you have at CityLight. If we don't manipulate this in our favor, you can say goodbye to everything you think you know. Including any hope of a relationship with your dad."

The words cut deep. If I wasn't entirely dependent upon his help, I might fight the low blow he just dealt. But the problem is that he's not wrong. If I sabotage this case, Dad won't ever forgive me, even if he was a major catalyst for this catastrophe.

Josh drops into the chair behind his desk and types something into his computer. "Be here at one-thirty. In the meantime, keep this whole thing to yourself," he barks without even looking at me.

The familiar feeling of being dismissed as the burden I

am snakes itself tightly around my lungs. "Alright. We'll see you then."

I stride to the elevator and feel a prick behind my eyes. I blink furiously and will away the rush of emotion. The doors *whoosh* open, and I step inside. When I get to the main floor, my eyes feel dry but not as dry as my hope.

My fickleness isn't lost on me. There's a hope I can taste, a sense of security that feels just within my grasp, and yet I feel as though the more I reach for it, the more I push it away. When I burst through the building's entrance, my flushed skin prickles in the cool air. I reach for my phone, and when I pull up Charlie's contact info, I feel a weird sense of peace.

I realize I want to talk to her. Inexplicably, I feel drawn to Charlie. I've known her less than twenty-four hours, but there's something familiar about her. I want to hear her voice, to feel that fiery presence of hers that is bold and sure and unapologetically *real* next to me. As much as I don't want to invite her anywhere near Josh, I type the text anyway and press send.

I lean against the brick exterior of the law firm. The air is chilly, though the sun emerging from the cloudy day and hitting me directly in the face is warm. Something eases in my chest.

"Can You make this alright?" I murmur as I turn my face toward the source of the warmth. "Is that really something You can do?"

My mother always seemed to believe so. Charlie does too.

Maybe God really does care enough to help.

12

Charlie

My head spins as I step off the stoop into the chaotic wonder of my first morning in New York City. I haven't yet adjusted to the energy of the air in the big city. The vibes here are so different than at home, and my tiny Vermont town feels like it's a million miles away.

The ambient city noises never seem to rest, not even in the middle of the night when I lay tossing and turning on the (surprisingly) comfortable bed in the apartment I'm borrowing from Andrew for a few days. Wiped out from the flight and the events of the day, I should have been sleeping. But every little squeak and noise in the building kept me staring wide-eyed at the ceiling in the darkness. Before I changed into pajamas, I made sure the doors were securely locked, but still . . . And as if I don't have a thousand other things hurtling through my brain like a cyclone, I had to go and spend an hour of precious sleep time looking up comp homes on the Upper East Side like a Nosy Nellie.

Andrew is either secretly a billionaire, or the man has invested incredibly well.

As I stand and gaze up, down, and all around the morning views of the tree-lined street, I can't help but marvel at the sight of the city in autumn. It never occurred to me that anywhere other than Vermont could be this stunning in the fall. The last of the drifting leaves are awash with the colors of the sunset. Crisp air bites my cheeks, turning them as red as a Pink Lady Apple, but I'm cozy and comfortable in my rust-colored knit cardigan sweater, jeans, and favorite walking boots from home.

There are so many things I need to do, but I have no idea where to start. My stomach rumbles, reminding me that at some point today, I need to feed it more than coffee and sugar.

Despite my reminder to eat a real meal today, when I catch a faint scent of apple cider and cinnamon donuts coming from the direction of the woodsy park down the street, I follow my nose and the rumblings of my stomach. Even though I know I need something more substantial, I justify my urgency for pastry with the fact that I woke up alone in a strange apartment in a strange city, stomach growling, and with a deep need to feel some sense of the comfort of home as I struggle to orient myself here.

But truth be told, I am used to waking up alone, even back home. Ever since Mom and Dad . . .

I've been accustomed to the heavy silence of my cottage for years. This morning felt different, though. Since I haven't quite gotten my city-sea legs yet, donuts feel like a good place to start.

I am not quite sure what to do with myself this morning. Andrew reassured me last night before I left his apartment that everything was going to work out. He asked me to trust him with the details. I'm not normally a trusting person. Stepping off a plane in New York and putting the fate of my quest to regain the rights to my book into the hands of a complete stranger wasn't exactly the plan.

Even if—by all things contrary to my usual personality— something about said stranger's warm chocolate eyes and confident (even though it is a little too flirty) smile instantly set me at ease. *Trust me*, Andrew's vibe says. Oddly enough, I find my natural inclination to bulldoze over all obstacles in my path to justice soothed in his presence.

And besides, what *was* my plan in coming here?

Did I plan to storm into CityLight and demand the return of my intellectual property, which they would immediately acquiesce to because of the powerful energy and force of my will? I saw how that plan worked out just yesterday morning when Mattias prevented me from entering the building. If Andrew hadn't come along and rescued me when he did, I probably would have ended up spending the night in a NYC county jail for disturbing the peace.

My boots kick up crisp, bronzed leaves as I meander down the path into the park-like setting. I'm still honed in on the scent of cinnamon, toasted sugar, and warm pastry. I woke with my fingers itching to bake this morning, but although I rooted through every cupboard in the remodeled apartment's picture-perfect kitchen, there wasn't a bag of flour or sugar in sight. When stress-baking is a girl's go-to coping method, she'll settle for donut cart goodies instead.

I catch sight of a small concession stand just ahead and make a beeline for the source of the delicious smells wafting through the air. I'm so focused on my mission that I nearly jump out of my skin when a horse whinnies just to my rear. Spinning and leaping aside, I gawk at the small, horse-drawn carriage rolling down the path. Seeing horses in public spaces isn't all that uncommon in my part of Vermont, but they are the last thing I expect to see in the city. And a horse drawing a carriage nonetheless as if I've just stepped into England at the turn of the nineteenth century.

As I look around the lush setting, it hits me with a rush. I was so lost in thought that I didn't realize I had just stumbled into Central Park. And it is so much more beautiful than I've ever imagined. Instantly enraptured, I do a three-sixty and drink in the sights around me: rolling, grassy knolls just beginning to be touched by the cold fingers of fall, miles and miles of paths leading to who knows what deliciously delightful places, and hundred-year-old trees watching solemnly over it all. Piles of leaves carpet the ground, and squirrels dash about, hiding away their nuts for the coming winter. The whole effect is charming.

And apple cider cinnamon donuts to top it all off. After the man at the concession stand hands me a fresh bag of hot mini donuts and a steaming cup of coffee, I can't help but smile as I turn away and walk through the park, nibbling the sweet pastries and sipping the coffee in turns. Despite the stress, despite *everything* the past few years, this is what a girl's autumn dreams are made of. There is an energy pulsing in the air as I trail down the woodsy paths. It intoxicates my senses, and I try to absorb everything at once.

Mom and Dad had been the ones with the travel bug.

After traveling often on mission trips with them as a young girl, I used to want nothing more than to wake up every day in my warm, comfortable bed and not have to fly around the world anymore. And then, when they so tragically passed away in a car accident overseas, my fears and anxieties around traveling intensified. I haven't ventured outside of Vermont in a long time. I don't know if I could ever leave my small hometown, with our tiny Main Street and quaint shops, where everyone knows everyone and a *hello* usually turns into a five-minute conversation, where the trees crowd in, and the pastures stretch wide and verdant, but this . . . *Could I ever get the courage to spread my wings and fly away from home?*

Could I ever be like Mom and Dad? Called away from comfort to serve others in a way I can only imagine. Am I doing enough to honor their legacy and the values they instilled in me?

My thoughts begin to turn pensive, a dark cloud of anxiety threatening to descend. But before my musings can turn too troubling, a ringing that comes from inside my purse sends me scrambling to find a spot to set down my coffee and donuts. Nate's face fills up my screen as I swipe to answer with a quick, "Hey."

"Hey," he replies. "I'm just checking in with you to make sure you're doing okay after the other day."

Am I doing okay? I take a moment to gather my thoughts before I spill the events of the past twenty-four hours in one continuous, uninterrupted breath. I plan to tell him about booking a last-minute flight out of Burlington, nearly getting kicked out of CityLight's offices, my motel room getting flooded, and Andrew coming to my rescue. Before I can form the words, Nate speaks again.

"Where in the world are you right now? That doesn't

look like home."

I breathe in deeply. "You'll never guess what I've gone through the past day and a half. I'm in New York right now, and I'm staying here until I get my book rights back."

The surprise on Nate's face is evident even through the phone screen. "Charlie, what are you doing?" he says quickly, his tone much more confused than I would expect. "Have you even thought this through?"

His tone puts me on the immediate defensive. "Yeah, Nate. I have thought this through. Thank you very much. I'm doing what you told me to do. I'm being proactive about something that belongs to me."

"I meant to hire a lawyer and go through the proper channels. If you just waltz in there and demand your book back, they are going to think you are some crazy wacko from off the street. There are steps. You have to prove that you wrote that book, win your case in court."

"I can do that." I ignore what he says about seeming like a crazy wacko because . . . too late.

"Have you even retained a lawyer?"

"Not yet."

Nate shakes his head. I hear him sigh deeply. "Tell me you didn't impulsively buy a plane ticket and storm their offices already? I know how you are, Charlie. You've always been impulsive and gone off half-cocked without thinking things through, and it doesn't always work that way in the real world."

"So what if it was sort of an impulsive decision?" I scowl at him. Nate has been one of my closest friends since childhood, so it shouldn't be a surprise that he is telling me his true opinion. Today, though, his words carry an extra sting. "At least I know when to take action instead of overanalyzing every decision at the pace of a snail and never making any changes at all."

We both know I just crossed an unspoken line, but Nate only shakes his head. "I can tell you are in a whole other headspace right now, so I'll catch up with you later. Talk to an attorney specializing in plagiarism claims before you take any other steps, Charlie."

He disconnects the call. I'm left to process the immediate feelings of guilt. Add them to the pile of decidedly uncomfortable feelings I've been experiencing lately. I feel like fuming, and I am tempted to text Nate with a snarky, *"Thanks for ruining my perfect autumn morning walk."*

But rather than damage our friendship further, I open the web browser on my phone instead. My fingers dash across the screen as I search for plagiarism attorneys in NYC. There is no shortage of lawyers advertising their services across the search engine. I pick one at random and dial the number to the firm's office.

As it rings, I feel a second twinge of guilt, remembering Andrew's assurances that he would straighten the whole mess out. But not involving lawyers only works in CityLight's favor, not mine. Nate is right about that.

—

It turns out that lawyers tend to be busy in good ol' New York City. Only a few have appointments available for later this week, but the prospect of sitting around and waiting for Andrew to realize I'm technically on the opposing side doesn't feel right. I've just dialed the fifteenth firm of the day, and I'm praying that this one can talk to me immediately. I just want to talk to someone who knows the law and can tell me what to expect.

"Baker Legal Firm." A man's voice answers after the fourth ring.

"Hello," I reply. "My name is Charlie Blaire, and I would like to talk to someone about a plagiarism claim. Would your firm have any appointments available for today?"

A beat of silence passes. "My eleven o'clock canceled," the man finally replies. "Can you get here by then?"

"Uh, yes." I glance at the time on my phone's screen. "I'm just at Central Park, so I will grab a taxi and head over."

"Good." He disconnects the call, and I am left with the sense that half of the conversation is missing. I feel a little flustered and unprepared, but can it be helped? Regretting that the last of my donuts and coffee are now only lukewarm, I gather everything and walk briskly toward the entrance to the park, hoping that Andrew doesn't hate me for not giving him a heads-up first.

A half hour later, I feel like I've crossed to a whole new city, which turns out to be the case when my directions app quietly informs me that the taxi I'm sitting in just entered downtown Brooklyn. I gave the driver my destination, but the paranoid part of me wanted to make sure we actually headed in the right direction, so I entered the address in my phone.

When the taxi stops, I find myself dropped into a decidedly urban environment. There aren't as many pretty tree-lined streets and houses over here. Baker Legal Firm occupies a small corner office of a weathered building whose once-vibrant bricks have faded into a pale approximation of brownish red.

Once I'm inside, a dingy gray carpet leads me down a long hallway filled with doors. Each has had the name of the business inside stenciled on the frosted glass windows. After climbing a flight of stairs and rounding the corner, I stumble across unit 205: Baker Legal Firm.

The utilitarian office space isn't quite what I've been envisioning when I think about embarking on a crusade for justice, but I remind myself that it isn't the office that makes the lawyer. Hesitantly, I knock, unsure of the protocol I'm supposed to follow here. Do I just walk in?

Ten seconds later, the door swings open to the sight of a short, bouncy man in his mid-to-upper fifties. He is dressed in wrinkled slacks and a faded blue button-down shirt. "Charlie Blaire?" He leans forward expectantly, and I'm reminded of a terrier mix I once trained back home.

I nod. "Mr. Baker?"

"Sam Baker. You're late." He turns on his heel and speed walks back to a desk on the far side of the frugally outfitted room. A desk, a set of bookshelves, a filing cabinet, two chairs for guests, and a table set up with a water cooler, mini fridge, and coffee pot are the only things in the office.

"I'm sorry," I reply, though I silently disagree with the label of late. "Thank you for meeting with me on such short notice." I sink into the chair he points to while he walks to the other side of the desk.

"I take it you called a bunch of other firms, and they didn't have openings for consultations today?" He gets right to the point.

The assumption makes me blush. "Well, yes. That is true. But I'm grateful nonetheless."

Sam Baker leans forward and plants his elbows on the desk. "Here's the deal, Ms. Blaire. I have a deposition across town in one hour. Accounting for traffic that gives you twenty minutes to tell me what this is all about to see if I can help you."

At a wave of his hand, I take a breath and dive into my story. I tell Sam of the novel I wrote during countless sleepless nights and through many heart-wrenching tears after my parents were killed in an accident delivering food and medical supplies to a hazardous zone after a tsunami swept across an unsuspecting Indonesian coastline. Their story is one of love and devotion, of two people who were never supposed to meet until God created good out of their troubled journey of faith. They were committed to a mission far greater than the comforts of a safe home in the countryside of Vermont, where I breathlessly awaited news after their cell phones went silent for the last time. My parents' story is one of tragic loss and immeasurable sacrifice. But it is also a story of anticipation and of the hope of our heavenly reunion that may take decades to arrive, but of which, I am sure.

As I'm explaining to Sam that I discovered my own book already published in a bookstore quite by accident, something inside my chest prevents me from naming CityLight as the culprit. I still feel a nagging sense of guilt that I'm seeking legal counsel before I've warned Andrew of the potential media storm that will ensue if news of my claim leaks to the press.

When I've finished giving Sam a basic overview of the past few days, he leans back and looks at me. "That's quite the story. I'm assuming you have some way of proving this book is yours?"

"I have the word processing file with the original manuscript."

"Hmm." He looks at the notebook on his desk that he's been scribbling in for the past ten minutes. "Not a lot to go off. I'm sure you understand that."

I nod. I feel my mouth turning down in the corners more and more as he frowns and doodles on the notebook. "I suspected it might be more challenging, yes."

Sam's head snaps up, and he looks at me with two small, round, blue eyes. "I don't do pro bono work. I require ten percent of the contingency fee as upfront payment. The rest I take after the lawsuit is settled."

Every second that passes in the small, cramped office makes me more and more uncomfortable. My heart sinks, not only because I'm going to have to break into my rather small savings account to pay the retainer but also because I don't trust my own ability to make this decision. Is Sam the right person to represent me against a firm like CityLight? I may be just a small-town girl with next to no knowledge of legal proceedings, but even I know that CityLight probably keeps the best team of lawyers on call. But do I really have another choice?

Just as I'm about to open my mouth to reluctantly agree to Sam's terms, my phone buzzes in my hand. Instinctively, I glance down to read the text message.

ANDREW: Hey. It's Andrew! I wasn't sure if you'd saved my number last night. Are you free for a meeting with one of our lawyers this afternoon?

I'm probably making a mistake, but relief floods over me. I look at Sam, who is watching me closely. My voice is surprisingly firm as I rise from the chair. "I'm going to take some time to think about all of this, Mr. Baker. I'll let you know when I decide to move forward with a lawsuit against the company who stole my book."

13

Andrew

Charlie's cheeks burn a blistery shade of red, and the dimple in her cheek winks as she chews her bottom lip. The nondisclosure agreement has been signed. Josh is closing out his convincing and hard-hitting spiel.

"CityLight will maintain the legacy of integrity it has cultivated for four decades. We will not hesitate to dig deep to find out the truth. Sometimes, things come up in cases like these that aren't very desirable for the claimant. And anyone who brings false claims against our client will face the full force of the law and the considerable financial repercussions of a countersuit." He fixes Charlie with a glare that could melt steel.

I'm leaning against the bookshelf, wishing I could halt this whole legal farce and blurt out the truth right now. Briefly, Charlie's eyes flicker toward me. I realize I've been staring at her profile. I offer her an encouraging nod as though I'm not a creep admiring her lone dimple as she bobs her knee underneath the desk and quivers in distress. She's trying not to show it, though, her chin lifting in defiance as she glares right back at Josh.

"I am fully prepared to answer any questions and provide any files you may require, Mr. Lance. Why don't we get A.C. Frost in this office for a face-to-face meeting and settle this right now?"

Josh clears his throat. "That's not possible right now because the author in question has an ironclad nondisclosure agreement in place with CityLight. In essence, they have chosen to remain completely anonymous, and it is going to take a very clear-cut trail of evidence on your part to legally bring them into the spotlight."

Abruptly, Josh stands from his desk and reaches out to shake her hand, signaling the meeting's end. Hesitantly, Charlie stretches toward him. As soon as he lets go, she bolts from the room. The door slams shut behind her. My eyes glued to the back of her rust cardigan, I follow her across the room through the office window as she nearly sprints to the elevator.

Josh blows out a deep breath and brings his hands to his hips. Pursing his lips, he shakes his head at me. "You realize what this could mean for CityLight, right?"

I rake a hand through my hair and slump into the chair Charlie just vacated. A guttural groan slips through my lips. I let my head fall into my palm. "I know. I know."

"You'd better hope we can make this go away. There's always a magic number with this type of case. Hopefully, we can make her an offer and settle this discreetly."

He sits at his desk. The computer screen illuminates his

121

scowling face. "This will crush your dad when he finds out. You've got to buy me time to spin this in our favor."

"How am I supposed to do that?" We're talking in harsh whispers now.

He nods toward the glass that overlooks the hallway. I follow his gaze and see Charlie. She's still waiting for the elevator, her back to us. I watch her bounce on her toes with a nervous energy she doesn't seem able to contain.

"Sweet-talk her," Josh says. "Use those good looks and that charming smile of yours and get her on our side. Find out any dirt about her you can. We're going to be digging into her home and family life, her social media, you name it, regardless. The more she likes you, the more likely it is that you can find something that will give us an advantage over her."

My heart sinks, and nausea rises in my stomach. "That's manipulation. I can't do that."

"You know what they say," Josh continues as though he didn't hear me. "Keep your friends close and your enemies closer."

I scowl at him. "She is not our enemy. She's the only innocent one in all of this."

Josh releases a sigh of disgust. "She's our enemy, Andrew."

"So you want me to lie to her as if I don't know that her book has one hundred percent been unintentionally plagiarized by my own father?"

A dark look passes over Josh's face. "That's exactly what I want you to do. The future of your father's company hinges on you this week. If you can hold her off, maybe I can figure out a strategy before the Winters' Wonder Gala so that she doesn't end up owning your inheritance. Don't mess this up."

To my annoyance, I realize he is right in one regard. Putting this on Dad's plate this week, of all weeks, is the last thing I want to do. "What do I do now?"

Josh points in Charlie's direction. I look over my shoulder to catch the swing of her long, dark hair as the elevator doors slide open. "I'd go after her and keep her busy if I were you. And Andrew . . ."

I'm already standing in the doorway but look back at the stern urgency in Josh's voice.

"I saw the way you were looking at her in this office. She's a beautiful woman, and I know how you are with the feisty types. Don't you dare fall for her."

I throw him an angry glare, but I don't have time to deal with his words. Sprinting across the main floor, I catch the elevator doors with my hand just as they are closing. They slide wide open again, and I step inside. Charlie quickly swipes at a tear on her cheek and pulls her shoulders back. She lifts her chin with what I suspect is a façade of confidence. The act breaks my heart.

"Hey," I say quietly.

Curtly nodding in response, she presses the button to make the doors close again.

I want to offer her an encouraging word, to tell her everything will be okay. But the taste of my own lies is growing more bitter by the second. Neither of us speak, the only sound the humming of the machinery as we slide toward ground level.

When we glide to a stop, I sneak a glance at her. Her face is set in stoic lines. As soon as the doors open again, she strides out briskly and makes her way through the building and onto the front steps. The sidewalk is bustling with people. Charlie lingers on the top step. I see her whip her phone from her purse. Her brow puckers as she stares at the screen. After a moment, she glances up and acknowledges my presence at her side. But a second later, she looks down at her phone again, her thumb furiously scrolling.

"What are you doing?" I ask coolly, though even I can detect a faint strain of worry in my voice.

A harsh scoff escapes her lips. "Josh said this Frost person has chosen to be completely anonymous. Then what's the story behind Frost's Instagram account, huh? That's not anonymous."

She shoves her phone screen in my face. The bogus A.C. Frost Instagram page stares incriminatingly back at me. I swallow hard.

Unbeknownst to me, Ava has been running this account for several months at Dad's request. She'd built up the shadow account with random photos from around the city, generic inspirational quotes, and the occasional food photo. It was enough to create a sense of mystery, but the account had very little substance in reality. Last week, Dad threw the responsibility for managing Frost's Instagram feed onto my shoulders. But there was no way I could stomach the task. Whatever was posted today was thanks to Ava setting up a third-party app to post at peak hours.

The blare of a horn down the street does nothing to drown out Charlie's shriek.

"Seven minutes ago!" She gasps and holds up her phone again. "This is . . . I know this place! Strand Bookstore! It's here in New York City! And Frost just posted a photo with the caption: *'Tis a good day to browse. Wonder what treasures will make it home with me today.'*"

She gapes at me and waits as though she expects a specific response, though I'm not sure what I'm supposed to say. "Okay?"

"What do you mean 'okay'? You're just going to stand there?"

"As opposed to . . .?"

She yanks my arm. "Let's go!"

She's so much smaller than me that her tugging only moves me a step. "Go where?"

"To Strand!"

"To do what?"

She releases my arm. Her fists settle onto her hips. "Do I have to spell it out for you?"

I stare at her.

"Come on, Andrew. Surely, you're brighter than this?"

My lips form a thin line. "Go ahead. Spell it for me like I'm in kindergarten, why don't you?"

She takes a deep breath. "You and I are going to Strand to find this fraudulent piece of trash and confront him . . . or her."

I groan and pinch the space between my eyes. "You can't possibly think that's a good idea."

At my discouraging words, she promptly turns on her heels and marches down the steps, a girl on a mission doomed from the start. Fists clenched, she weaves in between pedestrians and moves with determination.

"Charlie, you can't . . ." *Hear me*, I think to myself. I sigh and stride after her. I cover the distance quickly, catching her by the arm.

"Charlie—"

"I'm doing this. I don't care what you or Josh Lance or CityLight or anyone says."

"Oh, yeah? And what about the NDA you just signed?"

Her face falls. I know I can tell her the truth right now. I have the power to stop this whole ruse. But I know what is at stake. It isn't my reputation I'm worried about. It's Dad, every employee at CityLight, and even Josh at the firm. Ultimately, it's my mistake, and I will see that it's fixed. But I hear Josh's nagging voice in my head begging me for more time, and I know I can't tell her the truth just yet.

Charlie lifts her chin. Her face flashes with a determination I admire. "I have to at least check if Frost is at the bookstore. Don't worry. I'll play it cool."

"Whatever. But can you at least turn around?"

Her brown eyes narrow at me. "Why, Andrew? Why can't you just let me try to figure out who Frost is and prove to all of you that I'm telling the truth?"

She's adorable. Her passion and fierce determination draw me in and pulls a wry smile onto my lips in spite of my guilt. "Because you're going the wrong way," I reply slowly.

"Okay, then." She doesn't miss a beat and clasps her hands together. "How about you lead the way then, Mr. New York?"

It's a wild-goose chase, but at least it's a distraction and gives me a way to buy time while Josh figures out how to break the news to Dad. The city murmurs a thousand words between us as we silently make our way toward Strand. Cigarette smoke billows through chain link diamonds as we pass a construction site and inhale far too much sawdust and burning plastic than could possibly be safe. The smell of cooking oil from a nearby restaurant saturates our clothes, and a homeless man curses at us for no reason at all. We wait at the final crosswalk, and just before it pings, Charlie eagerly steps off the sidewalk. I yank her back in time once again.

"Do you have a thing for near-death experiences or what?" My arm has ended up around her shoulders, and a puff of sweet breath escapes her lips as she stares up at me.

A sudden mist fills her eyes, but she blinks it away. "Maybe I have a thing for giving you heart attacks." She rights herself and offers a sheepish smile.

"Well, you're really good at it, but if you could please stop, that'd be great."

The crosswalk pings, and out of instinct, I grab her hand. "I am now officially on crosswalk duty. Come on, kid."

I must admit that her hand feels warm and natural in mine. Her palm fits perfectly, and her fingers curl into me when I thread mine through hers. When we reach the other side of the road, it takes me a moment to let her go.

Once her hand is free again, Charlie pulls out her phone and looks at the photo she doesn't realize is already weeks old. "Okay, it's only been twenty minutes since Frost posted that photo. I'll bet she or he is still here. No one can leave a bookstore that fast. Come on."

The red awning curving around the corner of the building announces our arrival. We approach the store, and she barges through the door. Inside, it's a busy morning, per usual. Her eyes sweep around the space like a hunter looking for prey. Curiously, I watch her. Will she be so bold as to walk up to a random person and accuse them of CityLight's crime? The fierceness in her eyes burns. I fear she may tackle an unsuspecting victim if I don't manage this situation just right.

I need to intervene. I nudge her arm. "Easy, tiger. What's your game plan here?"

She takes a deep breath. "First, I'm going to do a lap."

"Okay, you do that. I'll be over here checking out these western romances." She throws me a look. I walk a few steps to a display of books as she makes a beeline for the bestsellers section. Out of the corner of my eye, I watch her as I absently pick up a random book from the shelf.

"That one is really good," I hear a gentle voice speak to my left.

My eyes hesitate to leave Charlie as I follow the dark bob of her head across the floor, but I tear my eyes away long enough to see a woman standing a few feet away. She holds a stack of books in her arms, a thick blonde braid resting on her shoulder.

"*Song of the Valley*," I read the title aloud. "You've read it?"

"I have," she affirms. "And I read *a lot*." She giggles and lifts the stack in her arms.

"I see that," I reply before the smile I begin to offer falls short when I spot *Love Between the Pages* tucked among her stack.

My ears tuned, a noise pulls my attention back to Charlie. I see her leaning across a display toward a woman on the other side. Her intense chocolate eyes are probably piercing into this stranger's face right now as she attempts to speak with her.

"There goes my kid acting up again," I call over my shoulder to the woman. "Gotta go. Thanks for the recommendation."

I approach the bestsellers section and overhear Charlie

speak to a different customer. The man is, unfortunately, reading the back of *Love Between the Pages*. "That's such a great book, I've been hearing. Are you familiar with it?"

The man sets the book down. "I am not. But I take it you are?" He leans his body flirtatiously against the display, angling in such a way that his attraction to her is obvious.

I hang back near a group of shelves and watch the interaction. Charlie reaches for the book and flips it open, reading a passage at random. We really need to get out of here, but how am I ever going to convince her to leave? Suddenly, the weight of my phone feels like an anvil in my pocket. A plan forms in my mind. I pull out my phone and find the log in credentials that Ava sent me. I quickly update A.C. Frost's Instagram story to a recent photo I took of Central Park. The feed struggles to update as my phone isn't connected to the store's Wi-Fi.

I tuck my phone away and hope it posts just as Charlie finishes her read aloud. "What an author, right?" she says, and I feel every bit of her sarcasm in my bones. "I mean, anyone who has a way with words like that"—she saunters a step closer to the man and bats her long eyelashes—"surely must do well with the ladies. Don't you think?"

My jaw drops. She's trying to flirt her way into a confession. And it seems to be working. I straighten my posture and stride forward just as a smug smile crawls onto the man's lips. He reaches over and playfully brushes her arm.

I don't think so, buddy. I don't have time to hear his verbal response as I dive between the pair and grab hold of Charlie's arm.

"Okay, girlie," I whisper into her ear and steer her toward

the back of the store. "Let's get you to another section before you wind up on *Unsolved Mysteries*."

"Hey, that guy was about to crack!" She tries to peer over my shoulder at him, but I move to block her view. Her bottom lip juts out in a pout. "Andrew . . ."

"Your terrible flirting skills won't work on me, so don't even try."

Her mouth falls open. "Terrible? Oh, come on. I wasn't even trying back there. Okay, well, like, maybe a little, but it wasn't for romantic reasons. And romantic flirting is different."

"Oh really? So, then what does that look like?"

I regret asking immediately. Josh was right. Charlie is beautiful. My heart flips over as she turns her face up to me. Her deep eyes sparkle as they lock onto mine, and I hear the slightest hitch in her breathing. A shy smile causes her soft, full lips to part, but before she can speak, her phone *dings!*

"Hold that thought," she says. Looking down, she digs the device from her purse, and her eyes widen.

"Oh my gosh! Okay, we're leaving." I feel her warm fingers thread through mine as she grabs my hand. "Frost is at Central Park!"

14

Charlie

As I burst out of Strand, it takes a second for the intoxicating scent of old and new books to fade away and be replaced by the distinctly-not-intoxicating smell of the city. I could have lingered in the bookstore forever, perusing the miles and miles of books, but hunting down Frost is more important right now. I pause to get my bearings, head spinning.

"I can't believe it! Frost lives in New York. I knew it," I exclaim. The noisy street corner takes my voice and whips it away. Andrew is a tall and comforting presence next to me as we emerge into the hazy sunlight. When the firm plane of his stomach bumps against the back of my arm, I realize with a start that his fingers are locked between mine in a vice grip. A flush heats my face as I look up, but I don't drop his hand right away. His palm is strong and warm, just like it was earlier when he led me across the street . . . after he rescued me from a traffic accident for the second time in two days.

He doesn't seem to mind, though. In fact, he hasn't seemed to mind any of the drama I've dropped into his lap by showing up and trying to open a plagiarism case against CityLight. Working for the company suddenly accused of the heinous crime of stealing another author's work has got to be a complicated scenario. Yet, Andrew claims he is on my side. He's done all the right things. He's connected me with their lawyers. He's given me a place to stay. He's listened to my claims and hasn't called the authorities to take the crazy lady away. Acts of kindness he is not obligated to do.

The warmth in his eyes greets mine without hesitation, but I detect caution too. It's an echo of the same voice in my brain telling me to be careful. Technically, I'm still in enemy territory over here. CityLight and all its associates will be guilty until proven innocent, in my opinion.

Despite my skepticism, it's incredibly difficult not to feel grateful that Andrew has been by my side the last couple of days.

Saves me from trying to navigate this city by myself.

"I knew it," I repeat, raising my voice to be heard over the din. "Now, which way is Central Park?" I drag him behind me, pushing through the crowded sidewalk like a proper New Yorker. I'm catching on fast in this city.

"Whoa, whoa, whoa." Andrew tugs me toward a pretty clothing boutique nestled among the storefronts. I let him pull me to a stop in front of the picturesque window display. A mossy-hued evening dress draped over a mannequin in the window catches my eye, temporarily distracting me. I've always had a soft spot for the shade.

"What is it that you knew?" He has to lower his head toward mine to be heard, and it's like he is whispering in my ear. I catch a whiff of his aftershave. Hints of caramel and forest and cozy cabins tucked among the trees on the Green Mountains make me want to lean in and take a second breath. He's everything autumn and spice and bonfires, and it's delicious. I want to memorize his scent and go home and bake it into a cookie.

A shiver rustles over me, probably from the sudden chilly breeze that catches my neck. I have to ask Andrew to repeat what he said before I can reply.

"What are the statistical odds that Frost is only visiting New York exactly the same time as me?" I demand. I hold up the Instagram post on my phone as if it unequivocally proves my point. "This was just posted and tagged at Central Park. If we hurry, maybe I can figure out who posted it. Maybe Frost is having lunch there or reading the book he just bought from Strand in that spot?"

He studies the post for a moment, bending lower again to get a better look. I watch as a shadow crosses his face. His lips press into a firm line as his eyes flash up. He catches me in the act of studying him.

I immediately blank my expression. "Why are we still standing here? We're wasting time that we could be using to walk," I say, a little sharper than I intend. I want to distract myself from his unnerving nearness.

"We won't be walking to Central Park," Andrew says firmly.

A feeling of immediate annoyance flashes through me. Just when I thought he was on my side. Yanking my fingers from his, I step back and cross my arms. My lips purse, and I shake my head. "You don't have to walk there. I can go by myself. Just point me in the general direction, and I'll find my own way."

I never had any right to expect him to traipse all over the city with me, but I'm somehow also hurt that he is refusing to. I turn away so that he can't read the expression written across my features. I've never been good at hiding what I'm thinking.

"Charlie, it isn't that." His voice finds my ear.

"I know you probably have to work today," I reply, staring down the street, suddenly very interested in the architecture of the building a hundred yards away. "I'm already keeping you from your responsibilities. I'll deal with this myself, Andrew. Don't worry about me."

But when I feel him pull away, a wave of anxiety hits me. I whip around to locate him again, finding his broad-shouldered form just a few feet away instantly. He's dressed in dark jeans and a white t-shirt, with a thick open cardigan instead of a jacket. The simplistic attire suits him well, emphasizing his caramel highlights as he watches me with a look I don't know how to interpret. Suddenly, I wish I knew him well enough to know what he's thinking right now.

"Central Park is four miles away," he calls to me. "It would take us over an hour to walk there. Let's just get a taxi."

He crosses to the edge of the sidewalk and raises his arm until a yellow taxicab cuts over to reach the curb. When he holds open the door and turns back to wave me over, I spring forward, my heart lifting with the gesture. He waits for me to slide in first.

"Central Park," Andrew says to the driver, who waits only a moment before pushing into a traffic gap despite a few protesting horn blares.

"See?" Andrew glances at me, lips twisted into a smirk. "Beats walking, yeah?"

"Um, yes." I nod, looking at him. The musty interior of the cab fills my senses, but I'm too grateful to mind. "Thanks."

"I've got you." He winks.

A little jolt of electricity pings in my stomach. "Thanks," I mumble again.

To distract myself, I stare down at my phone. The screen is still open to the photo Frost posted less than ten minutes ago. Vainly, I try to hold in my impatience.

"Do you know where this spot is?" I blurt out, holding the photo up to Andrew again. To my surprise, he doesn't even glance at it.

"It's the Conservatory Garden," he says without hesitation.

"How do you know that?" I study the photo again. In the corner is what looks like the base of a fountain. Looking up when Andrew doesn't answer my question, I see his head turned away from me as he stares through the window at the street beyond.

A beat passes before he says, "I grew up exploring the park almost every week with my mom on our walks. Now, I still go there to decompress or catch up on my reading."

"That's probably exactly why Frost goes there," I muse under my breath. Leaning forward, I tap the driver on his shoulder. "Could you drop us as close to the entrance of the . . . Conservatory Garden as you can?" I glance at Andrew for confirmation, and he gives me a single nod.

In the rearview mirror, the driver glances at me briefly. I get the feeling that is the only acknowledgment I will get.

"How much farther is it?" My knee begins to bounce with the nervous energy growing each extra minute we're in this cab. Frost could be making an escape right now. There's no guarantee I'll get another opportunity like this again. And I can't remain in the city forever while my plagiarism case pends investigation. Already, there are responsibilities and commitments back home that I've had to put off this week. My best chance of proving that *Love Between the Pages* is mine is to hunt Frost down and make him (or her) admit the truth.

"We're close," Andrew mutters as traffic comes to a dead halt in front of us. My leg can't stop moving. A crushing wave of dread washes over me as the driver brakes again.

I reach for the door handle. "I can't just sit here when Frost could be so close. Is it close enough for me to run to?"

A look crosses Andrew's face that I don't have time to analyze.

"Is it close?" I ask again, my tone insistent, impatience wearing me down. He gives me a half-nod of his head and motions toward the grove of greenery I can see rising ahead. That's all I need. Impulsively yanking the door handle, I leap from the cab and dart through rows of idling vehicles toward the sidewalk.

"Charlie, wait . . ." Andrew's shout reaches me.

I ignore him and keep up a brisk stride. I've left him stuck with the taxi fee, but I reassure myself that I'll pay him back later. The pathway is too crowded to sprint, but I'm pushing the limits of a half-jog as I approach 105th Street. Somewhere in the back of my mind, the faint memory of a narrator's voice from some TV travel show reminds me that there is an entrance gate on the east side. I round a group of meandering pedestrians and spot a glimpse of wrought iron ahead.

The massive gate looms before me. It stands open, and I dart through. Before me spreads the lawn of a magnificent Italian-style garden. Past a row of yew hedges, I see a fountain spouting into the sky, but as I glance again at the photo Frost just posted, the view doesn't match.

Rather than waste time searching this garden, I take a chance and veer south, trying not to sprint along the path. The faint voice of the narrator in my head reminds me that the conservatory has three distinct gardens, one in the center and two at the north and south points of the space. I can only hope I've headed in the right direction this time. Everyone else on the pathways appears to be enjoying a leisurely afternoon stroll, so I force myself to slow my pace a little and avoid getting kicked out for disturbing the peace before I've even had a chance to find the correct fountain.

Lonely weekends spent eating freshly baked scones with dollops of lemon curd and Devonshire cream while binge-watching period dramas finally pays off when I spot an English-style garden just ahead. "Thank you, *Pride and Prejudice*," I mutter, recognizing the distinctive shrubs and autumn foliage covered trees of the South Garden.

The lush space is quiet and peaceful as I enter. In light of my anxiety, I can't help feeling like I've entered a secret garden, hidden from the rest of the world. My shoes sound too loud on the path, so I force myself to walk softly—though briskly—toward the center. Despite the tranquil atmosphere, the garden is far from empty. I spot several groups of people and many solo walkers meandering along the pathways. Though the trees and hedges prevent me from seeing most of them clearly before they disappear again.

I walk along, scanning the garden for lone figures

reading or writing or otherwise doing something that says: *"It's me! I'm the fake who stole an entire manuscript and published it under my own name and didn't even bother to hide my theft by rewriting the most important parts in my own words."*

I wonder if plagiarists have a distinct look or if they manage to blend into society like shapeshifters. As I approach the center of the garden, the sound of water catches my ears first. The outline of a fountain comes into view. My breath hitches a little as I catch sight of a beautiful sculpture of two childish figures in the center. A row of benches flanks the hedge surrounding the fountain. If I wasn't on a mission, I would linger in this magical spot all day and let the words pour out into my notebook. But I force myself to tear my eyes away from the fountain and double-check the photo I've been referencing.

"This is it." The words slip out a little louder than I intend. I duck my head in embarrassment. No one around me seems to have noticed though. Quickly, I begin scanning the faces of the people lingering by the fountain.

I don't see anyone who particularly screams "plagiarizer" until a beautiful woman with magnificent, curly, dark brown hair catches my attention. She is seated on a bench, her long legs crossed, her head bent as her pen darts across a leather journal held open on her lap. I watch her, unable to tear my eyes away.

Could this be A.C. Frost?

The possibility that I've been successful on my quest causes my breath to catch. My knees suddenly buckle. A pit forms in the pit of my stomach. Now that I am faced with the person who may have stolen the words I labored over for years, I don't know if I have the courage to approach her.

Accusing someone isn't as easy as I assumed it would be.

Determined not to let my natural timidity hold me back, I square my shoulders and force my heart rate to slow. I won't miss this opportunity. I may never get it again.

"It's such a lovely day. Do you mind if I sit on this bench for a bit?" The words are out of my mouth before I think twice about them.

The dark-haired woman glances up. She startles when she sees me standing so close to her, but she nods politely. Her expression is friendly and open. "Of course. Please feel free."

I sit on the other end of the bench. She smiles at me and glances toward the fountain. "It's such a beautiful spot to sit and think."

"The fountain is really inspiring," I agree. My words continue to stream out impulsively. "I'm Charlie. Charlie Blaire." I watch her expression closely for any hint that she recognizes my name from my manuscript pages, but I can't tell.

The instant smile she flashes lights up her entire face. "It's great to meet you, Charlie. I'm Demi." She places her pen in the journal and reaches toward me. Her handshake is as delicate and refined as she is. "Are you an NYC native or simply visiting?"

"I'm visiting on business for the week. How about you?"

"Just here working," she laughs. "My family are all ranchers in Montana, but I've lived here a few years now modeling for a couple of companies."

"How fascinating." I lean toward her, assessing her eyes for any sign of alarm. I reach into my purse, searching for the hard edges of *Love Between the Pages*. "I'm actually a writer . . ."

"Charlie!" Andrew's voice interrupts the tranquility of the garden. Spotting him across the hedges on the other side of the fountain, I watch him lift a hand. I wave him over, trying to use my eyes to convey the situation. He approaches Demi and I with obvious caution. "You seem to have found your way around here quickly," he says as he closes the distance. "I was afraid you might get lost on these winding pathways. Did you make a new friend?"

"Sorry for ditching you back there," I admit, realizing that my impulsive dash from the taxi was probably unnecessary. He must have jogged the whole distance to find me so quickly.

"Who is your friend?" Andrew asks, glancing at her. He runs a hand through his hair, disheveling its smooth waves a bit more.

"Demi." She's returned to her journal but glances up when Andrew speaks. "Your girlfriend and I were just chatting about how lovely this water feature is."

"It's a work of art, for sure. One of my favorite spots in the city," he replies. It startles me that he doesn't immediately correct her assumption about us.

"Andrew works for CityLight Press," I blurt out.

Demi's friendly eyes cast themselves toward me, then back up to him. "That must be an exciting job. Is that why you love this particular fountain? For its bookish history?"

"It has definitely influenced my appreciation of it." Andrew smiles at her, his white teeth flashing.

He chuckles, and she laughs, the sound a melodious addition to the quiet garden. The sudden realization that I have no idea what they are referring to sends a spike of annoyance through my chest. When her smile doesn't fade, I wave my hand between them.

"Um, excuse me. Demi and I were having a conversation before you interrupted."

Andrew swings toward me, holding out his hand. "May I speak with you for a moment, Charlie?"

I glare up at him. When I don't move, he wiggles his fingers. Reluctantly, I place my palm in his. Instantly, his fingers close as he draws me up. He pulls me to his side and leads me toward the far side of the fountain. When my back is to the water, he leans in close.

"What are you doing?"

"That's A.C. Frost," I insist. "I know it's her. I'm going to get a confession out of her, but I may have to become friends with her first. When she trusts me, she'll admit the truth."

Andrew shakes his head. "That is not Frost. I guarantee it."

"You have literally no way of knowing that. Unless you haven't been telling me the truth, and you already know whether Frost is a man or a woman?" My eyes flash furiously as I stare up at him. A dark wave of suspicion begins to build in my chest.

We're so close that I can smell his aftershave again. It mixes with the woodsy autumn scent lingering throughout the garden, distracting me from my annoyance.

Andrew shakes his head again. His fingers squeeze mine gently. "Why don't you just ask her? If she says no, we'll keep looking." His free hand lifts, cradling my elbow in his warm palm.

Jerking my arm away, I take a step back, shaking my fingers to make him let go. "I get it, Andrew. You don't have

141

to be part of this if you don't feel comfortable. But I have to do this my way. Feel free to go home, go to work, or do whatever you have to do today. I'm fine on my own."

The toe of my walking boot clinks as it hits the walkway.

"Charlie," Andrew says. His voice is a warning.

Instantly alarmed by his change in tone, I take another step backward. Andrew lunges forward. His stride easily crosses the distance between us, and I see his hands reaching for me.

"Stop." My voice rises in pitch. I realize that I'm on the verge of making a scene. "I'm okay, really." Another step back.

"No. Charlie, you're going to fall into the . . ."

Too late. The back of my knees hit the fountain's edge. I lose my balance, falling through the air as my arms try to wheel me to firm footing again.

My gaze connects with Andrew's, and I register the horrified look on his face. "Catch me, please . . ." The cry is muffled as I tumble right down into the cold water.

15

Andrew

Disaster often happens in slow motion. Charlie takes a devastating final step, sealing her fate. Her panicked arms flail. A cry for my help escapes from her lips. But although I lunge forward, I can't reach her in time. She plunges backward into the fountain. Water splashes up and rains around us as Charlie flounders in the water.

I hiccup–yes, hiccup–as I'm caught between stifling a laugh and wanting to help her. It takes intense mental focus to suppress my smile and knit concern between my eyes. I extend my hand, intending to make a joke about this not being a water park. But my stomach drops when I see the shadow of shock and the burn of embarrassment on her face. My jaw goes slack. This poor woman is hundreds of miles from home, in a city foreign to her, fighting futilely for justice, only to find herself humiliated and swimming in a cold pond instead.

Shame sloshes over my heart. Water continues to heave up and over the fountain's edge as Charlie tries to regain her footing.

Her eyes betray everything she is feeling right now. They hit me with intensity. What I feel coming from her right now is the same emotion that I could sense on the page the night I sat down and first read her manuscript. It's clear to me that this woman, who feels less and less like a stranger, is more than this floundering damsel in distress. She is more than the book flying off shelves and crowning bestseller lists. She is the writer who moved me to tears as she captured the depths of a human soul. Through her words, Charlie captured my feelings of loss and the desperate questions that plagued me after Mom passed away. Questions I would never have been brave enough to explore on my own.

Her fingers reach up to grip my outstretched hand. Protectively, I close her delicate hand in mine, as though to say, *"You're safe now."* Our hands fit perfectly together, and I wish I could safeguard her from the hurt and betrayal about to come to light.

I don't want to continue this ruse anymore. I don't want to hurt this beautiful woman. It's time to give this up and make it right.

Because she deserves better than this.

"Come on, Ariel. Time for legs, not fins." I hoist her to her feet and help her step over the edge of the fountain. Water saturates my leather loafers as she drips all over them, but I pull her closer anyway. Charlie shivers in my arms. Her clothing is soaked clear through. As a breeze whips through the garden, I realize the crisp fall day isn't going to do her any favors either.

"Thanks," she mumbles.

Suddenly, her eyes widen. Her shaking ceases for a moment. She spins away from me, her movements jerky and frantic. I follow her gaze toward the bench, which is now empty. The dark-haired woman is gone. "She's gone? What?" Her voice is desperate. "I . . . I can't believe this! My chance! I had her right here, and now—"

"Charlie." I take a step toward her. "Stop. That wasn't—"

"But what if it was?" Her voice cracks. She folds her arms over her chest. Water drips relentlessly on her boots. "How could she leave?"

"Call me crazy, but I don't think she was prepared for her tranquil afternoon in the garden to turn into Shamu's splash zone."

Fire ignites her cheeks. The panic on her face dissolves into a cringe. "I'm acting like a crazy person, aren't I?"

I pinch a small space between my thumb and forefinger and hold them up in front of her. "A little bit. But I can't blame you. Here—" I shrug off my sweater and drape it on the back of the bench. I point toward her dripping cardigan. "May I?"

She wraps her arms around her waist and hugs herself tight. "It's fine."

"No. Come on, let's get you out of that. You can't traipse through the city in a soaking wet sweater. Number one: That's far too embarrassing for me," I tease. "And two: You'll catch pneumonia." The chilly air catches my now-bare forearms, sending goosebumps across my skin.

Finally relenting, she struggles against the heavy wetness of the knitted cardigan. I tug one sleeve to help. In a swift, unexpected motion, she yanks her arm free and almost

145

stumbles back into the fountain. This time, her laughter fills the garden. It's a bit hysterical, but the sound sends a spark down my spine. My lips split into a smile that feels genuine for the first time all day.

"Let's get you away from that thing and into the sun." I steer her away from the fountain and drape my sweater around her shoulders. I rub my hands along her arms to warm her up. "How's that? A little better?"

She burrows in, takes a deep breath, and nods. She closes her eyes for a moment. The last of the afternoon sun's rays bask across her cheeks. A few beads of water linger under her eyes. Instinctively, I reach up and brush them away with the pad of my thumb. She doesn't even flinch, though her breath catches at my touch.

"Your hand is warm," she murmurs. "It feels so good."

I let my palm rest on her cheek, aware now of my own heat. I shouldn't let myself get this close, not when I hold the power to hurt her the way I will when I tell her the truth. But in the moment, I sense something forming between us. There is a story woven as I watch her lashes flutter under the sunlight, and I can't pull away.

As soon as her eyes open all the way, I drop my hand and shove it into my pocket. Guilt snakes in my stomach. There's something else too, and it forces me to look away from her consuming chocolate eyes. I retrieve her soaked sweater from the bench. Its chilly soppiness is a relief to the heat flaring within my veins.

When I turn back to her, a smile has formed across her pretty lips. It's almost infuriating how adorable she looks bundled in my far-too-big-for-her cardigan. I can only hope I don't ruin that smile forever.

"What's the matter?" When she sees my face, her smile turns downward. "You look so sad."

I realize now how heavily the corners of my own mouth are pulling toward the ground. I attempt to smile, but a stinging that suddenly pricks my eyes threatens to give me away.

"Nothing. I, uh . . ." *Andrew, come on! Think!* I give her a look, my lips pressed together in mock sadness. "I was just thinking about all the whales still in captivity, you know?"

Her lips twist. "Is that so?"

"I'm glad you're finally free from that life." A grin breaks free now, but it's only thanks to the one plastered across her laughing face. We begin to walk toward the entrance. I can see that she's embarrassed by the skeptical looks thrown our way by everyone we pass, but she holds her head up high, nonetheless. "Come on, Free Willy. Let's get you back to the apartment and clean you up. We're taking a break from sleuthing for the rest of the day. Is there anything I can get you to make you feel better?"

Charlie doesn't even hesitate. "Homemade butterscotch cookies."

"Okay . . . I can try to make someth—"

"No," she interrupts, one eyebrow rising toward her hairline. "*I* will bake them. Baking is my therapy. Don't worry, though. I'll share them with you."

"Is this about that crummy cookie they served you at the coffee shop?"

She snorts and hugs my cardigan around herself. "I can outbake them in my sleep. I'm telling you."

"We'll see about that. How about I pick up the ingredients after I get you home safely? You can dry off and

147

change. Sound good? Maybe I'll pick up a pizza or something too?"

"That sounds perfect." She prances next to me with seemingly genuine enthusiasm. "A New York style pizza, homemade cookies—oh and maybe we'll stream a movie? What could be better after a hard day?"

My laughter suddenly can't be contained. Proposing a cease-and-desist on (fake) hunting for A.C. Frost across the city seemed like a long shot. But to my surprise, it seems as if Charlie actually wants to continue spending the day with me.

"What's so funny?" She shoots me a glare, and man, is she cute.

"Just remembering the look on your face as you fell into that fountain."

"Shut up."

I playfully nudge her with my elbow as we walk. "It sounds like our evening is all set. You focus on not smelling like a washed-up seal, and I'll get everything else ready."

She slugs me in the arm, and I honestly should have expected it. It doesn't hurt. Instead, it only makes me laugh more.

"Stop laughing at me!"

"You're laughing too!"

She twists her mouth to stifle her grin and ends up pulling the collar of my cardigan over her mouth to conceal her mirth.

"Come on, Nemo."

Another slug.

Another round of laughter.

—

Dad doesn't answer the first or second time I call. I pace my living room, my eyes trained on the city's skyline. The inklings of golden hour are just beginning, and I wonder how many sunsets I have left here because once we come clean, we may leave the city for good.

My mouth goes dry, and I feel the familiar, old nagging deep in my gut, the dull ache at the base of my sternum. Why should Dad take the most blame for this? He was only trying to do right by me. It's ultimately me. My fault. My ineptitude. Thoughts incoherently flood my brain and overwhelm me. Everyone knows I'm the weak link in the Ketner family chain. How can I face my family, my friends, and everyone at CityLight when they find out what I'm responsible for? I'll be a pariah after the truth comes out, a social outcast. But that's fine. Because the prison of being trapped with this secret and continuing to hurt the girl currently getting dried off and cleaned up down the hall is much worse than the judgmental whispers behind my back from Dad's country club cronies.

I dial Dad again but only reach his voicemail. I don't want to do this over the phone, but this time I leave a message.

"Hey, Dad. It's me. We, uh, have something really serious to"—barking pierces the air as Sergio charges the glass balcony door, aiming for a bird perched on the railing—"talk about. Sergio! Enough! Call me when—Sergio, stop! Call me when"—Sergio's bark intensifies as he scratches against the glass in a frenzy—"you can. Bye."

I throw open the door just to get Sergio out of the space and then collapse on the sofa. Charlie is in her temporary home down the hall, showering away the chill of fountain water and bits of dead leaves in her hair. By cultivating a friendship with her, I'm leading a lamb to slaughter. The thought makes me physically ill. She deserves the truth, not to be strung along by a guy who doesn't have her best interest at heart. But I must reach my dad first. I need to prepare him for what's about to happen with the company before I divulge everything to her and a media storm hits.

She'll be knocking on my door soon. We agreed to hang out in my apartment tonight since my kitchen is outfitted with more essentials than hers. The bag of baking ingredients she requested from the market sits on my island counter next to a massive pizza box from one of New York's most iconic pizza joints. I paid extra to have it delivered in record time. The scent wafts to me now as I groan in agony on the sofa. If it weren't for the birds taunting Sergio out on the balcony, he'd be jumping up on the counter, doing his best to snag the pizza before we get the chance.

Sergio whines to come back inside. I change into a pair of sweats and a t-shirt, then grab my journal and a pen before flopping back onto the sofa. It occurs to me suddenly that Dad left last night on a business trip to Toronto. Of course he's not answering. I groan and begin pouring my thoughts onto paper. I'm not sure how much time passes as I lay there scribbling away, dissolving into nothingness. A knock at the door brings me back to reality. Sergio barks and bounds for the front door.

"Oh my goodness, I can smell that pizza from out here," Charlie says as soon as I open the door. She greets Sergio and enters my home like it's the most natural thing in the world. She bustles toward the kitchen. "Did you preheat the oven?"

"Yep. Four hundred and fifty degrees, just like you said."

Her mouth drops open in horror, and I point to the oven, where three hundred and twenty-five is displayed in red numerals on the screen. She shakes her head. "You about gave me a heart attack."

"Come on. I'm not *that* bad at following directions. I also set out a few things I thought you might need."

She looks over the utensils, bowls, and baking sheets I placed on the counter. Some of them are things I didn't even know I had. "Three cookie sheets? How much do you think I'm going to bake?"

"You said stress-baking was your therapy." I shrug. "My stomach was semi-hoping you were on the verge of a psychotic breakdown."

"Wow. Thanks for that. Want to find a movie for us to watch while I whip these up and stick them in the oven?"

"On it." Anything to get out of the kitchen. I dive onto the sofa and pick up the remote. I flick through my streaming services and movies options as I hear a frenzy happening behind me. From the sound of things, Charlie is making herself right at home. "Do you like old movies?" I holler.

"Love them!"

A smile rests on my lips. Of course she does. Because she's . . . I don't allow myself to even say the word in my mind. *Don't go there, Andrew. You have to get all this sorted out first. And why would she want anything to do with you once she knows what you've done?*

I hear the oven door open, the clang of the metal rack as the tray slides inside, and the thump of the door closing. The oven beeps as she sets the timer. Charlie claps her hands. "Alright, prepare to be amazed in . . . nineteen and a half minutes."

"And until then?" I stand and walk toward the kitchen to grab the pizza box.

"Until then, try memorizing what your life was like before you tried my famous butterscotch cookies."

"Are they really famous?"

She snorts and reaches for a wad of napkins. "No, but they should be."

We sit on my couch with the pizza box on the coffee table in front of us. To my surprise, Sergio listens to her command and lays at our feet. I press play on the TV remote and shove the first bite of pizza into my mouth but catch Charlie staring at me. I freeze. Bite half in my mouth, I ask, "What? Did you want this slice?"

A smile tugs at the corners of her lips. "Absolutely not." She turns away and drapes a nearby throw over her lap, the same soft smile teasing me all the while. She reaches into the box for her own slice.

"What is it?"

"Nothing." She turns back to the television. The opening scene of *An Affair to Remember* fills the screen.

"Come on. Tell me."

She shrugs and lifts the slice to her mouth. "This is what you picked? You have a great taste in movies."

"Thanks. I attribute that to my mother. This was one of her favorites."

"Well, your mother had good taste as well, then. Because this is also one of my favorites."

We devour the pizza, both hungrier than we realized, and just as Terry McKay turns to Nickie Ferrante and says, "This is what's known as fooling the world," the oven timer beeps. Pausing the movie, I follow her into the kitchen, the now empty pizza box in hand.

"I'm ready to be amazed," I say, leaning both elbows onto the countertop.

"They have to cool first," she replies. She dons my oven mitt, which has probably only been used once before tonight, and takes the cookies from the oven. The butterscotch aroma fills the room even more than it already had, and I feel myself salivate.

"If they taste even half as good as they smell, I'll be a happy man." I watch her remove the cookies one by one with a spatula. She lays them onto a cooling rack, another piece of kitchen equipment I'm surprised I have. "What got you so into baking anyway?"

Charlie pauses for a long moment, her eyes trained intently on the sheet tray of golden cookies. "Um, when my parents passed away, the nights were way too long and dark and quiet. I kept remembering the weekends Mom and I would spend whipping up desserts for our family Sunday dinner. I think I started baking their favorite treats to cope, and then it turned into the thing I would do whenever I felt stressed or sad." She laughs, and the soft sound is jarring in my quiet kitchen. "I guess I felt sad and stressed a lot because I'm really good at it now."

Silence falls for a few minutes as she cleans up. When she's piled a handful of cookies onto a plate, she turns to me. "Ready?"

I lift my brow skeptically. "You're bringing all of those to the sofa?"

She lays her hand over her heart in mock sorrow. "You doubt me, Andrew, and that hurts my feelings. I'm not joking when I say you'll be so amazed you won't be able to stop at just one."

"Or two or three or four or five, apparently."

She laughs. "Grab us a glass of milk?"

"Sure I shouldn't just bring the whole gallon over?"

I hear a small snort as she walks away. Once we are resettled in the living room, and she has deemed the cookies cool enough, I take my first bite. I chew for about five seconds and pause the film. "What did you put in these?" I demand.

A satisfied smirk settles onto her face. "Told you."

Instead of reaching for another cookie, I pull the whole plate onto my lap.

"Hey! You cannot claim all of those!"

I bat her hand away. "You said *baking* is your therapy, not eating. Eating is mine."

Charlie leans over and swipes two cookies from the plate. She waves them tauntingly in front of my face. I make like I'm going to bite them right out of her hand, and she squeals.

"Down, boy. You're worse than Sergio. Were you the inspiration for Cookie Monster?"

I pop another bite of warm cookie into my mouth. My eyes roll backward at the explosion of caramelized brown sugar and butter on my tongue. "You should be famous," I mumble, realizing quickly that her fame should be for more than just baking.

I'm determined to make that happen.

I watch Charlie more out of my peripheral vision than I watch the movie. Seeing her stare dreamy-eyed as she watches the romance unfolding is far better than any scene that flashes across the screen.

At one point, I overhear her quiet murmur, "I've always wanted to stand at the top of the Empire State Building."

I snap my fingers. "That's right. It's your first time in the city, isn't it?"

She gives me a small, sheepish nod and tucks the throw under her chin.

"You have to experience more than just cabs and dirty sidewalks while you're here. How would you feel about me taking you to one of my favorite dinner spots tomorrow after I get off work? Somewhere that only the real locals know." I hold my breath as soon as the words come out.

Charlie lets a small gasp slip from her lips. "Really? You're not tired of me already? I really am okay on my own if you have other things to do."

I ponder for a moment. From what I've seen, it would be hard for anyone to get tired of this charming, adorable woman, with her quick comebacks and even quicker smile. Her presence beside me feels so natural; it's as if I've known her far longer than the couple of days she's been in New York. And that's when it hits me: I have known her longer. At least in the form of writing, in the stolen glimpse I got into her soul from her book. There's a reason she immediately felt so familiar to me and why I experience so much comfort in her presence.

But she doesn't know you, Andrew. She doesn't know who you really are . . .

I shake the dark thoughts away. I'm going to make this right. I will.

"Yeah, I'd love to take you to dinner," I hear myself say. "You might as well have a little fun and experience New York while you're here."

16

Charlie

Accepting Andrew's dinner invitation was not part of the plan.

The plan was: Storm New York City, right the injustice done to my parents' legacy, and then skedaddle back to my quiet, cozy life as a dog-trainer-slash-amateur-baker in rural upstate Vermont. That was the plan. *Simple, right?*

Except it isn't simple. Guilt surges through me, coming to rest in the hollow of my stomach. I feel like I'm letting everyone down. I booked a flight to NYC filled with faith that God was planning to move in a big way. I couldn't help but feel that He allowed me to stumble across my own, albeit stolen, book for a reason.

When I lost Mom and Dad in a car accident overseas, my heart was broken for months. Left alone as a young woman still learning to navigate the world, I struggled to sleep, not used to the heavy silence of my new normal. As I tossed and turned in the dark, remembering every word my parents ever said to me, a deep longing to renew my faith and restore my hope drove me to read for hours in the Bibles they left behind. Dawn broke day after day, finding me hunched over our breakfast table, obsessively studying the notes they each wrote in the margins, which now felt like letters they had inadvertently left me.

It took months, but eventually, the fresh light of morning broke on the horizon of my heart. Hope blossomed, my faith was restored, and the assurance that all was not lost, but on the contrary, that one day I would be reunited with them in a home far greater than any earthly place began to take root.

Their book was the first manuscript I ever fully finished among half a dozen projects I started and stopped throughout the years.

But I've been in the city for three days and feel no closer to accomplishing my mission than when I first arrived. Sure, the ball is rolling. Things are getting done. But it's a big ball, and I'm not sure my arms can hold on until I've seen my mission through. I'm not sure my faith is strong enough to stand against the roadblocks in my way. Questions have begun to pile upon questions. And the biggest question of all is Andrew.

I stare at my reflection in the large designer mirror of the bathroom in the remodeled apartment that he is graciously allowing me to occupy while I'm in the city. Winters Tower boasts a deep and quiet sense of wealth that is so much more luxurious than anything I'm used to back home. My idea of luxury up until now has been buying a pint-sized container of good ice cream from the market and eating the entire thing in one sitting instead of making it last the whole week.

Is Andrew my benefactor? Did I somehow land right-side up in a Bronte novel, and he is my Mr. Rochester? It's an intriguing possibility and one that I ponder until I remember with a start that there is so much more to Mr. Rochester than meets the eye. Secrets. Dark secrets that threaten to burn the whole house down around them. Is there more to Andrew than golden retriever eyes, goofy one-liners, and a smile that makes me tingle every time he flashes it in my direction?

This afternoon, I curled my hair and actually tried to apply a bit of eyeshadow and contour, feeling an inexplicable need to prove that I'm more than just flannel and denim and serviceable boots. Fluffing my long, dark waves for a third time in five minutes, I stare at the dress draped over my figure disapprovingly. I'm glad I thought to pack the black sweater dress and a pair of ankle boots at the last minute, but something still feels as if it's missing from my ensemble. I know what it is. Andrew is just so ridiculously handsome and effortlessly elegant, yet he is also cool and down-to-earth at the same time. I wear a dress exactly four times a year: on Christmas, Easter, my parents' anniversary, and my birthday. The rest of the year, I'm too busy wrangling rowdy dogs to find myself in anything other than pants and a t-shirt. A flannel is dressing up.

Yet here I am, staring into a mirror, wondering if I'm pretty enough to be seen with Andrew tonight.

"He's just being nice." My voice echoes loudly in the marble bathroom. I fix myself with a stern glare in the mirror. My lips feel sticky and unnatural with the red lipstick I painted on. "You made him feel sorry for you with your sad story and your futile attempts to find this elusive, mysterious, fake author. And then you go and make a fool of yourself by falling into a fountain after you've crazily accosted some poor, strange woman trying to enjoy her afternoon. Andrew is just a nice guy, and this dinner is happening because he feels sorry for you."

I would believe myself, except that yesterday afternoon, when Andrew pulled me out of the fountain, he drew me close, and there was something in his eyes that I can't explain. A look. A longing. Something on the tip of his tongue that he wanted to say.

His instant concern for me, the way he'd draped his sweater over my shoulders, choosing to walk in only a t-shirt through the chilly autumn air, the way the pad of his thumb had brushed the droplets of water away from my cheeks, and then his quickness in proposing a quiet evening to help me recover . . . it felt like something.

Something that I can't explain, yet I can't help but wish to explore. And wondering what could be behind that *something* scares me more than anything I've faced so far.

"Leaving my heart behind in New York City was not the plan, Lord," I breathe the prayer under my breath as a firm knock at the door signals Andrew's arrival. "It would be so easy to get swept away in all this. Please protect me, and let Your will be done."

—

Twinkling bistro lights, the clink of crystal, a touch of warmth from the fire crackling in the stone hearth . . . after my nervous musings that continued until Andrew knocked on the apartment door to pick me up for dinner, I didn't know I could feel this relaxed. He picked a quiet restaurant in Greenwich with a Provençal meets New England food vibe. We're tucked into a corner of the garden, away from most of the other diners, and the scenery is pure magic. After all the stress I've felt since discovering my book, a good meal and good company is exactly what I needed.

I feel my spirits lift with a renewed confidence that everything is going to work out okay. Perhaps the magical feeling is from the soft music cascading out of the hidden speakers or the nutty brown butter and lemon sauce of my perfectly crisped sole meunière that pulls me in for bite after bite. Or maybe it's from the warm sourdough bread spread with salty, rich butter that I keep reminding myself to recreate when I'm back home.

Or perhaps it's the company. Andrew has kept me laughing all evening with tales of his international travels and how one encounter with a stray dog in Venice started the chain of events that brought him to Sergio.

"So, how did you get into dog training?" Andrew asks.

"It was something I picked up from my dad, and then when I got older, it turned into a business."

Just as Andrew opens his mouth to speak, his phone rings. He pulls it from his pocket and glances at the screen. It would be impossible for his sudden frown to go undetected. He silences the call and tucks his phone away, but within seconds, it's ringing again.

"If you need to get that . . ."

He switches his phone to silent mode and shakes his head as he puts it back in his pocket. "It's fine." There's a dark cloud hanging over his face, but with a quick return of his smile, he casts it away. "So anyway, think you could give me some pointers for Sergio sometime? It's almost like he's on his best behavior when you're around, but I'd like to be able to take him out without worrying he is going to get us into trouble. There are group lessons offered in the park, but until he calms down some, I think it would end up being a disaster."

"I would be more than happy to help," I reply with a grin. "I'm not really sure who needs training more, though, Sergio or you." I intend for my tone to be teasing, but as the words leave my lips, I hear a flirtatious edge to them. Ducking my head in instant embarrassment, I slather another slice of bread with a thick layer of butter.

Andrew throws his head back and laughs. He doesn't seem to mind my teasing or notice my painful attempt at flirting. "Hey, I've watched plenty of YouTube videos, and I've tried. He's gotten me into some embarrassing scrapes because he's an unruly fellow who refuses to be trained, but I wouldn't trade his crazy, goofball self for any other dog in the world."

Glancing up through my lashes, I watch him scoop another spoonful of the seafood stew he ordered. The delicate scent of the carrot and saffron broth carries temptingly to me across the table. Our eyes meet, and the grin on his face widens. His eyes sparkle warmly, sending shivers up and down my spine. I don't think my reaction to his smile is normal in any way.

"It's crazy how fast those little furballs wiggle their way into our hearts." I drop my own gaze and run my finger across the rim of my water glass as we fall into silence. It isn't an awkward silence though. I noticed that immediately with Andrew. Our silence has the oddly familiar atmosphere of two people comfortable with each other and themselves. I feel as if I've known him for years, but it's only been a few days. Something has been niggling my curiosity about the man ever since we met, so I am the first to speak again.

"Tell me how you got started at CityLight. Have you always wanted to work in publishing?"

Andrew's spoon drops with a jarring clatter into the bowl, splashing the saffron-colored broth over the side. He apologizes and fishes it out, attempting to wipe the handle with the linen napkin before his head lifts again. When he does, he wiggles his eyebrows. "It's really very boring, I assure you."

I lean forward. "But I really want to know. It's such a dreamy vocation for a book lover, but I've never known much about the inner workings of a publishing house. Were you a big reader growing up? Did you go to school for public relations and then apply at CityLight?"

Andrew leans against the back of his chair. I hear the crack of his knuckles under the table. It takes him a moment to speak. "I'm afraid it's a really sordid tale of nepotism," he finally sighs dramatically, pressing a hand to his chest and heaving as if he's just revealed a secret. "My family has connections within the company, and it was because of that connection that I was given the job after I earned a public relations and marketing degree. I am a big reader. My mom encouraged me to read a lot growing up to help manage my anxiety. Believe it or not, I actually went to university for a degree in English Literature, but it was felt that a different degree would suit my path in life better."

I can't resist swiping some of the bread through what remains of the buttery lemon sauce on my plate and popping it into my mouth. "Why in the world aren't you part of the editorial staff? That seems much more fitting for your appreciation of literature."

"My father didn't feel that I was ready to take on a role like that," he replies, reaching for what is left of his bread too.

I pause in my second swipe. My eyebrows pull together as my head tilts to the side. "But what business is it of your dad's what you do with your career?"

Andrew's hand freezes over his bowl. He opens and shuts his mouth and then shrugs. "Honestly, my dad has always been involved with my life decisions, perhaps more than a normal family. He has opinions about my career, where I went to school, my reputation, and my work ethic. There isn't a lot that he doesn't have an opinion on." He ends with a short laugh. I watch as he places the uneaten bread back on its plate.

"That's nice that he cares to be involved in your life." I test the waters as carefully as I can.

Andrew shrugs again. "It seems nice on the surface. But in reality, try as I might, it seems to end more often than not with me making the wrong decision and upsetting him. I suspect he wants to be involved more as a safeguard against me embarrassing him than because he's actually proud of me."

The hurt that flashes across Andrew's face is foreign to me. My parents beamed with pride over every little accomplishment their only child made. My school awards, writing assignments, and report cards were proudly displayed on our family corkboard. After they were gone, I found dozens of faded awards and papers and short stories I'd written tucked away neatly year by year in their office filing cabinet.

When I lost them, I lost my biggest cheerleaders. At least Andrew's dad still has a chance to become his.

It must be the soft lights and music making me emotional, but I reach across the table and smooth the tips of my fingers over the back of his hand. He startles, his eyes flashing up to stare straight into mine.

My voice is soft. "Obviously, I don't know the ins-and-outs of your relationship with your dad, but keep working on him. There's going to come a day when he'll choose to tell you how proud he is of everything you've accomplished."

Andrew's hand shifts, and I expect him to move it away from me, which is okay because I know I might have overstepped my bounds. Instead, he moves his warm palm over mine and interlaces our fingers. His eyes go from their usual mischievous chocolate to a rich, deep brown. My chin lifts to fully meet his gaze. He leans forward, bringing our heads closer together across the tiny table. At his movement, a spark flares in my chest. My lower lip falls open just a little as I catch my breath.

He exhales, the soft whoosh of air warm as it brushes my cheeks.

"Charlie . . ." Andrew begins.

17

Andrew

My nerves have been on the fritz all evening. Dad's attempts to return my calls and Charlie's questions about my job and family aren't helping. Internally, I've been teetering on the verge like a powerline transformer, ready to blow at the slightest tip of the scales. It isn't the first time I've felt a panic attack brewing, and it won't be the last. Hello, anxiety, my old friend. But with her hand nestled so softly in mine, the tension and fear that's been brewing under the surface stills.

Against my will, my eyes drop to her parted lips. When I bring my gaze back to hers, I feel her fingers flinch in my grip and catch the flush that spreads across her cheeks. I don't want to break this moment, and I certainly don't want to break this woman . . . but it's time to come clean. As much as I wanted to warn my father first, I can't keep stringing her along.

"What is it?" Her voice is as rich and smooth as the

buttery sauce we just devoured with our meal. She leans forward, and on instinct, I do as well. Our faces are only inches apart, and my head swirls with the jasmine scent of her perfume and the sheen of bronze in her eyes.

"You're so beautiful." The words come out of their own volition, and I scramble to jam them back from where they emerged. "I . . . I'm sorry. I didn't mean . . ."

She unlaces her fingers from mine and sits back, one eyebrow quirked toward her hairline. "You didn't mean what you just said?"

"Yes. No." I shake my head and take a deep breath. *Come on, Andrew. You don't have to mess everything up. You can do this.* I struggle against the rope of anxiety tightening around my chest. "I did. I . . . I absolutely did." There's no denying that truth. "I just, uh, I didn't mean to say it out loud. I was going to say something else, but you, uh, distracted me."

"With all my beauty?" She snorts, and her lips split into a grin.

The nerves return but in the rare form of butterflies rather than fear. I marvel at the way this woman both unravels and remedies me at once.

"Is suave Andrew tongue-tied?" She feigns a shocked gasp and folds her arms across her chest. Satisfaction dances on her lips, and I hate myself for how badly I wish I could kiss her right now. Not that I ever can or will. There's no way my almost-peeing-my-pants-like-a-middle-school-boy vibe is working on her. Especially considering that it is coupled with the deceit that lingers like an ugly stain just below the other compliments I wish I could lavish upon her.

I rack my brain for something witty to say, for some way to get this derailed train back on its tracks. *Focus, you idiot!* I clear my throat and open my mouth, though I don't entirely trust myself with what might come out. "Let me start over. That okay?"

"I hesitate to agree. Seeing you squirm like this is adorable."

Adorable. Just how I want her to see me. Silently, I groan. But then reality hits. It doesn't matter how she sees me, because after what I'm about to say, her opinion about me being *adorable* is going to change. My gut aches.

"Are you . . . Is everything okay?" She studies me with wide, concerned eyes and rests her elbows on the table, leaning toward me just enough for her perfume to reach me once again.

"No, actually. Look. I need to tell you—"

My elbow catches my glass as I lean toward her. *Crash!* It tumbles to the floor, shattering into a million pieces as my drink saturates the tablecloth and the immaculate Spanish tile floors. Charlie and I both fly to our feet, only narrowly missing becoming human napkins. In an instant, a waiter is at our side, assuring us that, "These things happen all the time."

Yeah, I'm sure they do . . . not.

"I'm so sorry," I apologize, but the waiter waves me off as a busboy arrives with cleaning supplies. "Here, I'm happy to help." I reach for the mop but am shooed away immediately. The waiter instructs us to follow him to a new, clean table just around the corner.

"We were practically finished, weren't we?" Charlie pipes up.

The waiter stalls and gives us a questioning look. "Would you like a new table, or no?"

We *had* finished our meal. I glance at Charlie, and she shrugs one shoulder. "Are you . . . Did you get enough?" I ask.

"Yes. I mean, you might owe me a treat while we're out on the town later."

"Out on the town?" I can't help but laugh.

"Well, yeah. This night isn't over, is it?" Her mocha eyes twinkle with hope.

I turn to the waiter. "No need to seat us. We're ready for the check. In fact, here." I pull a card from my wallet and hand it to him.

We wait near the hostess stand for my card to be returned and bundle into our coats in preparation for the chilly autumn night air. The waiter returns, and I take my card and sign the receipt, leaving a hefty tip to ease my conscience.

The city is bright and brisk, the promise of experience at our fingertips as we leave the restaurant. Charlie's hands are shoved into her coat pockets, and as much as I want to yank one out and lace her delicate fingers back into mine, I can't. And not simply because of altruistic reasons, since Charlie is currently sprinting toward a churro stand down the street.

She dodges people like a true New Yorker and whirls around with a grin plastered across her face. "Remember that treat I mentioned?"

How could I say no? She goads me into ordering one for myself, and despite the pit in my stomach, I oblige. We walk side-by-side through The Village, munching on belly-warming churros with matching cinnamon-sugar dust sparkling all over the outside of our coats.

The early November chill sneaks up on us as we stop to throw the wrappers away. A shiver shakes down my spine, and I know I can't keep running from my confession forever.

"It looks like you were attacked by a fairy," Charlie says brightly as she takes the liberty of dusting away the churro's evidence from my collar. "So, where to next?" She frowns when she sees the pain on my face. "What's wrong?"

I swallow hard. *Just be a man and say it.*

"Charlie . . ." The words spin in my head, my confession a jumbled mess hurtling around like an asteroid bent on total annihilation. "Look, uh. You . . . you asked me earlier about my job and my parents. The thing is—"

"Wait." She thrusts out a hand and grabs me firmly by the forearm. "Are you about to tell me something sad?"

The question catches me off guard. Someone bumps into me as they pass, and I step closer to her. "It's . . . Well, yeah. In a way. It's sad and . . . painful."

Something passes over her face. I know this confession is going to wreck both of us more than I've even anticipated. Still, I open my mouth to let the truth gallop into freedom, but she holds up her hand.

"Stop." Her voice is firm and unflinching.

"What do you mean stop?"

Charlie drops her hand and tucks it back into her pocket. "I mean . . ." In the glow of the city lights, I see a gleam spark in her eye as she chews on her bottom lip. "I don't want pain and sadness tonight, okay? I've felt too much of that recently. Too much of that throughout the last few years. For one night, I just want to be free."

Free? *But the truth sets you free.* A faint echo of Mom's voice repeating the words to me pings through my brain.

"But Charlie—"

"Please." Her voice cracks. The tiny fracture nearly

shatters me entirely. "There's no news big enough or urgent enough that should ever be allowed to—"

"—ruin a perfect night."

Her eyes widen as we recite the line from her book in unison.

"So, you really *have* read my book?" she asks with an air of awe.

"More than once," I murmur. I know the line. And I know the pain out of which it had been born.

"Andrew, maybe it's this city at night, or maybe it's something else entirely, but at the expense of sounding like a complete loser, I haven't felt like this in a long time. Maybe . . . even ever."

"And how exactly do you feel?" My heart pounds. I can hear it whooshing in my ears. Charlie tilts her chin upward toward me, and I'm glad to see the spark of pain from earlier replaced with wonder twinkling in her eyes.

"I feel like"—she searches my face for something, but for what?—"I want you to take me to the top of the Empire State Building." Her boldness rips through the air like an electric current. If I thought I was about to burst earlier, I was wrong. She takes a step toward me, close enough now for me to touch her if I dared, her eyes full and clear. "Will you take me on an adventure, Andrew?"

18

Charlie

There's a look that passes over Andrew's features when I say the words that I can't quite explain. I feel it tingle through my limbs in electric waves. His eyes drop to my lips for the briefest of seconds before flashing up again. For once, he isn't smiling. My heart seizes. *Did I just make a complete fool of myself? Does he think that I . . .?*

I'm instantly too embarrassed to even think the words in my own head. We've known each other for mere days, and as much as I keep getting this uncanny sensation that I've known Andrew all my life, the reality is that it isn't so.

I begin to turn away, intending to laugh off my request and hail a cab for the ride home. It isn't late, but I can say that I'm tired. I'm well aware that I've barged into this man's life like a cyclone. He probably has his own weekly activities to get to. Maybe he won't accompany me back to the apartment. Maybe he takes lots of women to intimate dinners at charming, dimly lit restaurants tucked away in iconic NYC neighborhoods. I've never even asked if he has a girlfriend. Maybe he says, "You're so beautiful" in that voice, with those eyes, to other women all the time. Maybe I can spend one more night in the apartment he has lent me for the week. I'll find new accommodations in the morning so I can get back to the thing that brought me to this city in the first place.

I tell myself that the unexpected stinging at the corner of my eyes is just the cutting autumn wind that suddenly whips through the lamplit streets of Greenwich Village.

"Charlie, wait." Andrew's strong fingers wrap themselves around mine. Gently, he draws me back until my shoulders hit his chest. His arm goes around them, and he holds me in place while he hails a cab with his free hand. In an instant, my heart goes from seizing up to melting into a puddle at my feet. The pressure of his touch is gentle but firm. There's nothing pushy or forward about the way he embraces me. It's like I belong in this space, tucked against him, warm and held and . . . safe.

I want to laugh when the word flashes across my brain. *Safe.* I always feel safe in my sleepy little Vermont town. I've nestled into the quiet, cozy home I grew up in, burrowing in and refusing to pursue a life outside of Pleasant Hollow because . . . I don't trust anything beyond its borders after what happened to Mom and Dad. Writing has also been my safe place, my way to explore the world. In the words I've penned, I've hidden away my deepest thoughts and fears, the questions that have kept me awake at night until I'm forced to get up and write them down.

Yet here in the sprawling concrete wilds of New York

City, I suddenly feel safer than I've felt in years. As unrealistic as it is, given the scope of our days together, Andrew makes me feel safe to be myself, to be honest, to be vulnerable again.

That's a new kind of safe.

We don't speak as we wait for a cab to finally acknowledge our presence and decide to take our fare. We don't speak as a soft drizzle of rain begins to shower gently around our shoulders, dusting us with the lightest of raindrops, like shimmering fairy dew on the moss in the woods behind my home. We don't speak as he holds open the back door of the cab when it pulls toward the curb. He cradles my fingers, never letting them go, even after we're tucked into the seat, and he's told the cabbie, "Empire State Building, please."

It's a short drive in the deepening gloom of night. Red taillights and golden streetlamps light our way. The shower took everyone by surprise. I watch as New Yorkers turn their faces away from the drops, shielding their clothes and shopping bags from the threat of dampness. The back window of the cab is cracked a few inches. I turn my face up to the invigorating chill of the evening air, not minding the drops that fall from the sky.

I know we've reached our destination when I catch sight of the pale white twinkle of lights illuminating the exterior of the magnificent building. It's early November, and I'm glad I missed the display of lights for Halloween that typically rule the night in late October. I wouldn't want to see the Empire State Building any way other than this: an incandescent, shining beacon on this perfect night.

"You can just let us out up here," Andrew instructs the driver, his voice as deep and rich as pure maple syrup in the quiet cab. He hands the man a tip. We idle near the curb. Andrew steadies me as I step onto the damp pavement. The city seems slower here. As we approach the monument, my palm stays tucked securely within his. We pause in front of it. My head tilts back, all the way up . . . up . . . up to the tip of the building where it disappears into the night sky.

"What do you think?" Andrew's breath brushes past my ear.

"It's the nearest thing to Heaven we have in New York," I whisper the iconic line, the memory of my favorite classic movie stars making my heart ache for the undeniable romance of this place . . . this moment.

I hear him hum approvingly in my ear. "Shall we take the elevator to the hundred-and-second floor then, Terry McKay?"

Even though we just watched the movie together over pizza and butterscotch cookies last night, I thought I was the only person who appreciates movie lines quoted in real life. My face turns up to him in shocked, yet pleased, surprise as a happy flush brushes over my skin. I open my mouth to comment, but before I can speak, we're moving again. Andrew pulls me toward the doors leading into the building.

As we enter, I assume the landmark is rarely this quiet, even at night. The showers have driven everyone away, it seems. We pass security then stop at the ticket booth. We don't have reservations, but Andrew has a flex pass. After a few words, we make our way to the elevators. Our footsteps tap a steady rhythm on the marble floors. My eyes dance across the gold and gilded space. It's like Andrew and I stepped into the opulent brilliance of New York in the thirties, when Art Deco was all the rage, and lovers came to linger in the only space so beautiful it rivaled their own passion.

Once we are inside the elevator, Andrew wraps his arm around my shoulders again. The warm puff of his breath tickles the hairs at the nape of my neck. My shoulders are pressed against his chest. Although we are rising hundreds of feet into the sky, I've never felt more grounded and secure.

We bypass the main observatory deck on the eighty-sixth floor and ride the elevator to the pinnacle. As the elevator pauses on the hundred-and-second floor deck and the doors slide open, Andrew steps out first. I hesitate, struck with a sudden fit of nerves. He looks back with a quizzical expression.

"I'm nervous to step out and suddenly discover I'm afraid of heights," I say with a half-laugh, half-rueful shake of my head.

Andrew crosses back over the elevator's threshold. He leans over me, wrapping my fingers securely in his once again. His voice is deep and throaty as he says, "I'm right here with you, Charlie. I've got you."

And that's enough. I follow him across the observation deck. My eyes are immediately drawn to the panoramic views from each floor-to-rooftop glass panel. The city at night is breathtaking. Even through the soft descent of darkness, downtown Manhattan glows with the twinkle of a million lights. My breath catches. I begin to feel an old, familiar ache work its way into my throat.

The tears are already slipping down my cheeks. As much as I adore Pleasant Hollow with its quaint covered bridges, the thousands of trees awash in the colors of the sunset every autumn, and the aching memories stored in every square mile, I could get addicted to this magic. Something calls to the writer in me here. This city and all its inhabitants—but especially the one standing beside me—are both strange and familiar all at once. We're alone at the top of the world, and it feels like this is what was always meant to be.

My hand lifts to wipe away the tears coursing down my cheeks.

Andrew is instantly worried. "Hey, hey." I don't resist as he wraps his arms around my waist and turns my face into his shoulder. "Why are you crying?"

I tilt my head back and look at him, my laughter bubbling up unexpectedly. His eyes are a puddle of soft concern. Instinctively, my arms slide up. It's crazy, but it feels like the most natural thing in the world to twine my hands around the back of his neck. "'Beauty does that to me,'" I murmur in my best Terry McKay imitation. "I have a dozen reasons not to be, but I'm just so inexplicably happy right now. Can you explain that to me, Andrew?"

His lips twist into a smirk. "It's probably the churro you just ate. Who wouldn't be happy after that divine concoction of cinnamon and sugar?"

I roll my eyes, but a giggle bubbles out again as I throw my head back. The laughter feels good. When I regain my composure, I still have tears rolling down my face, but they are tears of laughter and not of pain. Andrew is looking at me strangely. "Do I still have cinnamon on my face?" I ask with amusement.

His mouth twists into his characteristic smirk, but the expression doesn't reach his eyes. I'm acutely aware of the soft pressure of his strong arms wrapped around my waist. My hand drifts to his cheek, the dark golden stubble on his jaw rasping against my palm. He tilts his head into my hand, his eyes closing for a moment. When he opens them again, he trains them intently on me, and his voice is gentle and husky.

"In all the places in all the world, I don't think I could find another woman quite like you, Charlie Blaire. I haven't told you this yet, but . . . your book helped me through a dark time. It gave me a glimmer of hope again when I thought all hope was lost. I know I don't have all the answers I need yet, but maybe someday I'll see the world the way you see it."

"You will," I breathe. "Keep your eyes on the Light, Andrew. It'll bring you home."

He doesn't reply, but his eyes speak volumes in the soft, golden light of the twinkling city as we stand on top of the world.

19

Andrew

Am I crazy for giving the door code to my apartment to a woman I barely know? Probably. But it sure doesn't feel like I barely know her. Charlie is . . . an enigma. An unexpected spark of light. An anomaly. And all I can think as I climb the front steps to CityLight's building and the revolving front doors open before me is her hand on my cheek last night and the look that filled her eyes as I told her what her book had done for me. Heat rushes through me. All at once, I feel young and old at the same time.

Mattias is dutifully standing guard this morning. I nod to him but ensure I don't hold his gaze too long. I don't want to leave any room for questions about the not-so-crazy lady who has me feeling all sorts of crazy myself right now. I step into the elevator as thoughts of her flutter through my mind. Her lips, so soft and trusting, the sweet jasmine scent of her perfume—

"Andrew Ketner!"

The words hit me as I step off the elevator on the floor below my office, intending to grab a coffee from the employee lounge first. The sound of my name ringing through halls feels like cold water crashing over me. Ava steps from her office just ahead. She waves first, then sets her hands on her hips. Her tortoiseshell glasses are perched on top of her head, and her eyes have turned into narrow slits. Sweat gathers at the nape of my neck as I slow down and veer toward her.

"Hey, stranger," she says, her eyes still narrowed. "How was your night?"

My guards rise at the question. "What's with the scrutiny?" I do my best to ease the words out in a joking manner, but inside, I quake.

She snorts and shakes her head. Her blonde ponytail swings behind her. I've known Ava since college. I trust her to fill me in on anything I need to know. "You'd better come up with a better response than that before you face your father."

The world comes to a grinding halt. *Dad?* I can feel the fear rise in the back of my throat. Has he already found out somehow? Did the story break before I've had the chance to make things right? That's what I'm here to do this morning. Am I . . . too late?

My stomach churns, an acidic reminder of my deceit. I'm here this morning to come clean. Last night, as Charlie and I stood together marveling over the beauty of the cityscape, I knew more than ever that my deception has already run too long. I have a plan. I am going to make this right. Today.

Ava looks at me now with a mixture of pity and curiosity.

I can feel my heart plummeting into my stomach.

"What do you mean?" I manage to ask.

Her lips twist into a wry smile. "According to the gossip from Joyce upstairs, your dad is pretty angry about last night."

"Last night?" My heart might jump out of my chest and flop onto the floor like a dead fish at this point. Last night was one of the best nights of my life, and yet . . . Was this my punishment? Did Josh tell Dad I've been running around the city with the woman about to launch a lawsuit against us for plagiarism? Josh was the one who told me to wait a couple of days until he had time to come up with a strategy and to keep Charlie busy to buy some time.

Dad had tried to call four times during my evening with Charlie last night, leaving no voicemails. It had been far too late for me to return his calls by the time we returned home. And besides, breaking the news to him over the phone feels like a cruel move, considering how important the gala this weekend is to both of us. Some news just has to be handled in person, which is why I came straight to the office to do so this morning. But it looks like someone beat me to it.

Ava's mouth falls open. "You mean, you really forgot?"

"Forgot what?"

Her eyes widen into saucers.

A sigh escapes me. I cross my arms. "Look, Ava. Can you squash the whole playing coy thing and just tell me what's up?" My voice goes up a little, and I feel a few pairs of eyes turn toward us from other areas of the office.

Shaking her head, she takes a step back and motions for me to follow. Inside her office again, she says pointedly, "Now that we're not suddenly having a fight in front of all the other staff . . . All I know is that there was some important meeting with some media guy last night, and you never arrived, so your dad had to handle the entire interview himself."

"Important meeting . . .?" I rack my brain, and it hits me. Two weeks ago, Dad emailed me about an interview Docu Wise Productions wants to film for an upcoming documentary about family-run businesses that have held out against mergers and buyouts in modern-day North America.

My breathing suddenly goes tight. Lifting my hand, I thread my fingers through my hair, feeling tiny pinpricks of pain as I tug on the roots. No wonder Dad was trying to call me last night. He was busy running our company and saving face during an interview that we were both supposed to be involved in. Father and son. When I didn't show up, he must have figured I'd disappointed him yet again.

My voice emerges with an edge of panic. "That interview completely slipped my mind."

Ava stares at me in visible shock. "What's the deal, Andrew? Half the time, you show up and pretend to give at least fifty percent of your attention to your work. The other half of the time, you're off doing who knows what. Do you not care about your job?"

"I care, okay? More than anyone knows." I drop into the lounge chair in the corner of her office, my legs beginning to feel shaky. The room spins around me. I can hear the blood pounding through my ears.

Ava leans against her desk. Her eyes drill into me. "What's the deal with you? Be honest."

"Be honest about what exactly?" I mutter. Does she want me to admit that ever since Mom passed away, I've been a complete failure? Or how about the fact that because of my selfish need to prove myself to Dad, I'm about to bring a storm of trouble down on the company he's put every bit of himself into over the years? Should I tell her I'm somehow falling in love and being crushed by heartbreak at the same time? Everything I touch turns to dust. Everyone I try to protect ends up leaving anyway.

With a flash, Charlie's pretty face as she stared up at me last night floats into my mind. Despite the turmoil raging in my chest, just the thought of her sets some of my nerves at ease.

"Spill the beans, mister. I've known you for years, and even this level of screwup is abnormal for you." Ava gasps and covers her mouth. "Wait a second. Andrew Clark Ketner, did you . . . meet someone?"

My eyes snap up to meet hers. She's looking at me with a puzzled expression. "Why would you think that?"

"For one thing, when I saw you walking through the office, you looked all distant and starry-eyed. Your shirt is wrinkled. I've never seen you with a hair out of place in the last ten years of knowing you . . . *except* when you're dating someone, and it isn't going well. And now you're blushing."

"Am not," I blurt out. Instinctively, I cup my jaw.

She gasps. "I'm right, aren't I?"

"No," I sputter. "I . . . My shirt is wrinkled because—"

"You slept over somewhere?" She arches her brow. Her expression is skeptical. She knows me well, but it's clear she's starting to have doubts.

"No," I say the word firmly. "I'm not that type of guy, but thanks so much for the accusation. My shirt is wrinkled because I slept in and didn't have time to iron before I needed to run out the door. *My* door."

It's true. I stayed up so late thinking about Charlie and this mess I'm in that by the time I put my journal down and fell asleep, it was already morning. I'd fallen into such a deep slumber that I didn't even hear my alarm for minutes after it began to ring. I had just enough time to throw on some clothes, take Sergio outside to do his business, slip my door code into Charlie's hand, and run downstairs to catch my ride. Charlie is currently under the impression that I have a full day of work. She has kindly agreed to walk Sergio during my absence today, not knowing that I came into work to break the news to Dad.

"Fine." Ava folds her arms against her chest. "Explain the starry-eyes and the blushing then."

"This is stupid." I stand and attempt in vain to smooth out my button-down.

"Ketner's in love . . . Ketner's in love . . ." Ava teases in a singsong voice.

Shaking my head, I step toward the door. "If you'll excuse me, I don't have time to partake in foolish office gossip. I have work to do."

"Do it while you can before your dad gets ahold of you," she mutters as I make my escape.

Knots twist in my stomach as I climb the stairs to the upper floor. I don't have the patience to wait for the elevator. Not today. Every second I let this mess unravel further is another reason that Charlie won't ever forgive me. Desperation builds in my throat as I take the steps two-by-two and speed down the hallway upstairs straight toward Dad's office.

I nearly bowl Mark over when he steps in front of me.

He grabs my arm and steers me toward the conference room.

"Dude, I thought you were pulling a no-show today on me too." He shoves a file folder at my chest.

Frazzled, I glance at the watch on my wrist. Mark is on CityLight's public relations and marketing team with me. The folder falls open, and I realize my morning meeting is scheduled to start in five minutes. Dad is just going to have to wait until after it's done. I can't fail yet another of my duties.

"No, I'm here. Of course . . . I'm here." The words come out flat and unconvincing.

"Alright. Get yourself together, Ketner. You look terrible."

I brush away from him and take a deep breath to steady the racing beat of my heart before I enter the conference room that is already full and waiting.

The meeting drones on longer than any of us expect. By the time it's over, I'm rushing into another. It's well near one o'clock by the time I finally get the chance to make my way toward my father's office.

Joyce, his secretary, looks surprised to see me as I approach. Her face cycles through shock, dismay, and disappointment in a three second span. I resist the urge to barrel through my father's closed office door and pause at her desk just outside.

"Mr. Ketner," Joyce greets in her high-pitched voice. "Good afternoon, sir. What can I do for you?"

"I need to see my dad. Alright if I head in?"

Her thinly drawn brows crinkle together. "Oh, I'm afraid he . . . took a personal day." Her voice trails off, and I know what she's thinking, but I choose to ignore it.

Dad and "personal day" have never before gone together in the same sentence. "What are you talking about?"

She hesitates. "He arrived early yesterday evening from Toronto and went straight to the Docu Wise Production meeting. He sent me a message this morning stating that he planned to handle a few last-minute details for your mother's benefit gala this weekend and then would be heading to find you. I think your, uh, absence from the Docu Wise Production meeting last night left him rather . . . unsettled." She raises her eyebrows and gives me a look that is at once pointed and pitiful.

"He's planning to find me?"

Her words are confirmation enough of how Dad is handling my failure to show up last night. He must have assumed I wasn't going to even show up for my job today. Well, there could certainly be worse times to deliver bad news, I suppose. Might as well pile it all on at once. I swallow the dry lump in my throat. "Wait. Where is he supposedly looking for me?"

She shrugs. "Wherever he might think you'd be. Perhaps at home?"

Home.

Charlie.

I smack Joyce's desk as I turn and sprint toward the elevator. My phone jostles in my pocket as I run. There's little chance it will work inside the elevator, so I wait, nerves spiking mercilessly until I reach the ground floor. Hands shaking, I dig it out and dial Dad's number. It takes six rings for him to answer.

"Andrew! My boy!"

The joy in his voice brings me to a halt on the steps in

front of CityLight's high-rise. The crisp November wind nips my cheeks. It's a gray day, the sky overcast and gloomy, though I'm hot, panting, and, at the moment, genuinely confused.

"Dad?" I huff into the phone. He certainly doesn't sound mad at all. "Wha . . . Where are you?"

"Funny you should ask. I came by to make sure you are alive and to see if we could have that talk you wanted. So, I'm at your apartment now and having the nicest chat with your girlfriend."

20

Charlie

I lean against the counter in my borrowed apartment. Morning traffic blares faintly, a cacophony of big city noise on the distant streets. Still dressed in my plaid pjs, I nurse my second cup of coffee of the morning along with a heaping spoonful of regret. Nothing happened last night that would cause me to hang my head. It was what didn't happen (though I wish it had) that has left me reeling with a confusing sense of thrilling butterflies and nervous anticipation.

My murmured prayer is a soft echo against the sounds of the morning. Talking to God aloud as if He is right in the room with me is a habitual routine, and I jump in without preamble. "I never expected to show up here and find such a distraction, Father God. I'm sorry if I'm missing the steps You are telling me to take to get the rights to my book back. Please help me to listen for Your still, small voice, even when this growing attraction I feel for Andrew feels so confusing and yet strangely . . . wonderful."

I've just met the man, but after last night, I found myself drifting off to sleep dreaming of what could be . . .

A soft knock startles me from my anxious thoughts. I almost gasp when I press my eye to the peephole and see Andrew on the other side. The thought crosses my mind that I should call through the door and tell him I can't talk to him right now, but such an excuse seems childish.

I pull the door open and try to hide behind it, wondering if I should have at least run a brush through my wild mane of morning hair before facing my neighbor. "Uh, hi," I greet him with an unexpected air of shyness.

"Good morning. How did you sleep?" The way his deep and husky voice draws out the words sends an involuntary shiver down my spine. His face shifts to a look of amusement as he takes in my disheveled morning appearance. "Rough night?"

Why does his stupid face have to be so handsome? I think with a touch of resentment. *Why does he have to stand here first thing in the morning looking like a cover model just off the runway? And why do I feel like I'm going to melt right into the floor every time that little smirk creeps over the corner of his mouth when he's teasing me?*

These are the words in my head. Aloud, I roll my eyes and force an overly sweet smile on my face. "Well, if someone hadn't kept me out until the wee hours of the morning, I might have gotten my full eight hours of sleep."

Andrew chuckles, the sound rich, golden, and throaty. "Some of us grew up in the city that never sleeps and are used to staying up past midnight like normal people instead of going to bed with the sun like you Vermonters." He leans forward. One forearm rises to rest on the doorframe just above my head. My breath makes a little hitching sound because the flecks of gold in his eyes sparkle in the morning light.

"That must be it," is all I can manage to squeak out.

He leans in closer. His warm gaze studies me, and in that space of time, my brain goes temporarily blank. Finally, his lips part again. Words come out, which I have to ask him to repeat while I gather my mental faculties again.

"I have to run to the office to get some work done today." He rubs the back of his neck. "I might be gone most of the day. Would you be able to take Sergio for a walk this afternoon so he isn't cooped up all day? I hate to ask . . ."

An unfamiliar sensation of disappointment surges over me. Not seeing him all day feels . . . wrong.

I smile and nod. "I am happy to take him out for you. I'll probably be headed out myself here shortly. I have a meeting, and I need to get some things in order. I'll come back around noon if that's okay?"

He pauses, studying me again. "That works. Here's a code that will open my door. His leash and doggy bags are hanging next to the pantry." Andrew hands me a scrap of paper with a few numbers written on it. I watch his Adam's apple bob with a quick swallow. "Are you . . . do you have a lead on A.C. Frost?"

I wave my hand nonchalantly. "To be honest, I have some things I'm working on, but I don't think it would be wise to divulge them just yet. Legal stuff for moving forward, you know."

I think I see a flash of hurt in his expression. However,

he quickly covers it up with a smile. Stepping back into the hallway, he gives me a nod. "I guess I am still working in the enemy's camp, aren't I?"

I open my mouth to protest but quickly shut it again. He is the one who just said it, not me. I did come to New York to get a task done, after all. Still, I can't resist the urge to blurt out impulsively, "I'll see you later though, maybe? I could cook dinner for us?"

He nods slowly. "I'll let you know if I can make it. Have a good day, Charlie."

And then he walks away, and I am left with the uncomfortable feeling that we've just had a fight and aren't on speaking terms. The rest of my morning is taken up with a meeting I managed to schedule with a well-rated (and extremely expensive) copyright lawyer in the city, as well as digging the web in one more futile attempt to hunt down any clues to the identity of the elusive A.C. Frost.

—

"Hold your horses. Don't break the door down," I call through the heavy door as the sound of anxious scratching reaches me from the other side. The key code Andrew left me this morning doesn't work the first time, so I double-check the digits and enter the numbers a second time more carefully. As soon as I push the handle, a barreling bundle of soft auburn fur and wild doggy kisses launches itself at me.

Sergio nearly topples me over in the hallway, but I manage to right myself before he trips me. His fur is warm and silky under my hands as I scratch behind his floppy ears and try to prevent him from jumping up and licking my face.

"Come on, boy," I laugh, wiggling my fingers so the dog will follow me back into Andrew's apartment. He pauses just outside the door for a moment, looking at me with a confused expression. One front paw is raised in the air as if I am the one who is supposed to follow him toward unknown and exciting explorations. He quickly relents, however. Sloppy tongue hanging, Sergio bounds over the threshold after me.

It's odd to step into the lofty, quiet space alone. I've only been inside Andrew's home a couple nights this week and haven't ventured past the kitchen and living spaces. I try not to look around too much, hurrying toward the kitchen alcove where Sergio's leash dangles on a hook above his food and water bowls. I grab the leash and a few baggies, managing to clip the leash onto the wriggling dog with relative ease.

"Are you ready for a walk, boy? Your dad asked me to step in to make sure you got to handle your business and stretch your legs this afternoon since he isn't going to be back in time." It feels silly to say the words aloud, but the awkward sensation of being alone in Andrew's apartment makes me want to justify my intrusion.

Sergio proudly struts down the hallway. His fluffy, curled tail waves high in the air with the thrill of going on a walk. I'm pleased he didn't bat an eyelash at my sudden appearance outside his door. We've quickly become friends. With the right training, I am confident that his wild, exuberant nature can be molded into something slightly more polite and less jumpy.

Once outside, Sergio wastes no time in dragging me to his favorite spots. He's strong and low to the ground. The law of physics works against my attempts to curb his rambunctious ramble. I let him lead us to the park and take care of business before I rein in the leash. Quickly, while he sniffs a nearby trash can, I modify his lead into an easy training tool, looping it and slipping it around his muzzle. I snap my fingers to bring him to attention. Sergio bounces up, already trying to reach the treats I purchased at a nearby bodega and stashed in my pocket as a training reward. As he leaps, the lead tightens slightly. At the unfamiliar pressure, he falls back to the ground, obvious confusion on his face.

"Time to get some training in, big boy, and make your dad proud he adopted you."

It's a struggle at first to get the oversized, playful dog to realize that if he walks calmly at my side, he'll get a treat. But within thirty minutes, we're walking together through Central Park, Sergio heeling with relative compliance at my side. We'll tackle basic commands another day. For now, I look around the lush, grassy space and nearly pinch myself with the giddy realization that I'm doing what I love in Central Park. It's autumn in New York City. The sky has been overcast all day, but nothing can detract from the vibrant sunset-hued piles of drifting leaves. For the last half hour, the sun has been trying to peek through the drizzly sky. I look up at it through bared branches while a crisp breeze plays with my hair. The moment feels like it freezes around me as I commit it to memory.

All at once, I'm struck with the realization that if I'd never picked up *Love Between the Pages* in Bluebird Books or if Lora had never decided to feature it in her autumn bestsellers display, I may never have realized my book had been plagiarized. I would never have flown to New York. I may have never walked through Central Park in autumn. Would I have ever ridden to the top of the Empire State

Building at night? Would I have ever met—

"Let's get you back home, boy." Suddenly uncomfortable, I interrupt my own train of thought and tug the shaggy dog in the direction of home.

Back in Andrew's apartment, Sergio gulps the water I pour into his bowl with his usual gusto. It's only after I've carefully replaced his leash where I found it that I gather the courage to glance around Andrew's kitchen without feeling awkward. The space is modern, sleek, and beautiful, featuring none of the rustic charm that fills my own kitchen back home. I risk taking a peek into the luxurious butler's pantry. Apart from a paper bag tossed into the corner and stuffed with overflowing takeout containers from a place called Gustinelli's, the kitchen looks like it just stepped out of an HGTV episode.

My curiosity and my courage grow as I wander through the apartment. "I'm not snooping," I call out and laugh at myself for my own silliness.

Andrew's living room is a bit more relaxed. I already know how cozy the sectional sofa is. In one corner, a desk sits amid a row of wooden bookshelves. Its surface is mostly bare, save for a closed laptop, a mug filled with pens, and an expensive-looking leather journal and pen tucked to the side. The placement of the ribbon bookmark shows that he uses it frequently. I'm tempted to open the journal and peek inside, curious as to what Andrew's most private thoughts are. But I refrain, feeling guilty enough for snooping through his apartment.

Instead, I turn my attention to the wall of photos hanging above the desk. A smile spreads over my face as I see Andrew featured in most of them. His caramel hair is messy in some; his million-dollar smile is displayed prominently in most. I see his diploma framed and hung over the desk too.

Columbia University. Impressive, I think. "A master's degree in public relations with a minor in marketing awarded to Andrew Clark Ketner, 2018," I read aloud.

Twenty-nine. He's only two years older than me. The thought of Andrew in a university lecture hall setting makes me smile as I continue examining the frames scattered across the wall. An older man who looks like a version of Andrew thirty years in the future is featured in several photos in the collection. In one photo, Andrew stands between the older man and a very pretty woman with soft gray hair and a pair of milk chocolate eyes that I recognize immediately. He has his arms around her, and they are both laughing at the camera. I've only heard him mention his mother a handful of times. Instinctively, I know that this is her, that she's gone, and that her absence has left a wound in Andrew's heart that he tries to hide behind a carefree demeanor and a goofy smile.

Why am I so confident? Because my own heart bears the same scars. I searched my parents' Bibles for months for answers to my pain, pouring over its words and the notes they left behind in the margins. Notes that felt like letters of wisdom written directly to me. While I've found comfort in an unshakable faith that not only will I see my parents again, but we will also spend eternity together in the joyous unity of our heavenly home, I can tell that Andrew doesn't have the same assurance. I want him to find it. He and I share the same ache. He hides it behind a carefree smile. I've hidden it by burrowing so deep into my childhood home that I may never have the courage to face the world again and writing aching love stories by candlelight on stormy nights.

Emotion stings the corners of my eyes. I quickly pull them away from the beautiful woman with the familiar eyes. My attention is immediately drawn to another photo on the wall. This one is of Andrew with a tall, slim, could-be-a-model young woman. They're both in cap and gown. College friends. He has his arm draped casually over her shoulders. I purse my lips at the sight, leaning closer to get a better look at the pair. It isn't lost on me that they look like they are made for each other, all golden skin and hair and beautiful smiles.

Something nags at my subconscious. The woman looks familiar. I lean over the desk again. My fingers brush the edge of the leather journal. Why *does* she look so familiar?

I pull my phone from my pocket, but before I can do any sleuthing, the door chimes. Instantly, Sergio erupts into a spinning, barking ball of fluff. A man steps through the door. I freeze in front of the desk. My memory jogs, and I recognize the handsome older man from the photos on the wall.

It's obvious my presence catches him off guard. We stare at each other awkwardly, neither of us saying a word. Somehow, I recover first and step forward, putting distance between myself and the desk. I stretch out my hand.

"You must be Andrew's dad?" I say hoarsely. Nervously, I paste on my best smile, hoping that he doesn't report to his son that it looked like I was just snooping through his desk. Which I totally was. "I'm Charlie, a friend of Andrew's."

I don't know how else to explain why I'm in his son's apartment alone in the afternoon. Sergio bounces up, attempting to earn a head rub.

The man returns my smile graciously, extending his

hand to shake mine firmly and politely. "Gary," he says. He gives me a once-over, but the inspection doesn't give me any creepy vibes.

"I think you have me at a disadvantage, young lady. Are you the one who has been distracting my son lately?" The words are said with a teasing wink, but there's a sharp curiosity in his eyes that I don't miss.

I blush. "I don't know that I'd count myself a distraction, but I have been keeping your son busy this week. He's helping me with something."

Gary leads the way to the kitchen. I trail after him aimlessly, unsure how to make my escape.

"Andrew went into the office this morning and asked me to walk Sergio," I say, still hoping to explain what I'm doing here.

Setting a cardboard tray with two to-go coffee cups onto the marble countertop, Gary turns to face me and shakes his head. "He went to the office today, you said? We've been playing phone tag. My son has suddenly become very mysterious. He told me he had to speak to me on an urgent matter, but it had to be in person. He was supposed to join me last night for an important meeting, but he never arrived."

A gasp escapes me, and I move my hand to cover my mouth. "Oh, no. I am so sorry. I might be a distraction after all." I cringe, guilt suddenly swirling in my belly. "Andrew was, um, showing me around the city last night. I had no idea I was keeping him from something so important. We got caught up with dinner and the Empire State Building, and I—" I realize I'm babbling and snap my mouth shut.

Gary eyes me, the corner of his mouth turned up in a

familiar smirk. "I wonder if you are the urgent matter he wants to discuss with me?" He reaches up to smooth his hand over his jaw.

I've suddenly turned into a blushing machine because my cheeks heat up again. "Oh, I . . . I really don't think it could be about me. I've only been visiting for a few days. When my hotel accommodations fell through, Andrew invited me to stay in the vacation unit he owns down the hall. I'm not . . . I'm not staying here." More blushing.

"Oh, you don't live in town?"

I shake my head. "No, sir. I am just visiting this week from Vermont."

"Please. Call me Gary. Vermont, did you say? I didn't know Andrew had a friend in Vermont." He leans forward and pushes a coffee cup toward me. "Here, Charlie, why don't you drink this before it gets cold? I'll catch up with my son later. So, are you in town for the gala then?"

"The gala?"

A look of confusion passes over Gary's face. "Has he told you about the gala this weekend?"

"No, he hasn't mentioned it."

Gary feigns shock. "Well, it's only the premier event to launch the upcoming holiday season. Will you be in town for the weekend?"

Will I? I shrug, suddenly feeling like I've completely lost my footing in this conversation. "I . . . I might. I mean, it depends how things go with Andrew this week. Well, you know, not just Andrew, but other things that I'm doing this week . . ." I'm floundering. *What am I saying?*

"Well, then, you absolutely must attend as my guest."

"It sounds like a lovely event, but I don't . . . " I stutter.

Gary waves his hands and adjusts his glasses. "I won't accept no as an answer. Every year, we throw this gala in honor of my late wife around the time the first frost arrives because she said there was no magic quite like it. She loved the winter season almost as much as she loved books and always threw a huge party to bring in donations for the children's fund."

I try to pull myself together. "It really is an honor. Thank you for the invitation."

"The Winters' Wonder Gala launches the holiday season around here. Puts everyone into a good mood right before Thanksgiving." Gary winks. There's been an electronic buzzing sound for a few seconds. It continues as he pulls a phone from his trouser pocket. "Andrew! My boy!" he says into the receiver. Gary mutes his phone for a moment and leans toward me. "Oh! And Charlie, let's not mention your invitation to my son. Let's keep it a little surprise for him between you and me, shall we?"

I nod helplessly as he straightens and winks at me again. He unmutes his phone and speaks into the receiver. "Funny you should ask. I came by to make sure you are alive and to see if we could have that talk you wanted. So, I'm at your apartment now and having the nicest chat with your girlfriend."

21

Andrew

"My . . . what?"

My head spins as I try to process what Dad just said. *What is happening?* I scan the block for a nearby cab, but the energy coursing through my body is not something that can or should be contained inside a small vehicle right now. As my messenger bag flaps against my leg, I book it down the sidewalk. Adjusting the phone to my ear again, I say, "Dad? Hello?"

"Hey, yeah. Sorry, Andrew. I got distracted. Turns out Charlie is much better to talk to than you." He laughs like the joke is his very best. Heat rushes through my body.

Is he not mad at me for missing the meeting? Why is he talking to Charlie?

Have. To. Get. Home.

"What's even . . . What are you . . ." I pant. My mind reels with all the possible outcomes of their encounter. How much is Charlie telling him? Has she honored the nondisclosure agreement? Has Dad told her he's the CEO of CityLight? I'm going to have a hard time explaining that one to her. It wasn't that I initially planned to hide my parentage from Charlie. When I handed her my card in the lobby, I fully expected her to recognize my last name. Being a Ketner was something I planned to use to my advantage as I navigated the tricky scenario. But when the name never seemed to register in her eyes, and she stuffed my card down into her purse, I just . . . put off mentioning it.

But of all the things to come of a meeting between Charlie and Dad, I certainly did not expect that he would ever think of her as my *girlfriend.*

Dad is speaking on the other end of the line. "I stopped by your apartment to have whatever conversation you so desperately needed to have with me and to find out what prevented you from attending that Docu Wise meeting last night. I certainly think I have answers to both questions now."

I hear rustling. He says something to Charlie, though I can't quite hear the words over the rush of city noises around me and my own heavy breathing. I push myself forward. My loafers are not exactly the best running shoes, but I have to make it home and interfere with whatever is happening at my apartment.

"It was great to meet you, Charlie," Dad's voice rises, and I picture him calling the words over his shoulder.

"Dad!"

"What? I'm just leaving your apartment now. We'll catch up later."

"No, Dad," I huff. My feet pound over the pavement. I

dodge an older woman carrying a grocery bag. "I really need to talk. You don't understand."

"Are you at the gym?"

"No." I want to chuck my phone into the uncovered manhole I'm forced to leap over as I sprint across the street. This has to be a joke.

"Look, I think I understand what's going on perfectly, Andrew. As ready to wring your neck as I might have been last night, nothing can stop a young man falling in love. I remember that very season with your mother." There's a slight break in his voice at the painful memory of Mom.

The mention of her is a knife to my already burning chest. Everything else only further confirms what an idiot I am.

"Oh, shoot," Dad says. "So sorry. I have an important call coming through. I have to go, son. Let's have dinner soon. Maybe after the gala. You know how slammed this week is."

Before I can reply, the line goes dead. I come to a grinding stop on the sidewalk, my right shoe narrowly missing a piece of freshly spit-out gum. I just want this whole ordeal with Charlie to be over.

Charlie . . .

I picture her standing in the doorway of her temporary apartment, her hair a mess and those tiny dots of mascara sprinkled below her lower lashes. She was so beautiful this morning. I'm so glad I've met her, and yet by the end of this, she will wish she'd never met me.

It's a quick leap from Charlie to my mom. Dad's mention of her and the upcoming gala this weekend brings everything into sharp focus. It feels like I have a thousand things to do in preparation for Winters' Wonder in a few days, and I've done next to none of them. This week is supposed to be dedicated to honoring Mom and the legacy she left for this city. Of all the things I've messed up lately, this can't be one of them.

A pain pinches behind my ribs. I try to convince myself that it's caused by sprinting across the city. But I know that is a lie, even if I can't admit it. Mentally, I'm too afraid to even approach the truth.

If I'm honest, the closest to something akin to healing I've felt since Mom's death was ironically found amid the pages of the very manuscript CityLight stole from Charlie. *Love Between the Pages* . . . She wasn't wrong. Through the darkness of last winter, Charlie's writing was provocative enough to make me cry, which I hadn't allowed myself to do since I watched Mom slip into eternity. Her words were honest enough to make me consider my own spiritual future, or lack thereof, and thoughtful enough to put back together some of the pieces that shattered within my heart when we lost Mom. Charlie's words have lingered. I've pondered them, and because of them, I have felt the blossoming of a tiny root of hope for what lies beyond this life.

It's no secret that Charlie is a stunning woman. I would go so far as to say she is drop-dead gorgeous. But her striking outer beauty holds no candle to what she looks like inside. She is at once both gifted and a gift to the world. The epitome of perfection. And she deserves recognition for that. Everything I ever hoped to find in a woman, that's Charlie.

The trouble is, she's the one woman I have no right to pursue.

I stare at my phone. Pedestrians swarm around me, breaking like a river as I stand like a boulder in the path. A bead of sweat rolls down my spine in spite of the chilly November air. What did Dad say to her? Should I call her? Determination burns in my chest. I just want to make things right for her, for Dad and me, for CityLight. But if I get her on the phone right now, will I just blurt it all out?

I have to wait until the Winters' Wonder Gala is over. For Dad. Dad doesn't have the capacity to deal with news like this beforehand. I take a deep breath. It's only a few more days, but my heart is tired. I feel it rotting more every day with the lies I've told and continue to tell.

But maybe I can remedy something in the meantime . . . An idea begins to form in my mind. It's not that there's even much to remedy romantically speaking. From the look on Charlie's face in the doorway this morning, her features seemed to cringe with regret about our date last night.

What did I think the outcome would be? Wining and dining her. Taking her to the top of the Empire State Building. Spilling my heart to her while we looked out at the most romantic view in the city. What right did I have? None! I'm literally the enemy. The kingpin. The villain. The CEO of her demise. My hatred toward myself flares.

Charlie and I were never supposed to meet. But now that we have, I wish there could be something between us that isn't destined to end in disaster. I shouldn't pursue her. I really need to get that fact through my thick skull. Regardless of the bleak future our relationship has, I want to show her how absolutely sorry I am for the mess that she doesn't even know I've caused yet.

And yet . . . I have to wonder: What did she say to my dad for him to assume she is my girlfriend?

My finger hovers over her name in my phone. Just as I

move to press call, a text pops onto the screen.

CHARLIE: Hey, so . . .

My heart constricts, and I wait. But nothing else comes.

ME: . . . so you met my dad?

CHARLIE: Yeah . . .*facepalm emoji* . . . I think there's been a misunderstanding.

I begin to type: About my dad or about us? But I quickly delete it. Of course, she means both. She's obviously realized how grave of a mistake we made last night. In spite of my logic, my heart deflates.

ME: I apologize for anything my dad misconstrued. That's Dad for you.

The little blue dots appear and then disappear. She's stopped typing. My fingers fly across the screen again.

ME: Do you want to get lunch? I have some time before my next meeting. Promise there won't be any awkward dads there . . .

CHARLIE: I think I'll brave the city on my own this afternoon, but thank you.

I blink at the screen. Why does her rejection hurt so much?

ME: Oh, okay. No problem.

CHARLIE: I'm still happy to make dinner tonight like I offered, though.

I sigh. I don't want to be an obligation to her.

ME: I won't hold you to that. Enjoy your day out. Spread those Vermont wings of yours.

CHARLIE: Oh. Do you . . . not want to have dinner together?

Someone bumps into me, but I don't take my eyes off my phone. Confusion swirls in my brain.

ME: Do you want to?

CHARLIE: I asked you first.

ME: What are we? In middle school?

CHARLIE: *laughing emoji*

I shouldn't type the next words, but among the intricate web of lies I've already spun, I can't help but share some truth too.

ME: Charlie, I'd love nothing more than to have dinner with you. But how about we cook together instead?

CHARLIE: It's a date.

An ear-to-ear grin spreads across my face. I may have an afternoon meeting, a hundred emails to catch up on, and last-minute Winters' Wonder preparations to make, but for a split second, the day doesn't seem half bad. I steer myself back toward the office, but before I start any work, there's an even more pressing matter I must attend to.

Step one of earning Charlie's forgiveness.

22

Charlie

The job title proudly displayed in her bio says she is a production editor for CityLight Press, New York City, New York.

My breath hitches, and I feel a painful thump as my heart skips a beat. Anger, confusion, and sadness war for the upper hand.

After Andrew's dad left the apartment, I gave Sergio a quick head rub and hurried back to my own borrowed home for the week. It felt too weird to linger in Andrew's apartment any longer. The feeling of familiarity in Ava's face hadn't left me as I chatted with Gary. Her serene beauty is memorable. I knew I'd seen her before, and recently.

Safely locked in my apartment again, I went to A.C. Frost's Instagram account, which I've unashamedly poured over the past few days. There weren't any new posts. It was the tagged section I was after, anyway. Thumb scrolling rapidly, my eyes darted over the screen.

And there she was. A golden-hued beauty, smiling boldly, holding *Love Between the Pages* proudly up to the camera on a post whose caption read:

"Five stars! This book is so good, you guys! Maybe one of the best books I've ever read. If you are a romance and fated-star-crossed-lovers girlie like me, add this to your TBR immediately. Bring the tissues!"

@foxybooklady is her handle's name.

I assure myself it is only curiosity that leads me to click over to her profile.

Ava Camille Fox.

A.C.F.

Her name is the first thing I see.

"Wait . . . what?" I say out loud in the quiet apartment. My vision blurs for a moment, and I reread her bio carefully.

Senior production editor, CityLight Press, New York City, New York.

My heart begins to pound uncomfortably in my chest, and a hot wave passes over my skin before leaving me trembling with an icy chill. Rapidly, I scroll through her feed. Her social media presence seems dedicated to a carefully curated book-lover-slash-day-in-the-life-of-a-big-city-editor-style content. It takes scrolling eight months back before I find her excited announcement:

"This day was HUGE, you guys! Your girl just got promoted to production editor at work. Acquisitions was fun, but I'm ready for the chance to prove my skills. First up: A secret project that I can't wait to share more about."

She worked in acquisitions less than a year ago. Had my manuscript come across her desk? While my laptop boots up,

I study every post on Ava's feed carefully. Setting the phone aside, I pull up a search engine and type in her name. It isn't hard to find her in today's everything-is-online-and-accessible-to-anyone world. The past five years of her employment history have been spent at CityLight.

Has he known this entire time?

In the haze of what feels like a profound discovery, I'm startled to realize that's what hurts the most. Almost everything about the days since I discovered my book sitting on the display table in Bluebird Books has been a blur, except for Andrew. He stands out in crystal clear, a-little-too-handsome-to-look-straight-at, took-me-to-look-at-the-city-lights-on-the-top-floor-of-the-Empire-State-Building-like-we're-in-a-romance-movie contrast to the confusion of everything I've been experiencing. Has he meant anything we've shared? Or has it all been a ruse to delay me discovering the truth that Ava is the anonymous author of *Love Between the Pages*? Or rather, she is a thieving plagiarizer, smiling for the camera like she hasn't stolen someone else's dream. Whichever label works better.

Because he has to know, doesn't he?

I examine the evidence that I have so far.

1. Ava's initials are literally A.C.F. Does it get any more obvious than that?
2. She's clearly read and worked hard to promote *Love Between the Pages* on her social media feed.
3. They seem to have known each other since college.
4. They work for the same company.
5. There's nothing easier than to hide the truth in plain sight.

Someone at CityLight knows exactly who A.C. Frost is.

Am I really going to believe that someone would keep news like this from her friend?

"He doesn't owe you anything, Charlie," I mutter to myself. "Let's say best case he only suspects the truth. He's probably just been trying to figure all this out, just like you are."

I want to believe my own words so badly.

Hiding in plain sight.

Her life looks so perfect it makes me feel a little ill. Ava's feed primarily features her charming, aesthetically pleasing apartment, lattes in coffee shops, and beautifully photographed book content from iconic locations all around the city. A few of the posts are shockingly similar to the posts on A.C. Frost's feed. And maybe CityLight simply pays her well, but she doesn't seem to be lacking any creature comforts despite the high cost of living in the city.

Royalties?

One of her most recent posts catches my eye, and I click on it eagerly. I spy a paper coffee cup with The Drip's logo stamped on the side and a crumbly butterscotch cookie I instantly recognize. Of course, all the staff probably get their overpriced lattes from the coffee shop since it is just down the street from CityLight's offices.

I stare at the phone screen, chewing on my lip as I debate the likelihood I could catch her there at nearly two o'clock in the afternoon. It's worth a shot. In an ideal world, I'd have a chance to observe Ava before I come forward with my accusation. In consideration of the nondisclosure agreement I signed with CityLight's law firm (I make a mental note to check in with them), I want to be totally sure before leveling a plagiarism claim against one of their employees.

True to form, I jump right into an audible (though slightly one-sided) conversation without introduction as if God is sitting on the sofa next to me.

"Lord, did you give me the chance to see this today? If it wasn't Ava who submitted my manuscript as her own, who could it be? She has direct access to hundreds of manuscripts and insight into all of CityLight's inner workings. She knows exactly what they look for in a future bestseller. Is Ava the bookish bandit I've been looking for?"

I don't hear an audible answer. But a warning flashes across my brain. Accusing her wrongfully will taint every act of kindness Andrew has shown me. If she is his friend, I want to be one hundred percent sure before I tell him what I suspect.

Standing, I grab the heavy green flannel shacket I brought to guard against the autumn's chilly temperatures, which seem to have dipped lower each day I've been in New York. Boot laces tied firmly, cream-colored wool beanie pulled over my ears, I shoulder my bag and resolutely leave the apartment to head toward a mission that may signal certain disaster.

—

Catching Ava at the coffee shop was such a long shot I can't even be upset that I've overshot it by a mile. I've been sitting at a corner table, laptop open in front of me, pretending to be immersed in writing while I sip an overpriced espresso that would have tasted better made in my Moka pot back home. The caffeine buzz has already worn off. I'm starting to entertain the idea of hunting down her email and asking for a face-to-face meeting. And with each moment that passes, I'm getting more and more nervous that Andrew himself is going to walk in and catch me here.

And that's when she walks in. The bell jingles. My gaze pops up. I can't even help that my lower jaw drops as I recognize her instantly. Apparently, my instincts were right. A fellow coffee lover knows the lure of the afternoon java break, especially when you're busy making and breaking the dreams of writers around the world.

Instant panic erupts in my brain. I stop myself from calling out her name.

Think, Charlie, think.

Only one scenario makes sense. More coffee.

I stand, grabbing the book sitting conspicuously on my table, and join the line directly behind Ava.

She is tall and willowy, with a sense of fashion that immediately makes me feel like the frumpy country-mouse cousin in my jeans and flannel. A perfect match for Andrew, for sure.

Too bad she's a thief.

I force myself to shake off the invading insecurities and clear my throat rather loudly behind her. In response, Ava angles slightly and casts a look in my direction. Her striking aqua eyes sweep over me. I'm prepared for her to look down on me disdainfully, like a proper big city snob. To my shock, a smile breaks out like sunshine across her face.

She points to my hands. Her expression is eager. "Have you had a chance to read that book yet? It's one of the best books I've read all year," she says, her voice both soft and friendly.

The weight of *Love Between the Pages* in my hands is almost as heavy as the weight on my heart. I force myself to return her smile. "Yes. The author is a brilliant writer."

"I know, right? I'm not sure if we've seen this kind of talent since Steinbeck or Hemingway or Fitzgerald."

The bored-looking barista motions Ava forward. Quickly, she orders a pumpkin-caramel latte, turning back to me as she hands over her card to pay. "I mean the pure vulnerability in the words, the rawness, the ache when Danny and Margot crash, and they aren't sure if anyone will ever find them . . ."

She pauses. The story she is describing sweeps over me with the same emotional intensity it had as I was writing it to honor my parents' legacy. I quickly order another espresso, handing the barista a ten-dollar bill and murmuring for her to keep the change as I follow Ava to the pick-up counter.

"The writer certainly seems to know how to tap into the emotions of his or her readers." I'm the first to speak this time. "Too bad A.C. Frost chooses to stay anonymous. I'd love to know who wrote one of my favorite books."

I look at her, my expression firm and pointed. I'm hoping she'll crack, but her eye contact doesn't falter.

"You and me both." She leans toward me and lowers her voice. "Want to know a little secret? I work at the firm that published that book." There's a look of glee on her face.

I feign shock. "No way. You must know A.C. personally, then?"

Ava shakes her head. The barista slides her to-go latte across the counter just then. "I have no idea. Literally no one knows who Frost really is."

I don't believe her. In the age of insta-information and no privacy, someone always knows.

"That's wild," I say aloud. "What an incredible job either

way. I'm a writer myself, and I've been wondering what steps I need to take to land an agent to represent me for publication at a big firm. I'd love to pick your brain if you have time."

Ava looks at me regretfully. "I am so sorry, but I am late for a meeting already. I just ran to get a coffee to fuel myself for it. I wish I could stay and chat. I really do . . ."

She reaches for my hand, and I realize she is asking for my name. I grip her soft, elegant hand and give it a shake. "Charlie. Charlie Blaire." My eyes bore into hers as I try to see if my name strikes recognition.

"Ava," she replies. "I'd love to stay and chat, Charlie. Perhaps we'll run into each other another time." She turns away.

"I'll be here tomorrow," I blurt out without thinking. "I'm only in the city for a few more days."

Ava spins back to me. "You don't live in New York?"

"No, Vermont."

"Ah, Vermont." Her gaze shifts toward a tiny tornado of leaves swirling outside the window. "I'll tell you what. I will probably walk over for a coffee around eleven tomorrow. I'll save a few extra minutes if you'd like to chat."

"I would love that." I'm aware my voice is too eager, so I try to restrain myself. "I'll be here."

"It's a book lovers' coffee date then." She grins and gives me a little wave, her graceful hand poised to push open the door.

"Thank you." It comes out awkwardly, but I don't know what else to say. *You stole my manuscript, but thank you for giving me time to find out your identity and prove the truth so I can take you and your company to court?*

213

"Until tomorrow." She flashes me another million-dollar smile, then she's gone, disappearing quickly among the pedestrians on the sidewalk leading back to CityLight.

Until tomorrow, A.C. I exhale with a heavy sigh of relief that Andrew didn't walk in and catch me talking to her.

—

"I'm sorry. I had just brought Sergio back in from his walk, and your dad surprised me here." I walk from the kitchen when I hear the chime of the door and wait with an appropriately apologetic, I-know-this-is-awkward expression on my face as Andrew enters his apartment.

He shakes his head, trying to move past the entryway, where Sergio bounces up to greet him enthusiastically.

"Sergio, down," I say firmly, practicing a new command I've been teaching the boisterous dog for the past couple hours. Thinking he's about to receive a treat, the fluffy beast drops to all fours expectantly, allowing Andrew to move toward me unimpeded. He approaches me with what I see is an equally apologetic expression.

"No, I'm sorry," Andrew replies. "We've played phone tag this week, and I guess he thought I was here. Dad can be a bit . . ."

"Eager?" I offer.

He throws me an appreciative glance. "I was going to say overbearing and pushy."

"He was nothing but kind to me . . . despite probably initially thinking he'd caught a burglar in his son's house."

"If I walked in and caught you in my house, I would probably be so distracted by your pretty eyes I'd tell you to help yourself to whatever you wanted." There's an undeniable flash of admiration in his eyes, and it makes me blush.

Before he can see how his compliment affects me, I wave my hand and turn back toward the kitchen. A soft jazz track plays from the overhead speaker, which I finally learned how to operate about twenty minutes ago. "Go get comfortable. I have predinner snacks and drinks waiting in the kitchen."

"Be back in a flash." Andrew's voice fades in the direction of the bedroom.

I use the next few minutes to gather myself after the heart-pounding, emotions-fluttering reaction he just sparked in my chest. I've decided that tonight has to be the night I reestablish my purpose in coming to the city and stop allowing my feelings for the enemy to run away with me.

I shouldn't have wrapped my arms around Andrew's neck last night. Shouldn't have let him hug me. Shouldn't have lingered in his arms at the top of the Empire State Building, pretending that the daydream of it all could last forever. But I'm a hopeless romantic, and the combination of our delicious dinner, the sparkling drops of rain, and the magic of seeing the city lit up at night must have addled my brain just a little. When he left me at my door in the wee hours of the morning with a long, lingering look, I hadn't wanted him to leave. He only went a few doors away, but it was too much for my heart. Tonight, I know what I must do. I've made sure my heart is prepared for the shattering it will probably endure.

At some point during our dinner, I must tell Andrew that I know about Ava. I have to tell him what I suspect her of doing. He has been too kind to me this week to hide what I plan to do. I owe him the courtesy of a heads-up.

"It smells incredible in here." His deep voice fills the small space as he walks into the kitchen. "I've been starving

215

all afternoon waiting for dinner tonight." He walks up to lean one hip against the counter next to me.

It's strange how just his voice makes my heavy heart soften a little. But it turns into a full-on puddle when I gather the courage to tilt my chin up and meet his gaze. I freeze when I see the way his eyes are studying me intently. It feels as if he is trying to memorize every detail of my face. A spark flutters up through my stomach, coming to rest in my throat.

My voice is suddenly raspy and hoarse. "We'd better get you fed then. I wouldn't want Sergio to have to defend me if you turn into a grumpy, hungry bear."

He sneaks a finger into the pot I'm stirring, swiping a taste. He winks at me. "Let's be honest, Charlie. If either of us is going to turn into a grumpy, hungry she-bear, it'll probably be you."

23

Andrew

Charlie flutters around my kitchen like she owns the place. The scene reminds me of moments in childhood, before Dad shoved me into the arms of corporate America, before Mom's health took a turn, back when I had integrity . . . Rather than employ a chef (which we easily could have afforded), Mom was always in the kitchen. She would whip up the most delicious meals from scratch, which we would eat around the table as a family most nights. Cooking for us and watching our faces as we ate was her joy, she always said. I would stand in the kitchen, much as I am doing now, watching in amazement as she'd carry on a conversation with me while simultaneously doing five other cooking-related tasks at once.

Ever since she passed, I've resorted to takeout, ready-made meal services, dining out, and occasionally the mercy of friends most nights. Cooking for myself reminds me too much of good memories I'll never experience again. Tonight is the first home-cooked meal I'll have in a while.

Charlie moves with confidence. I can tell she's already made herself familiar with my space. Her obvious comfort in my kitchen instills an ache behind my ribs and an ease in my heart all at once.

There's an energy to her tonight. It's something I can't quite put my finger on, but she moves with a nervous excitement like she's drifting on a caffeine high. I can't help but wonder if it has anything to do with our evening last night and the fragility of the house of cards on which our relationship is built.

"Are you just going to stand there, or are you going to help me cook our dinner?" She playfully bumps me with her hip as she sashays to the refrigerator.

This is the punishment I get for letting her believe I cooked our pasta dinner the first night we met. I move aside and lean against the marble countertop, plucking an olive from the charcuterie board she crafted for our predinner snacks.

"It seems like you have a perfect handle on things. Plus, these snacks over here look lonely." I pop the olive into my mouth.

She pours a drizzle of oil into a preheated skillet and shoots me a wry smile. "Not as lonely as I am over here cooking all by myself."

Heat flashes in my core. I can't help but admire how adorable she is as she tosses her long, dark hair over her shoulder and turns away, a light pop of pink appearing on her cheeks.

"I don't want to be in your way, so why don't you just

tell me exactly what you'd like me to do," I reply.

That was always my job with Mom. *Andrew, can you hand me the flour? Will you throw this away? Grab the heavy cream, please.*

Charlie points to a head of lettuce and various fresh salad toppings sitting beside a cutting board and knife. "You can chop those."

When I don't move, she sets her hands on her hips. One of her dark eyebrows arches toward her hairline in mock surprise. "You do know how to chop veggies, don't you?"

"Of course I do." I scoff. I'm confident I can fudge my way through the task. How hard can cutting something into pieces be? "I'm just . . . waiting for the magic word."

"The magic word," she repeats with a deadpan expression. "Please, pardon my bossiness. Let me try that again." She walks a few steps over and tilts her chin back to look up at me. There's a look of mischief brewing in her eyes. "Andrew, will you, with those strong, capable arms of yours, please do me the favor of dicing those veggies right over there?"

"Well, when you ask like that, how can I say no?"

She rolls her eyes and points a spatula at me. "You are so . . ."

"Yes?" I pick up the knife and make my first slice through a cucumber.

Charlie's lips pull into a funny smile, and quite honestly, I'm not sure what it means. But she shakes her head and turns back to the sizzling pan in front of her. "Never mind," she murmurs.

I've never wanted to know what she has to say more.

We work in comfortable silence for a few minutes. I chop

the veggies for our dinner salads. She caramelizes onion and garlic in the pan while seasoning two breasts of chicken. I'm assuming she found a grocery store to stop at today because I know she didn't find these ingredients in my kitchen. Finally, I present my work to her using the cutting board as a platter. I kneel before her like a peasant to a queen.

"Your veggies, your Royal Highness."

She takes the board from my hands. I look up at her with an impish expression, still kneeling on one knee. She pretends to inspect the veggies piled onto the board.

"Impeccable work," she finally says.

I rise and take the cutting board from her. I finish preparing the salad as she stirs the contents of the skillet. I wait until she turns away from the stove before I speak. "So, is there anything else you need my strong, capable arms to help with?"

Briefly, her mocha eyes widen. The burst of pink returns to her cheeks. I thought my little joke would make her laugh, but as I feel my own cheeks redden, I realize the comment does nothing to smooth over the lingering awkwardness from last night. I could feel it in the air when I came home. We've managed to behave with relative normalcy up until now.

"I didn't mean . . . You know, I've been thinking about . . ." The words catch in my throat. *Last night.* Does she feel like a romantic jaunt to the top of the Empire State Building was a mistake too? Does she remember how my arms felt around her waist? Does she . . . wish she could kiss me right now as badly as I wish I could kiss her?

I shove the distracting thoughts away as Charlie carefully tends to our meal. The glorious scent of browning chicken and garlic waft toward me. I see her glance my way a few

Danseureau & Howard

times. Just when I think she's going to say something and save me from this awkward silence, her phone rings. She sets her spatula aside and pulls her cell phone from the back pocket of her black jeans. It's the same pair she wore when I first met her a few days ago. She's wearing the same pretty, palest-of-soft-pinks sweater as well, I notice.

The ringing continues. Charlie takes a long look at the screen, then silences the call and shoves it back into her pocket.

Suddenly, I feel like a stranger in my own home.

"Would you mind setting out some plates for us? Maybe setting the table too? Dinner is almost ready." Her voice breaks the silence gently. I have to wonder if she's just trying to ease the blow.

You don't deserve her anyway, Andrew, I remind myself, trying to ease the pain of losing something I've never even possessed. I don't want my heart to ache the way it already does at the thought of her going away soon. Not that I've ever had Charlie at all . . . The most I can hope for is that she doesn't hate the memory every time she thinks of me.

But maybe . . . after she sees what I've been working on . . .

I hate the way hope buoyantly rises in my chest.

I do as Charlie asks and set the table while she dishes up our plates. Together, we sit across from each other, and it isn't lost on me how normal this moment feels. As I pour each of us a glass of wine and sparkling water, I realize that Charlie is looking at me with an expectant expression on her face.

When she knows I'm paying attention, she folds her hands together in a prayer position. "Do you mind if I say a blessing over the food for us?" she asks.

"Absolutely," I reply. I'm less caught off guard by her

221

request to say grace than I am by how thankful I actually feel deep down in spite of everything that's going on.

We bow our heads, and Charlie gives thanks for our meal. It feels right to be sitting here with her, and even the unfamiliarity of prayer feels like a comfort rather than a burden. When she opens her eyes, she visibly startles to find me watching her. But her face softens as our eye contact lingers. An understanding passes between us. Her eyes turn soft and pleading as though she can see right into my very heart.

"Want to hear a really sad secret?" I break the silence.

Her brows pucker. "Only if you feel like sharing."

For some reason, I actually do. "I haven't said grace since before my mother passed away. We always said it as a family at every Sunday dinner together. But when she was gone, I stopped."

"Why did you stop?"

"For the same reason I stopped praying in general, I guess. I didn't feel that I had much to be thankful for anymore."

A small, audible gasp leaves Charlie's lips. She frowns. "Andrew, I'm so sorry."

I can't tell her that her manuscript found me when my heart was dark with doubt and grief. Or the way her words of hope and the reignition of her own faith after grief sparked new life into the dying embers of my soul. Or the hunger it awoke in me to have the same confidence that one day, what was lost to me would be restored.

Instead of the truth, I say, "It's okay." I want to change the subject away from my mother. The Winters' Wonder Gala in her memory this weekend is going to be hard enough. "Want to hear another secret? This one's a bit embarrassing."

She nods with bright eyes as she lifts a forkful of chicken to her mouth.

"The other night, I didn't actually make dinner. I, uh, ordered in takeout from Gustinelli's. I'm somewhat of a regular there."

Her giggles cascade like music into the room. She covers her mouth with her hand as she finishes chewing, holding up a finger for me to wait.

"What's so funny?" I ask.

She points toward the butler's pantry. "I may or may not have already suspected as much based off what I saw in your trash can."

I purse my lips. "Wow. Nothing slips past you, does it?"

Only after the words come out, do I realize what I said. My mouth tastes bitter. I cut a bite of chicken that is swimming in a garlic-based cream sauce whose richness and flavor rivals the best restaurants I've ever been to.

She eyes me with a sparkle in her eye. "What else have you lied to me about?" she teases.

Her words are spoken playfully, but my blood immediately runs cold. Slowly, I wipe my lips with a napkin and feel the weight of every second slipping past. The sparkle seems to fade from Charlie's eyes as she watches me.

In a curious voice, she asks, "Andrew, why did you lie about the food? I wouldn't have cared whether it was takeout or not."

Why did I lie? It's a good question. I try to gather my thoughts, but there are too many ping-ponging around in my brain to pull them together into anything coherent. From the moment I met Charlie, I've built our entire relationship on lie after lie. Shame burns deep within my core.

"And please don't lie about it now," Charlie adds.

I close my mouth tightly and nod. "You want to know why I lied about the food from Gustinelli's?"

"Yes."

"Okay," I reply, my voice low. I press as far into the truth as I can manage. "I wanted to impress you."

She squints at me from across the table as though trying to determine my level of honesty. "You mean you wanted to charm me. You know, to get your enemy off your back?"

Enemy. Is that what she thinks she is to me? I snort. "No. That wasn't it at all. I . . . Never mind."

"What?"

"It's not . . ." I want to blurt it all out right now. My irresponsible action that caused this whole mess in the first place, my growing and confusing feelings toward her, my plan to make everything right. I'd spent half the afternoon juggling work emails and meetings while arguing with Josh about this situation over the phone. The other half I'd spent working on a surprise for Charlie, using up the only shred of hope I have left.

As much as I want to tell her how she makes me feel inside, I can't lead her on. I won't let these feelings grow between us. Not when I know I am only capable of breaking her heart.

"Andrew." Her voice is low, almost a growl. It snaps me to attention.

"Yes, Charlie?"

"Tell me the truth, please. Did you really just want to impress me?"

I nod.

"But why?"

"Because I was afraid you'd turn into a werewolf again if you weren't fed properly."

She doesn't laugh at my joke. "Do you not know how to be honest?"

Inside, I squirm. Heat prickles the skin on my neck. "Sometimes honesty can cost you everything."

"The truth is free. It's lies that cost everything," she counters. "So, what's the truth?"

A battle wars in my mind. Two more days. Two more days. I close my eyes. To my surprise, a passage from Charlie's book floats into my mind.

"*And though their paths were never meant to cross, courage fueled by love forged forward with unbridled hope, paving the way for a future full of a radiant glory neither of them could have imagined.*"

When I lift my head, our eyes connect. Resolutely, I hold her gaze and say what I have no right to say, "The truth is that I'm falling for you, Charlie. And I know I shouldn't be. There are so many lines I'm crossing here, but I can't help feeling like I've known you much longer than a few days."

Her back hits her chair. Her lips part, her cheeks burning with that familiar shade of pink. A glimmer appears in her eyes. "Well," she begins softly, "that's ironic, because I feel the same way about you."

The world grinds to a halt as if a master pause button has just been pressed. Silence falls over the dining table. I wonder if she is just as lost as I am on how to proceed. But the silence doesn't last for long. Sergio must realize that Charlie and I are both too stunned to move. He jumps at the table, his big, clumsy front paws rattling the dishware as he capitalizes on the nearly untouched chicken on my plate.

"Sergio!" I yell at the same time Charlie commands, "Sergio, down."

Sheepishly, he listens to her, making for the balcony with

a giant bite of chicken in his mouth. Instead of making his escape, he runs smack into the glass door, which he obviously assumed was open.

I facepalm myself and shake my head. "Ladies and gentlemen, Sergio." Quickly fetching a rag, I clean what mess hit the floor as Sergio lays in front of the balcony door, guilty muzzle resting on his paws.

"Don't feel too bad." Charlie comes over to help me. "I've seen far less-behaved dogs than him."

"Oh, yeah? Name one." I shake my head, still frustrated that Sergio interrupted the moment.

She whips out her phone and moves closer to stand beside me. Her hair smells fragrant. I have to pull my attention away from her to concentrate on what she is showing me.

"Here, I'll show you." Charlie scrolls through her pictures and videos until she finds one of a Bernese Mountain Dog chasing after a biker while its owner is literally being dragged behind on the leash.

"This is a dog you've trained?" I ask.

She laughs and replays the video. "Yes."

A FaceTime notification pops up from someone named Nate. Charlie immediately declines the call.

"Do you need to get that?"

Before she can respond, a text banner appears across the top of the screen. I catch myself reading it before I realize what I'm doing.

NATE HOPKINS: *Don't tell me NYC has stolen you from me. I've been trying to . . .*

And that's all the text I can see. Quickly, Charlie swipes the banner away and tucks her phone into her back pocket.

"If you need to—" My voice sounds gruffer than I

intend it to.

"No, it's fine. It's just a friend."

A pang of jealousy rattles my ribcage. It's completely unwarranted. What right do I have to be jealous over a girl I'm not even dating?

A dreadful thought occurs to me. What if Charlie is only flirting with me in order to get me to help her with the lawsuit against CityLight? She doesn't seem to have any idea who my dad is, but maybe she is playing me? It wouldn't be the first time a woman has used me for ulterior motives, especially where money is involved.

Charlie has every right after all I've stolen from her. Yet my heart shivers at the thought that she might not be interested in me at all. Once she gets this situation ironed out, she'll forget about me and go back to Vermont. She'll probably live happily-ever-after with the adoration of this Nate guy who probably also isn't a scum-of-the-earth-lying-wannabe-writer.

"There's more food, by the way," she says, breaking me from my thoughts. "I made plenty. I can replace whatever Sergio ate."

I don't want to eat anymore. "It tasted amazing, but maybe I'll save those leftovers for a midnight snack later."

Disappointment clouds her beautiful face. "Midnight snack? You have some late-night plans that are going to keep you up?" Her voice sounds almost hopeful at the end.

My only plans are finishing the surprise I have for her, though it may take an all-nighter if I'm going to finish it by tomorrow. "Yeah, I actually have some work I have to catch up on," I reply.

"Oh, okay. I understand. I'm sure dealing with me all week hasn't exactly been good for your schedule."

"Charlie."

She looks at me, the gleam in her eye telling me she's suddenly struggling with her emotions. "Hmm?"

My voice is earnest and sincere. "There's nothing I would have rather done this week. And by the way, I chatted with A.C.'s lawyers today. Everything is going to work out. I promise."

Her jaw drops. "You talked with someone today and haven't bothered to tell me until now?" Elation fills her face. "Well, come on! What's the scoop?"

"I . . . I can't say anything more than that right now. I'm sorry. But early next week, you should—"

"Early next week?" She walks away from the table and drops onto the sofa. Her eyes flit back and forth as her mind runs rampant with conclusions. "So, it's good news for me?"

My steps toward her are slow and measured. "Look, I really can't say too much, but it's going to work out." *Though it might shatter our hearts in the process.*

Charlie beams and leaps from the sofa, tossing her arms around my neck. The scent of her perfume makes me dizzy. Slowly and hesitantly, I wrap my arms around her waist, pulling her up and into me with gentle tenderness. I don't want this hug to end. Not now, not ever. I close my eyes and hope that my best will end up being good enough in the end.

She pulls away first and looks up at me with a smile on her face. It occurs to me that Charlie's days in my city are limited. The whole charade will come to an end, and it's going to end soon.

"By the way . . ." I'm surprised by the sudden shakiness in my voice. I clear my throat. "What exactly are your plans? Do you think you'll stay in the city a while longer then?"

"Well, I really have no idea." She smooths a hand over

her sleek hair. "But if something is happening as soon as next week, then yes! I mean, of course, only if your apartment is still available. Am I overstaying my welcome here?"

"No, not at all. It's yours for however long you need."

"Thank you. Truly, thank you for everything, Andrew."

Her appreciation nearly guts me. The only way through this is forward. Courage, I remember.

I take a deep breath before jumping in. "Look, I don't want to leave you hanging, but the next few days are a little crazy. I need to work all day tomorrow. Saturday evening, I have a family commitment. But I have something planned for us for tomorrow night. That is, if you're free?"

She smiles as she takes a few steps backward and dramatically flops onto the sofa. The back of her hand covers her forehead. At the motion, Sergio forgets he is in trouble and bounds over like a woolly bear to lick her face, which sends her into a giggling fit.

The comical scene demands my laughter too. I wish things were different because I can picture myself doing this every day. Charlie just fits. From what I've gathered of her life in Vermont, it is wildly different than my own, yet somehow, she seems to fit perfectly into my life too.

"So, is that a yes for tomorrow, or . . .?"

Charlie pushes Sergio's giant head away and wriggles out from beneath his tongue. She regards me thoughtfully. Her hair is now a mess of wild locks. If I'm not mistaken, there's slobber across her cheek. She grins.

"It's an absolute yes. For the first time on this trip, I actually feel something akin to hope."

24

Charlie

I never got around to telling Andrew of the fraud I suspect his friend of committing last night. The right time never presented itself, and then when he told me that he met with A.C. Frost's lawyers, I just couldn't bring myself to ruin such a happy moment.

I still plan to gather evidence of who Ava really is to strengthen my case. In case she tries to deny what she has done.

I'm an hour early for my meeting with Ava at The Drip. Rather than putting my mind at ease, it turns out to be sixty minutes of torture. My screaming nerves cause my knee to bounce up and down as I pretend once again to work on my laptop. As if I could concentrate on writing when every cell in my being is wondering if Ava will even show up at all.

It was impossible to tell if Ava recognized my name yesterday afternoon. I couldn't get a read on whether or not she realized she was speaking to the very woman whose book she stole ten months ago. Her soft, pleasant smile didn't shift. I didn't see an instant panic glaze over her eyes. And she'd agreed to meet with me today.

Was she that forgetful or that devious?

I still don't have a plan for exactly how I'm going to prove Ava stole my manuscript. I'm telling myself today is just reconnaissance. It's the first move in a long line of actions to reclaim my book. I'm trying to be logical and coolheaded about the situation. I don't want to end up tipping my hand to her too early.

And I realize it is entirely possible that she just told me what I wanted to hear and doesn't intend to show up for our meeting at all. After all, I'm just some gal from Vermont in the city for the week. If she really didn't recognize my name, she may skip our meeting altogether.

I haven't quite figured out what my next step is if Ava never shows. That is a hiccup I don't even want to consider.

Regretfully, I realize staking out the coffee shop so early comes with another downside. I've claimed a table in full view of the door and corner window. Ava isn't the only CityLight employee who likes to get a java fix here. Andrew frequents this coffee shop as well. And I have no idea if he is at the office this morning. His potential proximity is jarring.

Hours ago, I heard the jingle of Sergio's collar pacing past my condo. It could have been my imagination, but the jingle seemed to pause and linger in front of my door for far longer than necessary. I wanted to walk over and open it. I wanted to ask Andrew in for coffee. The urge to ask if I could walk with the two of them to revel in the crisp autumn air of an early morning in New York was strong. Maybe we could both play hooky from reality and explore The Big Apple like two tourists who don't have a care in the world.

But I knew it was a foolish instinct, born of his irresistible smile and the lingering memories of our moonlit date on top of the Empire State Building. I must stay strong. Getting distracted by thick, swoopy hair, kind eyes that crinkle at the corners when he laughs, and strong hands that have stopped me from stepping in front of a taxi more than once now would derail everything I've come here to do.

I'm not here to fall in love. This isn't a movie.

It's more like a nightmare.

I keep finding myself muttering a prayer under my breath that today, of all days, Andrew doesn't walk through the door. At eleven o'clock, my eyes are glued to the entrance. I forget to breathe for whole chunks of time. At eleven-oh-eight, she walks in.

Ava spots me, and an immediate smile beams across her face. Her vibrant, take-over-the-room energy is instantly contagious. And I'm so relieved she is here that I forget I'm supposed to be angry with her. I smile back despite myself.

"You're still here," she says, walking toward me. "I'm sorry I'm a bit late. Meetings all morning. We have a big event this weekend. Everyone is scrambling to get ahead on our projects so we don't have to come in until Monday."

I rise, trying to look taller next to her willowy presence. Despite my good posture, I still feel underdressed in my flared jeans, white cotton t-shirt, and brown plaid blazer that always cuts the mustard in small-town Vermont business meetings but feels underwhelming in chic NYC.

"I hadn't even glanced at the time," I say, waving my hand in a grand gesture of easygoingness. "Can I buy you a coffee?"

"Let me buy you a coffee," she exclaims, moving toward the counter before I can protest. "What are you drinking?"

"Double shot espresso," I mumble, sinking back down in my chair as she chats amiably with the barista. I watch her closely, trying to find the visage of a plagiarist in her vibrant, expressive face. *People hide their true nature all the time*, I remind myself. Though, if I'm honest, a tiny flicker of doubt begins to make me wonder if I've completely misread the situation.

Ava returns a few minutes later with a tray. "We might as well nibble a few little treats while we're here," she laughs. "Do you mind if I take a picture of it? It's all so pretty."

I stand back as she swiftly and efficiently arranges the items across the table in what I must admit is a very aesthetically pleasing display of boutique coffee shop offerings. Standing over it, she snaps a few quick photos on her phone, then slips the device back into her purse.

"Bookstagram has me in such a chokehold, I swear," she laughs again, a faint hint of pink rising on her cheeks.

"You must read all the latest viral books because of your job." I sit back down.

"Yes and no." She lifts her latte up to her lips and takes a sip. Even from across the small table, it smells like pumpkin spice with a hint of cinnamon whip. "Honestly, I sometimes feel like I spend so much time creating bookish content for my social media account that I don't even get to read the books I feature." She lifts one elegant shoulder. "I miss just reading for fun."

"Still, it's a dreamy job getting to work with books all day." I feel clever for redirecting the conversation so casually.

She grimaces. "Well, again yes and no."

I lean forward. "I'll bet authors can be challenging to work with." I let a sparkle slip out of my eyes, signaling what I hope is an unthreatening appeal for the local office gossip.

"What do you mean?" Ava eyes me quizzically.

I wave my hand nonchalantly. "Oh, I mean the really demanding, want-it-their-way-or-the-highway, finicky ones."

Ava laughs. "We do get those on occasion. And now that I'm on the production side of things, it's even worse because I'm also facilitating artists and marketing and scheduling. Although, it's mostly a great experience."

"There are always challenges in any industry. Have you worked other departments?" I ask, leaning back and sipping my espresso. I set the cup down on the saucer again when I can't stop my hand from trembling.

Ava reaches forward and breaks off a piece of pumpkin chocolate scone. She nibbles on it and chews, nodding in response to my question. "I was in acquisitions for a few years before this."

Now, the conversation is getting somewhere. I put on my best casual-but-interested expression. "How exciting. Did you handle the acquisition of A.C. Frost's book as well?"

Ava shakes her head. Her green eyes widen. "I wish. I'm not sure who pitched Frost's book initially. It's a long story, but I did end up getting to work on the production side of things. In early February, it's all anyone in the office could talk about, but we were all told to be super hush-hush about it. There was so much hype for it even then, though. And then, it hit the bestseller list barely a month after it was published."

Now it's my turn for my eyes to widen. "How does that happen so quickly?"

Ava shrugs. "Luck and a good marketing team, I guess. Our marketing department is really putting in the work to promote it on TikTok. I think it just hit the right notes and took off."

She drains the final sips of her fragrant pumpkin latte and glances at the gold watch on her wrist. "But enough about my job. You wanted to ask if I have any pointers about landing a book deal."

I get the hint that she's running out of time. It's a challenge to pull myself out of investigator mode, so I say the first thing that comes into my head. "That's right. Is there anything that sets a manuscript apart and gives it an edge?"

"Do you have an agent yet?" she asks, nibbling the last bits of the rich, crumbly scone. The scent of ginger, nutmeg, and chocolate tantalizes me, and my stomach growls. I couldn't even think about food this morning. "The last thing you want to do is send off unsolicited manuscripts and then never know why you didn't get any interest."

I freeze. "Um, no. I don't have one. I haven't really had the budget to hire an agent yet."

"Well, they pick you more than you pick them," she explains kindly. "You send a query to them, and if they like the sound of your novel, they may ask to read the rest of it. If they think they can pitch it, they'll offer to represent you and try to get it sold. Have you finished your manuscript and had it go through developmental and copy edits with a professional editor yet?"

I try not to let myself look like the bumbling idiot I feel. "Uh, no, not exactly."

From out of nowhere, the truth comes pouring from my mouth before I can stop it. Or at least, it is almost the truth.

"I had a finished manuscript that took me several years to finish. But someone stole it from me and is trying to publish it under their own name." I watch Ava carefully for her response.

Her mouth falls open with a look that seems like pure shock and consternation. "Charlie! How is that possible? Can you get the rights to your book back?"

I shake my head, wondering how she can seem so genuinely shocked by the news, considering . . . "I don't know if it will be possible to get it back. I have to jump through hoops to prove that it's mine. I'm devastated."

She reaches across the small table to press her hand onto my arm. I flinch at her touch. "I am so sorry," she says earnestly. "When a writer pens a book, it is like their heart comes to life on each page. Have you contacted a lawyer to pursue your rights? If you haven't, you should think about retaining one immediately to represent you. Then I would go after the thief to the fullest extent of the law."

Her words fluster me. I don't know how to respond. How can she possibly push me to retain a lawyer when she knows full well that she stole my manuscript and published it under her own pen name? Ava Camille Fox. A.C. Frost. It just fits. I have no idea what meaning the name "Frost" holds for her. Maybe she just loves winter? Unless . . .?

I lean forward, ready to press on and figure out the truth. "Ava, I have to be honest about . . . this is all very unexpected—" My words are cut short by the familiar flash of a coat across the picture window that looks onto the street. It's a long, wool camel coat that was wrapped warmly around my shoulders just the other night. A coat that belongs to my very-temporary, very-handsome, very-much-doesn't-know-what-I'm-up-to-today neighbor.

It will ruin everything if he catches me here. I jump up. "I have to use the restroom. Will you excuse me, please?" Without waiting for a reply, I bolt toward the door that indicates the facilities, disappearing just as the bell jingles cheerfully over the entrance.

25

Andrew

Notifications ping off like popcorn along the bottom corner of my computer screen, but I ignore them. As behind as I am, work requests and emails can wait today. The task at hand is far more important.

Scribbling furiously, the pen scratches across the page in front of me. The morning isn't over yet, but I feel like I've been at the office forever. After several hours and a hand cramp, I write the final words into my journal and lock it inside my desk drawer. Logging out of my computer, I go downstairs to find Ava. She is the only one I trust with this part of my plan.

Rather than find her ensconced in her cozy office, diffuser steaming while she reaches for yet another piece of candy from the dish on her desk, when I reach her door, it's closed and locked. The lights are off.

I look around the main floor of the office but don't see

her with any of the other editors or production team at work on various projects. My best guess is that if she's anywhere, she's down the street grabbing a coffee at The Drip. When I actually make it into work, we often walk to grab a cup together from our favorite shop when the late-morning slump hits. I wouldn't mind a stronger coffee right now myself. The brown water they brew in the employee lounge isn't cutting it today. After only managing a few hours of sleep last night, my eyelids are starting to droop.

I retrace my steps to my office, grab my coat, and head out of the building for the coffee shop just a couple blocks away. A street sweeper is working to clear the pavement of the brown, crisp, woodsy-scented leaves that have nearly completed their life cycle. I find myself wishing that New York didn't work so hard to sweep away the traces of their presence so quickly but rather left them to linger, covering the ground protectively like a blanket of rich ochre, auburn, and purple for the coming winter frost. *Just like they do in Vermont.*

I catch myself and resolutely turn my mind away from a certain flannel-wearing, brown-eyed girl from the woodsy state and back to the task at hand. Mentally, I run through today's checklist as the crisp autumn air bites my cheeks.

1. Ask Ava for a giant favor and hope she says yes.
2. Guzzle espresso and down a pastry in lieu of the water and proper lunch I should probably make time for.
3. Pick up gift-wrapping supplies.
4. Have that meeting at one-thirty.
5. Check in with Dad to see if he needs any help

finalizing the details of the gala. He probably won't, but he'll appreciate the gesture.

6. Pick up my tuxedo from the dry cleaner.
7. Bring a bouquet of pink roses to Mom's grave and tell her that I met a girl just in time for her gala, but I can't invite her because if she finds out who I really am, the jig is up.
8. Prep for a date this evening with Charlie.

A rush of chilly air accompanies me as I open the door and walk inside The Drip. Instantly, I spot Ava's blonde head at a table near the window. Her back is to me. With quick strides, I walk toward her. The chair across the table is empty but pushed away as if the occupant left in a hurry. A half-empty cup of cooling espresso lingers behind, and there's a closed laptop on the surface.

I tap Ava on the shoulder once. She jumps and arches around to see who just accosted her.

"Andrew, hey!" Her bright smile lights up.

"Hey, I thought I'd find you here. I need some help," I say, not wasting any time getting straight to the point.

"Help?" Ava's eyebrows lift. "Are you . . . in trouble?"

I'm in more than just trouble, I think to myself. Aloud, "No, I just . . . I need your help with something." I glance around us and lean down toward her. "I actually have a huge favor to ask of you."

She eyes me skeptically. "Okay . . . shoot."

"Is your uncle still working at the Botanical Garden?"

"He is. Why do you ask?" She reaches for her coffee and starts to take a sip, but the cup is empty. She gives it a disappointed little shake. From the lingering scent, I'm guessing she switched to a pumpkin spice latte with extra cinnamon whip when fall began. I'll have to bring her one weekly until the season ends to pay her back for this favor.

"I don't have time to get into all the details right now," I reply to her question. "But I am hoping he can get me in for after-hours access?" I press my palms together in a begging manner.

She sets the empty cup on the table and narrows her sharp eyes at me. "Tonight? That's rather short notice."

"Yes, tonight. I looked, and there's nothing on the calendar event-wise for this evening."

Her lips twist into a smile. She crosses her legs, and I sense the teasing already on its way. "Wait," Ava says. "This doesn't have anything to do with that romantic interest of yours, does it?"

This response is exactly what I feared would happen. I hem and haw around for a few seconds until finally replying, "If I say yes, does that increase the odds you'll help me?"

Ava grins. "Oh, absolutely it does. You know I'm a sucker for anything romantic."

"Great. Then that's what it's for."

"And you waited to ask for my help at the last minute because . . .?"

"Because I'm Andrew, a perpetual moron." I give her a blank look.

"I guess what else could I expect from the guy who put off his senior project until the night before it was due."

"Exactly. That's me. So, what do you say? Can you help me?" I clasp my hands together and give her my best pleading, puppy dog eyes.

Ava taps one manicured finger on her lips. "You realize I can't just clap my hands and make this happen, right?"

"Sure you can. Because you're Ava Fox, the girl who organized an entire surprise birthday party in one afternoon because she already had themed Pinterest pages with every detail accounted for. Aren't there some strings you can pull for me? Can you ask your uncle for this favor?"

She stills for a moment, then sighs. "I guess that *is* me. I'll text you his number, and you can ask him yourself. He always remembers and asks about you for some weird reason anyway."

A weight is lifted from my chest. I'm so relieved that I bend down and wrap my arms around her. "You're a gem. Thank you."

She pats my shoulder and says, "Just be prepared to pay back the favor one day."

I snort, straightening again. "The mysterious Ava Fox doesn't date."

Her jaw drops open. "Hey, I might fall in love one day."

"And I might win the lottery."

"You realize you're at my mercy right now, don't you, Drew?" She waves her hand in a circular motion and works her jaw. "And besides, you winning the lottery would just be unfair. Leave some for us peons who have to work for a living."

I laugh. "You know you really are a catch."

"And you know you're like a pesky brother who won't get out of my hair."

"Never said I wasn't your pesky older brother." I glance at my watch and note the time. "I've got to run, but I'll see you soon."

She sends me off with a wave and a promise to text her uncle's number to me right away. I move to the short line and order an Americano and cheese Danish to go. I glance at Ava as I leave, but she's still sitting alone.

Once I'm back at the office, I call Ava's uncle. When I end the call twenty minutes later, I practically slam dunk my phone. He's agreed to help me tonight. My energy recharged, I move like a madman, furiously responding to PR and book campaign related emails and making necessary phone calls to extinguish last-minute gala fires after Dad gives me a short list. He seems pleased, though also shocked, at my offer to help. He didn't come to the office today. Everyone knows he is home, overseeing the preparations and fussing over the words for his speech and toast to my mother.

I put off opening the small bag of supplies for as long as I can. Once I'm ready, I thoughtfully smooth my thumb over the surface of the journal I've been writing in for the better part of a year. Almost every page has an entry. This morning, I wrote the final words. Carefully, I wrap it in the pretty paper I picked up from a stationery shop not far away. The paper is rich and velvety, custom-made, and worthy of the woman I plan to present it to. As best I can, I wrap a silky ribbon around the middle and tie a bow in it. I'm well aware this is my last Hail Mary, my one shot to win over Charlie's heart before the truth breaks free and I lose her completely.

If she will just read this journal, I may have a small but fighting chance.

———

The cemetery's wrought iron gate screeches on its hinges as I push it open. A carpet of maple leaves spreads before me, crunching beneath my boots as I trek past rows of headstones and monuments. In my hand, I clutch an overflowing bouquet of pink roses, my mother's favorite flower. Visiting

Mom at the cemetery is something I try to do often. The last time I was here, though, was at the beginning of this nightmare, back when Charlie Blaire was only a name on paper rather than the woman who is capturing my heart more and more every moment I spend with her.

As I approach Mom's grave, a chilly wind whips through the still, quiet property. It rustles under the collar of my coat and sends a single pink petal fluttering to the ground. I stoop and pick it up, rubbing the velvety surface between my fingers. Its softness is a keen reminder of my own mother's gentle beauty that housed a strong and resilient spirit. While she and Charlie are nothing alike, the quality of a gentle, quiet strength is something that I sense Charlie possesses too.

A carpet of colorful leaves blankets Mom's resting place. The thought of her fragile form under the weight of dirt and grass has often bothered me. But according to Charlie and the words she penned in her book (words I'm now realizing were inspired by a faith in God's Word that carried her through a storm that tried to crush me), my mom—her real self—her soul isn't here anymore. She lives in a place whose existence I am beginning to comprehend fully.

Kneeling next to her grave, I guide the rose stems into the in-ground vase and arrange the flowers carefully.

"You already know how badly I've messed up, Mom." The words sting on their way out. I've been faced with my shortcomings lately in a way that I never anticipated. My failures have carried reverberating effects to those around me, hurting everyone from my own family to the woman who has somehow already staked her claim on my heart. "I didn't mean for this to happen, but Mom, I'm trying to fix it. I'm trying to have the faith that I watched you demonstrate."

As if in response, the leaves rustle around me. I hear them whisper encouragement. It's like the warmth of Mom's voice surrounds me, and I can hear her saying, "Give it your best, Andrew, but more than that, give it to God."

I've been wrestling for control for so long, fighting for a place on the pedestal of my dad's good opinion as proof of my worth. And where has that landed me? In a hole that feels impossible to claw my way out of. And maybe it is. Maybe this whole situation is only the beginning of my demise. But as long as I have breath in my lungs, I have the ability to try to make it right.

"I'm going to give it my best," I whisper. I think of my parents, of the love story that brought them together. It's a classic tale of a poor boy meets rich girl. They were never supposed to meet, and the tides of social connection and her family's wishes were against them. Eventually, her family grew to love him, and against all odds, their love survived. Their choice to defy the odds and pursue love anyway is one reason Charlie's story captured my attention in the first place.

As I turn to leave, my pocket vibrates. When I pull out my phone, I see a text from Josh.

JOSH: Please tell me you haven't gotten romantically involved with Charlie.

The text feels out of place, and I'm not sure what to make of it. But my feelings for Charlie are none of his business, I quickly decide. Rather than respond to him, I open my text thread with Charlie and type out a message.

ME: I hope you're ready to see a side of NYC you've only imagined.

She responds just a few moments later.

CHARLIE: Looking forward to it!

The corners of my mouth tug into a smile. I feel myself beginning to hope. Maybe we aren't as star-crossed as we seem. I tuck my phone back into my pocket and stare for a moment at Mom's headstone. Her absence still doesn't feel real. In this moment, though, her presence certainly does.

Leaning down, I pluck a single rose from the vase on a whim and tip it toward her engraved name. "I'll make sure to tell her this is from you."

26

Charlie

I feel like an idiot for peeping through the crack in the door to spy on Ava and Andrew, but this is what it seems I've descended to.

"Please, please, please, make him leave quickly. And please don't let her mention my name," I murmur the prayer under my breath.

Their heads are together. It's obvious, even from my limited viewpoint, that they are both familiar and comfortable with each other. A surge of something painful begins to stir in my gut. I'm too preoccupied to stop and analyze if it's . . . jealousy. Of course, it's not jealousy. Andrew isn't mine. The feelings that have flitted in and out of my consciousness the past few days whenever I'm around him can't possibly mean anything. We've just been thrown together during this crazy time, brought together by a book that I never expected to cause this much drama and chaos in my life.

Andrew has been so kind, taking me under his wing like the perfect gentleman. It isn't his fault that I've practically locked myself in my house the past couple of years, stress-baking and watching classic movies from the fifties and daydreaming about the day that I'll feel whole again. At this point, any kindness from a man starts to feel like romance . . . And the fact that if he had tried to kiss me the other night in the Empire State Building, I wouldn't have objected hasn't helped matters any.

As I strain to overhear their conversation, something else continues to nag at the peripheral vision of my subconscious. Something that I don't want to think about, not now, not ever.

Does Andrew know the truth about Ava's identity as the elusive A.C. Frost? Has he known all along that she plagiarized my manuscript? Has he been trying to protect not only CityLight but also his friend from a very public fallout?

The thoughts pestering my brain are too uncomfortable to deal with right now. Instead, I press my ear to the door crack and listen harder to catch their voices. Hopefully, no one walks up wanting to use the restroom because that is going to cause an awkward scene.

Snippets of their conversation float to me through the ambient murmur of the coffee shop. "…help me…? strings you can pull for me…? this favor…"

A few minutes later, they seem to part ways. My heart pounds as I spy on Andrew as he grabs a coffee and pastry to go. He looks a bit frazzled this morning, his hair less perfectly swoopy and more messy, the lines around his eyes a little deeper, the corners of his mouth turned down in a frown.

What favor did he ask of Ava? Up until now, he has said all the right things, but do I really trust him to see justice through if doing so involves people he is close to?

Would I betray my friends and business colleagues if a random stranger showed up in town claiming fraudulent activity?

I wait a minute after he's gone to be safe. Once I'm sure he has left the building for good, I rush back to Ava and quickly gather my things. "I am so sorry to rush off, but I have to go."

She looks at me with surprise. "Is everything okay?"

I pause and stare at her. I try to analyze her expression, uncertain of everything I am feeling and experiencing right now. "No, it's not. But I hope that someday it will be."

I know what I came to New York to do, but actually doing it is going to end up being harder than I expected. Despite what I suspect Ava has stolen from me, she's been kind. I hate that I have to resort to such extreme measures, but her advice to secure a lawyer and go after my rights has given me the courage. And though my heart aches at the thought of it, my next course of action is probably going to ruin the memory of these last few days with Andrew. But I must follow through with what I set out to do. The importance of honoring my parents' legacy is too great to sacrifice.

—

Too late into my impulsive mission, I realize I probably should have called Sam Baker first. It is not until I step out of the taxi for the second time in front of his faded building that I realize he never really confirmed he even wanted to take on my case. Nevertheless, I walk over the grubby gray carpet and knock on his office door anyway. At his low-toned

"Come in," I open the door.

He doesn't look surprised to see me. "Knew you'd be back," he states matter-of-factly. "Couldn't find a fancier lawyer to take your case? Or one you could afford. Told you it was going to be almost impossible."

The words are said in a gruff tone, but I choose to ignore it.

"I'm not ashamed to admit I'm on a budget, but I think this case is worth your while. I've exhausted all the possibilities for fixing this myself. I need someone with expertise to help me regain the rights to my book."

Still grumpy, Sam harrumphs. But the flash in his eyes tells me he is secretly intrigued. "Well, for starters, why don't you sit down and give me all the facts? And I want names. Enough of this beating-around-the-bush nonsense. Tell me who we're going to sue. And remind me of your name again."

The way he rubs his palms together makes me uncomfortable. For a moment, I second-guess my decision to come here. Maybe I should wait for Andrew to come through on his promise to fix the situation. I don't want to sue anyone. I don't want any of this. My only hope was to someday publish the story of my parents' love, devotion, and faith so that if someone else out there was mourning the loss of a loved one, their story could be a comforting reminder that the goodbyes of this life aren't the end. As deeply as I've grieved, my heart hums with a steady assurance that I will be reunited with my parents someday because we have another, greater, eternal heavenly home to look forward to. Sharing that faith with the world seemed like the right thing to do.

But someone else published that story before I had the

chance to do so, and that's why I'm here. That's why I'm forced to go after the publishing house that employs both the woman I must count as my adversary if she truly stole my book as well as the man who has been nothing but kind to me since I dropped into his lap like a tornado. If I'm the victim here, why do I feel like I'm the one about to steal someone else's future?

Sam clears his throat when I don't reply. "Let's get on with it. I have other cases to work on today."

Somehow, I doubt it. But I swallow past the lump in my throat and pull a copy of the nondisclosure agreement I signed from my bag. "This all started when my parents passed away, and I decided to document the story of their lives and never-ending faith in God . . . "

—

Two hours later, I emerge from the Baker Law Firm in possession of both a new attorney to represent my claim against CityLight and a heart heavier than ever. I stand outside of the faded brick building and try to gather my thoughts while I wait for my ride share driver to arrive. I've told Sam Baker everything, including my suspicion that Ava Camille Fox is the real A.C. Frost. He was intrigued, to say the least. While he didn't make any bold or outrageous assertions of what I could expect moving forward, he did offer to represent me in the fight to get my book rights returned.

"The first step is to find out if there's any real connection between her and this mysterious author," Sam said. "People try to hide their trail, but it's really impossible if you know where to look. I'll start digging to see what I can find."

While it's a relief to know someone with no ulterior

motives is finally in my corner, the annoying nag of guilt still swirls around in my brain. Have I done the right thing? Is there a better way to discover who has stolen my book and the dream I had for a future as an author? Have I betrayed the trust Andrew has given me?

As I sit quietly in the back seat on the drive back to the heart of the city, I scroll through A.C.'s profile on Instagram. It's like it operates on a timer. There is little disruption to the flow of the feed. Photos of the city, current reads, and other moments I must assume are from A.C.'s life pop up in regular posts. It's a bit maddening to see how little my claim has affected her life so far. It's like she doesn't even know. Like no one has told her someone showed up at CityLight this week claiming she's stolen a book that belongs to someone else.

When the truth breaks, will it affect anyone's life? Or does all this turmoil and second-guessing and striving for answers exist only in my little bubble.

By the time we enter Manhattan, I know what I need to do.

"Could you drop me off at this address instead?" I rattle off the address of the legal firm that represents CityLight Publishing.

I don't call ahead. I don't give Josh any warning that I'm dropping in. Instead, I march straight up to the receptionist behind her desk and ask for Josh Lance. Her sharp eyebrows form the exact exaggerated "V" shape they took on the first time I arrived. I wonder if it's just the expression she uses for all her interactions with humans.

"Do you have a meeting scheduled?" she replies with icy politeness.

"No. But I think he'll want to see me," I reply firmly. She looks skeptical.

"It's okay, Julia." A voice speaks behind me. "I'll talk with Ms. Blaire. Please hold my calls." Josh is suddenly standing directly behind me. I whirl to face him and find his hand outstretched, a genial smile plastered across his face. Reluctantly, I shake his hand and follow him into his spacious office. We both take our seats.

"What brings you in today?" He doesn't waste any time getting straight to the point.

I pause to gather my thoughts before I speak. "I just came to say that while I understand it's your job to protect CityLight, I know now that you should never have asked me to sign that nondisclosure agreement without my lawyer present. I've tried to be reasonable and give you and this firm the benefit of the doubt this week. I'm done waiting for action to be taken. I know the truth. I've discovered it, and I have proof. I've retained an attorney. I just want you to know that I intend to see this lawsuit through. To the fullest extent of the law if I must."

It's a long speech for me, and I struggle to even get the words out. I think I see Josh's face turn a shade paler. He gives no other outward sign that my announcement perturbs him. Instead, he nods. I watch his eyes narrow.

"I'm going to cut right to the chase here, Charlie. May I call you Charlie? Retaining your own attorney is within every right of yours, but have you stopped to ask yourself why we pursued an NDA so quickly?"

I shake my head.

Josh continues, "I may represent CityLight in a legal capacity. But more than just being its lawyer, I care about

Andrew because he is my friend. He screwed up by talking to you and offering to help you in the first place. I've watched him struggle with his own challenges for a couple of years. He's a good guy. I will not allow his future to be placed in jeopardy. Decades ago, CityLight committed itself to bringing the gift of the best books to the world. It has remained true to that commitment. When you go after CityLight, you're going after Andrew. I don't think you realize the damage you could do to him by exposing this."

As my mind whirls with fresh confusion, Josh leans across the desk, staring intently at me. "Is that what you want, Charlie? Do you want to hurt Andrew?"

"Of course not. He is an amazing person." My response is instinctive and immediate, and I instantly regret giving away such a key piece of my inner thoughts.

Josh's eyes sharpen as if he just caught a mouse. "By agreeing to help you, Andrew has jeopardized his own reputation and future," he says. "He's made mistakes. Big ones. But does he deserve to have his life ruined? Before you pursue this further, I suggest you stop and decide if you have it in you to be responsible for that."

I'm shaken and confused. His words spin in my head, but I can't seem to grab onto them enough to make sense of Josh's meaning. Rising abruptly, I stand and stare at him, feeling like I'm missing an important piece of the puzzle. "It has never been my intention to cause any harm to Andrew through all of this."

Hurriedly, I excuse myself and rush from Josh's office.

I don't even bother to hail a taxi once I emerge into the crisp air again. I need to walk. I need time to think. I need to clear my head of this feeling of cobwebbed confusion the same way I usually clear it at home. Walking for miles in the open air is the best therapy in my experience. "Walking cures most things," Dad used to say.

At the forefront of my troubled thoughts is Andrew and what my quest for justice could mean for him. But does he even deserve my concern? If he already knows about Ava and has been buying time to get ahead of my lawsuit this entire week . . . What does that mean for us?

The truth is that there is no us. We are just two strangers who were never supposed to meet, but I can't help feeling a glimmer of happiness that we did.

By the time I reach Winters Tower, my feet are sore, but my heart hurts more. When I walk into my borrowed apartment, its air of luxurious city living feels cold and shallow. I miss my cozy home tucked away between the trees. I miss my furry clients. I miss baking in my too-tiny but sweet and cheerful kitchen. I miss my friends in town. I miss the animal shelter where I volunteer each week so that nothing stops those homeless stray pups from finding their forever homes.

My life is quiet. I've rarely let myself venture out of Pleasant Hollow for years, feeling safest and happiest in the home I shared with my parents. But I consider my life a rich, full life, nonetheless. Writing gave the long nights meaning. What does this life mean if it isn't for a greater purpose? I thought I was honoring my parents' legacy. But am I really just betraying my new friend?

I don't know if I've been standing in the middle of the living room for five minutes or an hour when there is a soft knock at the door. Startled, I walk across the floor automatically to answer it. Did Josh tell Andrew that I came in and threatened CityLight? Is he here to confront me and tell me to leave? Distracted, I open the door without looking through the peephole. A long ecru box leans against the frame. I look down the hall, but the person who delivered it is already gone. The box isn't heavy, so I pick it up and move it inside.

To my shock, the card has been addressed to me. Untying the pretty velvet ribbon holding the box together, I lift the lid to discover layers of delicate tissue paper and another card, this one handwritten.

Dear Charlie:

This dress reminded me of the forests of Vermont. It would look stunning on you at the Winters' Wonder Gala tomorrow night. If you like it, please wear it for this momentous occasion. And remember: Don't tell Andrew you're attending. It's our secret. My son won't know what hit him.

~ Gary

I tear through the layers of tissue to find the most exquisite mossy green dress I've ever seen. It has been sewn from miles of flowy gauze and the softest silk, in a color that makes me ache for home. I lift it out of the box and hold it up, tears sparking in my eyes as I realize what a complicated mess I've gotten myself into by coming to New York.

He thinks Andrew and I are dating, and he wants me to feel welcome, I think, dread blooming in my chest. *He's trying to be a supportive dad.*

My phone buzzes on the table, lighting up with a message from Andrew.

ANDREW: I hope you're ready to see a side of NYC that

you've only imagined.

My eyes shift from his message to the dress. Everything is confusing me right now, but I am sure of one thing. I want to go on this date with Andrew tonight, if only to have one more perfect night with him before it all comes crashing down. One more moonlit date on a perfect autumn night in New York with a man I could see myself falling for if things were different. There will be time for the truth another day. Resolutely, I type my reply.

CHARLIE: Looking forward to it!

27

Andrew

Charlie is quiet in the town car, but her energy fills the air with palpable electricity. Her legs are crossed. Her foot bounces up and down—suede ankle boot jiggling so fast it's blurring in my peripheral. Something about her mood is different tonight.

Is she nervous? Does she not want to be here? Is this about the strange text message from Josh or the voicemail he left me right as I was knocking on the apartment door to pick her up?

On the floor, my leather messenger bag rests against my leg. The wrapped gift tucked inside—my personal journal chronicling my world from the night I first read Charlie's manuscript until now—has made me anxious in my own right. I think of Dad. It's risky to give Charlie ammunition against my father's company before the Winters' Wonder Gala. For a moment, I wonder if I should stick to the original plan until after the gala is safely over tomorrow night. But the weight of my secret is crushing my chest. I can only hope that Charlie plays along and trusts me when I tell her not to open my gift until tomorrow night.

Charlie casts a nervous-looking glance my way and attempts a smile.

I clear my throat. "What did you do today?" The question is lame, but the ice in this car desperately needs to be broken.

A flash of what looks like guilt strikes across her soft features. Charlie looks down and picks a stray reddish hair from Sergio off her black leggings. "Oh, I just did some exploring around the city. A little, um, research on Frost too."

My gut twists sharply. "Find anything interesting?"

I don't plan to bring up the cryptic voicemail and text Josh left about her earlier.

"Umm . . ." Her face blanches. She searches her leggings for another stray dog hair and purses her lips. The car brakes unexpectedly. We lurch forward. The moment is broken, and we both fall silent.

I don't know if my stomach is in knots because of our driver's erratic road skills, because of how desperately I want tonight to go well, or because I'm scared Charlie is putting the dots together before I get the chance to tell her the truth myself.

"So, do I get to know where we're going yet?" She angles her body toward me now, a smile plastered across her pretty lips. I have to wonder . . . is the smile real or fake?

"Not yet," I reply. "But I can give you a clue."

"A clue? I do love a good mystery."

Carefully, so as not to expose the gift inside, I reach into my bag and extract the pink rose I took earlier this afternoon from Mom's bouquet. I'd trimmed the stem down considerably before leaving the house.

"Here." I reach over and tuck the rose behind Charlie's ear. The soft pink petals pop magnificently against her dark hair and warm skin. I watch in appreciation as her cheeks turn a color similar to the blushing rose.

"Thank you," she murmurs softly.

My gesture seems to soothe the tense energy in the car. A sweet smile plays on Charlie's full lips as we pull into the New York Botanical Garden. The striking white and glass palm dome rises ahead of us toward the dusky sky. There are few cars left in the small parking lot.

Charlie looks at me quizzically. "Are we too late? Is it closed?"

Slinging my messenger bag over my shoulder, I get out and hold the door open for her. "Not for us," I reply with a grin.

I bid our driver goodbye, giving instructions for his return time. Together, we walk to the entrance. Quickly pulling out my phone, I dial the contact Ava gave me for her uncle. Within minutes, the after-hours guard lets us in. The gardens are well lit, even as dusk wanes. Soon we're strolling among paths dotted with fairy lights. While much of the fall foliage has faded away this late in the season, vivid bursts of crimson, purple, and gold still whisper to us in the fading light of the immaculately kept garden.

I nudge Charlie's arm. "Since this is your first time in New York, I thought this was one place you shouldn't miss."

"This is gorgeous," Charlie murmurs. She spins in a circle, her neck craned to take in every inch of the place. "It does make me miss home, though."

I study her face. "Oh, yeah?"

She smiles. "Fall in Vermont is a special time of year."

I shove my hands in my pockets and nod. "I've heard a rumor or two," I tease. "I bet you're dying to get back, huh?"

"Yes," she says softly. Her eyes drink me in. "It turns out though that New York is also pretty special this time of year. I've had a much—let's just say—more pleasant time than I expected to."

"Have you?" I press her. "I mean, this trip isn't exactly a vacation."

She twirls away from me and shrugs as she reaches out to touch the petals of a bright yellow rose thriving despite the soon-approaching frost. "It hasn't been a vacation, but not exactly torture either." Charlie pulls out her phone to snap a picture. I watch her open a text first and catch the nervous glance she throws my way.

"Everything okay?" My mind drifts to the voicemail from Josh earlier. What happened this afternoon? I don't want anything to ruin my last night with Charlie, but anxious curiosity nags at me.

She finishes taking the photo. Sliding the phone into her purse, I hear it chime a second time. This time though, she ignores it.

We keep walking and come to a tranquil pool of water. Together, we lean over to peer inside. In the reflection, I see Charlie's face. The water reveals a troubled expression across her features. Something is definitely wrong. I wish I had the right to take her in my arms and promise her that I will make everything right so she can smile again.

Jokingly, I jut an arm out in front of her instead. Startled, she casts me a sideways glance. "What are you doing?"

"I don't trust you around bodies of water," I reply solemnly.

She bites her lip to keep from laughing. "Oh, so that's how you're going to be. I'm perfectly fine, thank you." With playful force, she pushes my arm out of the way, but her strength seems to take her off guard. She spills forward.

On reflex, I grab her by the elbow. She teeters on the edge, her body angled over the still water. "You were saying?"

"Pull me back. Pull me back," she whispers, her wide, brown eyes scouring the water that would claim her if I was to let go.

I tug her toward me. Softly, she collides against my chest. Her hands come up to grip my forearms, and she peers up at me with a grin that makes a lone dimple pop in her cheek. Her eyes crinkling up, she dissolves into laughter. The sound is a melodic burst in the quiet garden.

"One day, you're not going to need to save me, Andrew," she finally says.

That's what I'm afraid of, I think to myself. Pain swirls in my chest, and I gesture for her to follow me down the rustic paths through the forest of trees.

The vibrant beauty of autumn surrounds us on all sides, and I am struck with how rich the ending of a season can be. There is beauty to be found even in loss. Just like Charlie wrote about in her book.

"You know, my mom used to take me here a lot as a kid," I begin to speak without preamble.

"So, this is a special place to you?" Charlie takes a step closer to me.

"Yeah." I chuckle a bit at the memory I'm about to share.

"For a while, I thought I might like to be a botanist, but that dream was soon swapped for another."

"What then? A public relations specialist for a big publishing house?" Her laugh makes me smile.

"No. I wanted to be an author. I used to envision myself sitting on one of those tranquil benches with my notebook like some contemporary Hemingway planning the next great American novel as people meandered past."

Her wide eyes search my face expectantly, as though she's waiting for the punchline to a joke. "You really wanted to be a writer?" she finally says. "Why?"

My shoulders shrug, the sudden vulnerability internally shaking me like an unpleasant cross wind. "I grew up in the book world. It's always been part of my life. I guess I have always had an appreciation for the way words could be strung together with such power. Words have the ability to unite, connect, and heal people. I wanted to be part of that. But maybe more so it was because I wanted to fit in. I wanted to make a mark and give people a reason to pay attention to me."

Dusk is nearly swallowed up by night now, but the garden lights illuminate Charlie's face. The pink rose still tucked behind her ear is like a wink from the other side of eternity, encouraging me to keep going. I point to a nearby bench. "Will you sit with me?"

She obliges. Her small form tucks next to mine, and I treasure the warmth of her presence as we look over the gardens.

Clearing my throat, my voice is raspy as I begin. "I want you to know, Charlie, how much meeting you has meant to me. I'll be the first to admit that my faith has struggled since my mom passed away. The questions you had after your parents' accident were the same questions I was left with."

I pause for a moment and gather my thoughts. "Mom was always the one with the unstoppable faith in God. Dad and I just accompanied her to church every Sunday. I thought I didn't have to know much about Him because she would always be there to guide me. But then she wasn't, and I fell into such a deep darkness of the soul. But while I don't pretend to know much of these things, I believe God brought you to New York so that I could meet you."

She makes a gasping sound and shifts on the bench to face me better. Her face is shadowed in the gloom, but I sense her warm, fervent eyes trained intently on me. "Your book, Charlie, it restored my hope that there really is something greater than this earth to look forward to after this life. I don't have all the answers to my questions yet, but I'm going to keep looking. I'm going to search for Him like you did. You've looked grief in the face, but you've fought to find the light again. I want what you have."

Her fingers reach for mine. I wish I could hold onto them forever.

"Andrew," she says, and I hear tears in her voice, "you have no idea how much this means to me. I've prayed countless times that God would use my words to bring a hurting heart back to Him. That He would restore that which was lost. If He used this whole undesirable situation just to be able to put my book in front of you, that is worth every bit of heartache to me. I will be praying that one day you will have an unshakable faith in Him too."

She curls into my side, and it feels natural to slide my arm around her shoulders. If I only get to hold her one time, this is the moment. "I would give anything to be able to heal hurting hearts with my words like you, Charlie Blaire."

"You can," she whispers.

I shake my head against her hair. "I don't want to pretend to be someone I'm not anymore."

Her chin tilts up to look at me. Our eyes lock. "So, you're giving up on your dream to be a writer? I know it's hard to push through and finish a draft, but—"

"Actually, I have been writing something," I interrupt her.

She raises her eyebrows. "Really?"

I can practically feel my journal about to explode in my bag. "But I want to talk to you about something first."

"Wait. I do, too," she says. Pulling away from me suddenly, she stands up from the bench. She paces in front of me as my heart plummets.

My hand rests on the clasp of my bag. "Do you want to go first?"

Her feet stop moving, and she faces me. "I have a feeling that I know what's really been going on."

My mouth goes dry. A painful tremor constricts my lungs. "What do you mean?"

"Look, I couldn't just sit around to wait and hope and trust you. Not that I don't, Andrew. I just . . . I need to look out for myself, you know? So, I got a lawyer today. And I met with Ava at The Drip." She folds her arms as though her words are steeped in triumph.

"Wait. Who? Ava-from-CityLight-Ava?" I scratch my head. Well, that explains Ava's strange presence at The Drip this morning. I thought it seemed like she had been engaged in conversation before I arrived at the half-empty table. "That was your laptop I saw sitting there?"

"Yeah." There's an edge to her tone now. "Is my meeting with her an issue?"

I'm utterly lost. "Did you . . . tell Ava everything?" If Charlie broke the NDA, there could be serious trouble for both her and us.

"No, but I don't think I have to."

"Charlie, can you please just explain what you're talking about?"

"I've put two and two together, Andrew. I know by talking with Ava that she was in acquisitions when I stupidly sent my manuscript into CityLight. At the time, I knew next to nothing about how publishing works. I should have gone about it a different way, but my entire life has been punctuated by a certain sense of impulsivity. It's something I know I clearly need to work on. That being said, I have reason to believe Ava is the one who intercepted and published my manuscript."

She says it with an air of finality that has me floored. My jaw drops, and I scrub my face with my hand. "No, Charlie. Ava did not—"

"And you've been covering for her, haven't you?" she interrupts with a soft voice. "I get it. She's your friend. You guys have history together. But—"

"History? I don't even know what you're talking about. Charlie, will you please just listen to me when I say—"

"Will you listen to me?" A hint of exasperation creeps into her tone. "I'm trying to tell you what I've discovered, and you aren't even willing to listen!"

My confession is ready to leap off my tongue. But I have to try to protect Dad for as long as I can. My bag is still next to me. Reaching for it, I unclasp it. I must give this to her now. It's the only way to stop this. She may not honor my request to wait until tomorrow night to unwrap and read my journal, but the truth belongs in her possession.

"I have something for you," I say as I reach inside the leather bag.

To my surprise, Charlie takes a step back on the path. "No," she says firmly. "I don't want your gifts. I don't want any more of you buttering me up. Please, just save it." Her voice cracks. "Saying goodbye to you is going to be hard enough."

Ignoring her, I slide the gift out anyway. It's too late. The pink rose slips from Charlie's hair, bouncing on the graveled path as she storms away.

I leap up. "Charlie! Stop!"

Already yards ahead of me, she whirls around. "I need some space right now, Andrew," she yells. "This is all too much. I . . . I don't need you saving me anymore. I'll find my own way home."

"Please wait!" My voice breaks, but Charlie moves quickly, creating more space between us.

Dismayed by this turn of events tonight, I take a few steps and stoop down to pick up the rose. An unseen thorn hidden under the petals nips at my finger. Funny how something so soft and beautiful can still cause so much pain.

28

Charlie

Waves of disappointment crush my soul one turbulent crash at a time. Hot tears slip freely down my cheeks, dragging the mascara I'd carefully applied earlier tonight down in charcoal streaks. I'm not crying because I'm angry with Andrew. I'm not. Who knows what I would have done in his position?

At this point, I'm not even sure he knows what Ava did. Or what I think she did. His response to my accusation told me nothing. I was expecting at least a flash of guilt on his face, if not a full confession. Rather than walk away with a clear path forward, I'm more confused. And disappointed. I'm disappointed in everything.

"Are you okay, miss?" The driver glances at me in his rearview mirror, concern apparent in his eyes. With the back of my hand, I smear the tears off my cheeks and nod, mumbling that I'm fine.

After I left Andrew at the bench, I walked a few blocks from the Conservatory in the dark before I could gather myself enough to open my phone and call for a ride. I spent the short interval hoping Andrew would appear, but also praying he wouldn't chase after me. It would not have been a surprise to see him racing around the corner, coming to rescue me like he has done all week. But he never appeared.

As much as I hate to admit it to myself, that's what I'm disappointed in the most. It feels like further confirmation of what I already feared.

My inner mental dialogue is harsh as the driver weaves through the streets back to my temporary home. Probably even more temporary because I've just provoked a fight with its owner. *What were you thinking, Charlie? You were in the middle of a very beautiful evening, and you ruined it. You couldn't have waited until tomorrow to make your accusation against one of his friends and colleagues? Why didn't you gather more evidence or get Ava to confess first? Once again, you walk away looking like the crazy one.*

As I dig deeper, I realize that I'm the most disappointed in myself. Impulsively blurting out whatever I'm thinking has been the bane of my existence for years. Just like my decision to send my unsolicited manuscript to a bunch of different publishers or my decision to confront CityLight with no legal representation has resulted in a less-than-desirable outcome, being impulsive has once again come between me and something I long for. I tell myself that the bubble I've been in all week had to break sometime. I just didn't expect to be the sharp point of the pin that popped it.

Please forgive me if I haven't shown wisdom in my decisions lately. Through Your strength, I will work on listening to You better. But was I crazy to think You brought me here for a reason, Lord? To think that You had planned some wild story of goodness coming out of all the heartache and pain I've experienced?

The prayer floats softly through my brain as my ride pulls up to double park along the curb. I pull myself together enough to thank the driver. When he pulls away, I stand motionless on the tree-lined sidewalk. Tilting my head back, I peer upward, trying to catch a glimpse of the stars that populate the night sky by the thousands back home. I always feel comforted when I stare up into the heavens and remember the vastness of my Savior's mercy and grace for my shortcomings. To my disappointment, the stars are faded and dim against the glow of the city lights.

I shiver against the chilly wind that seems caught between the surrounding buildings. Suddenly, I feel out of place and exposed. My heart calls for the comforting shelter of the trees and open space of Central Park down the street, but I don't dare venture toward its dark and foreboding presence at this hour. If I were home, I would go for a moonlit ramble through the meadows, walking out my feelings and praying aloud on the empty roads. But I'm not home. I wish I was.

"We aren't in Kansas anymore, are we Dorothy?" I murmur. Reluctantly, I glance down the street one more time, hoping to see a tall, familiar, broad-shouldered figure with perfectly swoopy hair, dreamy eyes, and a heart-melting smile walking toward me. But I am only greeted by darkness and shadows.

Sighing, I turn toward the steps that lead into the

building. There's no one around to hear me say, "Maybe it's time for Dorothy to take herself home where she belongs?"

—

I hear his footsteps pause outside my door early Saturday morning. His shadow lingers. For a breathless minute, I hope he is going to knock. I never expected to long for a man I've known less than a week to pull me into the safety of one of his warm hugs, but that's what I want. I want him to laugh his big laugh and reassure me that A.C. Frost is some lonely hermit up in Alaska whose cold heart matches his or her terrible deeds. I want Andrew to promise he'll fix it. That he'll fix anything that's broken if it means we are going to be whole.

But that would require me to open the door, and I know that I need to wait patiently for circumstances to work themselves out.

Though his footsteps linger as if he is listening quietly to see if I'm inside, he doesn't knock. And when his shadow moves away from the apartment door, I stay frozen in my seat on the loveseat. My duffel bag is flung open and nearly full on the floor before me. I started packing at seven in the morning. The fuller my luggage gets, the heavier my heart feels.

I don't know what I expected to be the result of storming New York City to demand the return of my book rights and the vindication of the injustice done to me, but it wasn't this. I never expected to stumble across the exact person I needed to pull me out of the slump that has been dragging me down ever since Mom and Dad . . .

My heart constricts as I realize what I will lose by storming back home to fight this battle alone . . . again.

Last night, he set up the perfect date in the perfect place. He shared words that every writer who hopes one day her words will touch someone's heart longs to hear. He took me to a forested, plant-lover's dream. To find out it was the place he visited often with his mother . . . to share that with me after we've shared the loss of so much. It meant something to me.

I saw the grieved expression flashing across his face when I accused him of hiding the truth from me.

I don't want to be the cause of anyone's pain. I never want to cause pain for him. Because despite his mistakes, I know in my heart that Andrew is a good man.

I don't want to lose whatever beautiful thing has begun to blossom between us because I pridefully allowed my hurt and anger to get in the way. Even after everything said last night, I still wonder if God brought him across my path for a reason.

The mossy green dress Gary sent me yesterday afternoon hangs on the bedroom door. In the soft morning light filtering through the windows, it seems to glisten with a sparkle that reminds me of the magic in the green-soaked forests back home after the autumn rain falls. The dress won't fit into my duffel bag for the return flight home. Guiltily, I wonder if Gary will think I didn't care about his kind invitation.

There's no one in the apartment to hear me. I say the words out loud anyway, bowing my head and closing my eyes.

"Right now, I don't have all the answers to all the confusing questions playing in my head, Heavenly Father. But You do. You brought me here for a purpose, and maybe it was for nothing more than for me to know that the book You inspired me to write helped a hurting heart to begin to heal. If knowing Andrew is the only thing I walk away with after all this, I think he's worth the risk of trusting. And if not, I trust You to protect me and bring me home."

Peace that passes all understanding echoes in my head as my phone buzzes beside me. I jump. My heart begins to race. "That was fast, Lord," I whisper as I lift the device to look at the screen.

It's hard not to let my heart drop in disappointment when I realize the text is from Nate.

NATE: Just reaching out to check on you. Are you still mad at me?

He answers on the second ring. "Are you calling to chew me out, Charlie Blaire?" Behind his amused tone, I hear the hesitation in his voice. In all our years of friendship, we've rarely had a spat. I take full responsibility for our disagreement earlier this week.

I smile, hoping he'll hear the peace in my tone. "Now, why would I do that to one of my closest friends? Even if he did leave me in Vermont and move over 3,000 miles away."

"Hey, some of us like a little saltwater therapy to go along with our forest bathing." The lightness reenters his voice. My smile grows as he continues. "Are you still in New York? What's the news?"

Without missing a beat, I dive into a full rundown of everything I didn't get the chance to tell him a few days ago. I tell him about spilling coffee all over Andrew's shirt, which led to us meeting and him offering to help. I tell him about running through Central Park trying to catch Frost red-handed and beginning to suspect a CityLight employee of stealing my book. For some reason, I don't mention tonight's invitation to the gala or the dress hanging in front of me.

Nate takes a deep breath when I finish. "I can honestly say I didn't expect you to say any of this. Do you still think it's this Ava-chick?"

I shake my head even though he can't see me. "I don't know. Maybe. I've retained a lawyer like you suggested, and I'm waiting to hear back from him. I'm hoping he can dig and find out more about Frost's online presence. I don't know how it all works, but I'm trying to trust the process and trust God to get me through this."

"The old trust exercise: Will He catch me when I fall headlong into the unknown?" Nate laughs.

I'm about to elaborate more on the events that have unfolded this week when a brisk knock raps on the door. My heart leaps into my throat. For a second, I freeze. "Nate, I'll catch up with you later, okay? Someone just knocked on the door."

He came back for me.

Joy fills my heart.

I pad toward the door in my socks and don't even bother to check the peephole before I fling it open. The first thing I see is a pair of trouser-clad legs and loafers standing behind a massive bouquet of pink roses.

"I'm so sorry, Andrew," I blurt out. "You were right. I should have trusted you. I don't want this to come between us. I should have waited . . ."

A startled, clean-shaven face peeks around the bouquet, a face decidedly not Andrew's bearded one. "Charlie Blaire?" he says, clearly afraid I'm going to launch myself into his arms after that speech.

Wordlessly, I nod, unable to gather my faculties enough to speak. He shoves the bouquet toward me. I take it with a mumbled "Thank you" before I back away in embarrassment and shut the door.

The bouquet easily holds a hundred soft pink roses, their stems nestled in an intricate crystal vase. It's extravagant and over the top and exactly like Andrew to go to such lengths. I carry it to the coffee table. My heart pounds as I set it down and pluck the cream envelope from the holder. I slide out the card from inside.

The note is simple, written in Andrew's bold script.

Charlie,

I have so much to say, but I don't know how to say it. From the moment we met, there has been something about you that feels as though I've known you for years. I had to help you even though I know it is not in my best interest to do so. And though I know that whatever began brewing between us the moment you spilled that cup of coffee on me couldn't stay hot and fresh forever, I can't let go of you yet. I have so much more I want to tell you, but I need one more day. Can you give me one more day to make things right?

I have a family event tonight, but can we have brunch tomorrow at your place? I'll place the takeout order. If I knock on your door at eleven and you don't open it, I'll know your answer. And I'll forever remember the week I got to meet the real Charlie Blaire.

~Andrew

My stomach flutters as I read the note a second, third, and fourth time. There's still hope. There's still time for our story to begin. If everything that has happened was to lead up to this point, it's worth it. I glance up at the dress hanging gracefully in the doorway, then down at my nearly full duffel bag.

"Well, Charlotte Blaire, I guess if you're ever going to buy a fancy pair of heels and get your hair styled and your makeup professionally done, there's no better place for it than The Big Apple." I set my hands on my hips resolutely. "If only the folks at home could see me now."

As I rush around, throwing on fresh clothes and gathering my things, my phone buzzes with another text from Nate. I only glance down briefly at the message before rushing out the door.

NATE: Remind me of the name of the guy from CityLight who's been helping you this week? Did you say it was Andrew? What's his last name?

29

Andrew

I adjust the cuff links on my tux clumsily. My fingers fumble with the clasp as my mind swirls with ever-consuming thoughts of Charlie. Nothing can pull my mind away from her. Live piano music drifts from the great room. Well-dressed guests mill through the house. Snippets of conversations fall on my ears, and professional servers bustle around my father's estate, balancing flutes of champagne and tempting canapes on silver trays. But my mind drifts back to her every few seconds.

We haven't spoken since last night, when everything seemed to fall apart. I nab a flute of sparkling water from a passing server and swallow past the lump in my throat. My hope seems to slide down with it. It was foolish to mess with Charlie in the first place and even more foolish to let myself develop feelings for her.

There are no winners in this game I've forced us all to play.

"Andrew." Dad catches me on the shoulder. I turn to face him and see that while a smile lingers on his face, there's sadness behind his eyes. This is a bittersweet night for both of us. "Mind greeting guests?" he says.

I nod. This night is for Mom, a night intended to honor the work she did in the community to promote literacy. Years ago, when I was just a boy and anxiety began to hit, she would read aloud to me to kill off the monsters in my head. She cultivated a love for books that stuck with me. Yet, as much as I want to remember her legacy, the ache of heartbreak reins me in. I want to do justice to her tonight. I can't let my emotions cloud my vision anymore. This is for Mom.

"Sure thing, Dad." I begin to walk away, but he stops me with a hand on my forearm.

"And Andrew? I know we haven't had much of a chance to talk lately about the snafu with Docu Wise Productions, but I want you to know you're the only one who matters to me. Soon, I hope I can prove how proud I am of you." He winks and walks away. Within a moment, he is already embracing one of our many guests.

I'm left a little floored. When I arrived this morning, there was already a bustle of caterers, musicians moving in their instruments, and decorators adding the finishing touches to the estate. There wasn't any time or opportunity to address the elephant in the room between Dad and me. It's a relief to know it isn't going to be an issue standing between us. I doubt he'll be as gracious when he finds out I inadvertently put him in a position to plagiarize an unsuspecting author's book, and we're about to pay the piper. My only hope is that someday he'll be able to forgive me if I take full responsibility.

I move toward the wooden, oversized, double front doors and welcome the rush of cool air coming into the house. The night is rapidly growing chillier, but I feel flushed and overheated nonetheless. Outside, valets slide into luxurious Benzes and Maseratis as guests climb the wide front steps leading toward the door. Our circular driveway is now lined with waiting cars. All our guests are arriving at the same time.

Mom did so much for the community, passing her love of reading onto the next generation. Her father invested well as a young entrepreneur and later founded CityLight in the eighties. But Mom didn't hoard her wealth. She was generous, setting up a foundation to raise money for underprivileged kids with limited access to books and educational materials, as well as setting aside resources for those with reading disabilities. She carried herself with a classic charm and a genuine love that people could feel. The community, whether they were personal friends, foundation members, or CityLight employees, carry on the tradition of the Winters' Wonder Gala to pay their respects and celebrate the merging of fall and winter just as the magical morning frost begins to touch the landscape, her favorite part of the approaching winter season. Dutifully, I shake familiar hands and guide them into the house.

Clusters of guests gather on Dad's perfectly manicured lawn, making small talk in the brisk air before heading inside. I grew up on this estate. It is a sprawling five acres of grass, gardens, and trees. The house, a luxury stone manor built in 1906, caps out at 4,000 square feet.

It's not beyond me that I grew up far more privileged

than most, having the ease of luxury and anything I wanted at my fingertips. Years ago, I didn't understand at first why Dad made me earn a master's degree at Columbia and then take a position as a junior public relations strategist in CityLight's marketing department. For years, it felt like he deliberately kept me in the shadows, rarely pulling me in for press conferences or important business decisions. Considering I am destined to run CityLight someday, I used to resent my position in the company and, I thought, in Dad's heart.

I am beginning to understand now the growth and maturity I've needed to pursue this entire time.

Without Mom here to fill the giant gap her absence creates, everything feels a bit more empty, hollow, and frivolous. I'd trade all of this to make things right with Charlie.

Amid the flashy sports cars and embellished SUVs dotting the graveled drive, I spot a bright flash of yellow coming down our private lane. The taxi pulls in front of the wide limestone steps. One of the valets throws me a confused look.

The cab idles for a minute. Finally, the back passenger door opens. The pale golden glow of the lamp posts lining the driveway reveal a pair of silver heels and a shimmer of mossy green fabric first. The heels hit the pavement as the hem of the dress barely brushes the ground. When the passenger rises fully to her feet, my gaze lifts. I lock eyes with a beauty so exquisite that my state of uprightness is threatened.

Autumn's gentle breath plays with the soft, wispy curls framing Charlie's face. The rest of her dark hair is swept into an elegant low bun. I see her full, glossy lips part as her eyes latch onto mine. Slowly, she breaks my gaze, turning to shut the door to the cab. I drink in the sight of her slender, exposed neck and the subtle sparkle of a dainty necklace resting in the hollow of her throat.

She takes one hesitant step toward me as the cab pulls away. The motion sways the voluptuous tulle skirt of her dress.

Nothing about her arrival or appearance makes sense to me right now. But nothing matters except her. I was not expecting this tonight, and it is the best surprise.

At the top of the steps, I hear my name. I can't drag my eyes away from Charlie, though. Nor do I want to. I step toward her and hold out my hand.

"You're stunning." The words leave my lips like I was born to say them. "But that's nothing new."

She finally takes my proffered hand and allows me to guide her up. The glow from the house lights up her face, and I see how her dark eyes study me. I stare right back because I could drink in the sight of her forever.

"And you're . . . here?" I finally ask, the fog in my brain beginning to lift. How and why is she here?

"I'm here," she replies softly. Her eyes dart up to my childhood home. Her dimple pops as she purses her lips. "Here at this palace, apparently. *This* is your childhood home?"

"It is." I pull her hand into the crook of my arm, nestling it there. We begin to climb the front steps together.

"You're really not in Kansas anymore, Charlie," I overhear her mutter under her breath.

I can't help but smile. I don't think I was supposed to

hear that. "Don't you mean Vermont?"

She takes one more step and pauses to regard me, her cheeks a radiant shade of pink. "I am, um, way out of my league here. I feel like an imposter coming to crash the royal ball."

"And yet, somehow, you put everyone else here to shame." The compliment elicits an eye roll from her, and I wish she knew how deeply I mean it. She is stunning. The green dress drapes over her form like it was sewn just for her, and the mossy color complements her skin and hair like I imagine they would a forest nymph. "Charlie, why are you here tonight?"

Panic creeps across her face. She snatches her hand from my grasp. "Is it not okay that I am?"

"I'm thrilled you are." And if I'm honest, both relieved and terrified to have her by my side again. "I'm just confused at how you—"

"Got here? By cab, silly." A smile finally breaks across her face. "I was given a personal invitation."

"By whom?" I realize I don't need her to answer. This has Gary Ketner written all over it. An anvil drops in my gut. Has he done or said anything else I need to know about?

"Obviously not from you," she says pointedly. "Honestly, I don't blame you though. Andrew, I am so sorry for how I acted last night. I'm so overwhelmed with everything right now. I . . ." Her lips stay parted for a moment as though she's going to continue, but then they press firmly together. I wonder if she couldn't find the courage to say what's on her mind.

"I'm sorry too. For everything." *Every. Single. Thing.* The urge to wrap her in my arms and whisk her away from this lively party to the quiet countryside overwhelms me. I take a deep breath and ask, "Did you get my note?"

"I did." Her answer is simple, yet she gives no indication of her answer. I don't press her. It's enough that she is here now. I guess I will find out when I knock on her door tomorrow morning. "So, how does this whole thing work tonight? Tell me what to do so I don't embarrass your family."

I laugh. "Charlie, there is nothing you can do to ruin tonight. You have no idea what it means to me that you came." My mind swirls with acute awareness of all the ways this night could go off the rails. Her presence means there's still hope though, and I'm going to hold on to that. After last night, I thought hope for something between us was more than gone. "As long as you don't go near the fountain in the courtyard, you'll be just fine."

Her hearty laughter rings out. "You're never going to let me live that down, are you?"

I take her hand and pull it through my arm again. "Not for the rest of our lives."

There's a hitch in both of our steps at my words, as though we both just stumbled into a conversation neither of us have been brave enough to broach. It might be more awkward if I correct myself, and I don't feel the desire to either. My heart will soon be filleted open for Charlie to see. I might as well start showing her pieces of myself now.

I hear her small, suppressed gasp as we walk inside my father's home. She isn't bashful in the way she takes in the massive foyer: the cathedral ceilings and diamond chandelier hanging overhead, the double bridal staircase welcoming guests upstairs to the ballroom, the fire burning warm and bright in the fireplace between the stairs.

"I have no words," Charlie whispers.

I lean down to reply, but I'm pulled aside suddenly by the head chairman of the Winters' Wonder Foundation, Warren Hartfield. He tugs on my arm, loosening my grip on Charlie's hand, and sweeps me into conversation about fiscal matters that only half reach my ears. I've sat on the board for several years, though my heart hasn't been fully invested in the responsibility. Out of my peripheral vision, I watch Charlie spin and bump into a server carrying a full tray. The man hardly budges, though Charlie still apologizes profusely as she delicately lifts a flute from the tray.

"—but the foundation's lasting effects echo far beyond their contributions. Wouldn't you agree, Andrew?"

I have no idea what Warren just said, but enthusiastically nod as I keep an eye on a man I don't recognize as he swoops to Charlie's side. My gaze returns to Mr. Hartfield, and I realize I'm still nodding.

He slaps me enthusiastically on the back. "We've missed you at the meetings this year. Your opinions are always valued, Andrew. Your mother was always so proud of you. Will we see you next month?"

I don't need to be reminded of my failures. Guilt has already eaten its way through me, like a worm through an apple, affecting every aspect of my life. When she was alive, I served on the board eagerly, happy to help her with something that brought her so much joy. After she was gone, it seemed like an empty pursuit. Who was I to try to help anyone? I've always struggled to give my full self to anything, forever captured by the fear of not being good enough should I truly give it my best effort. Self-sabotage and incompetence have always felt like a form of protection. In reality, I'm recognizing that I've only imprisoned myself.

It's time I grow up. Man up. Change for the better.

For Charlie.

For my mother.

For myself.

"I'll be there, sir," I say to Warren. He pats me on the shoulder as though pleased with my answer and excuses himself to greet someone else. I turn to find Charlie and catch Josh glaring at me from across the room instead. Alarm grips my chest at the sight of him. In the distraction of seeing her, I forgot he would be a staple presence here tonight. Josh points a firm finger toward her, and I follow his direction to see her now across the room in conversation with a group of people. The man I didn't recognize earlier lingers at her side. I see him snake an arm behind her, his palm alighting on the small of her back.

I recognize the familiar motion. He's staking his claim on her as the target of his interest for the rest of the evening. I realize with shame that I've done the same thing to other young women in the past. It's infuriating to watch. My heart pounds in my chest as I tear my gaze back to Josh's furious face. First things first. I make my way through the crowd to speak with him.

He yanks me aside when I'm close enough and hisses in my ear. "What are you thinking bringing her here? Do you want to kill your father's reputation and company all in one night?"

Roughly, I push his hand away from me and straighten my collar and bowtie. "Look—"

"No, man," he seethes. "You look. I'm doing my best to

get you out of this mess, but I told you not to get involved with her. You were supposed to just keep her busy all week. She's going to tell everyone everything."

The reality is that Josh is only doing his job: protecting the company he gets paid to protect. Yet I can't help the fire that burns in my chest. It's Charlie who deserves the protection, not me.

I keep my voice low so no one overhears. "This is between her and me, Josh. Don't get involved tonight, okay? I'm warning you. I'll do everything I can to protect Dad and CityLight. But don't you dare mess anything up between us."

Josh works his jaw and looks at me like I'm the biggest idiot he's ever seen, which probably would not be far from the truth. His eyes dart away, then back to me. He thrusts his chin in the direction over my shoulder. "You should be less worried about me and more worried about him."

I flip around, expecting to see the mystery man escorting Charlie upstairs to the ballroom. Instead, I see her leaving the room, her hand tucked on the arm of my father.

30

Charlie

The man's hand slips around the small of my back. I feel a tickle as his pinky just grazes the exposed skin at the top of my ball gown. Its off-the-shoulder design has left my back and upper shoulders exposed. Someone whisked away my wrap when Andrew and I entered. I was too entranced by the gorgeous home to notice anything other than the warmth of Andrew's arm as he pulled my hand through it.

Now, though, I feel the brisk autumn evening chill coming through the flung open double front doors. The stylist I visited this afternoon insisted that I wear my hair swept into an updo. Right now, I'm sorely missing the protective warmth my long hair usually affords me.

Darn this backless dress, Gary, I fume inwardly as the strange man draws me closer to his side. I'm tempted to pull away and put him in his place, but for all I know, he is one of Andrew's relatives.

And where is Andrew? We've gotten separated in the swirling eddy of gala-goers. The crowd mingles with each other amid happy laughter and the clinking of champagne glasses. Rising onto my toes, I finally spot him a few feet away, engaged in conversation with a distinguished-looking older man.

"Hello, lovely. Have we met before? I know for sure I'd remember you in this dress anywhere." A husky voice hits my ear just as his arm slips around my waist. I turn to find the stranger with no sense of personal space leisurely trailing his gaze up and down my figure with an appreciative glint in his eyes.

"It's new," I reply, allowing my tone to take on an icy chill. I try to force a polite smile across my lips. Though, baring my teeth might be a more accurate description of my expression. "So, you must be thinking of some other girl in another pretty dress." I shrug, hoping to move his arm away from me without causing too big of a scene at Andrew's fancy gala.

"You know, you could be right." The stranger snaps the fingers of his free hand. "But I definitely saw you in my dreams last night wearing this exact same dress."

"Leave the lady alone, Benton. She doesn't have time to put up with your nonsense." A teasing, slightly familiar voice breaks in between us. Gary appears at my side. He places his arm gently around my shoulders and tugs me away from Benton's grip, saying he wants to give me a tour of the house before the night slips away.

"Thank you," I whisper as he rescues me from Benton's unwanted attention. "I wasn't quite sure what to do back there."

"Standing up for yourself is a learned skill, my dear." Gary winks down at me. He removes his arm from my shoulders, pulling my hand through the crook of his arm instead. "But if you don't mind, I really would love to show you something. I have a feeling you'll appreciate it."

"Oh . . . of course." I glance back over my shoulder in Andrew's direction, hoping to catch his eye, but I can't spot him as we sweep down the hall.

"I guess it's true what they say. The woman really does make the dress."

I blush, realizing my lapse in manners. "I cannot thank you enough for it, sir. I truly wish you hadn't sent it, but now that I'm here, I'm so glad you did."

Gary squeezes my hand. "I'm so glad you wore it." He opens a wooden door inlaid with an intricate gold pattern and ushers me inside.

I gasp as warmly lit sconces on the wall flicker on. I drink in the sight of the breathtaking room. Fabric-bound books occupy built-in wooden bookcases that stretch from floor to ceiling. A metal spiral staircase leads to a cozy loft upstairs, where I see more paperbacks stacked on shelves. Cozy seating is placed all around the room, begging for a reader to curl up in an armchair for a few hours. Floor-to-ceiling windows look over the gardens, which are lit with torches that press back the gloom of the chilly November evening.

It is the color inside the magnificent library that strikes me at once. With both hands, I grasp the fabric of my dress and lift it above my ankles. I can't help but do a little twirl across the soft cream rug. "My dress!" I exclaim.

The wallpaper, the bookshelves, the armchairs, and even the heavy velvet drapes that hang from the windows are all soft variations of the same mossy green shade of my dress. It is exquisite and stunning and earthy and comforting all at once. The effect is of stepping into a cozy forest filled with books.

"How did you match the color so perfectly?" I spin to look at Andrew's dad with a look of confusion on my face .

"I didn't," he laughs. Gary steps toward a small frame sitting on a side table. I recognize the same beautiful, fragile woman from Andrew's gallery wall. "I happened to notice that dress in a boutique window in the city near one of our business offices. It reminded me of the color my wife insisted the decorator use for this room over twenty years ago. And then, when I invited you to this gala we host every year in her honor, I remembered the dress, and somehow, it seemed fitting."

He says it simply, but I detect the emotion behind his words. "I'm honored. From what Andrew has told me, your wife was a very special woman," I say softly.

He smiles at me. "She was. She was the glue that held our family together. I've done a terrible job at managing since her passing. Everything I am is because of her. She saw something in me one day and gave me a chance to know what love was despite how little I deserved it."

I feel the urge to cry pressing itself against my throat. "That's the best kind of love, sir. The kind we never deserved."

"It is. But enough of this 'sir' nonsense. Please call me Gary." He beams at me. My breath catches as Andrew's familiar, warm smile looks out at me from his father's face.

I smile back at him. "Well, thank you then, Gary."

"Hope I'm not interrupting anything." Andrew's head

pokes through the door. His eyes shift rapidly between us before settling on me. Music and laughter tinkle in from the rest of the opulent mansion. It sounds like the party is well under way out there.

"Not at all," Gary replies. "I do need to get back to our guests, though. Andrew, can you take over here?"

"My pleasure." His son steps forward and extends his hand for me to take.

There's a smoldering flame in the depth of his brown eyes, which haven't left mine yet. I hardly notice Gary slipping from the room as Andrew pulls me closer. The din of the party outside lessens as the door swings shut.

"Dad's showing you around, huh?" His voice is husky as it surrounds me.

"I've never seen such a beautiful room." My reply is equally low and soft. Andrew looks so handsome in his black tuxedo that I can hardly keep my thoughts straight. He trimmed his beard this morning. The five o'clock shadow now looks smooth and soft, and my fingers itch to run themselves across his jaw.

My hand is warm and secure in Andrew's strong grasp. "This room is very special to us because it was my mother's favorite place in the whole world," he replies. "She and I spent a lot of time in here together. I love books because of her."

I pull my eyes from his face and rove them across the room. My heart is beating faster than usual, and I'm not sure why. "You probably spent hours reading in one of those cozy chairs over there." I point toward the window seating with my free hand.

"Not exactly." Andrew's breath whooshes past my ear.

"Let me show you."

He leads me deeper into the room, toward the farthest side. I catch sight of a pair of doors built into a bookcase.

"Go ahead. Open it and peek inside," he instructs.

Curious, I pull the mini doors open and peer into what appears to be an ordinary, old-fashioned wardrobe. I look over my shoulder toward Andrew, feeling a quizzical smile creep across my face. "What is this? There's nothing here."

He grins. "Look deeper."

I turn back and peer again into the space. Leaning forward a little, I realize that a pair of mossy velvet drapes are covering the back of the wall. Reaching out to touch them, I exclaim in surprise when they part. I catch a glimpse of a room just beyond. Without hesitation, I take two steps forward. Suddenly, I emerge in a cozy pocket room under the loft. The ceiling is lower than normal. The walls have been painted with scenes from Narnia, and the room is set up just like I've always imagined Mr. Tumnus' house would be.

Andrew steps in after me. I notice how much he has to stoop to avoid hitting the ceiling.

"What is this magical place?" I breathe the words.

Andrew passes his hand over his jaw. He clears his throat before he speaks. "When I was a boy, I was always anxious and afraid. I'd overheard the doctor talking about my mother's weakened heart on accident one day. It started a pattern of several years where I would wake up with night terrors, dreaming that she'd left and gone away, and I never saw her again.

"Almost every night, Mom would bring me into the library and read aloud to me to soothe my fears. *The*

Chronicles of Narnia was one of her favorite series. We must have read it a dozen times. She had this room built for me because she said I could go into it and shut the door and never be afraid while I was here. She would always say with this knowing little smile on her face, 'Who could be afraid in a land where Aslan, The Great Lion, would lay down his very life to protect you?' And it was true. In here, it always felt like the cares of the world were very far away."

I hear the emotion in his voice as he finishes the story. It feels like the most natural thing in the world to step closer and wrap my arms around his waist. I sigh as he wraps his comforting arms around me in return. "Andrew, that is the most beautiful memory. I can see why you treasure your mother so much."

"I don't think I've been in this little hideaway since she passed," he whispers, his breath hot against the top of my head. "Thank you for giving me a reason to return to my childhood safe space and remember what it felt like to be in Narnia."

"Anytime." I smile as I pull away. I tilt up my chin to look at him. "Though I think maybe I should have taken you to Brobdingnag and left you with the giants because you might fit in better there."

He laughs. His palms slide across my back as he pulls me closer, grazing the skin at the top of my dress. It tingles warmly under his touch. "Okay, Gulliver. Now tell me, would you ever consider dancing with a giant?"

I tilt my head back and forth as if I'm carefully considering. I shrug one bare shoulder and purse my lips. "Maybe. If said giant was a good dancer."

"He had dance lessons when he was a kid."

"I think I can work with that."

—

I feel like a princess as I ascend the grand staircase on Andrew's arm. At the top of the stairs, a pair of ornate doors have been flung open. My senses are so filled with the glitter and glam of an actual ballroom that I can hardly take it all in. Groups of people in beautiful ball gowns and elegant tuxedos mingle, talking and laughing and sipping from their drinks.

It's the décor that takes my breath away for the second time tonight. The grace of autumn meeting the ethereal beauty of the first frost seems to be the theme for the night. Hanging from the chandeliers on one half of the room are gorgeous sprays of autumn foliage and ornamental grasses. On the other half of the room, the vibrant displays are overtaken gradually by a dazzling wash of sparkling frost until, finally, only snow-covered branches and cascades of origami snowflakes remain. The effect is exquisite. I feel a stinging behind my eyes as I take in the rest of the scene.

Well-dressed waitstaff wind among the mingling groups, expertly carrying trays piled with scrumptious-looking hors d'oeuvres above their shoulders. Against the far end of the room, a stage has been constructed. A mahogany dance floor takes up the middle of the space.

The ballroom is opulent and gorgeous and utterly overwhelming.

"Who are you people?" I glance incredulously up at Andrew. The library downstairs may have been a book lover's dream, but this . . . this reaches a level of wealth I've never even imagined.

He laughs, and I repeat, "No, seriously. Who are you?

Never in a million years would I have guessed this was your childhood home."

Instead of answering my question, Andrew extends his hand and bends in an exaggerated bow. "Miss Blaire, would you do me the honor of a dance?"

I roll my eyes but can't help the flush that heats my cheeks at his gentlemanly gesture. For one night, I plan to feel like a Jane Austen heroine and enjoy every moment with him. I drop into a quick curtsy. "It would be my pleasure, good sir."

And I mean it. As Andrew draws me into his arms and sweeps me onto the dance floor, I can't help but silently express my gratitude that somehow, at the very moment I felt the most lost and unsure, this man stumbled into my life. Or rather, I stumbled into him and spilled coffee all over his crisp white shirt. From the looks of things, the dry cleaning bill probably wasn't a hardship.

Despite the devastating discovery that brought me to New York City in the first place, I'm almost glad it happened. Even if I lose in the fight against CityLight to regain the rights to my book, everything I've gained this week may be worth it. I want to take the memory of this magical week and this wildly unexpected man home to Vermont with me.

Inwardly, my heart drops a little as I remember that my sojourn in The Big Apple isn't forever. Soon, I'm going to have to return home. As much as I miss my tiny cottage and rambling through the woods, I wonder if I'll be able to tear myself away from the city.

Lord, I know You promised to work all things together for my good, but is meeting Andrew just too wild and crazy to be from You?

Suddenly, my heart feels a little heavier.

Andrew seems to sense the shift in my mood because his arms tighten around me. I lift my chin to look at him. He gazes down at me, that smoldering expression present again in his dark, moody eyes.

As we waltz, I notice we are making our way ever so gradually toward the wall of French doors that lead out to what looks like a terrace built to overlook the property. All at once, the grand ballroom feels too stifling, too full of people.

I stretch onto my toes to reach his ear. "What do you think about stepping outside for some fresh air?"

His lips turn up into a smirk. "I was just thinking the same thing."

31

Andrew

The November night wanes with a hint of frost in the air as we slip through one of the French doors leading outside. All I feel is heat coursing through my veins. As Charlie rushes onto the terrace, her dress swooping around her ankles as if she is a princess, I carry two flutes of champagne I nabbed from a waiter just before stepping outside. Thankfully, the chilly air has prevented guests from loitering on the terrace. For now, we're alone.

"This view is spectacular," Charlie breathes, gliding to the railing and overlooking the courtyard below. I set her flute on a nearby table, taking a sip from my own. She gazes at the ornately kept garden, hedges trimmed into perfect shapes, scattered with flower beds that rival the botanical garden we wandered through last night. A pond is the focal centerpiece, a large fountain spraying from its middle.

"There's that fountain you warned me about," she says in a teasing tone. She twists her body toward me, a coy smile playing on her lips.

I hold up my palms. "Don't get any ideas, Flipper. I'm not diving into that to rescue you tonight. Uh-uh, no way."

"Oh, please. I'm a phenomenal swimmer. I wouldn't need your rescuing." She shrugs one bare, pretty shoulder.

I reach for the billowing tulle of her gown. "Even in all this?"

Purposely, she sways to and fro, swishing the hem around her shoes. "Perhaps not. Maybe I would let you come to my aid then."

"Jack Sparrow and Elizabeth Swann style?"

"Aligning yourself with a pirate now, are you?" She arches her brow.

"Well . . ." Immediately, I falter. Though my crime was unintentional, I am a thief, aren't I? And I haven't disclosed my crime, which makes me a liar. Inwardly, I wince.

Charlie doesn't seem to notice my hesitation. Her charming voice continues, "Because I had quite the crush on Jack Sparrow back in the day."

She throws me a glance, then turns away from me, gripping the railing to peer over. When she reaches up to rub the prickle of goosebumps on her arms, I jump into action. Shrugging out of my tuxedo jacket, I drape it over her bare shoulders. Charlie visibly melts.

"Thank you," she murmurs, hugging my jacket around herself. "What is this lined with? Silk? It's so soft and warm. Thank you, Andrew."

My name on her lips lingers like a spark in the air. The thought that this moment is probably the closest I'll ever get to holding her again is crushing. As if she can sense my shift in mood, Charlie steps toward me. The space between us shrinks. She leans gently against the railing next to me. Head tilted sideways, she peers into my face. I can see the moon's reflection in her espresso-shaded eyes.

"Andrew, what's your deal?" she asks without preamble. The question is spoken without animosity but rather with immense curiosity.

"My . . . deal?"

She gestures toward the overflowing ballroom just inside the French doors. "There's a literal mansion full of sophisticated, well-to-do people, not to mention an especially attractive pool of seemingly single women in there. Yet you're choosing to be out here all alone with me in the cold. I guess I'm wondering . . . what's wrong with you?"

Her laughter cuts through the air. Gently, she grabs my forearm, and her touch is like a flame licking through my white dress shirt. The echo of her giggles carries into the night. I ride them like a wave—a wave that will inevitably come crashing onto shore once the truth is known.

"That is . . . a loaded question," I say carefully. "I wouldn't even know where to begin."

"Oh, come on." She licks her lips. If I'm not mistaken, her eyes flutter with a quick glance at my own. "You are the kind of man one only reads about in fairy tales."

The words wound me more than she could ever know. Sure, I am the kind of man in fairy tales—the villain.

"I am the furthest thing from Prince Charming," I reply, shaking my head. "But . . . Charlie?"

Her hand is still pressed into my arm. She leans closer to me now. "Hmm? Yes, Andrew?"

Her chin lifts slightly, bringing her lips closer to mine.

Her eyes glaze with a haze of yearning. Reaching up, I cup her chin and brush the pad of my thumb across her perfect lips. I can't pretend I'm not spinning in a haze myself.

The truth is a whispered breath between us. "I'm out here alone with you because there's no one I'd rather be with."

She draws in a quick, sharp breath as the *chink! chink! chink!* of a fork hitting expensive china in the ballroom carries outside to us. I glance toward the floor-to-ceiling French windows that line the length of the room and see guests congregating. It is speech time. I tip my head toward the house.

"Shall we?"

Charlie's disappointment is apparent, and I wish I could tell her I feel the same way. As much as I want to take this woman in my arms and kiss her, it feels wrong to follow my instincts while still harboring a secret that will tear us apart once she knows.

Instead, I take her fingers in mine and lead her inside. She slips off my coat and hands it back to me as we enter the ballroom again. Some of our guests are seated at the tables scattered across the room, while others gather close to the stage where Dad is already standing, microphone in hand. He is entertaining the crowd with a charm only Gary Ketner possesses, working them for their donations to Mom's foundation. And that's when I hear him call my name.

"Andrew, join me up here, would you please?"

It's not unusual for me to say a few words every year about the importance of literacy skills and making books accessible to all children. And for Mom, I'll do anything. After I finish this speech, I plan to whisk Charlie out of here to someplace quiet where I can have her all to myself for the rest of the night. Squeezing her soft hand, I leave her standing in the crowd and make my way up the stairs of the stage to stand at Dad's side.

He claps me on the shoulder a few moments later. I see a gleam of something I don't recognize in his eyes. "As many of you know," he begins, "it's been a big year for CityLight Press. Many records have been set and then broken, and most can be attributed to a single, very special book."

My heart drops into my shoes. What is Dad doing? We don't ever talk about CityLight during the Winters' Wonder Gala. This night has always been devoted to Mom, the one day a year we don't bring up business. And out of nowhere, Dad is now holding up a copy of *Love Between the Pages*, a proud smile beaming on his face. The sunset-hued cover stares at me incriminatingly.

Dad continues, "Andrew, I think it would be fitting if you would do us the honor of reading a passage from this powerful novel that I think your mother would have loved to read."

Suddenly, there might be a limit on what I am willing to do for Mom. My stomach drops again, and I feel the eyes of our guests pressing into me. I lean toward Dad and whisper into his ear, "I don't think we should do this."

Dad only shoves the book into my hands and says into the microphone, "He's delighted to read for us! Andrew, the floor is yours." He holds out the mic for me to take. Instantly, I feel as if I've gone from a six-foot-three stature to two feet tall.

The truth dawns on me. Dad will never take no for an answer, no matter what I say. My voice will forever fall on deaf ears. My words will only mean to Gary Ketner what he wants them to mean.

I take the mic. It feels like lead in my grip. When I lift my gaze, my eyes instantly find Charlie. She offers a thumbs-up paired with a dorky grin. Her sweetness is astonishing. I wonder how hard it is for her to watch this unfold, her chart-topping novel being read aloud to a room full of people who have no idea who she is. As I stare at her, I almost forget I have a crowd waiting for me to speak. I'm going to get through the reading of this passage, and then I'm taking my girl away from here. A wave just behind Charlie catches my attention. I see Ava cheering me on too.

Courage fueled by love forged forward with unbridled hope. The words float into my mind as a reminder as I lift the microphone to my lips.

"Good evening. To echo Dad's sentiments, thank you all for coming tonight. In each of your smiling faces and by your support for the Winters' Wonder Foundation, I feel my mother's presence. Her absence has created a hole in my heart that I never believed was capable of mending. But to my eternal gratitude, this book has offered me exactly that."

My gaze lands once again on Charlie. There's a sheen in her eyes now. A smile plays across her face that I never want to forget. I continue, "I have a specific passage in mind I'd like to read from, one that spoke to me in my lowest of moments."

I crack the book open, flip to the page that I have nearly memorized, and begin to read.

"'It's not the end. You slipped away, but it was only to the next room. While the echo of your voice fades, the warmth of your words surrounds me. Sometimes I forget, and I listen for the steady beat of your footfalls around the corner, the lilt of your sweet voice calling my name. Your presence lingers, filling the air with a sense that you are merely out of sight, on a temporary errand from which you will soon return, your smile wide with the anticipation of a secret surprise only you have seen. 'Come with me,' you'll say, hand outstretched. 'You won't believe what they've got waiting for us there.' It's not the end. And when I step away from this lonely earthside place, I'll look for you first in our heavenly forever home.'"

I close the book and feel the prick of tears behind my eyes. Blinking the threat away, I look for Charlie again as I finish my speech for the evening. "Tonight, as we gather to celebrate the beauty of the written word and its far-reaching, long-lasting impact through generations, I find myself pausing and untangling myself from the luxury of the night. Because the truth that I'm in the season of learning is that all of this will turn to dust. We can't take with us our fortunes, possessions, or the ranks we climb in our careers. Nor can we take the approval of others." I can't help but steal a glance at my father before continuing.

"Wealth and having everything we want does not equate with happiness. Things don't prevent us from losing those we love. The only thing we can be sure of is . . . Heaven. And maybe not everyone in this room feels that alongside me right now, but this book"—I hold it in the air as my eyes lock with Charlie's—"is a masterpiece not only in its exquisite prose and execution but in its ability to show the reader what truly matters."

The room melts away, and I can't hear anything over the pounding of my own heart as Charlie and I speak a thousand words to one another with our eyes. The short length of time in which we've known each other feels multiplied by infinity. All I can think as Dad takes back the microphone is how deeply and fully I want her heart.

32

Charlie

Everyone in the ballroom fades until it is just the two of us.

Or at least that's how I feel as I stare up at the handsome man on stage. Andrew smiles at me, causing the nerve endings across my skin to tingle again. My heart is still fluttering from the words he whispered to me on the terrace. Across my lower lip, I can still feel the gentle pressure of his thumb as he used it to brush over it softly. There was something in the way he leaned toward me, something in the look in his eyes as he lessened the distance between us . . . it mirrored exactly how I feel. The sensation of his lips on mine is as tangible as if he already claimed them as his. I know what I want. I want Andrew to kiss me and keep kissing me until the end of forever.

I can hardly keep my mind focused on the men on stage. It takes me a minute to process what Gary is saying.

". . . big year for CityLight . . ."

CityLight? The name jars me out of my dreamy reverie. Inwardly, I cringe. Anything but CityLight in this magical moment. The seriousness of business and impending lawsuits and stolen books is the last thing I want to be reminded of right now. *Is he bringing up CityLight because of Andrew?*

At my side, the small handbag I'd purchased this afternoon to complement my dress tonight vibrates with an incoming call. I feel the buzz against my hand, but I can't tear my attention away from the stage to glance at the caller ID. Even from a distance, my eyes register the telltale autumnal colors of my book as Gary holds it up on stage.

". . . reading a passage from this powerful novel that I think your mother would have loved . . . " He turns toward the crowd and throws them an exaggerated wink.

I watch Andrew lean toward his dad and whisper in his ear. His body language is tense and awkward. Why Gary would insist on him reading a passage is lost on me, but my focus is on Andrew. When he throws me a distressed glance, I wonder if he is thinking of how uncomfortable this moment is for me.

Before I can blink, Andrew is holding my book. He flips through the pages. His eyes find mine again. His expression is clearly anxious. I don't want him to experience discomfort over this on account of me. I'm a big girl. I can handle hearing my book read aloud, as awkward and unnecessary as it seems. Andrew's tanned face has gone as pale as a ghost. I give him a thumbs-up and flash him an encouraging smile.

It's okay. I'm okay. I try to convey my thoughts with my facial expressions.

Falteringly, Andrew begins to speak into the

microphone. I feel a rustle beside me. Looking up, I find Ava standing next to me. Her eyes connect with mine, and I see the instant flash of surprise. I'm just as surprised to see her. *Didn't she say she was going to a work event this weekend?*

She smiles, warmth blossoming across her face like a flower in spring. "Hey, stranger! I never in a million years thought I would see you here tonight. Do you know Andrew?" Her voice is soft and low. She glances toward the stage, confusion competing with her smile.

I clear my throat, sensing a very awkward conversation in the near future. As much as I suspect her of stealing my book, Ava is so warm and genuine and kind that it is hard to think she could do such a heinous thing.

"Yes. Andrew and I met this week," I whisper in reply. My handbag vibrates again, the buzz tingling against my hand.

She nods. Her next whispered question is the one I'm dreading. "Have you found anything out about the person trying to steal your book?"

I'm spared the pain of answering right away because Andrew's voice pulls my attention back to him.

". . . one that spoke to me in my lowest of moments." He flips a page. I knew it was coming, but it startles me nonetheless to hear his strong, smooth voice reading aloud words that I wrote in one of my own lowest moments, when hope and faith warred with my grief. The words clutch themselves around my heart again, as emotional in this moment as the day I put them to paper.

"'And when I step away from this lonely earthside place, I'll look for you first in our heavenly forever home.'"

Tears spring freely to my eyes as Andrew lowers my

book. There's a breathy moment of silence before the entire ballroom erupts in applause. Andrew lets them clap, and my heart constricts as it dawns on me that the applause is for me. They may not know it, but each guest's enthusiastic cheers bring a little more healing to my wounded writer's heart.

When Andrew raises his hands to quiet the crowd, I open my handbag in search of a tissue. I'm certain that if I don't get my emotions under control, I'll look like a raccoon in about two minutes. My phone jostles against my fingers as I dig around. The screen lights up from the movement. I see a series of missed calls and a few text alerts flashing across the screen.

Curiosity tugs at me. Lifting the phone, I take a quick glance at the call log.

Nate. He's called me three times since I arrived at the gala.

Alarm spreads through my chest. Nate is levelheaded and cool, the complete opposite of me. It isn't like him to try so many times to reach me. Something must be terribly wrong. His family still lives in Pleasant Hollow, and I hope they are okay.

I see that he has texted me too. As Andrew's voice fills the room again and tugs my attention back, I spare a quick glance at my message folder. I'll feel better if I know what is causing Nate's urgency.

At the top of today's message thread between us is a link to an article. I register "CityLight Press" in the title of the piece. Rather than click on it, I skip below to Nate's messages.

NATE: Charlie, you said the guy from CityLight who has been helping you is named Andrew, right?

NATE: I can only find one Andrew listed on the website's staff bios. Is it Andrew Ketner?

NATE: Are you aware that Andrew is Gary Ketner's son?

NATE: Gary is the current CEO of CityLight Press. The company was founded by his wife's father. Did his son disclose that to you?

NATE: Something about this feels weird. Call me, Charlie. And don't do anything until I talk to you. We need to make sure you don't get completely screwed in whatever mess is going on. I hope you're okay.

My heart seizes painfully. I feel like I am going to be sick. I sit at an open table. Ava takes a seat next to me, but she's focused on Andrew who is still speaking on stage. His eyes lock with mine. As our eyes speak, I wonder if he can see the panic and confusion writing itself all over my face.

Instantly, everything feels . . . wrong.

Why didn't he tell me? Has anything that happened this week been real, or has Andrew been trying to manage me so he could prevent me from wrecking CityLight's reputation? Did he ever plan to tell me the truth?

Rapidly, doubt creeps in. I feel the itching of anger beginning to rub at my brain.

". . . a masterpiece not only in its exquisite prose and execution but in its ability to show the reader what truly matters." Andrew concludes his speech to more applause. Gary steps forward immediately to take the mic from him.

He knows who A.C. Frost is. They both do. The realization flashes over me like a tidal wave. *How could I have been so stupid? So naïve? It was all a ruse. All fake. He's been hiding Frost this entire time.*

My chest heaves as I try to control my breathing. Still

clutched in my fingers, my phone buzzes again with another text from Nate. I glance down instinctively, and my heart drops again as the words register.

NATE: Andrew's late mother was named Alexandra Celeste Winters. Her favorite time of year was when the first frost touched the trees, and every year, she would throw a huge gala to celebrate the coming of winter. Sounds a lot like A.C. Frost to me, Charlie. I wouldn't trust this guy if I were you.

Gary's sonorous tones carry across the room. "That was a treat, wasn't it? Thank you, son, for writing these deeply profound words for all of posterity to read. I'm so proud of you, and I know your mother would be too."

I leap to my feet as Gary continues.

"And on behalf of the Alexandra Celeste Winter's Foundation, I want to thank you all for coming out tonight. The first frost was always my wife's favorite time of year, and we've tried to bring that magic into the room tonight. Your generous donations to the children's literacy fund are going to make such a difference to her beloved cause. As hopeless book lovers around here"—the crowd laughs—"it's always an exciting day at the CityLight offices when we get to deliver that check. Now, let's enjoy the rest of this party."

My vision turns red.

The band strikes up again. Couples swarm onto the dance floor.

"Charlie, are you okay?" I hear Ava's soft tone and feel the brush of her hand as she reaches out for mine.

But I'm already moving forward. My feet carry me across the floor toward Andrew's approaching figure. A charming smile is plastered across his mouth, but all I see is a lying, manipulating traitor. My blood boils, running hot and rampant through my veins.

When he reaches me, Andrew tries to take me in his arms. With all my strength, I plant my hands on his chest and shove him back. We are the only immobile figures on the dance floor as people shimmy around us to the latest pop hit.

"Don't touch me," I seethe, not bothering to moderate my tone. My chin thrusts upward angrily at him, and I rise onto my toes, trying vainly to match our heights. "I know who you are. I know about your dad and CityLight. I know you are A.C. Frost. I know everything."

Andrew's face pales, but he tries to reach for me again. "Charlie, I can explain."

I don't want an explanation. Darting around him, I rush for the stage. I nearly trip on the hem of my gown as I speed up the stairs and grab for a microphone.

"Ladies and gentlemen," I shout into it, not caring that my voice sounds like a shriek hurtling itself into the room. The band slows. The dancers, confused at the sudden interruption to their fun, turn to look up at me in confusion.

I lower my voice a decibel. "If I can get your attention, I have an important announcement."

There's a sudden, painful pressure on my elbow. I try to yank my arm away, craning my neck to see Josh at my side. Anger is written all over his stern face. Of course, he is here. He does CityLight's dirty work.

"I'm warning you, Miss Blaire," Josh says in an undertone meant for my ears only. "You signed an ironclad nondisclosure agreement of your own free will. If you break it right now by exposing anyone in the firm I represent, you will be liable in court for the damages. And believe me, we will win." He whispers the words, his breath hot and clammy against my skin.

I shiver at his threat. My impulsive instinct to expose everyone at CityLight as the lying, cheating frauds they are deflates a little, but my anger still rages strong. "You coerced me into that," I hiss back.

"Try to prove it."

Andrew darts up the stairs behind him, pausing on the top step with a look of distress on his features that would have sent me rushing to comfort him a minute ago. But now…

Love Between the Pages sits conspicuously on a stool to my right. I grab it and flip to a page I memorized long ago. Locking eyes with Andrew over Josh's shoulder, I lean forward and begin to speak into the mic. The ballroom is still watching me.

"Since we are all such great book lovers here, I'd like to read one of *my* favorite passages from this globally bestselling novel." I'm aware of the dripping sarcasm in my tone as I clear my throat and begin to read.

"'There was never a question or a choice for Danny. He knew what he had to do. Saving Margot by sacrificing himself had been written into his destiny. What else could they expect of him? Loving her meant he would sacrifice himself a thousand times over if by doing so she and their unborn baby would live just one more day. Because that's what love was. Love was sacrifice. Love was courage in the face of fear. Even when the world made you feel broken, love made you whole.'"

I don't need to look at the page. I speak the words slowly

and clearly, eyes locked on Andrew. When I'm done, I replace the mic on its stand and walk calmly past Josh to the end of the stage.

"I told you to keep her busy, not to fall in love with her," I hear Josh mutter under his breath to Andrew as I pass.

Heat flares in my cheeks, his comment only further confirmation of their sick and twisted plan. I hand Andrew the book . . . my book . . . and harden my heart to the pleading look he gives me.

I stare up at him and refuse to let anguish show on my face. "Congratulations, Andrew. I guess you really did become a writer after all."

With that, I sweep down the steps and across the dance floor. The confused crowd parts for me as the band picks up its song as if nothing had interrupted it. I head straight for the ballroom doors, longing for the chilly freedom of night, and freedom from the man I just left behind.

33

Andrew

The live music resumes. The ballroom renews its expected merriment as though the world itself didn't just fall apart, as though Dad didn't just let my darkest mistake slip as he concluded his speech.

The lights from the chandeliers begin to blur. My lungs constrict. I can feel the pulse of my heart in my throat.

Helplessly, I watch Charlie move with the fury of betrayal toward the open ballroom doors. Her mossy dress swirls around her ankles. Casting my eyes around the room, I briefly catch a look of dark confusion and anger that Ava shoots me before she strides after the fleeing woman.

But my legs are frozen. The sudden sensation that I'm six years old again hits me painfully. I'm on the verge of one of my childhood panic attacks, this time with no mother around to help me through it.

"No," I murmur breathlessly. My mind struggles to wrap

itself around what just happened. Charlie knows. The jig is up. My failures have come home, ready to collect. "No, no, no . . ."

Sweat slicks across my skin beneath the tux. A familiar flush creeps over me. For most of my adult life, I've been able to control the onset of a panic attack by simply running in the other direction whenever something rose to challenge me. But I can't run away from this. I squeeze my eyes shut to stave off the spinning. When I reopen them, Charlie is out of my sight.

Fighting to regain my ability to move, I finally manage to stumble down the stage's steps and rush for the door. I fumble and lurch among the dancers but make it across the dance floor. The doorway calls to me. Before I can reach it, a strong hand grips my shoulder and yanks me into the shadows of the room. Josh's surly face glares at me.

"So, remind me again of how you didn't need my help?" he seethes. "You're lucky no one else seems to be aware of what just happened!" His hand grips my shoulder harder. I shove him away.

"This isn't how it was supposed to happen, Josh." My voice is weak. My lungs are still unable to take a full breath. I try to leave, but he stops me again, this time more forcefully. His aggressive behavior sends my blood into an instant boil. The air begins to feel even thinner than before, and I know if I don't get out of this room soon, the consequences won't be pretty.

"Stop," he warns me. "Leave well enough alone, man. You're going to have enough of a fight in the courtroom."

"Well enough?" My face contorts. I feel some of my strength returning as the instinct to protect Charlie and try to fix the unfixable surges across my skin. Taking my forearm, I push Josh roughly against the wall, pinning him there. My eyes are daggers as I glare down at him. "Do you know what we've done to her? I'm going to explain everything, and don't you dare try to stop me." The words come out with a force I didn't know existed inside of me.

He wipes the spittle from his face, glowering darkly. I give him one more shake against the wall to prove my point and then stalk out of the room. Once I'm out of sight of any guests, I barrel down the stairs and sprint for the front doors.

As I spill through them, the bitter chill of a New York November night smacks me in the face. I see her on the graveled drive. She's still here, waiting while Ava gently strokes her back.

"Charlie!" I yell, flying down the steps. She spins around to face me.

"Stop!" she screams.

I obey immediately. Her face is blotchy and streaked with mascara-stained tears. She lifts the skirt of her dress and stomps a few steps toward me. My breath freezes. A pressure builds in my chest, like a sob quickly making its way to the surface.

Charlie pauses a few yards in front of me, her small frame shivering. "I trusted you, Andrew! I *trusted* you!" She throws her arms in the air and then helplessly lets them fall back to her sides. "How could you do this?" Her voice grows weak. She wipes her red nose.

I take two tentative steps toward her. "Charlie, please. I can explain everything."

Her face darkens. "Okay, then do it. Explain your way out of this, Andrew. Give me another round of lies, why don't you?"

I take another step. "I'm serious, Charlie. I never meant for this to happen. Please. I . . . I almost told you so many times, but—"

She shakes her head, tendrils of dark, silky hair falling across the nape of her neck. "Almost isn't enough. Like how I *almost* thought you were one of the good guys? How I *almost* fell in love with you? How I *almost* thought you could be the one? But *almost* means nothing." The words come out like venom and almost bring me to my knees.

She swirls before me. I do my best to blink the mist away, but tears well up in my eyes, falling like bombs. The crisp air crusts them to my face like ice. I reach for her, but she holds up her arm to halt my movement as a valet driver pulls up with Ava's Kia.

Charlie holds my gaze a moment longer, and the brokenness on her face shatters my heart.

"I'm so sorry." My voice is barely above a whisper.

"Sorry is a lot like almost," she says. "Worthless." She turns and climbs into the passenger seat of Ava's car.

I lurch forward, willing to do anything to prevent her from leaving. Ava stops me before I can reach Charlie. Planting herself in front of me, my friend shields the passenger side of her car with widespread arms.

"No, Andrew," she says firmly. "I'm taking her home. You need to walk away. I don't know the extent of what you've done yet, but if it is what it seems . . . I have no words for you right now." She shakes her head.

I stare off with one of my longest friends and see the reverberating effects of my selfish actions splinter into our friendship. It seems that the poison I can inject into a relationship reaches no end, a domino effect of the many sins of which I am guilty.

"Please." My voice falters. "Ava, please, let me—"

"Who are you, Andrew?" Ava's glowing skin turns to ashy stone as she stares at me. Her look is of absolute disgust. She walks around the car and climbs in. The engine is already purring. I make another desperate grab for the passenger door, but Ava drives off quickly, leaving me standing on the drive like the imbecile I am.

Raking my hands through my hair, I stagger backward. I've felt heartache before, but this heartache feels like death.

"You need me to grab a car, mate?" the valet says to me.

With a shake of my head, I say, "I've got it."

My feet can't carry me fast enough to Dad's eight-car garage. I punch in the code, but I am shaking so hard I do it wrong the first time and have to enter it again. Finally, the door glides open. I dive into the nearest vehicle, a Land Rover. Flipping down the visor, the keys fall into my lap.

Putting it in reverse, I peel out of the garage and fly around the circular drive, speeding down the lane leading to the road. A few snowflakes land on the windshield as I zip through the suburbs toward home. In the far distance, the glow of the city's lights is a beacon calling to me. Almost there . . . Almost . . . Almost . . .

A fresh round of tears stings my eyes. Ava's words creep into my mind. *Who are you, Andrew?*

An imposter.

A screwup.

A fool.

My life has been punctuated by the inability to be the person I am supposed to be. I sniff and wipe my nose with the back of my hand. The bridge hums beneath me, almost like it's trying to tell me something, as if I'm on the cusp of learning something I desperately need to know.

With every mile I get closer to Charlie, I know I'm only falling farther behind. Nothing I can do will fix this. Nothing can stop what my failure set in motion.

I press the gas harder. I don't want to be this person anymore. The man who runs away and allows things to happen, the one who doesn't take control of his own life, the one who can't stand up for what he believes is right. The man who hides in the shadows of whom he believes he ought to be, the one who dips in and out of life as he sees fit, the one who can't man up and face the hard stuff.

The Upper East Side welcomes me home, and I double park just down from my building. The elevator is too slow, so I take the stairs three-by-three. I hear a bang as I rush past Charlie's door. I'm taking it as a good sign. She may be punching holes into my walls, but at least she's in there. I barge into my own home. Sergio goes ballistic when I enter.

"I'll be back, bud." I give him a pat on the head as his front paws land on my chest. Charlie's still perfectly wrapped gift sits on the kitchen island. Grabbing it, I rush for the door. Sergio whines and tries to follow me, but I block his attempt to escape and shut the door behind me.

Just as I reach Charlie's door and lift my hand to knock, it flings open.

We stand face to face. She's changed out of the dress and into a simple black sweatshirt and leggings. Her hair is still twisted into a beautiful bun, but her face has been mostly scrubbed clean of makeup. Her eyes brim with tears again. She shakes her head with fury, but words don't leave her

319

trembling lips, as though she's too angry and hurt to even speak.

I'm not here to make excuses or try to stop her. "This is what I wanted to give you last night. It explains everything." I extend the wrapped package toward her.

She yanks it from my hand and tucks it under the arm that carries her duffel bag. She tries to dart around me, but I block her in the doorway.

"Keeping a journal has been something I've done for years. And ever since I first read your manuscript months ago, and I couldn't get it out of my head, I've been writing down all my thoughts. All the darkness. All the grief. All the questions that plagued me. The truth is all there. But the ending isn't written yet, Charlie. You'll have to be the one to finish writing this story."

A confused look passes over her face. She sniffles. "I have a flight to catch, Andrew."

I nod and step out of her way. She brushes past, and without another look at me, Charlie moves down the hall and turns toward the elevator, disappearing from sight. I hear Sergio's paws hit my door down the hall. A long, exaggerated whine follows.

I freeze in place, hoping for a foolish moment that she will turn around, that this won't be the end. But I hear the *ding!* of the elevator and the *swoosh!* of its closing doors. Suddenly, I'm alone with no one but myself in the hall.

Andrew Ketner, folks.
The one and only.

34

Charlie

There is no comfort in life quite like the comfort of home.

I step out to the deck built onto the back of my cottage and hold the door open for Hank to follow. The shaggy black and brown border collie mix bounds after me, grateful to be released from the warm confines of the house. Last night, I relented and brought him home from the animal shelter because I knew I needed the presence of a dog to soothe my aching heart.

I may also be missing a certain oversized golden dog's wild antics and sloppy kisses.

A cozy home and doggy cuddles, the age-old magical cure for heartbreak. It wasn't working for me anymore though, apparently.

We had showers last night, enveloping Pleasant Hollow in a delicate gown of raindrops and mist. The first touches of winter have officially moved in and made themselves comfortable. Winter has scattered the white and gray paint on her palette far and wide, her icy breath already tingeing everything with frost. Her chilly touch is just a reminder that the season of darkness and rest is coming. The deep, cold, often lonely months will soon settle in, both inside and out.

Instead of going to sit on the soggy summer lounge chairs I still need to bring into the storage shed before the season fully changes, I stand in front of the railing, watching Hank explore the yard, warming my hands on the hot mug of coffee I just freshly brewed.

Sleeping has been an issue lately, and coffee seems to have become my new best friend. Not that it ever wasn't. It was either start drinking too many cups of coffee or spend my life savings in stress-baking supplies. Coffee was cheaper. But it is also probably why I'm not sleeping well. Although, I know the reasons for my insomnia reach far beyond my caffeine consumption. Its cold fingers have wound themselves tightly around my heart and won't let go.

I flew home days ago. I cried when I walked in and saw the cozy green velvet sofa in the living room, the swivel reading chair next to the bookshelf, the faded kitchen table with all its scratches and dings, the too-tiny kitchen, and the press of the meadow and forest just beyond the yard. I fell face down on my bed and cried for the lifetime of memories stored in this house and the lifetime of memories I carried home with me from New York.

And still, days later, I feel as if I am in mourning, but I can't identify the exact cause of my grief. It isn't as if I lost someone precious to me . . .

Ava and Gary have reached out several times and so has Sam Baker. The only calls I've answered have been from Sam.

He is turning out to be a pretty good lawyer, a far better advocate than I could have hoped. The ball of justice is rolling, and it makes me sick to think of it.

I know I need routine again. I need my passions and pet projects. I need to start working again. But I feel too tired to care anymore. The only thing that has felt worthwhile this week was visiting the dogs at the shelter. Their joy at the sight of me was like a group of old friends rushing to greet me. I asked Maeve if Hank could come home with me for a few days . . . or maybe forever. She simply peered at me over her glasses and gave me a sympathetic nod that said it all.

"Come on, Hank. Come inside, boy." I call to him. He obediently bounds up the steps to the deck, his fluffy tail waving as he runs into the house. His fur is damp with mist, and I smile as he strides straight to the stone fireplace and plops himself down with a contented sigh on the cozy dog bed I placed in front of the crackling fire.

He looks so at home. I wonder why it's taken me so long to bring some new life into this quiet, empty cottage.

As I go to refill my mug, I studiously avoid looking at the kitchen table, where a wrapped paper package sits conspicuously in the center. If I look at it, I'll want to open it. A dozen times, I've been tempted to toss the whole package into the fire unopened.

That'll show him, I think. But when I go to pick it up, I can't go through with it.

I also haven't had the courage to see what's inside, though I feel the curiosity growing in the back of my mind. I know the moment is coming when I reach for it for real, but I'm not ready yet.

Later that night, after the sun has dipped behind the trees

with her final goodnight, I sense it's time. Mechanically, I prepare a plate of cookies from a recent baking session and a cup of cocoa. I refuse to go into this without courage in the form of sugar and chocolate. The plate holds both sugar cookies and pumpkin chocolate chip, a homage to autumn and a nod to winter. I don't think I will ever eat a butterscotch cookie ever again.

I bring the cookies and cocoa with me, along with the gift-wrapped package Andrew handed me as I stormed out of the apartment. As I settle in, Hank climbs onto the sofa next to me without invitation. I think he recognizes that I need all the comfort I can get right now, so I let it slide. His body is warm, and I tuck a crocheted throw over both of us. The fire crackles in the hearth, the only sound in my quiet living room besides the whisper of my heavy breath.

The beautifully wrapped package sits on my lap. It's a big step. It's an even bigger step when I slide my fingernail through the tape and break the seal.

I recognize the journal underneath immediately. The same leather cover that I nearly peeked under when I was snooping that afternoon in Andrew's condo. He said this journal contains all the answers to my questions. I take a deep breath with the realization that I nearly uncovered the truth all on my own.

I don't want to touch anything that *he* has touched. That he's written in, pondered over, pages that he's poured more of his excuses and lies onto. Or at least that's what I imagine this journal is full of. I can't imagine what else it can contain that will be worth my while.

But for my own peace of mind, I want to know exactly how Andrew justified his unspeakable wrong. I want to know how I was so deceived that I nearly began to . . . imagine something between us that was never meant to be. Resolutely, I let it fall open to the first page and begin to read.

Dear Charlie Blaire, it begins. *I just read your manuscript tonight. We've never met, but I wish that we could. I wish I could tell you what your novel has done to my heart.*

Two hours later, I've turned the last page. My hand is shaking as I close the journal. Hank, instinctively sensing my distress, nuzzles his nose under my hand. Absently, I stroke his soft fur. The plate of cookies sits discarded on the table next to me, cocoa gone cold long ago. Hot tears splash unhindered onto my lap, pinging off the leather cover before me.

It's all there. Not only has Andrew kept an almost daily journal since the week he found my manuscript discarded in Ava's office wastebasket, but he also journaled of the questions my novel raised in his mind: questions of hope, of life after death, of eternity. The journal is a journey of exploration, and I watch as Andrew's entries show the gradual blossoming of hope and a brand-new faith as he searches the Bible for the answers to the questions my book inspired. His entries take my breath away.

After the discovery that his dad had secretly published my novel on his behalf under a pen name, thinking the publication of a novel would be an encouraging surprise for his son, Andrew wrote of the dismaying discovery and his subsequent plan to make it right. But then I'd arrived before he had the chance to break the news to his dad. And the journal continues through the week we met, every lie, every bit of deceit chronicled by a man who felt trapped between a rock and a hard place.

He's made no excuses. He admits that he should have gone to his dad with the truth immediately upon his shocking discovery of *Love Between the Pages'* existence. I have everything I need for a full lawsuit to hold both CityLight Press and Gary and Andrew Ketner personally responsible for the damages done, including a handwritten note from father to son that Andrew tucked inside for me to read.

But though the journal is a clear admission of guilt—from the moment he took my manuscript from the wastebasket in Ava's office to the process of preparing it to leave on his dad's desk, thinking that Gary would finally see that he had what it took to contribute as a leader in CityLight's future, and the ultimate mistake in identity that allowed Gary to think Andrew had written a future bestselling novel—it's also so much more.

I've gotten to know Andrew—the real Andrew, full of flaws, anxieties, and faults—through these pages, just like he met me in mine.

The royalties that *Love Between the Pages* has earned are mine. Andrew hasn't touched a penny of it. His dad put it away into a separate account on his son's behalf, looking forward to the day he could present it to his son as a reward well-earned. His dad had hoped to repair the cracks in their relationship by surprising his son with a chance to prove himself as a writer. During the time I was still in New York City, Gary didn't even know the damage his mistake in identity had caused. Andrew felt that he had to wait until after the gala to break the news.

There is still the issue of the rights to the novel being returned to me, *but that's for the lawyers to hash out,* Andrew writes. He hopes that an agreement can be reached that preserves his dad's reputation as much as possible. *The fault is entirely mine,* he says. *It was never his.*

I can't stop crying.

And I scold myself for it because despite all of this, despite the lies, and despite what he's taken from me, my heart reaches out to him. I hurt with Andrew. Although I don't know if I can ever trust him again, I suspect that once I arrived on the scene, the situation just spiraled rapidly out of control.

If only we had met under different circumstances, maybe then . . .

But Lord, my broken heart protests, *why? I can handle someone maliciously stealing my book. Why did it have to be Andrew, though? Everything that I thought could be is ruined now. All I want is to go back to that first night in his apartment, when he snuck in takeout and pretended he cooked it just to impress me. When is it going to be my turn to be happy?*

I'm not sure how long I stare into the fading embers of the fire, Hank snoring at my side, before my phone buzzes next to my leg. It's late, the evening creeping toward midnight. Wiping the tears from my blurry eyes, I stare down at the phone, unable to pull myself away even though I tell myself not to look when I see her name appear on the message thread.

AVA: I know you have every right to hate all of us. You aren't taking my calls, and I don't blame you at all. But Charlie, please. There's so much going on here, and it isn't just for Andrew that I ask you to listen.

A second message buzzes in while I'm reading the first.

AVA: There are countless people at CityLight who had no idea what they were inadvertently involved in. What

Andrew is planning to do could destroy all our livelihoods.

I stare at the screen. We exchanged numbers the night of the gala, when Ava figured out I'd been telling her about a book that had already been stolen, and she put together the source of the theft from my reaction in the ballroom. As she drove me home, I blurted everything out, not caring if it was breaking the limitations of the NDA I'd signed. She listened and promised me she would do everything she could to help me make it right.

I had refused to speak to her since, not wanting to hear her voice because it reminded me of *him* and every promise he'd made and broken.

As I stare at the messages now, reading them over and over, I know what I must do.

She picks up on the first ring. "Charlie, thank you. Please hear me out. It's bad. He's planning to . . . Oh, but first of all, how are you? Are you okay?"

I inhale and exhale deeply, the knots in my stomach tightening. "I'm fine. No, honestly, I'm a wreck. It's been an awful week. I'm miserable."

"He's miserable too," she replies quietly, and I'm both happy and heartbroken to hear it.

"Tell me what's going on that calls for middle-of-the-night emergency texts."

Ava doesn't hesitate as she dives in.

35

Andrew

Sergio snuggles up to me and lays his block of a head on my chest, sensing my distress as tears splash onto the sofa cushions beneath me. Scratching his golden fur, I stare at the ceiling, mind swirling with agonizing regret. The buzzing of the intercom at the front door jolts me into an upright position.

Charlie?

Springing up, I rush over to answer the call. "Hello?"

"It's Ava. Let me in."

My heart sinks as reality hits that Charlie really is gone for good. The clear anger and disappointment in Ava's voice doesn't help much.

"It's unlocked," I mumble into the receiver, pressing the button to buzz her into the building.

Feeling the onset of a raging migraine, I put on a pot of coffee in the kitchen while I wait for Ava. I have a feeling we'll be needing it. Within minutes, her determined rap sounds at my door. Sergio lets out a soft bark and meets her at the door with a sleepy greeting. Even with all his energy, he's not used to so much commotion at two in the morning.

Ava's heels click against the hardwood floors as she strides inside. She's still dressed in the gown she wore to the gala tonight. Tossing her purse on the island, she squats down to rub Sergio's head. She looks up at me. Her eyes are rimmed with the telltale marks of exhaustion.

"I hope you're brewing that coffee extra strong," she mutters. She stands and rubs her temples. I lean on the counter, waiting for what I know is coming. Finally, she throws her hands into the air. "Andrew, will you please tell me what is going on?"

My brain is only operating at half-speed. I reach for two mugs and pour each of us a generous cup, then gesture for the table. Sergio lays down on the cool floor with a grunt and goes to sleep. Ava and I settle at the dining room table across from one another. Beyond the balcony, the sky is inky darkness, though the glow of city lights can be seen even from the twelfth floor. I stare into the empty blackness.

Ava drums her fingernails against her mug. "Okay. Spill the beans."

I stare into my coffee, the dark liquid reminding me in every way of Charlie. "I don't even know where to begin."

"Did you . . ." Ava falters. "Did you steal her manuscript? Are you A.C. Frost?" Though her tone has softened, her words are heavy with accusation.

"No," I reply quickly and vehemently. "Absolutely not."

I take a shaky breath and dive into the mess that my life has become. Once I've divulged everything to her, she sits speechless and motionless, her eyes bulging, frozen hand pressed across her mouth.

"Let me get this straight," Ava finally says after taking a moment to gather her thoughts. "First of all, unknowingly, all of the employees at CityLight have unintentionally plagiarized Charlie Blaire's book?"

I nod.

"And second, you discovered this right before Charlie herself found out?"

Again, I only manage a nod.

Ava frowns. "And Josh asked you to distract her so he could come up with a solution, which led to you lying to her all week while inadvertently starting to fall in love with her?" She rests her elbow on the table and presses two fingers to the space between her eyes.

I clear my throat. "In all fairness, I think my heart was destined to fall in love with Charlie before I even met her."

"Andrew, you can't . . ." Her words fall short. "You realize that your father's words tonight have convinced Charlie that you *intentionally* stole her book and have been playing her all week, right?"

"I know." My voice is weak, and my eyes burn. As uncomfortable as I am showing emotion in front of others, I can't stop fresh tears from welling up. "It's all such a mess."

"This is worse than I even thought." Ava stands and paces the length of the table, her heels a steady *click, click, click* against the floor, a stark reminder of the nails being driven into CityLight's professional coffin. "How do we fix this?"

The lump in my throat won't dissipate no matter how

much I try to clear it. "I don't know, but I'm ready to do whatever it takes."

—

The next few days bleed together like a series of wounds, one after another. Sleep evades me, as does my appetite. The hollows beneath my eyes deepen. My emotions swing like a pendulum. One moment, the anger I feel toward Dad overwhelms me. The next, I'm back to nursing my broken heart.

I returned Dad's car on Sunday, but our attempt at speaking only ended in a yelling match. I've tried reaching out to Charlie, but she's blocked my number. I don't blame her. Why wouldn't she? At this point, I'm sure she has dusted her hands and written me off completely. From the sounds of things, her lawyer is coming at us guns blazing, and rightfully so.

I roll over in bed and glance at the clock. Though it is barely five-thirty and the sky is still dark, there's no use in trying to get any more rest. I haul myself out of bed, change into running attire, leash up Sergio, and head out the door. As I step off the stoop, the cold air bites at my exposed face and skin. The early morning has the beginnings of winter already in its taste. The holiday season is around the corner. It's supposed to be a time of festivity and cheer. But I'm not sure if my heart can bear to say goodbye to fall just yet.

Because losing fall means losing Charlie.

It means losing my mother.

Losing . . . everything that's ever meant anything to me.

The darkness hugs me close, and I draw in as much of the crisp air into my lungs as I can. Sergio has to find ten sticks and mark seven bushes before he can run faithfully beside me. As the sun begins to rise over the eastern horizon, my mind feels the clearest it has felt since this mess began.

After I've run until my lungs are burning and my legs are sore, we settle our pace, walking through Central Park to cool down. Sergio's tongue hangs from his smiling mouth. The dog is happy whether he's running or snoozing in his bed. It's a kind of contentment I wish I could emulate. Taking my phone from the pocket of my joggers, I snap a photo of his goofy face, thankful to have his company now more than ever.

I catch sight of a waiting text from Ava on my phone.

AVA: This isn't good.

There's a link to an article attached to her message. I click to open it. The article is a recap of the Winters' Wonder Gala, which isn't unusual. We always invite the press to the event; their presence is great for marketing, raising awareness, and bringing in extra donations. I scroll through the write-up, and my just-settling heart begins to pound again.

In an unexpected turn of events, and perhaps the highlight of the evening, Gary Ketner revealed the identity of CityLight's mysterious bestselling author, A.C. Frost, to be none other than his own son, Andrew Ketner. We're unaware if Mr. Ketner meant to create a media storm with his unexpected revelation, but the cat is definitely out of the bag. The stunning announcement occurred just as Andrew himself was embroiled in an apparently dramatic lover's spat with a brunette beauty. The situation begs the question: Is Love Between the Pages *a quickly rising international phenomenon because of its own merit or because of the influence of a publishing family?*

The article continues, but I've read enough. I waste no time calling Dad. He's already heard the news.

"Where are you? At home or the office?" I ask as I jog back to my apartment, Sergio keeping pace at my side.

"Still at home," he replies grimly.

"Don't leave yet. I'm coming down there. We need to talk."

—

The tufted leather armchair lets out a groan as I drop into it. Dad takes a seat in the matching chair across from me as a fire crackles from the hearth. Even after the train ride out to Scarsdale, I'm too warm and too stressed to feel the chill in the air. Still in my running gear, I shrug off my hoodie and lean forward.

Dad remains rigid. He's stoic, his jaw hardened as he stares through the window to the gardens below. I feel steam building beneath me. Maybe this is his way of letting me have the floor. I begin.

"I have a lot on my mind, Dad, so I'm going to just say it. I . . . I let this go on far too long. When I realized the mistake you made, I should have hounded you until you decided to listen."

"Well, that certainly would have saved a lot of—"

"But you don't make that easy, Dad."

My words shut him up. I take a slow breath and go on. "Mom isn't here to be our go-between anymore. She was always our mediator, the one who ironed out all the wrinkles in our communication. But if we're going to have a chance to truly have a relationship—both as professionals and as father and son—something has to change on both ends. For me, I need to step up and show up. I need to devote myself to my responsibilities and stop hiding behind my fear of disappointing you. I need to stand up to people who try to steamroll over me."

"And let me guess? I need to stop steamrolling, eh?" Dad lets out a small chuckle, though the deep lines across his forehead aren't ones of amusement. He rubs a hand over his beard and sighs. "I really messed this one up, didn't I?"

"We both played our part."

Dad stretches a hand toward me but lets it fall back to his lap. "I know I'm hard on you, Andrew."

I lift a hand to stop him. "Dad, I don't mind you pushing me to be a better version of myself. But do you know what it's like to live in Gary Ketner's shadow my whole life? To feel like I might as well get used to mediocrity because my best will never be good enough?"

"Is that really how you feel?" He glances at me before his eyes dart toward the fire. A shadow passes over his face.

"Yeah." I swallow and clear my throat. "I don't often see the point in trying when I know I'm just going to fail in your eyes anyway."

"Son, you don't fail. You . . . you are tremendously talented."

"When's the last time you told me that, Dad? Aside from believing I'd written Charlie's book."

Dad's mouth closes. His brows furrow. His unspoken words say plenty.

"Here's the thing," I continue. "I know I haven't proven myself. I don't apply myself; I seem to skate by doing the bare minimum. But I want that to change, and I want a chance to make this right."

"You mean this plagiarism ordeal? There's no making it right, Andrew." He puts his head in his hands, and, for a moment, the ever-resilient Gary Ketner visibly crumbles.

335

"We'll settle this lawsuit privately and weather the storm the best we can. If the full truth gets out, we will obviously have a damaging story to spin, but that's where your PR expertise comes in."

"No." I shake my head stubbornly.

Dad straightens his back and tilts his head to the side. "It's your job," he says curtly. "What happened to pulling your own weight?"

"I know what we have to do. Or more so, what I have to do." I lick my lips, take a breath, and brace myself for his reaction to what I'm about to say. "I'm going to be interviewed on *Wake Up, USA* on Friday morning."

Dad's face drops. Slowly, he asks, "Why would you do that?"

"To take the blame for all of this."

"No, you're not. Cancel it."

"Hear me out—"

"Absolutely not." Dad rises and begins to pace across the rug. "Not when we have a nondisclosure agreement already signed and can settle this without further smearing our own name!"

"And does that make it right? Tossing money at a woman whose entire life has been turned upside down by our mistake? Is it fair to muzzle her while people are whispering about your unintentional little slip up at the gala? You might not be aware of how far this has already reached."

Pulling out my phone, I scroll to the social media posts I found on the train ride here. The bookish corner of the internet is a fierce force not to be trifled with. There are already numerous posts and videos about the situation, with loyal forces on each side. I pull up a post that features a photo of my face (where did they find the headshot, by the way?) next to the cover of *Love Between the Pages*. The caption reads, "Forget book boyfriends! Can we make author boyfriends a thing? Because hello, Andrew Ketner!" Three heart-eyes emojis follow.

I hold up the screen and show it to Dad. "There are plenty more where these came from. But on the other side of the spectrum are posts like this."

I flip to a video of a man asking, "What makes a bestseller?" On a green screen background is the article that Ava sent me earlier this morning. I press play and hold the phone up again for Dad to see.

"Nepotism in the workplace much?" the man in the video says. "To me, this seems like a conflict of interest. Has CityLight used its influence to quietly create a bestseller? I haven't read the book in question, but something about this doesn't sit right with me. What do you guys think? Let me know in the comments!"

I clear my throat. "If I go on television and shoulder the blame for everything before news gets out that this is not only a question of nepotism but a plagiarism scandal as well, maybe it will save CityLight from the worst of the consequences. You'll get off scot-free."

Dad shakes his head vehemently. "You're being rash. We'll figure this out. I can't allow you to do something like that." He sounds annoyed.

I pull up one final post on my phone and hand it over for Dad to read. "Tell me what you think about this."

Dad squints and reads aloud, "CityLight should be held to the highest accountability for plagiarism . . . When the truth comes out, you'll all be horrified." His face falls.

"Who is . . . @natetheghost . . .?"

"A public relations nightmare," I grumble. I have a hunch the poster is Charlie's friend, the one who contacted her when we were together last week.

Dad shrugs. "So what if one random person on the internet says this? People say junk online every day. It's not likely anyone will pay attention."

"It's more than one person. And what if they do? We don't know who Charlie told before storming into New York. Do you see what is at stake here yet?"

Dad hands my phone back. "I can't believe I let this happen. I . . . I . . ." His voice breaks.

I don't enjoy seeing him like this. Nothing has ever been able to bring down the Gary Ketner I've always known.

"You're not going on that talk show. I'll throw myself to the wolves before I let you mop up my horrible mistake."

I rise to my feet. "Charlie is never going to forgive me as it is, even though I'd do anything to make that happen. But if I can save anyone in this situation, I'm going to save you and the rest of our employees at CityLight. I'll take all the blame."

He scoffs. "You're willing to go on live television to ruin your entire reputation over this? Over her?" Suddenly, Dad tilts his head to the side again. He eyes me intently as if he is waiting impatiently to hear my response.

I don't hesitate to answer. "Yeah. Because that's what love is: sacrifice."

"Son . . . Do you love this woman?"

I'm not sure how we've sidestepped our way into my ruined romantic life, but I nod. "I know it sounds crazy, but I think I've begun to fall—"

"The best love stories always are."

I open my mouth, already prepared to argue, but falter before the words come. What did he just say? Dad takes one look at my confused expression and chuckles again.

"When I first read that manuscript you left on my desk—*Charlie's* manuscript—I thought you'd written an overdramatized, fictionalized version of my and your mother's love story. So many things were different, but you already know we were never supposed to meet. There were a million reasons to keep us apart."

Dad pauses and walks to retrieve a photo of them together from the fireplace mantle. He stares down at it with emotion brimming in his eyes. "But we knew we were destined for love from the moment we met, and we were determined to make it work. There simply wasn't any other option. From our supernova meeting to the last breath she drew, we loved each other. My love with Alexandra, the love between Charlie's parents . . . It doesn't seem that far off from the story currently being spun between you and Charlie. From the day I met her, I could tell she was someone very special."

He looks from the photo to me, his eyes misty. "Man, I miss her."

"I do too."

Dad passes the frame to me, and it's almost too painful for me to look at.

"I'm sorry you've lost your supernova, Andrew."

Mom's smiling face in the photo makes my chin tremble.

"Are you doing any of this to win Charlie back?"

I was hoping my journal might be a beacon of hope, that she might see past the Andrew who hurt her and, within my deepest thoughts, read the truth of who I am. I shake my head. "I don't know. It's all so painful and messy. But maybe if she sees . . ."

My words fall short. Why am I allowing myself to hope for her like this? I clear my throat and continue, "I just want to make this as right as I can. Sure, you pushed this book into publication, but I set the whole thing in motion by not communicating or doing my job well enough. I've been a liability to this company for a long time, and you know it. I know you love this company and want to protect it, Dad. I do too."

"There's something I love more than CityLight, Andrew."

"Imported wine?"

"You." He looks me in the eyes. "Leave this to me to make this right. I'm sure there's a way we can explain all of it."

"You realize how ridiculous this story sounds, right? Clearly, not even Charlie believes it." The armchair creaks as I shift uncomfortably. "Can you trust me? This is the new Andrew, remember? The version where I give it my all?"

"You really think going on a morning talk show is going to absolve your guilt and solve this problem? You think it will be a grand enough gesture to show her your true feelings?"

"I have to do everything I can to try."

Dad sighs and stares down at his hands for a moment. "As my employee, I can't give you my blessing to do this."

I shouldn't have expected his support. But the disappointment is crushing anyway.

"But as my son, I want you to know how proud I am of

you," he continues.

With a start, I look up at him. He's leaning against the mantle, staring down at me intently. Without hesitation, I rise and stride forward, my hand outstretched. As he pulls me in for a hug, all I can say is a heartfelt, "Thank you, Dad."

36

Charlie

Travel isn't my forte. Wanderlust belonged to my parents. When I was younger, it was a matter of course that I accompanied them on mission trips, working with various organizations to deliver supplies and aid to struggling communities both globally and within our own country's borders.

Our home base was always Pleasant Hollow, where my parents grew up. I used to treasure the weeks we spent at our country cottage. I would snuggle in front of the fire and ramble through the woods and meadows or attend as many activities with my friends as I could because it was only a matter of time before my parents were called away to serve another community in need, and we'd be gone a few weeks or sometimes months at a time.

As soon as I turned eighteen, I began to elect to stay home instead of accompanying Mom and Dad when the mission field called them to fly far, far away. As their world expanded, mine seemed to narrow. I began my dog training course and stayed close to home, building my business and not venturing far outside Vermont's state borders for the next few years. Our local church, my small group of friends, volunteering at the shelter, and coming home every night to the same cozy, quiet space was enough for me.

And when I got the call that a crash on the coast of Indonesia had stolen my parents' lives as they were delivering medical supplies after a devastating tsunami hit the region, my world narrowed even further. I hid myself away in the safety of my tiny village home and only explored the world through the stories I wrote to remember them.

So, it surprises me that I don't feel out of place as I step off the plane at the JFK International Airport for the second time in a matter of weeks. Instead of feeling crushed by the teeming mass of people darting to and fro, I make a beeline for the gate and the purpose that brings me back to New York City.

Ava is waiting for me outside of baggage claim. She's several inches taller than me, but she stoops and throws her arms around me, gripping me tightly.

"Thank you so much for coming. I know how hard this must be," she says, finally releasing me. We step toward her waiting SUV.

I'm silent as traffic moves at a snail's pace away from the airport. It's early in the morning, and commuters are still making their way to offices across the city. Ava drives silently for a few minutes. I can feel her getting antsy as she fidgets and murmurs about the other cars on the road.

Finally, it bursts out of her. She shifts to glance at me,

then back at the road, then back to me again. "Charlie, I am so, so sorry. All of this has been so horrible. We couldn't have made a worse mistake, and I'm partly to blame."

Her apology is appreciated but unnecessary. I shrug, lacing my fingers together and folding them into my lap. I see a few of Hank's brown hairs lingering on my pants from when I dropped him off with Maeve this morning. I pluck them away, hoping my newest housemate doesn't think I've abandoned him to the shelter. I'm already counting down the hours until I return and take him home with me again. I'd dressed comfortably for the flight: forest green leggings and an oversized cream sweatshirt paired with my trustiest pair of leather boots. I don't plan on staying long. I only packed an overnight bag and didn't even bother to do my makeup. I am here for one mission and one mission only.

To stop Andrew from unnecessarily ruining his, Gary's, and CityLight's reputation in one fatal, though well-intentioned, blow. His crime doesn't fit the punishment. No one deserves to have their lives ruined over this, least of all Andrew. I'm here to save him from himself.

"You don't have anything to apologize for, Ava. You couldn't have known the chain of events throwing away my unsolicited manuscript would spark. If anyone's to blame, maybe it's me for impetuously mailing off my book to a few random publishers just because the fancy struck me. I didn't do my due diligence on research, so I'm very much to blame for the confusion." I try to make the smile playing on my lips genuine enough to set her at ease.

"It's just awful. Your book . . ." She glances at me again, and I see the spark of unshed tears in her eyes. "It's everything that is good and pure and true. A story of love that knows no borders and puts no limits on the sacrifices it is willing to make. We're going to make it right for you, Charlie. I know it."

"I believe you." I nod. "I know my lawyer is working with CityLight. It's looking like the settlement will return the royalties to me and then some. We just still need to iron out the details of reclaiming my identity as the author. Maybe the book will be pulled from distribution and republished under my name?" I shrug. There are so many details that still need to be ironed out between the law firms, and I'm still trying to process it all. "Gary has reached out to me personally a couple of times, but I haven't had the heart to speak to him yet."

Sam Baker has warned me not to talk about the upcoming litigation as we go through the process of getting the rights to my book back. But there's something about Ava's soft, green eyes and gentle face that pushes me to be honest. If circumstances were different, I could see us becoming good friends.

There are a lot of things I could see turning out differently after my visit to New York if circumstances weren't what they are.

The *Wake Up, USA* studio looms ahead, the GPS guide announcing our impending arrival. My heart rate picks up as all the reasons I shouldn't have come ping themselves through my brain like a pinball machine. Ava presents her entry badge to the guard at the front gate, and we drive onto the lot. When she parks the car and turns to look at me, I know she already knows what I'm thinking.

"You can do this. He needs you to do this." She reaches across the console and grabs my hand.

I shake my head. "How can I face him again? He destroyed the trust we were just starting to build. It was all a lie. A lie from the beginning. However well-intentioned and stuck between a rock and a hard place Andrew was, my dream has still been stolen out from under me."

"It wasn't all a lie," she replies. "I've known Andrew a long time, and the only other person he's been willing to give up everything for is his mom. Whatever he feels for you, it started months ago when he first read your manuscript."

The car falls silent. I fidget with my fingers, staring down at them as if they hold the answers to every question I have. Ava clears her throat softly.

"Publicly coming forward as a plagiarizer before everything has been settled legally is going to ruin Andrew's reputation. As stupid as his choices were, I don't believe they came from an evil place. He is desperate to make this right, but I don't think he is a bad man at heart."

I suck in a breath and exhale heavily. My fingers come up to grasp the door handle, and I push it open. "That's the thing, Ava. I don't think he is a bad man either."

—

She's arranged for both of us to have press passes. We walk into the studio together. It's my first time in one, and I think of how often I used to dream of my first interview as a published author. It is a dream that faded long ago as I grew older and more content with my quiet home life, but to say that simply being here doesn't set my nerves tingling would be false.

Andrew's interview is scheduled to be in Studio B right after the late morning news airs at ten o'clock. It's now ten after ten, and we are rushing to make it on time. Ava's high-heeled shoes clatter down the concrete hallway. I try not to outpace her by too much since I have no idea where I'm going. I don't know much beyond the fact that Andrew plans to come clean on live television about the truth behind his role in *Love Between the Pages'* publishing journey. He plans to take the full blame on himself to prevent the backlash from hitting his dad and CityLight once the news breaks. And I'm here to stop him.

If I can reach him before it's too late. My heart races, pounding as we rush down the halls.

A red light announces our arrival at the entrance to Studio B. While Ava speaks quietly with the man standing guard at the door, I try not to fidget and let my nerves give me away. Finally, he cracks the door for us, and we slip inside. The set is deeply quiet, the only sounds coming from the small living room stage set up against a fake window backdrop under beaming studio lights.

A man is speaking on the set. My heart leaps because I instantly recognize Andrew's deep, smooth tones. Except today, there is an extra layer of sadness, a melancholy undertone that makes my heart constrict against my will.

I'm not here to make amends with the man who broke my heart. I'm simply here to prevent him from dragging everyone else down as the lies crumble around him. There are too many guilty parties and too many innocent ones. I think there's been enough heartbreak for one book already.

He's sitting on the edge of a small velvet loveseat, his hands planted firmly on his knees. For a man about to fall on his sword to protect his dad and the company he built, he looks resolute and determined, his strong jaw set and firm beneath the stubble of his dark golden beard.

That beard. Even from the shadowy shelter of the camera bay, it looks just as soft as I've imagined in my stolen daydreams, daydreams I've stubbornly shaken off as I've moved throughout the past week.

I tear my eyes away from his handsome face and force myself to concentrate on his voice, registering the words falling from his lips that will quickly condemn him.

"Thanks for having me on, Meg," he is saying calmly in response to her introduction. "There have been a lot of rumors floating around about the true origin of the global bestseller my father's company published earlier this fall."

Meg, the host, a pretty, brown-haired woman, leans forward eagerly. "Yes, do tell. There are a few rumors going around that have caused quite a stir online. My own daughter showed me some viral videos on TikTok that only demonstrate the great mystery surrounding *Love Between the Pages*. There's been a lot of talk lately about what makes a bestseller. Is it the book? Or is it the marketing campaign and the dollars behind it that propel a book into the spotlight? So, tell us what we're anxious to know. Are you the real A.C. Frost?"

Andrew passes a hand over his beard. "Before I tell you the truth of how the book came to be, I want to make it publicly clear that my dad had no idea what the public's response to the book was going to be when he made the decision to publish it. My dad has stood at the helm of CityLight Press ever since my grandfather stepped down. He has done a heck of a job maintaining our integrity and commitment to publishing only the best, most worthy books."

Andrew pauses to catch his breath, and Meg takes the

opportunity to lean a little closer. I freeze, watching the two of them closely.

"Are you A.C. Frost like the rumors are saying?" she says. "Did you write this novel and get your dad to publish and promote it for you?"

Andrew shakes his head. "I can't take credit for this novel. The person who wrote it is a brilliant writer and an even better person. But what the public doesn't realize is that an injustice has been done. The author hasn't gotten credit for *Love Between the Pages*. The truth is . . ."

I can see the gossip TV ratings skyrocketing as Andrew's words spill out. He takes a deep breath as I lurch forward, hands outstretched. My sudden movement catches his eye. His head turns toward me, and our gaze connects. Confusion and uncertainty spill across his face, but in his eyes is a flash of familiar warmth.

"Don't do it," I mouth, trying to telepathically communicate with him that he doesn't need to do this. The last thing I want is more damage being done because of my book. Especially not to someone that I care for . . .

Andrew smiles, giving me a subtle nod. I see everything he won't say in the intensity of his gaze. This is his way of giving me justice. His lips part. "I am here to confess that I sto—"

"Stole me," I shout, striding forward onto the set.

Meg jumps. She swings toward me. I freeze halfway into the faux living room, realizing what I just said.

Meg's eyes sharpen. She looks between me and Andrew. "I recognize you from a video clip taken at the Winters' Wonder Gala. What do you mean he stole you? Are you two . . . together?"

I sputter, shaking my head. Looking at Andrew, I reply in a tone meant only for his ears. "I mean, he stole my heart. But we're not together."

Before Meg can react, I turn to her. I take a few steps forward until I know I'm within sight of the cameras. "What I meant to say is that CityLight stole me away from any other publisher. They took a first-time novelist and gave her a chance to become a bestselling author. It's me. I am A.C. Frost."

A heavy silence falls over the set. Meg's face goes from startled to focused to shrewd in the space of two seconds. But I barely see her reaction as I focus on Andrew, now only a few feet away. He's looking at me with a quizzical expression I can't read, but his intense gaze envelopes me like a hug. The scene narrows until only the two of us are in the room. A warmth spreads across my limbs. Whatever the future holds, I know I've done the right thing.

Meg quickly recovers and waves me onto the set. She motions for me to sit on the small loveseat next to Andrew. "Is this true, Andrew? Is this A.C. Frost?"

He stares at me. Finally, his head nods slowly. "Yes, it is. This is the real A.C. Frost."

Meg leans toward me. "Is that your real name?"

"My real name is Charlie Blaire," I reply.

"Why would you keep your identity a secret? Why use a pen name?"

I ponder my reply for a long moment. "Because I wasn't ready to be an author. I wanted to stay hidden so that nothing could hurt me. This novel has taken me out of my comfort zone in many ways. I'm realizing now that what I thought was my comfort zone was just a rut I was stuck in because I was scared to let anyone into my heart and risk losing them again."

Though my eyes are fixed on Meg, my words are for Andrew.

"So why reveal your identity today?"

My words are barely audible. "Because courage fueled by love forges forward with unbridled hope."

What follows is a blur of an interview that leaves me reeling. I won't remember a word of what was said until I go back to watch the segment, and even then, I don't know if any of it will seem real. All I'll ever remember is the smile that crept across Andrew's face as he watched me with a telltale sparkle in his eyes.

—

Meg took the opportunity to land herself an exclusive interview with the global bestselling author, A.C. Frost. Which I guess is now me.

I've arranged for a one-night stay in a hotel uptown before I fly back to Vermont tomorrow morning. Instead of going directly to it, I ask Ava to drop me off near Central Park. She hugs me before I step out of the car, and without warning, I find myself inviting her to visit me in Pleasant Hollow if she ever finds herself out that way.

"I would love that," she replies emphatically.

I turn toward the park. I don't see myself returning to the city in the future, and I want one more walk through the sunset-hued carpet of fallen leaves.

The only thing missing is a fluffy golden dog and his handsome, bearded owner.

My mind is heavy, and my heart hurts.

Despite the deep chill that is settling into the New York

autumn days, Central Park is busy. It hasn't snowed yet, so New Yorkers are taking advantage of the chance to be outside. I am glad I brought my puffy winter coat to guard against the frosty air. I wander the trails, dodging other walkers and the occasional cyclist. It isn't long before I somehow find myself entering the Conservatory Garden, and my path veers instinctively toward the English side. I wander among the hedgerows, all that is left of the vibrant garden for the year. When I find the fountain again, I stop and stare, my mind buzzing as I mentally retrace every moment of that fateful week in the city.

"Has Ariel decided to exchange her legs for fins and return to the safe waters of her native homeland?"

I stare at the fountain, frozen in place, the familiar timber of his voice washing over me. My reply is slow and measured. "She tried it up here on land, but Prince Eric didn't turn out to be the person she thought he was, and she thinks it's safer back home."

"Charlie, can you ever forgive me?"

I spin on my heel and find him standing only a few feet behind me. His wavy hair is disheveled, and his breathing is heavy like he's been running. I can't help that my heart skips a beat at the sight of his face. I wish everything could be different.

"Don't be mad at Ava. I begged her to tell me where you'd gone. You left the studio so quickly that I didn't have a chance to say…"

"Say what?" I cross my arms over my chest and plant my heels. We're alone in the garden, and I allow myself to raise my voice a few decibels. "What is there to say, Andrew?"

He shakes his head and throws his hands out to the sides.

"What is there to say? How about I met an author through her words, but I had no idea the real version would be a thousand times better? How about you are one of the most talented people I know, but you've hidden yourself in that tiny town you call home because your idea of a good life is to curl up on the sofa eating butterscotch cookies and watching movies that break your heart?" He passes a hand over his face as a heavy sigh heaves deep within his chest.

"How about you came blazing into this city like a pack of yappy dogs, and you helped me to see that this life isn't the end? It's just the beginning." He takes a step closer to me, his hands reaching for mine. I let him take my fingers in his, the warmth of his strong grip going straight to my heart. His voice is a whisper now.

"How about you changed my life, and I want to spend my days getting to know you, showing my gratitude for everything your words have done for me?"

He presses his forehead against mine now. Our breath mingles, foggy in the chilly air. I try to harden my heart, but being near him is everything I never knew I wanted. My heart leaps for joy at his words despite every objection I shout at myself inside my head. My arms come up, and I twine them around his neck. He wraps his arms around me, pulling me up, holding me close, his face buried against my neck.

I could live in this moment forever.

"I never meant to hurt you," he breathes against my skin.

"I know," I whisper back. Untangling my arms from his neck, I push him away, careful not to fall backward into the fountain. He lets me go, and I both hope he won't and wish he would pull me back.

My bag is slung over my shoulder. Reaching into it, I pull

out the leather journal he gave me. I wasn't sure if I would ever give it back, but now that he is here, I have some things I need to say. "In this journal, you wrote of a struggle to hold onto faith when your heart was broken, a struggle I am all too familiar with. The thing with faith is that it requires your choice to trust that the end is what God says it is. If we knew everything He knows, there would be no need for faith."

Stretching out my arm, I extend the journal toward him. "You told me that I would have to finish writing this story. But I'm here to tell you that the only one worthy of your trust with the ending is God."

His voice is low and throaty. "I believe that, Charlie."

I know it's time to leave before I do something wild and impetuous that I'll regret forever. I'm learning to turn my impulsive nature over to the Lord. As much as I want to throw myself back into Andrew's arms right now and stay forever, I know we both have some growing up we need to do before anything can develop between us. If we're ever meant to be, it's up to the Lord to decide.

For the last time, I walk up to him and lay my palm across the soft stubble covering his jaw. He closes his eyes and leans into my hand.

"Goodbye, Andrew. Give Sergio a hug for me."

I don't let myself linger a moment longer. Turning on my heel resolutely, I walk out of the garden and don't look back.

37

Andrew

Spring. Five Months Later.

The blossoming cherry trees remind me that I did it: I finally made it through a New York City winter again without running away. Though the icy nights sliced through me like a knife, I stayed and battled through the pain.

The pain of losing my mother.

The pain of losing Charlie.

My triumph comes at the price of turbulent emotions, a few panic attacks, and countless nights on my knees in prayer. But I'm here. I'm breathing. I'm . . . living again.

A pink blossom drifts from a tree and lands on Sergio's golden back. I pluck it from his fur and rub the delicate petals between my fingers. Never far from my consciousness, Charlie's face floats through my mind.

Even after everything, I can't help but wonder how she is. She saved our company by stepping in on the day of the

Wake Up, USA show. Since then, the lawsuit has been settled. She was willing to settle quickly and privately, given the return of her royalties and the rights to her book. From what I've heard around the office from Ava (they are apparently friends now), she is continuing to write—and plans to introduce the public to her real name little by little: Charlie Blaire, writing as A.C. Frost.

She may be content to tuck herself away in her Vermont home, but she's rightfully making a name for herself in the book world. Her words continue to change lives. I know she certainly changed mine.

Sergio tugs at the leash, eagerly lunging for a bird. I make a clicking sound with my tongue, and his attention snaps back to me instantly.

"Good boy," I praise and toss him a training treat, which he readily catches in his mouth. His poor manners have improved somewhat over the past few months. I've had ample time to reevaluate my life and remedy things I had sorely neglected, including Sergio's lack of training.

Turns out, putting your head down and choosing to work actually pays off. At CityLight, I've transitioned to the editing department, starting at the bottom as a junior acquisitions editor. I'm determined to work my way up like Dad and earn my rightful place within the company. Truthfully, I don't think I would ever have taken a stab at editing in the past. I finally feel like I'm home, though, discovering new worlds within the manuscript pages like I did as a kid as I read countless books in the safety of Narnia with my mom.

Through the soft, balmy spring day, I walk Sergio back to my apartment and leave him with a bowl of kibble and fresh water before heading into the office. I arrive early now. Sometimes, I'm the first one through the doors.

Midway through the morning, a knock at my door tears my attention away from a manuscript pitch I'm crafting. Dad leans through the doorway.

"Hey. Got a minute?" He lingers, a folder thick with paper tucked under his arm.

While our relationship didn't magically repair itself overnight, things between us have been better. Dad acknowledges my renewed work ethic, my willingness to try. We've both been more deliberate with our communication as well.

I wave him in. He takes a seat in the leather armchair in the corner of the room. "What's up?" I ask.

"I have some news," he says. "Thought you should be the first to know this time around."

I laugh lightly and wait.

"As you know, Miss Blaire has continued to write. Over the past couple of months, she has been in talks with Ava about allowing CityLight to continue publishing her work. Over the course of the winter, she submitted another manuscript to us. It's a novel we would be honored to publish on her behalf."

"That's wonderful," I quickly reply.

I think of Charlie, curled up in a chair, laptop and blanket on her lap, homemade cookies within reach, pouring her heart into a fresh story over the frigid winter months. My heart twinges. Our love story was never meant to be. I realize that now. God put her in my path for a reason, but it wasn't for her to be mine forever—as much as I still wish things could be different. I almost ask Dad what her new book is about, but part of me is too afraid to know. I'm not sure I could handle knowing how fully she has embraced a future without me.

"We're offering her a contract," Dad says, a sheen in his eyes.

"The contract she deserves, I hope?"

"Absolutely." He watches me for a moment, and under his gaze, I'm afraid my perfect composure might crack. Finally, he continues, "Do you want to be the one to present it to her?"

I freeze. "What . . . what do you mean?"

A soft smile pulls on Dad's mouth. He looks at me with deep kindness. He sets the thick folder he'd been carrying on my desk. "Miss Blaire needs to read through this contract, sign, and return it. Of course, there are many avenues to make that happen. E-signatures, certified mail, etcetera. But some things are better hand delivered, don't you think?"

My heart begins to swell with the thought of seeing her again, with the prospect of extending an olive branch just as she did to me months ago. But she wouldn't want to see me again. She said goodbye after all.

"I don't know, Dad. I don't want to cause her any more heartache than I already have. She made it clear that she wasn't interested in having anything to do with me."

"Andrew, if I ask you to trust me, will you?" Dad drums his fingers across the folder. "Unless you have personal objections to the matter, I think this would be good for you. If seeing Charlie is too much, though, I understand."

I stare at the stack of papers in front of me, unable to come up with an answer. Charlie's feelings aside, can I face her? Will it be too painful? "She's in Vermont," I murmur.

"Since when have you ever been opposed to travel? Vermont is only a few hours away. Borrow one of my cars, book a driver, or take a flight. Just get this contract to her, would you?"

"Why are you asking me, of all people, to do this?"

"Ah." He holds up a finger. "That, my son, is where trust comes in."

My chest tightens. I open my mouth. "I'm not sure if I can—" I stop myself and remember.

Though the winter was filled with many hopeless days and endless nights, I am not shattered.

Though my relationship with Dad was riddled with conflict, we are healing.

Though my life had been marked with disaster and unfilled potential, I am not broken.

Before we even knew each other, Charlie showed me there is hope, that even the most difficult bridges can be crossed, that even when nothing makes sense, God still does.

Though seeing her may be as devastating as I fear, I realize I can do this.

—

The rolling countryside of Pleasant Hollow unfurls before me. Daffodils and tulips dot the sprawling land like a sea of bright confetti. Budding trees and hardy evergreens grace the Green Mountains. Slowly, I drive down Charlie's lane, the windows of my father's Land Rover rolled down to let the spring air in. I haven't experienced air this fresh and pure in far too long.

A cottage—*her cottage*—comes into view, and its understated beauty and warmth is everything I would describe Charlie to be. I take what's meant to be an anxiety-reducing breath, but even this six-hour drive hasn't been able to squash my nerves.

I park in her driveway and close my eyes, sending a silent prayer to the Heavenly Father who Charlie reminded me is always good. Contract in hand, I get out and walk up to her front porch. Two rocking chairs sit on the wooden deck, an unobstructed view of the quiet, breathtaking land before them. Briefly, I wonder if she sits out here with anyone. I imagine the creak of the chairs, the way her eyes might light up as she spots a gliding bird in the evening sky, the aroma of a strong coffee in her delicate hands.

I shake the thoughts away. It's none of my business with whom she shares her life.

Though I wish it were me.

I knock on the wooden door and wait. No answer comes. I knock again. When several minutes pass, I try one more time, then retreat from the porch. She's either not home or not interested in the person here to visit—me.

What was the point of this trip if not to see her? To make one last attempt at amends? To deliver the good news of her contract? I wonder if my dad knew she would be gone all along. Could he be so cruel as to send me here like this? Is this his way of testing how much I've healed?

I contemplate leaving the contract on her doorstep but decide against it. I tuck it under my arm, then take out my phone and pull up her contact info. My thumb hovers over the call button, but I can't bring myself to press it. She probably still has my number blocked, anyway. Sliding my phone into the back pocket of my jeans, I walk to the edge of her property, where a footpath trails into a vibrant, flower-studded meadow.

I'll take a walk, I decide, and then I'll try her door one more time. If she doesn't answer, then I'll know. I'll go home and let Ava or my father be the ones to fulfill this duty. After that, I'll let go of Charlie forever.

The city noises I'm accustomed to fade from my memory as the meadow envelopes me with its soothing magic. Spring speaks to me as I move along the trail, brushing my free hand over wild grasses and flowers. Like the shedding of a heavy coat, I feel myself continue to thaw from the harshness of winter. A winter that pressed me to grow and change in ways I never thought possible. I feel myself continue to heal, even in the face of today's dead end, even in the face of this next round of heartbreak.

As I approach the forested border of the meadows, a dog barks in the distance. I swing my gaze in the direction of the sound, peering across the meadow toward the base of a heavily wooded hill. The dog barks again, and this time, I hear a familiar woman's voice speak a command. My eyes search the land for any sign of *her*. Suddenly, I see a bounding ball of dark fur sprint across the meadow, heading directly toward me.

That's when I hear her voice cut through the stillness. "Hank! Come!"

Hank doesn't heed her command, only increasing his speed. I take my eyes from his fast-approaching frame and look up to see Charlie jogging in my direction behind him. From across the meadow, I see when her eyes catch mine. Her steps slow until she comes to a full stop. It hits me how overwhelmed I am at the sight of her. I never thought I'd see her again.

A fierce bark directs my attention back to Hank, and I

ensure my grip around Charlie's contract as I brace for him to lunge. The brown and black dog barrels closer, his speed building with every stride.

"Hank!" I hold up my palm and say his name like I mean it, though I have no idea what I'm doing. "Stop!"

To my shock, he slows and looks at me with distrust. I kneel and hold out my hand for him to sniff. He crawls toward me, still visibly unsure. "See? It's okay. I'm not going to hurt anyone. I promise."

Charlie whistles, and I register her approach. Hank darts away from me back toward her. I stand to discover that Charlie has closed the distance between us only to a few yards. Her warm, brown eyes are rich with curiosity. She tosses her long, dark braid over her shoulder as wisps of loose hair flutter around her face in the soft breeze.

My heart beats wildly in my chest. I wonder if hers is doing the same as we stare at each other, willing the other to speak first.

Eventually, she does. "Andrew."

My name is a simple two syllables on her tongue, yet with that one breath, I'm hit with a thousand emotions. I would change our trajectory if I could, but what I wish for is not what we were meant to be for each other. As much as I want to hear my name slip through her lips every day, as much as I want to give her the world—whatever that may mean to her—I know it's not meant to be.

I grip the contract tighter in my hand. At least I can give her this. And maybe to her, this is the world.

"Charlie," I breathe. For a moment, I'm unsure if I've spoken out loud or not.

"What . . ." Her voice trails off. She shakes her head.

"What are you doing here?"

I lick my lips and take in a deep breath of the sweet air. "I wasn't trying to hurt you, Charlie." My own words take me by surprise.

Her eyebrows pucker, and she tucks her hands into the pockets of her worn denim overalls. She watches me for a moment and then says, "I know."

"I was taken off guard in so many ways, and I know that doesn't dismiss how I handled everything, keeping the truth from you the whole week you were in New York. I should have told you what was going on right away, but I didn't know how. I just hope you know how truly sorry I am and, despite the circumstances, how much I loved getting to know you last autumn."

The words spill out of me like I'm journaling to her again, though this time, it's not on the page. I continue, "I might have been guarding a horrible secret, but every moment with you was genuine. I never faked how I felt. Not that it changes anything now, but I just thought you should know."

"You said this," she replies. "In your journal."

I purse my lips. "It's true, Charlie. It's all true."

Hank sits at her feet and whines. She doesn't flinch. A moment that seems to stretch into infinity passes between us, and I realize that it's time to do what I came here to do.

"I came here to present this to you." I extend the contract to her. Gingerly, she moves forward and takes it from my hand. "I've been told that you've written another stunning book, which is no surprise. I . . . I have no doubt you will continue to change lives. Congratulations, Charlie."

She breaks eye contact and thumbs through the contract

in the folder. "I've been working with Ava. She's become a good friend through all of this. She told me my contract would be coming through certified mail."

I shrug. "I got a promotion. Mailroom clerk."

Finally, Charlie laughs, and the sweet sound just about kills me. "You're not in the business of swiping manuscripts anymore, are you?"

"No. I left that life behind. I'm clean now."

The corners of her soft lips lift into a smile. "I heard from a little birdie that you are an editor now?"

"I am," I reply. How does she know? Has she . . . asked Ava about me?

"Good. It sounds like you're really good at your job. I mean, you did discover CityLight's best selling author after all." She bites her lower lip and grins as she clutches the contract against her chest.

"You deserve it all and more," I say. I slide my hands into my pockets and memorize the coffee color of her eyes. In the Vermont sunlight, they're the shade of a rich Americano.

I know God has big plans for Charlie Blaire. There's no question about it. I take a step back, ready to remove myself as a roadblock in her path. Charlie said her goodbyes to me last autumn in my hometown. It's time for me to say mine in hers.

"I'll be cheering you along in all you do, Charlie." I take another step backward. "Thank you for . . . everything."

I turn around, knowing I can't turn back no matter how badly I wish to. What I would give for a do-over, a different ending. But one thing I've learned is that sometimes walking away is okay.

Not when it's out of fear.

But when it's out of sacrifice.

"Andrew, wait!"

I've already begun to retrace my steps when she calls out to me. I slow and realize her footsteps are directly behind me. Her hand wraps around the pushed-up fabric of my Henley at my elbow. Her fingers slide along my forearm, her warmth a grounding force. I turn around. A span of only a few measly inches now separates us. Her proximity is a knife to the heart.

"What?" I ask softly.

Charlie reaches up and cups my jawline with her hand, dragging her nails gently across my shortly-trimmed beard . I close my eyes, remembering a moment not unlike this one in the English garden of Central Park. I lean into the warmth of her soft palm and prepare myself for one final goodbye.

"I've wondered if you'd ever be ready to write the rest of the story," she whispers. "Next time, can you just steal my heart, not my pages?"

My eyes flutter open in shock. She has leaned even closer now. Our breath mingles as she presses herself against me. Of their own volition, my arms snake around her waist. She surrenders into them as I draw her in. Suddenly, nothing makes sense, yet everything feels right.

Reaching up, I cup her chin gently and tilt her head toward mine. She leans closer. The contract drops into the wildflowers as she wraps her arms around my neck and lifts her lips to mine.

The past and the future hang within the tiny breath of air separating us. Everything draws together, and it's as if an ending that is more like a beginning takes flight.

And there, in a meadow under the witness of a thousand flowers, I do the very thing I never thought I would have the chance to do, the very thing I want to spend the rest of my life doing.

I lower my head and kiss her welcoming lips with a promise of love fueled by courage and hope and faith that cannot be shaken for all eternity.

Epilogue

Charlie

The Following Winter

"Are your eyes closed? Promise that your eyes are closed."

I can't help the laughter that bubbles up like a spring from within my chest. I tug on Andrew's hand, which is gently shielding my eyes from whatever is in front of us. "I promise, I promise," I protest, but my tone is filled with amusement. "I'll keep them closed, but will you focus on the road and driving us to this mysterious location, please?"

Trusting me, his hand drops away from my face. True to my word, I keep my eyelids pressed tightly together. I feel Andrew pull one of my hands from my lap, twining our fingers together while he uses the other hand to steer the Land Rover. The SUV's tires bounce, and I feel the ground change beneath us.

If someone told me a year ago that I would one day look forward to traveling between New York and Pleasant Hollow on a regular basis to visit my big-city boyfriend, I would have thought that person was crazy. I was the woman who spent years declaring that I would never leave my hometown. But here I am.

Since Andrew says he can't survive for more than a few days without seeing me, he rents a cottage down the road from mine. He's been promoted to senior acquisitions editor and splits his time between Pleasant Hollow and NYC. He visits me two weeks out of the month, though his cottage is used more for sleeping than anything else. I've turned him into a pretty good assistant dog trainer, though I have less and less time to devote to my business these days. Writing my next novel is taking up most of my time lately.

In the little over a year since I've publicly become a novelist, writing has taken over my life in ways I never expected. The royalties *Love Between the Pages* brings in has more than replaced my income. I'm writing full time now. CityLight published my second novel last year to rave reviews, and I'm working closely with Ava as I write my third.

When I'm in the city, I stay in the same apartment Andrew insisted I use the first time I visited New York. He says it is mine now and refuses to allow anyone else to stay there. When I found out that Andrew owns Winters Tower, plus a few other buildings on the Upper East Side, as part of his inheritance from his mom, I felt a little less guilty. Sergio and Hank race each other down the hallway between our doors.

We've just left brunch with Gary after attending church together where Andrew was raised. We have two church families now. My small country church community eagerly embraced Andrew the first time I brought him to Sunday service, and his church was equally happy to see him and Gary return home.

"How long do I have to sit like this? I feel silly sitting in a moving car with my eyes closed," I pretend to protest again.

"Just about . . . here," Andrew replies. The car stops. "Open your eyes."

Eagerly, I release my eyelids and look through the windshield. To my surprise, we're on a tarmac, a sleek, shiny, white jet purring on the runway just ahead. Based on the distance we just drove, my guess is that we are at the Westchester Airport. I turn to him, a quizzical look writing itself across my features.

"So . . . What are we doing here?"

His thumb rubs slow circles on my palm. He clears his throat nervously. "Okay, here's the thing. I know that you aren't the biggest fan of leaving Pleasant Hollow. It still means the world to me that you even come up to see me and Dad."

He makes a goofy expression, so I give him the lightest smack on the forearm with my free hand. "I come up to visit Ava and my friends at CityLight, you know that."

"I'll take what I can get," he laughs. He brings my hand up and kisses my knuckles. My heart skips a beat like it does every time he does that. "But I thought that this week we could do something a little different."

I wait quietly, my nerves suddenly spiking.

"How would you feel about visiting my family's home in Florida for the next couple of days? You'll have your own private suite, and it'll be just like we are under our own roofs but with the perk of getting to wake up on the beach together." He winks at me, making the heat rise in my cheeks. When it became obvious to both of us that we wanted to spend as much time together as possible, we agreed that though we might be inseparable during the day, until we made the ultimate commitment to each other, we would sleep alone in our own beds come nightfall. This would be our first time sharing one roof.

"And . . ." Andrew continues. My eyes flash up to him sharply. "We've been invited to work with a church organization working to build new homes for some of the families in need down there who are still reeling from the recent hurricane. We can spend the rest of the week helping them if you are up for it."

Memories of mission trips with my parents flash through my head in a series of vivid slides. What I wouldn't give to relive those days with them.

"But I don't even have any luggage."

"Already handled," Andrew replies. "I asked Ava to go into your apartment and pack a bag with everything she thought you would need for a week while we were in church this morning. Plus, I added a few extra things for warmer weather."

Shaking my head, I laugh. "A man with all the plans." I fall silent, staring out at the sleek private plane on the tarmac.

Andrew gives me time and space to process everything I'm feeling. Finally, he squeezes my hand. "So, what do you think?"

I turn to him, my gaze meeting his warm, comforting eyes. Despite the tendency to be a homebody that I'll probably always struggle with, I trust him. And where he goes, I want to go. Life with Andrew has proven to be an adventure from the first day we met, and I don't want to miss a moment of it. A grin spreads across my face.

"Let's do it!"

—

After the frosty chill that has enveloped both Vermont and New York since the autumn weather began to turn, the Emerald Coast is a balmy escape even as the evening sun begins to fade over the water. The sunset washes over the horizon, the sky ablaze with an ombre cascade of color.

Andrew brings my long cardigan down from the house. He wraps it around my shoulders as we stand on the beach, and once I'm snuggled in it and safe from the evening's drop in temperature, he moves to stand behind me, wrapping his arms around my shoulders and snuggling his beard into the crook of my neck. I only let him stay there for a minute before I wiggle around until we are facing each other. Wrapping my arms around his waist, I press my face to his chest, my head turned to watch the slow descent of the sun into the water.

"Did you ever think our story would end up like this the first time we met?" I say, tilting my chin up to look at his handsome face.

"To be honest?" He laughs, and his smile makes my insides melt. "I thought you were going to take your manuscript and smack me over the head with it like we were in *Anne of Green Gables.*"

My lips twist in pretend disapproval at the idea that I would ever be so impulsive. Laughing, he takes the opportunity to bend over me to steal a kiss. I lean into it, feeling safe and warm with his arms wrapped protectively around me.

"Our story is a really special one, isn't it?" he says when he breaks away. "Full of flawed humanity, to be sure, but also full of forgiveness and the rebirth of hope. I am so thankful for every day that I get to write my story with you." He pulls me closer, and I feel a rumble from his chest as he chuckles. "We should write a book about it together."

The words come out as a joke, but with a start, I stare up at him. "Andrew."

"I'm just kidding, my love," he laughs.

"I'm not." A sudden surge of excitement causes me to pull away from his arms. I dodge his reach, my feet dancing backward on the sandy beach. My hands lift to press themselves across my cheeks. "What an incredible idea. We should co-author a book!"

He looks at me with doubt. A wave of energy pulses across my skin, raising goosebumps all across it. I spin to face the water, my laughter bubbling up as I lift my arms and shout toward the waves. "We should co-author a book together!"

The silence behind me makes me spin back to face Andrew, determined to convince him of the brilliance of the idea. At the sight of him, I gasp. My knees go weak.

He has sunk to one knee on the sand, and a tiny mossy green box is extended toward me, its lid open in his hands. The ring inside flashes as it catches the sunset, a moss agate stone set between two diamonds.

"Charlie . . ." he breathes, his voice low and husky. "The only person I want to write my story with is you. And I want to write it with you for all of eternity and beyond. Will you marry me?"

I stumble toward him, sinking onto my knees in the sand

and throwing my arms around his neck. Through the tears already springing to my eyes, I manage to squeak out, "Yes, a thousand times yes."

The look on his face as he lowers his head to mine says it all. I stop him with a finger on his lips just as they are about to connect with mine.

"On only one condition, though."

"Anything." He pulls me closer.

"I get to name our book."

His chest rumbles again with laughter that never ceases to send sparks along my skin. "Well, now co-author. We might have to negotiate that. What's your idea for the title?"

I lift my lips to his. *"Love Beyond the Pages."*

Acknowledgments

All the glory goes to Jesus for inspiring this work of fiction. He took two authors and put in their hearts a mutual desire to write a love story that tackled real-life questions of faith after loss while pointing readers to the Source of all the answers. If you have suffered from the loss of a loved one and felt the hopelessness of grief, we want you to know that the future is bright and full of joy.

Jesus, the Only Begotten Son of God, chose to leave His Heavenly Kingdom, be born on this earth to live the sinless life we are incapable of, sacrifice His own life to repay the debt our failures and sins incur, and defeat death by rising from the dead so that we could be reclaimed as children of God. If you accept this free gift from Him, your future home is Heaven. When your time on this earth has come to an end, eternity is just beginning. God's desire for you (and our prayer for you) is that you choose to return to live with Him in your true home, reunited with your loved ones in the Kingdom of Heaven where sorrow, fear, pain, and death are banished forever.

This book was written to bring hope and comfort to those who have questions about eternity, who have suffered from grief, and who long to see their loved ones again. Whether you already know Jesus or are on a journey of getting to know Him, He loves you to eternity and back again. He's ready and waiting anytime you reach out to Him.

To our incredible community of book lovers, our promotional team, and our ARC readers, thank you. You have given us courage with your unending support, your overwhelming enthusiasm for this book, and your generosity in sharing it with others. We wrote this book to encourage you and to bring you joy. And (of course) for the adorable, lighthearted, autumn-inspired journey of Charlie and Andrew's love story.

Thank you for making this journey of being independent authors such a joy!

Erica and Britt

Britt's Acknowledgments

I couldn't have asked for a better partner to co-author a book with than my fellow author, sister-in-Christ, and dearest friend, Erica. My deepest thanks go to her for being an incredible friend and a brilliant writer, for having the sharpest sense of wit and humor, for being the most patient, hard-working, and joyful co-writer, and for making me part of this incredible journey. I'm so thankful I got to write a book with you, and I can't wait to write another one.

To the family and friends who never cease to encourage, praise, and support me, thank you! I write hoping you will find a new book to love. Mom, Gram, and Jeannette, you're the best.

And to my dear husband Joe, without whom I would never have found the courage to write, thank you for being the best life partner I could ever have asked for. Your patience for the long nights, your grace for the days when you leave and come home and find me in the same spot, your willingness to let me talk out plot and character development, and your enthusiasm for reading anything I write means the world to me. My heart will forever treasure hearing you say I am your favorite author. I love you.

Erica's Acknowledgments

To Britt, my co-author and beloved friend, you are such a blessing in my life. Writing this with you has been more fun than I could ever describe. Here's to the hours-long phone calls and endless text exchanges, brainstorming ideas and gushing about our characters. Thank you for all your hard work and for being such an amazing writer, editor, and friend. I can't wait to write the rest of this series with you!

To Patrick, the love of my life, your optimism, support, and steadfast faith keep me going every day. You're my favorite. Thank you for showing me that this type of love exists. You're the best cheerleader. Thank you for believing in me. I love you.

To my children, I pray that you always know the endless love of Christ and choose to walk in His light and rest in His love. The joy you both bring me cannot be measured. Mommy loves you, Leo and Nora!

To my family and friends, you all are the absolute best. Thank you for cheering me on and being lights in my life. I love you all so much.

To stay up to date with Britt:

Website: www.britthoward.com
Instagram: @britthowardauthor

Also available from Britt Howard

Song of the Valley, a contemporary western romance and the first book in the *McCade Family Series*

———————————————

To stay up to date with Erica:

Website: www.ericadansereau.com
Instagram: @ericadansereauauthor

Also available from Erica Dansereau

Come Forth As Gold, a Chrisitan historical fiction romance and the first book in *The Gold Series*

After the Water Brooks, a Christian historical women's fiction and the second book in *The Gold Series*

About the Authors

Britt Howard's goal as a writer is to create a thrilling tale that merges all the best parts of literature with a story that ultimately leads readers to a deeper relationship with God. She makes her home in Idaho with her husband and a very cute dog. Whenever she is not editing books for other authors or writing (or reading) new love stories, she heads to the mountains to recharge in nature.

Erica Dansereau currently resides in Idaho with her husband and children. Her desire as a writer is to point readers to Christ through her storytelling. Aside from reading and writing books, Erica loves spending time with her family, hiking, and having a nice cup of coffee or tea. The Bookish Bandit is her third novel.

Printed in Dunstable, United Kingdom